fly away

Kristin Hannah is a *New York Times* bestselling author. She is a former lawyer turned writer and is the mother of one son. She and her husband live in the Pacific Northwest near Seattle, and Hawaii. Her novel *Night Road* was one of eight books selected for the UK's 2011 TV Book Club Summer Read.

ALSO BY KRISTIN HANNAH

Home Front

Night Road

Winter Garden

True Colours

Firefly Lane

Magic Hour

Comfort and Joy

The Things We Do for Love

Distant Shores

Between Sisters

Summer Island

Angel Falls

On Mystic Lake

Home Again

Waiting for the Moon

When Lightning Strikes

If You Believe

Once in Every Life

The Enchantment

A Handful of Heaven

fly away

KRISTIN HANNAH

PAN BOOKS

First published 2013 by St Martin's Press, New York

This edition published 2014 by Pan Books
an imprint of Pan Macmillan
20 New Wharf Road, London N1 9RR
Associated companies throughout the world
www.panmacmillan.com

ISBN 978-1-4472-2954-4

9

A CIP catalogue record for this book is available from the British Library.

Printed and bound by CPI Group (UK) Ltd, Croydon, CR0 4YY

To Benjamin and Tucker,

who show me every day what love really means;

To my family—

Laurence, Debbie, Kent, Julie, Mackenzie,

Laura, Lucas, and Logan.

Each of you keeps me going,

and our memories tell our story;

And, lastly, to my mom.

We miss you.

Acknowledgments

✦

With every book I write, I seem to lean on my friends for the strength it takes to imagine a story and give it life. This journey was particularly rocky, and there were times I might have given up if not for my friends. I thank Susan Elizabeth Phillips and Jill Barnett for telling me that it was time to write this story, and to Megan Chance and Jill Marie Landis, I say, absolutely honestly, I couldn't have done it without you. Thank you.

Thanks also to Jennifer Enderlin and Matthew Shear for giving me what I needed most: time.

The charm, one might say the genius of memory, is that it is
choosy, chancy, and temperamental:
it rejects the edifying cathedral and indelibly photographs
the small boy outside, chewing a hunk of melon in the dust.

—Elizabeth Bowen

✦

If a man could pass through Paradise in a dream,
and have a flower presented to him as a pledge
that his soul had really been there, and if he
found that flower in his hand when he awoke—Aye!
What then?

—from the notebooks of S. T. Coleridge

fly away

✦

Prologue

✦

She is in a restroom stall, slumped over, with tears drying on her cheeks, smearing the mascara she applied so carefully only a few hours ago. You can see instantly that she doesn't belong here, and yet here she is.

Grief is a sneaky thing, always coming and going like some guest you didn't invite and can't turn away. She wants this grief, although she'd never admit it. Lately, it's the only thing that feels real. She finds herself thinking about her best friend on purpose even now, all this time later, because she wants to cry. She is like a child picking at a scab, unable to stop herself even though she knows it will hurt.

She has tried to go on alone. Really tried. She is trying still, in her way, but sometimes one person can hold you up in life, keep you standing, and without that hand to hold, you can find yourself free-falling no matter how strong you used to be, no matter how hard you try to remain steady.

Once—a long time ago—she walked down a night-darkened road called Firefly Lane all alone, on the worst night of her life, and she found a kindred spirit.

That was our beginning. *More than thirty years ago.*

TullyandKate. You and me against the world. *Best friends forever.*

But stories end, don't they? You lose the people you love and you have to find a way to go on.

I need to let go. Say goodbye with a smile.

It won't be easy.

She doesn't know yet what she has set in motion. In moments, everything will change.

One

✦

September 2, 2010
10:14 P.M.

She felt a little woozy. It was nice, like being wrapped in a warm-from-the-dryer blanket. But when she came to, and saw where she was, it wasn't so nice.

She was sitting in a restroom stall, slumped over, with tears drying on her cheeks. How long had she been here? She got slowly to her feet and left the bathroom, pushing her way through the theater's crowded lobby, ignoring the judgmental looks cast her way by the beautiful people drinking champagne beneath a glittering nineteenth century chandelier. The movie must be over.

Outside, she kicked her ridiculous patent leather pumps into the shadows. In her expensive black nylons, she walked in the spitting rain down the dirty Seattle sidewalk toward home. It was only ten blocks or so. She could make it, and she'd never find a cab this time of night anyway.

As she approached Virginia Street, a bright pink MARTINI BAR sign caught her attention. A few people were clustered together outside the front door, smoking and talking beneath a protective overhang.

Even as she vowed to pass by, she found herself turning, reaching for the door, going inside. She slipped into the dark, crowded interior and headed straight for the long mahogany bar.

"What can I get for you?" asked a thin, artsy-looking man with hair the color of a tangerine and more hardware on his face than Sears carried in the nuts-and-bolts aisle.

"Tequila straight shot," she said.

She drank the first shot and ordered another. The loud music comforted her. She drank the straight shot and swayed to the beat. All around her people were talking and laughing. It felt a little like she was a part of all that activity.

A man in an expensive Italian suit sidled up beside her. He was tall and obviously fit, with blond hair that had been carefully cut and styled. Banker, probably, or corporate lawyer. Too young for her, of course. He couldn't be much past thirty-five. How long was he there, trolling for a date, looking for the best-looking woman in the room? One drink, two?

Finally, he turned to her. She could tell by the look in his eyes that he knew who she was, and that small recognition seduced her. "Can I buy you a drink?"

"I don't know. Can you?" Was she slurring her words? That wasn't good. And she couldn't think clearly.

His gaze moved from her face, down to her breasts, and then back to her face. It was a look that stripped past any pretense. "I'd say a drink at the very least."

"I don't usually pick up strangers," she lied. Lately, there were only strangers in her life. Everyone else, everyone who mattered, had forgotten about her. She could really feel that Xanax kicking in now, or was it the tequila?

He touched her chin, a jawline caress that made her shiver. There was a boldness in touching her; no one did that anymore. "I'm Troy," he said.

She looked up into his blue eyes and felt the weight of her loneliness. When was the last time a man had wanted her?

"I'm Tully Hart," she said.

"I know."

He kissed her. He tasted sweet, of some kind of liquor, and of cigarettes. Or maybe pot. She wanted to lose herself in pure physical sensation, to dissolve like a bit of candy.

She wanted to forget everything that had gone wrong with her life, and how it was that she'd ended up in a place like this, alone in a sea of strangers.

"Kiss me again," she said, hating the pathetic pleading she heard in her voice. It was how she'd sounded as a child, back when she'd been a little girl with her nose pressed to the window, waiting for her mother to return. *What's wrong with me?* that little girl had asked anyone who would listen, but there had never been an answer. Tully reached out for him, pulling him close, but even as he kissed her and pressed his body into hers, she felt herself starting to cry, and when her tears started, there was no way to hold them back.

✦

September 3, 2010
2:01 A.M.

Tully was the last person to leave the bar. The doors banged shut behind her; the neon sign hissed and clicked off. It was past two now; the Seattle streets were empty. Hushed.

As she made her way down the slick sidewalk, she was unsteady. A man had kissed her—a stranger—and she'd started to cry.

Pathetic. No wonder he'd backed away.

Rain pelted her, almost overwhelmed her. She thought about stopping, tilting her head back, and drinking it in until she drowned.

That wouldn't be so bad.

It seemed to take hours to get home. At her condominium building, she pushed past the doorman without making eye contact.

In the elevator, she saw herself in the wall of mirrors.

Oh, God.

She looked terrible. Her auburn hair—in need of coloring—was a bird's nest, and mascara ran like war paint down her cheeks.

The elevator doors opened and she stepped out into the hallway. Her balance was so off it took forever to get to her door, and four tries to get her key into the lock. By the time she opened the door, she was dizzy and her headache had come back.

Somewhere between the dining room and the living room, she banged into a side table and almost fell. Only a last-minute Hail Mary grab for the sofa saved her. She sank onto the thick, down-filled white cushion with a sigh. The table in front of her was piled high with mail. Bills and magazines.

She slumped back and closed her eyes, thinking what a mess her life had become.

"Damn you, Katie Ryan," she whispered to the best friend who wasn't there. This loneliness was unbearable. But her best friend was gone. Dead. That was what had started all of it. Losing Kate. How pitiful was that? Tully had begun to plummet at her best friend's death and she hadn't been able to pull out of the dive. "I need you." Then she screamed it: "I *need* you!"

Silence.

She let her head fall forward. Did she fall asleep? Maybe . . .

When she opened her eyes again, she stared, bleary-eyed, at the pile of mail on her coffee table. Junk mail, mostly; catalogs and magazines she didn't bother to read anymore. She started to look away, but a picture snagged her attention.

She frowned and leaned forward, pushing the mail aside to reveal a *Star* magazine that lay beneath the pile. There was a small photograph of her face in the upper right corner. Not a good picture, either. Not one to be proud of. Beneath it was written a single, terrible word.

Addict.

She grabbed the magazine in unsteady hands, opened it. Pages fanned one past another until there it was: her picture again.

It was a small story; not even a full page.

THE REAL STORY BEHIND THE RUMORS

> Aging isn't easy for any woman in the public eye, but it may be proving especially difficult for Tully Hart, the ex-star of the once-phenom talk show *The Girlfriend Hour.* Ms. Hart's goddaughter, Marah Ryan, contacted *Star* exclusively. Ms. Ryan, 20, confirms that the fifty-year-old Hart has been struggling lately with demons that she's had all her life. In recent months, Hart has "gained an alarming amount of weight" and been abusing drugs and alcohol, according to Ms. Ryan . . .

"Oh, my God . . ."

Marah.

The betrayal hurt so badly she couldn't breathe. She read the rest of the story and then let the magazine fall from her hands.

The pain she'd been holding at bay for months, years, roared to life, sucking her into the bleakest, loneliest place she'd ever been. For the first time, she couldn't even imagine crawling out of this pit.

She staggered to her feet, her vision blurred by tears, and reached for her car keys.

She couldn't live like this anymore.

Two

✦

September 3, 2010
4:16 A.M.

Where am I?

What happened?

I take shallow breaths and try to move, but I can't make my body work, not my fingers or my hands.

I open my eyes at last. They feel gritty. My throat is so dry I can't swallow.

It is dark.

There is someone in here with me. Or some*thing*. It makes a banging sound, hammers falling on steel. The vibrations rattle up my spine, lodge in my teeth, give me a headache.

The sound—crunching, grinding metal—is everywhere; outside of me, in the air, beside me, inside of me.

Bang-scrape, bang-scrape.

Pain.

I feel it all at once.

Excruciating, exquisite. Once I am aware of it, of *feeling* it, there's nothing else.

✦

Pain wakens me: a searing, gnawing agony in my head, a throbbing in my arm. Something inside me is definitely broken. I try to move, but it hurts so much I pass out. When I wake up, I try again, breathing hard, air rattling in my lungs. I can smell my own blood, feel it running down my neck.

Help me, I try to say, but the darkness swallows my feeble intent.

OPENYOUREYES.

I hear the command, a voice, and relief overwhelms me. I am not alone.

OPENYOUREYES.

I can't. Nothing works.

SHESALIVE.

More words, yelled this time.

LIESTILL.

The darkness shifts around me, changes, and pain explodes again. A noise—part buzz saw on cedar, part child screaming—is all around me. In my darkness, light sparks like fireflies and something about that image makes me sad. And tired.

ONETWOTHREELIFT.

I feel myself being pulled, lifted by cold hands I can't see. I scream in pain, but the sound is swallowed instantly, or maybe it's only in my head.

Where am I?

I hit something hard and cry out.

ITSOKAY.

I am dying.

It comes to me suddenly, grabs the breath from my lungs.

I am dying.

✦

September 3, 2010
4:39 A.M.

Johnny Ryan woke, thinking, *Something's wrong.* He sat upright and looked around.

There was nothing to see, nothing out of place.

He was in his home office, on Bainbridge Island. Once again, he'd fallen asleep working. The curse of the working-from-home single parent. There weren't enough hours in the day to get everything done, so he stole hours from the night.

He rubbed his tired eyes. Beside him, a computer monitor revealed a frozen image, pixilated, of a ratty-looking street kid sitting beneath a crackling, on-and-off neon sign, smoking a cigarette down to the filter. Johnny hit the play key.

On-screen, Kevin—street name Frizz—started talking about his parents.

They don't care, the kid said with a shrug.

What makes you so sure? Johnny asked in the voice-over.

The camera caught Frizz's gaze—the raw pain and angry defiance in his eyes as he looked up. *I'm here, aren't I?*

Johnny had watched this footage at least one hundred times. He'd talked to Frizz on several occasions and still didn't know where the kid had grown up, where he belonged, or who was waiting up at night for him, peering into the darkness, worrying.

Johnny knew about a parent's worry, about how a child could slip into the shadows and disappear. It was why he was here, working day and night on a documentary about street kids. Maybe if he looked hard enough, asked enough questions, he'd find her.

He stared at the image on-screen. Because of the rain, there hadn't been many kids out on the street on the night he'd shot this footage. Still, whenever he saw a shape in the background, a silhouette that could be a young woman, he squinted and put on his glasses, peering harder at the picture, thinking: *Marah?*

But none of the girls he'd seen while making this documentary was his daughter. Marah had run away from home and disappeared. He didn't even know if she was still in Seattle.

He turned off the lights in his upstairs office and walked down the dark, quiet hallway. To his left, dozens of family photographs, framed in black and matted in white, hung along the wall. Sometimes he stopped and followed the trail of these pictures—his family—and let them pull him back to a happier time. Sometimes he let himself stand in front of his wife's picture and lose himself in the smile that had once illuminated his world.

Tonight, he kept moving.

He paused at his sons' room and eased the door open. It was something he did now: check obsessively on his eleven-year-old twins. Once you'd learned how bad life could go, and how quickly, you tried to protect those who remained. They were there, asleep.

He released a breath, unaware that he'd drawn it in, and moved on to Marah's closed door. There, he didn't slow down. It hurt too much to look in her room, to see the place frozen in time—a little girl's room—uninhabited, everything just as she'd left it.

He went into his own room and closed the door behind him. It was cluttered with clothes and papers and whatever books he'd started and stopped reading and intended to pick up again, when life slowed down.

Heading into the bathroom, he stripped off his shirt and tossed it into the hamper. In the bathroom mirror, he caught sight of himself. Some days when he saw himself, he thought, *Not bad for fifty-five,* and sometimes—like now—he thought, *Really?*

He looked . . . sad. It was in the eyes, mostly. His hair was longer than it should be, with fine strands of gray weaving through the black. He always forgot to get it cut. With a sigh, he turned on the shower and stepped in, letting the scalding-hot water pour over him, wash his thoughts away. When he got out, he felt better again, ready to take on the day. There was no point in trying to sleep. Not now. He towel-dried his hair and dressed in an old Nirvana T-shirt that he found on the floor of his closet and a pair of worn jeans. As he headed back into the hallway, the phone rang.

It was the landline.

He frowned. It was 2010. In this new age, only the rarest of calls came in on the old number.

Certainly people didn't call at 5:03 in the morning. Only bad news came at this hour.

Marah.

He lunged for the phone and answered. "Hello?"

"Is Kathleen Ryan there?"

Damned telemarketers. Didn't they ever update their records?

"Kathleen Ryan passed away almost four years ago. You need to take her off your call list," he said tightly, waiting for: *Are you a decision maker in your household?* In the silence that followed his question, he grew impatient. "Who is this?" he demanded.

"Officer Jerry Malone, Seattle police."

Johnny frowned. "And you're calling Kate?"

"There's been an accident. The victim has Kathleen Ryan's name in her wallet as an emergency contact."

Johnny sat down on the edge of the bed. There was only one person in the world who would still have Katie's name as an emergency contact. What in the hell had she done now? And who still had emergency contact numbers in their wallet? "It's Tully Hart, right? Is it a DUI? Because if she's—"

"I don't have that information, sir. Ms. Hart is being taken to Sacred Heart right now."

"How bad is it?"

"I can't answer that, sir. You'll need to speak to someone at Sacred Heart."

Johnny hung up on the officer, got the hospital's number from Google, and called. It took at least ten minutes of being transferred around before he found someone who could answer his questions.

"Mr. Ryan?" the woman said. "I understand you are Ms. Hart's family?"

He flinched at the question. How long had it been since he'd even spoken to Tully?

A lie. He knew exactly how long it had been.

"Yes," he answered. "What happened?"

"I don't have all the details, sir. I just know she's en route to us now."

He looked at his watch. If he moved quickly, he could make the 5:20 ferry and be at the hospital in a little more than an hour. "I'll be there as quickly as I can."

He didn't realize that he hadn't said goodbye until the phone buzzed in his ear. He hung up and tossed the handset on the bed.

He grabbed his wallet and picked up the phone again. As he reached for a sweater, he dialed a number. It rang enough times to remind him that it was early in the morning.

"H-hello?"

"Corrin. I'm sorry to call you so early, but it's an emergency. Can you pick up the boys and take them to school?"

"What's wrong?"

"I need to go to Sacred Heart. There's been an accident. I don't want to leave the boys alone, but I don't have time to bring them to you."

"Don't worry," she said. "I'll be there in fifteen minutes."

"Thanks," he said. "I owe you one." Then he hurried down the hallway and pushed open the boys' bedroom door. "Get dressed, boys. *Now*."

They sat up slowly. "Huh?" Wills said.

"I'm leaving. Corrin is going to pick you up in fifteen minutes."

"But—"

"But nothing. You're going to Tommy's house. Corrin might need to pick you up from soccer practice, too. I don't know when I'll be home."

"What's wrong?" Lucas asked, his sleep-lined face drawing into a worried frown. They knew about emergencies, these boys, and routine comforted them. Lucas most of all. He was like his mother, a nurturer, a worrier.

"Nothing," Johnny said tightly. "I need to get into the city."

"He thinks we're babies," Wills said, pushing the covers back. "Let's go, Skywalker."

Johnny looked impatiently at his watch. It was 5:08. He needed to leave now to make the 5:20 boat.

Lucas got out of bed and approached him, looking up at Johnny through a mop of brown hair. "Is it Marah?"

Of course that would be their worry. How many times had they rushed to see their mom in the hospital? And God knew what trouble Marah was in these days. They all worried about her.

He forgot how wary they could sometimes be even now, almost four years later. Tragedy had marked them all. He was doing his best with the boys, but his best wasn't really enough to compensate for their mother's loss. "Marah's fine. It's Tully."

"What's wrong with Tully?" Lucas asked, looking scared.

They loved Tully so much. How many times in the last year had they begged to see her? How many times had Johnny made some excuse? Guilt flared at that.

"I don't have all the details yet, but I'll let you know what's up as soon as I can," Johnny promised. "Be ready for school when Corrin gets here, okay?"

"We're not babies, Dad," Wills said.

"You'll call us after soccer?" Lucas asked.

"I will."

He kissed them goodbye and grabbed his car keys off the entry table. He looked back at them one last time—two identical boys who needed haircuts, standing there in their boxer shorts and oversized T-shirts, frowning with worry. And then he went out to his car. They were eleven years old; they could be alone for ten minutes.

He got into his car, started the engine, and drove down to the ferry. On board, he stayed in his car, tapping his finger impatiently on the leather-covered steering wheel for the thirty-five-minute crossing.

At precisely 6:10, he pulled up into the hospital's parking lot and parked in the artificial brightness thrown down by a streetlamp. Sunrise was still a half hour away, so the city was dark.

He entered the familiar hospital and strode up to the information desk.

"Tallulah Hart," he said grimly. "I'm family."

"Sir, I—"

"I want an update on Tully's condition, and I want it *now*." He said it so harshly the woman bounced in her seat as if a slight current had charged through her body.

"Oh," she said. "I'll be right back."

He walked away from the reception desk and began pacing. God, he hated this place, with its all-too-familiar smells.

He sank into an uncomfortable plastic chair, tapping his foot nervously on the linoleum floor. Minutes ticked by; each one unraveled his control just a little.

In the past four years, he'd learned how to go on without his wife, the love of his life, but it had not been easy. He'd had to stop looking back. The memories simply hurt too much.

But how could he not look back here, of all places? They'd come to this hospital for surgery and chemotherapy and radiation; they'd spent hours together here, he and Kate, promising each other that cancer was no match for their love.

Lying.

When they'd finally faced the truth, they'd been in a room, here. In 2006. He'd been lying with her, holding her, trying not to notice how thin she'd become in the year of her life's fight. Beside the bed, Kate's iPod had been playing Kelly Clarkson. *Some people wait a lifetime . . . for a moment like this.*

He remembered the look on Kate's face. Pain had been a liquid fire in her body; she hurt everywhere. Her bones, her muscles, her skin. She took as much morphine as she'd dared, but she'd wanted to be alert enough so that her kids wouldn't be afraid. *I want to go home,* she'd said.

When he'd looked at her, all he'd been able to think was: *She's dying.* The truth came at him hard, bringing tears to his eyes.

"My babies," she'd said quietly and then laughed. "Well, they're not babies anymore. They're losing teeth. It's a dollar, by the way. For the tooth fairy. And always take a picture. And Marah. Tell her I understand. I was mean to my mom at sixteen, too."

"I am not ready for this conversation," he'd said, hating his weakness. He'd seen the disappointment in her gaze.

"I need Tully," she'd said then, surprising him. His wife and Tully Hart had been best friends for most of their lives—until a fight had torn them apart. They hadn't spoken for the past two years, and in those years, Kate had faced cancer. Johnny couldn't forgive Tully, not for the fight itself (which had, of course, been Tully's fault), or for her absence when Kate needed her most.

"No. After what she did to you?" he'd said bitterly.

Kate had rolled slightly toward him; he could see how much it hurt her to do so. "I need Tully," she'd said again, softer this time. "She's been my best friend since eighth grade."

"I know, but—"

"You have to forgive her, Johnny. If I can, you can."

"It's not that easy. She hurt you."

"And I hurt her. Best friends fight. They lose sight of what matters." She had sighed. "Believe me, I know what matters now, and I need her."

"What makes you think she'll come if you call? It's been a long time."

Kate had smiled through her pain. "She'll come." She'd touched his face, made him look at her. "You need to take care of her . . . after."

"Don't say that," he'd whispered.

"She's not as strong as she pretends to be. You know that. Promise me."

Johnny closed his eyes. He'd worked so hard in the past few years to move past grief and fashion a new life for his family. He didn't want to remember that terrible year; but how could he not—especially now?

TullyandKate. They'd been best friends for almost thirty years, and if not for Tully, Johnny wouldn't have met the love of his life.

From the moment Tully had walked into his run-down office, Johnny had been mesmerized by her. She'd been twenty years old and full of passion and fire. She'd talked herself into a job at the small TV station he'd run then. He'd thought he'd fallen in love with her, but it wasn't love; it was something else. He'd fallen under her spell. She had been more alive and brighter than anyone he'd ever met. Standing beside her had been like being in sunlight after months of shadow-dwelling. He'd known instantly that she would be famous.

When she'd introduced him to her best friend, Kate Mularkey, who'd seemed paler and quieter, a bit of flotsam riding the crest of Tully's wave, he'd barely noticed. It wasn't until years later, when Katie dared to kiss him, that Johnny saw his future in a woman's eyes. He remembered the first time they'd made love. They'd been young—him thirty, her twenty-five—but only she had been naïve. *Is it always like that?* she'd asked him quietly.

Love had come to him like that, long before he'd been ready. *No,* he'd said, unable even then to lie to her. *It's not.*

After he and Kate had married, they'd watched Tully's meteoric rise in journalism from afar, but no matter how separate Kate's life became from Tully's, the two women stayed closer than sisters. They'd talked on the phone almost daily and Tully had come to their home for most holidays. When she'd given up on the networks and New York and returned to Seattle to create her own daytime talk show, Tully had begged Johnny to produce the TV show. Those had been good years. Successful years. Until cancer and Kate's death had torn everything apart.

He couldn't help remembering now. He closed his eyes and leaned back. He knew when it had begun to unravel.

At Kate's funeral, almost four years ago. October of 2006. They'd been in the first row of St. Cecilia's Church, sitting bunched together . . .

stiff and bleak-eyed, acutely aware of why they were here. They'd been in this church many times over the years, for Midnight Mass at Christmas and for Easter services, but it was different now. Instead of golden, glittery decorations, there were white lilies everywhere. The air in the church was cloyingly sweet.

Johnny sat Marine-straight, his shoulders back. He was supposed to be strong now for his children, their children, her children. It was a promise he'd made to her as she lay dying, but it was already hard to keep. Inside, he was dry as sand. Sixteen-year-old Marah sat equally rigid beside him, her hands folded in her lap. She hadn't looked at him in hours, maybe in days. He knew he should bridge that divide, force her to connect, but when he looked at her, he lost his nerve. Their combined grief was as deep and dark as the sea. So he sat with his eyes burning, thinking, *Don't cry. Be strong.*

He made the mistake of glancing to his left, where a large easel held a poster of Kate. In the picture, she was a young mother, standing on the beach in front of their Bainbridge Island house, her hair windblown, her smile as bright as a beacon in the night, her arms flung wide to welcome the three children running toward her. She had asked him to find that picture for her, one night when they lay in bed together, with their arms around each other. He'd heard the question and knew what it meant. *Not yet,* he'd murmured into her ear, stroking her bald head.

She hadn't asked him again.

Of course she hadn't. Even at the end, she'd been the stronger one, protecting all of them with her optimism.

How many words had she hoarded in her heart so that he wouldn't be wounded by her fear? How alone had she felt?

God. She had been gone for only two days.

Two days and already he wanted a do-over. He wanted to hold her again, and say, *Tell me, baby, what are you afraid of?*

Father Michael stepped up to the pulpit, and the congregation—already quiet—grew still.

"I'm not surprised so many people are here to say goodbye to Kate. She was an important person to so many of us—"

Was.

"You won't be surprised that she gave me strict orders for this service, and I don't want to disappoint her. She wanted me to tell you all to hold on to each other. She wanted you to take your sorrow and transform it into the joy that remains with life. She wanted you to remember the sound of her laughter and the love she had for her family. She wanted you to *live.*" His voice broke. "That was Kathleen Mularkey Ryan. Even at the end, she was thinking of others."

Marah groaned quietly.

Johnny reached for her hand. She startled at his touch and looked at him, and there it was, that unfathomable grief as she pulled away.

Music started up. It sounded far away at first, or maybe that was the roar of sound in his head. It took him a moment to recognize the song.

"Oh, no," he said, feeling emotion rise with the music.

The song was "Crazy for You."

The song they'd danced to at their wedding. He closed his eyes and felt her beside him, slipping into the circle of his arms as the music swept them away. *Touch me once and you'll know it's true.*

Lucas—sweet eight-year-old Lucas, who had begun to have nightmares again and sometimes had a meltdown when he couldn't find the baby blanket he'd outgrown years ago—tugged on his sleeve. "Mommy said it was okay to cry, Daddy. She made me and Wills promise not to be afraid to cry."

Johnny hadn't even realized he was crying. He wiped his eyes and nodded curtly, whispering, "That's right, little man," but he couldn't look at his son. Tears in those eyes would undo him. Instead, he stared straight ahead and zoned out. He turned Father's words into small brittle things, stones thrown against a brick wall. They clattered and fell, and through it all, he focused on his breathing and tried not to remember his wife. That, he would do in solitude, at night, when there was no one around.

Finally, after what felt like hours, the service ended. He gathered his family close and they went downstairs for the reception. There, as he looked around, feeling both stunned and broken, he saw dozens of unfamiliar or barely familiar faces and it made him understand that Kate had pieces of her life he knew nothing about and it made her feel distant to him. In a way, that hurt even more. At the first possible moment, he herded his children out of the church basement.

The church's parking lot was full of cars, but that wasn't what he noticed.

Tully was in the parking lot, with her face tilted up toward the last of the day's sunlight. She had her arms stretched wide and she was moving, swaying her hips, as if there were music somewhere.

Dancing. She was in the middle of the street, outside the church, dancing.

He said her name so harshly that Marah flinched beside him.

Tully turned, saw them coming toward the car. She tugged the buds out of her ears and moved toward him.

"How was it?" she asked quietly.

He felt a surge of rage and he grabbed hold of it. Anything was better than this bottomless grief. Of course Tully had put herself first. It *hurt* to go to Kate's funeral, so Tully didn't. She stood in the parking lot and danced. *Danced.*

Some best friend. Kate might be able to forgive Tully her selfishness; it wasn't so easy for Johnny.

He turned to his family. "Get in the car, everyone."

"Johnny—" Tully reached for him but he stepped aside. He couldn't be touched now, not by anyone. "I couldn't go in," she said.

"Yeah. Who could?" he said bitterly. He knew instantly that it was a mistake to look at her. Kate's absence was even more pronounced at Tully's side. The two women had always been together, laughing, talking, breaking into bad renditions of disco songs.

TullyandKate. For more than thirty years they'd been best friends, and now, when he looked at Tully, it hurt too much to bear. *She* was the one who should have died. Kate was worth fifteen Tullys.

"People are coming to the house," he said. "It's what she wanted. I hope you can make it."

He heard the sharpness of her indrawn breath and knew he'd hurt her.

"That's not fair," she said.

Ignoring that, ignoring her, he herded his family into the SUV and they drove home in an excruciating silence.

Pale late-afternoon sunlight shone down on the caramel-colored Craftsman-style house. The yard was a disaster, forgotten in the year of Katie's cancer. He parked in the garage and led the way into the house, where the faint scent of illness lingered in the fabric of the drapes and the woolen strands of the carpet.

"What now, Dad?"

He knew without turning who would have asked this question. Lucas, the boy who'd cried at every goldfish's death and drawn a picture for his dying mother every day; the boy who'd started to cry at school again and had sat quietly at his recent birthday party, unable to even smile as he opened his gifts. He felt everything so keenly, this boy. *Especially Lucas,* Kate had said on her last, terrible night. *He won't know how to miss me so much. Hold him.*

Johnny turned.

Wills and Lucas stood there, standing so close their shoulders were touching. The eight-year-olds had on matching black pants and gray V-neck sweaters. Johnny had forgotten this morning to make either boy take a shower and their shaggy haircuts were unruly, smushed in places from sleep.

Lucas's eyes were wide and bright, his lashes spiked with moisture. He knew his mother was *Gone,* but he didn't really understand how that could be.

Marah came up beside her brothers. She looked thin and pale, ghostlike in her black dress.

All of them looked at him.

This was his moment to speak, to offer comforting words, to give them advice they would remember. As their father, it was his job to turn the next few hours into a celebration of his wife's life. But how?

"Come on, boys," Marah said with a sigh. "I'll put *Finding Nemo* on."

"No," Lucas wailed. "Not *Finding Nemo.*"

Wills looked up. He took hold of his brother's hand. "The mom dies."

"Oh." Marah nodded. "How about *The Incredibles?*"

Lucas nodded glumly.

Johnny was still trying to figure out what in the hell to say to his wounded children when the doorbell rang for the first time.

He flinched at the sound. Afterward, he was vaguely aware of time passing, of people crowding around him and doors opening and closing. Of the sun setting and night pressing against the windowpanes. He kept thinking, *Move, go, say hi,* but he couldn't seem to make himself begin this thing.

Someone touched his arm.

"I'm so sorry, Johnny," he heard a woman say, and he turned.

She stood beside him, dressed in black, holding a foil-covered casserole dish. He could not for the life of him remember who she was. "When Arthur left me for that barista, I thought my life was over. But you keep getting up, and one day you realize you're okay. You'll find love again."

It took all his self-control not to snap out at this woman that death was different from infidelity, but before he could even think of her name, another woman showed up. She, too, thought hunger was his biggest problem now, judging by the size of the foil-covered tray in her plump hands.

He heard ". . . better place" . . . and walked away.

He pushed through the crowd and went to the bar that was set up in the kitchen. On the way, he passed several people, all of whom murmured some combination of the same useless words—*sorry, suffering over, better place.* He neither paused nor answered. He kept moving. He didn't look at the photographs that had been set up around the room, on easels and propped up against windows and lamps. In the kitchen, he found a clot of sad-eyed women working efficiently, taking foil off casserole dishes and burrowing through the utensil drawers. At his entrance, they stilled, quick as birds with a fox in their midst, and looked up. Their pity—and the fear that this could someday happen to them—was a tangible presence in the room.

At the sink, his mother-in-law, Margie, put down the pitcher she'd been filling with water. It hit the counter with a clank. Smoothing the hair away from her worry-lined face, she moved toward him. Women stepped aside to let her through. She paused at the bar, poured him a scotch and water over ice, and handed it to him.

"I couldn't find a glass," he said. Stupidly. The glasses were right beside him. "Where's Bud?"

"Watching TV with Sean and the boys. This isn't exactly something he can deal with. Sharing his daughter's death with all these strangers, I mean."

Johnny nodded. His father-in-law had always been a quiet man, and the death of his only daughter had broken him. Even Margie, who had remained vital and dark-haired and laughing well past her last birthday, had aged immeasurably since the diagnosis. She had rounded forward, as if expecting another blow from God at any second. She'd stopped dyeing her hair and white flowed along her part like a frozen river. Rimless glasses magnified her watery eyes.

"Go to your kids," Margie said, pressing her pale, blue-veined hand into the crook of his arm.

"I should stay here and help you."

"I'm fine," she said. "But I'm worried about Marah. Sixteen is a tough age to lose a mother, and I think she regrets how much she and Kate fought before Kate got sick. Words stay with you sometimes, especially angry ones."

He took a long sip of his drink, watched the ice rattle in his glass when he was done. "I don't know what to say to them."

"Words aren't what matter." Margie tightened her hold on his arm and led him out of the kitchen.

The house was full of people, but even in a crowd of mourners, Tully Hart was noticeable. The center of attention. In a black sheath dress that probably cost as much as some of the cars parked in the driveway, she managed to look beautiful in grief. Her shoulder-length hair was auburn these days, and she must have redone her makeup since the funeral. In the living room, surrounded by people, she gestured dramatically, obviously telling a story, and when she finished, everyone around her laughed.

"How can she smile?"

"Tully knows a thing or two about heartbreak, don't forget. She's spent a lifetime hiding her pain. I remember the first time I ever saw her. I walked across Firefly Lane to her house because she'd befriended Kate and I wanted to check her out. Inside that run-down old house across the street, I met her mom, Cloud. Well, I didn't *meet* her. Cloud was lying on the sofa spread-eagled, with a mound of marijuana on her stomach. She tried to sit up, and when she couldn't, she said, *F—— me, I'm stoned,* and flopped back down. When I looked at Tully, who was maybe fourteen, I saw the kind of shame that marks you forever."

"You had an alcoholic dad and you overcame it."

"I fell in love and had babies. A family. Tully thinks no one can love her except Kate. I don't think the loss has really hit her yet, but when it does, it's going to be ugly."

Tully put a CD into the stereo and cranked the music. *Born to be w-iiii-ld* blared through the speakers.

The people in the living room backed away from her, looking offended.

"Come on," Tully said, "who wants a straight shot?"

Johnny knew he should stop her, but he couldn't get that close. Not now, not yet. Every time he looked at Tully, he thought, *Kate's gone,* and the wound cracked open again. Turning away, he went up to comfort his children instead.

It took everything he had to climb the stairs.

Outside the twins' bedroom, he paused, trying to gather strength. *You can do this.*

He *could* do it. He had to. The children beyond this door had just learned that life was unfair and that death ripped hearts and families apart. It was his job to make them understand, to hold them together and heal them.

He drew in a sharp breath and opened the door.

The first thing he saw were the beds—unmade, rumpled, the *Star Wars* bedding in a tangled heap. The navy-blue walls—hand-painted by Kate to show clouds and stars and moons—had been covered over the years with the boys' artwork and some of their favorite movie posters. Golden T-ball and soccer trophies stood proudly on the dresser top.

His father-in-law, Bud, sat in the big papasan chair that easily held both boys when they played video games, and Sean, Kate's younger brother, lay asleep on Wills's bed.

Marah sat on the rug in front of the TV, with Lucas beside her. Wills was in the corner, watching the movie with his arms crossed, looking angry and isolated.

"Hey," Johnny said quietly, closing the door behind him.

"Dad!" Lucas lurched to his feet. Johnny scooped his son into his arms and held him tightly.

Bud climbed awkwardly out of the cushy papasan chair and got to his feet. He looked rumpled in his out-of-date black suit with a white shirt and wide polyester tie. His pale face, marked by age spots, seemed to have added creases and folds in the past weeks. Beneath bushy gray eyebrows, his eyes looked sad. "I'll give you some time." He went to the bed, thumped Sean on the shoulder, and said, "Wake up."

Sean came awake with a start and sat up sharply. He looked confused until he saw Johnny. "Oh, right." He followed his dad out of the room.

Johnny heard the door click shut behind him. On-screen, brightly colored superheroes ran through the jungle. Lucas slid out of Johnny's arms and stood beside him.

Johnny looked at his grieving children, and they looked at him. Their reactions to their mother's death were as different as they were, as unique. Lucas, the tenderhearted, was undone by missing his mom and confused about where exactly she'd gone. His twin, Wills, was a kid who relied on athleticism and popularity. Already he was a jock and well liked. This loss had offended and scared him. He didn't like being afraid, so he got angry instead.

And then there was Marah; beautiful sixteen-year-old Marah, for whom everything had always come easily. In the cancer year, she had closed up, become contained and quiet, as if she thought that if she made no noise at all, caused no disruption, the inevitability of this day could be avoided. He knew how deeply she regretted the way she'd treated Kate before she got sick.

The need in all of their eyes was the same, though. They looked to him to put their destroyed world back together, to ease this unimaginable pain.

But Kate was the heart and soul of this family, the glue that held them all together. Hers was the voice that knew what to say. Anything he said would be a lie. How would they heal? How would things get better? How would more time without Kate soothe them?

Marah rose suddenly, unfolding with the kind of grace that most girls would never know. She looked sylphlike in her grief, pale and almost ethereal, with her long black hair, black dress, and nearly translucent skin. He heard the hitch in her breathing, the way she seemed hard-pressed to inhale this new air.

"I'll put the boys to bed," she said, reaching out for Lucas. "Come on, rug rat. I'll read you a story."

"Way to make us feel better, Dad," Wills said, his mouth tightening. It was a dark, sadly adult expression on an eight-year-old face.

"It will get better," Johnny said, hating his weakness.

"Will it?" Wills said. "How?"

Lucas looked up at him. "Yeah, how, Dad?"

He looked at Marah, who looked so cold and pale she might have been carved of ice.

"Sleep will help," she said dully, and Johnny was pathetically grateful to her. He knew he was losing it, *failing,* that he was supposed to provide support, not accept it, but he was empty inside.

Just empty.

Tomorrow he'd be better. Do better.

But when he saw the sad disappointment on his children's faces, he knew what a lie that was.

I'm sorry, Katie.

"Good night," he said in a thick voice.

Lucas looked up at him. "I love you, Daddy."

Johnny dropped slowly to his knees and opened his arms. His sons pushed into his embrace and he held them tightly. "I love you, too." Over their heads, he stared up at Marah, who appeared unmoved. She stood straight and tall, her shoulders back.

"Marah?"

"Don't bother," she said softly.

"Your mom made us promise to be strong. Together."

"Yeah," she said, her lower lip trembling just a little. "I know."

"We can do it," he said, although he heard the unsteadiness of his voice.

"Yeah. Sure we can," Marah said with a sigh. Then: "Come on, boys, let's get ready for bed."

Johnny knew he should stay, comfort Marah, but he had no words.

Instead, he took the coward's route and left the room, closing the door behind him.

He went downstairs, and ignoring everyone, pushed through the crowd. He grabbed his coat from the laundry room and went outside.

It was full-on night now, and there wasn't a star in the sky. A thin layer of clouds obscured them. A cool breeze ruffled through the trees on his property line, made the skirtlike boughs dance.

In the tree limbs overhead, Mason jars hung from strands of ropy twine, their insides full of black stones and votive candles. How many nights had he and Kate sat out here beneath a tiara of candlelight, listening to the waves hitting their beach and talking about their dreams?

He grabbed the porch rail to steady himself.

"Hey."

Her voice surprised and irritated him. He wanted to be alone.

"You left me dancing all by myself," Tully said, coming up beside him. She had a blue wool blanket wrapped around her; its end dragged on the ground at her bare feet.

"It must be intermission," he said, turning to her.

"What do you mean?"

He could smell tequila on her breath and wondered how drunk she was. "The Tully Hart center-of-attention show. It must be intermission."

"Kate asked me to make tonight fun," she said, drawing back. She was shaking.

"I can't believe you didn't come to her funeral," he said. "It would have broken her heart."

"She *knew* I wouldn't come. She even—"

"And that makes it okay? Don't you think Marah would have liked to see you in there? Or don't you care about your goddaughter?"

Before she could answer—and what could she say?—he pushed away from her and went back inside, tossing his coat on the washing machine as he passed through the laundry room.

He knew he'd lashed out unfairly. In another time, in another world, he'd care enough to apologize. Kate would want him to, but right now he couldn't manage the effort. It took everything he had inside just to keep standing. His wife had been gone for forty-eight hours and already he was a worse version of himself.

Three

✦

That night, at four A.M., Johnny gave up on the idea of sleep. How had he thought it would be possible to find peace on the night of his wife's funeral?

He pushed the comforter back and climbed out of bed. Rain hammered the shake roof, echoed through the house. At the fireplace in the bedroom, he touched the switch and after a *thump-whiz* of sound, blue and orange flames burst to life, skating along the fake log. The faint smell of gas floated to him. He lost a few minutes standing there, staring into the fire.

After that, he found himself drifting. It was the only word he could come up with to describe the wandering that took him from room to room. More than once, he found himself standing somewhere, staring at something with no clear memory of how he'd come to be there or why he'd begun that particular journey.

Somehow, he ended up back in his bedroom. Her water glass was still on the nightstand. So were her reading glasses and the mittens she'd worn to bed at the end, when she'd always been cold. As clear as the sound of his own breathing, he heard her say, *You were the one for me, John Ryan. I loved you with every breath I took for two decades.* It was what she'd said to him on her last night. They'd lain in bed together, with him holding her because she was too weak to hold on to him. He remembered burying his face in the crook of her neck, saying, *Don't leave me, Katie. Not yet.*

Even then, as she lay dying, he had failed her.

He got dressed and went downstairs.

The living room was filled with watery gray light. Rain dropped from the eaves outside and softened the view. In the kitchen, he found the counter covered in carefully washed and dried dishes that had been placed on dish towels and a garbage can full of paper plates and brightly colored napkins. The refrigerator and freezer were both filled with foil-covered containers. His mother-in-law had done what needed to be done, while he had hidden outside in the dark, alone.

As he made a pot of coffee, he tried to imagine the new version of his life. All he saw were empty spaces at the dining room table, a car pool with the wrong driver, a breakfast made by the wrong hands.

Be a good dad. Help them deal with this.

He leaned against the counter, drinking coffee. As he poured the third cup, he felt an adrenaline spike of caffeine. His hands started to shake, so he got himself some orange juice instead.

Sugar on top of caffeine. What was next, tequila? He didn't really make a decision to move. Rather, he just drifted away from the kitchen, where every square inch held a reminder of his wife—the lavender hand lotion she loved, the YOU ARE SPECIAL plate she pulled out at the smallest of their children's achievements, the water pitcher she'd inherited from her grandmother and used on special occasions.

He felt someone touch his shoulder and he flinched.

Margie, his mother-in-law, stood beside him. She was dressed for the day in high-waisted jeans, tennis shoes, and a black turtleneck. She smiled tiredly.

Bud came up beside his wife. He looked ten years older than Margie. He had grown quieter in the past year, although none would have called him a chatty man before. He'd begun his goodbyes to Katie long before the rest of them had accepted the inevitable, and now that she was gone, he seemed to have lost his voice. Like his wife, he was dressed in his customary style—Wrangler jeans that accentuated both his thinning legs and straining paunch, a checked brown and white western shirt, and a big silver-buckled belt. His hair had checked out a long time ago, but he had enough growing in the arch of his brows to compensate.

Without words, they all walked back into the kitchen, where Johnny poured them each a cup of coffee.

"Coffee. Thank God," Bud said gruffly, taking the cup in his work-gnarled hand.

They looked at each other.

"We need to take Sean to the airport in an hour, but after that we can come back here and help," Margie said at last. "For as long as you need us."

Johnny loved her for the offer. She was closer to him than his own mother had ever been, but he had to stand on his own now.

The airport. That was the answer.

This *wasn't* just another day, and as sure as he stood here, he couldn't manage the pretense that it was. He couldn't feed his kids and drive them to school and then go to work at the station, producing some cheesy entertainment or lifestyle segment that wouldn't change anyone's life.

"I'm getting us the hell out of here," he said.

"Oh?" Margie said. "Where to?"

He said the first thing that came into his head. "Kauai." Katie had loved it there. They'd always meant to take the kids.

Margie peered up at him through her new rimless eyeglasses.

"Runnin' away doesn't change a thing," Bud said gruffly.

"I know that, Bud. But I'm drowning here. Everywhere I look . . ."

"Yeah," his father-in-law said.

Margie touched Johnny's arm. "What can we do to help?"

Now that Johnny had a plan—however imperfect and temporary—he felt better. "I'll go get started on reservations. Don't tell the kids. Let them sleep."

"When will you leave?"

"Hopefully today."

"You'd better call Tully and tell her. She's planning to be back here at eleven."

Johnny nodded, but Tully was the least of his concerns right now.

"Okay," Margie said, clapping her hands. "I'll clean out the fridge and move all the casseroles to the freezer in the garage."

"I'll stop the milk delivery and call the police," Bud said. "Just so they know to watch the house."

Johnny hadn't thought of any of those things. Kate had always done all the prep work for their trips.

Margie patted his forearm. "Go make the reservations. We've got you covered."

He thanked them both and then went into his office. Seated at the computer, it took him less than twenty minutes to make the reservations. By 6:50, he'd bought airline tickets and reserved a car and rented a house. All he had to do now was tell the kids.

He headed down the hallway. In the boys' room, he went to the bunk beds and found both of his sons on the bottom bunk, tangled up like a pair of puppies.

He ruffled Lucas's coarse brown hair. "Hey, Skywalker, wake up."

"I wanna be Skywalker," Wills murmured in his sleep.

Johnny smiled. "You're the Conqueror, remember?"

"No one knows who William the Conqueror is," Wills said, sitting up in his blue and red Spider-Man pajamas. "He needs a video game."

Lucas sat up, looking blearily around. "Is it school time already?"

"We're not going to school today," Johnny said.

Wills frowned. "Cuz Mom's dead?"

Johnny flinched. "I guess. We're going to Hawaii. I'm going to teach my kids how to surf."

"You don't know how to surf," Wills said, still frowning. Already he had become a skeptic.

"He does, too. Don't you, Dad?" Lucas said, peering up through his long hair. Lucas, the believer.

"I will in a week," Johnny said, and they cheered, bouncing up and down on the bed. "Brush your teeth and get dressed. I'll be back to pack your suitcases in ten minutes."

The boys jumped out of bed and raced to their bathroom, elbowing each other along the way. He walked slowly out of the room and down the hallway.

He knocked on his daughter's door, and heard her exhausted, "What?"

He actually drew in a breath before he stepped into her room. He knew it wouldn't be easy, talking his popular sixteen-year-old daughter into a vacation. Nothing mattered more to Marah than her friends. That would be especially true now.

She stood by her unmade bed, brushing her long, shiny black hair. Dressed for school in ridiculously low-rise, flare-legged jeans and a T-shirt that was toddler-sized, she looked ready to tour with Britney Spears. He pushed his irritation aside. This was no time for a fight about fashion.

"Hey," he said, closing the door behind him.

"Hey," she answered without looking at him. Her voice had that brittle sharpness that had become de rigueur since puberty. He sighed; even grief, it seemed, hadn't softened his daughter. If anything, it had made her angrier.

She put down her hairbrush and faced him. He understood now why Kate had been wounded so often by the judgment in their daughter's eyes. She had a way of cutting you with a glance.

"I'm sorry about last night," he said.

"Whatever. I have soccer practice after school today. Can I take Mom's car?"

He heard the way her voice broke on *Mom's*. He sat down on the edge of her bed and waited for her to join him there. When she didn't, he felt a wave of exhaustion. She was obviously fragile. They all were now—but Marah was like Tully. Neither of them knew how to show weakness. All Marah would let herself care about now was that he'd interrupted her routine, and God knew she spent more time getting ready for school than a monk devoted to morning prayers.

"We're going to Hawaii for a week. We can—"

"What? When?"

"We're leaving here in two hours. Kauai is—"

"No *way*," she screeched.

Her outburst was so unexpected he actually forgot what he was saying. "What?"

"I *can't* take off from school. I have to keep my grades up for college. I promised Mom I'd do well in school."

"That's admirable, Marah. But we need some time away as a family. To figure things out. We can get your assignments, if you'd like."

"If I'd like? If I'd like?" She stomped her foot. "You know *nothing* about high school. Do you know how competitive it is out there? How will I get into a good college if I tank this semester?"

"One week will hardly throw you under the bus."

"Ha! I have Algebra 2, Dad. And American Studies. *And* I'm on varsity soccer this year."

He knew there was a right way to handle this and a wrong way; he just didn't know what the right way was, and honestly, he was too tired and stressed out to care.

He stood up. "We're leaving at ten. Pack a bag."

She grabbed his arm. "Let me stay with Tully!"

He looked down at her, seeing how anger had stained her pale skin red. "Tully? As a chaperone? Uh. No."

"Grandma and Grandpa would stay here with me."

"Marah, we're going. We need to be together, just the four of us."

She stomped her foot again. "You're ruining my life."

"I doubt that." He knew he should say something of value or lasting importance. But what? He'd already come to despise the platitudes people handed out like breath mints after a death. He didn't believe that time would heal this wound or that Kate was in a better place or that they'd learn to go on. There was no way he could pass along some hollow sentiment to Marah, who was clearly hanging on by as thin a strand as he was.

She spun away and went into her bathroom and slammed the door.

He knew better than to wait for her to change her mind. In his bedroom, he grabbed his phone and made a call as he walked into the closet, looking for a suitcase.

"Hello?" Tully answered, sounding as bad as he felt.

Johnny knew he should apologize for last night, but every time he thought about it, he felt a rush of anger. He couldn't help mentioning her disappointing behavior last night, but even as he brought it up, he knew she would defend herself, and she did. *It's what Kate wanted.* It pissed him off. She was still talking about it when he cut her off with: "We're going to Kauai today."

"What?"

"We need time together now. You said so yourself. Our flight is at two, on Hawaiian."

"That's not much time to get ready."

"Yeah." He was already worried about that. "I gotta go." She was still talking, asking something about the weather, when he hung up.

✦

SeaTac International Airport was surprisingly crowded on this midweek October afternoon in 2006. They'd arrived early, to drop off Kate's brother, Sean, who was returning home.

At the self-service kiosk, Johnny got their boarding passes, and then glanced at his children, each of whom held some electronic device; Marah was sending something called a text on her new cell phone. He had no idea what a text was and didn't care. It had been Kate who'd wanted their sixteen-year-old to have a cell phone.

"I'm worried about Marah," Margie said, coming to stand beside him.

"Apparently I'm ruining her life by taking her to Kauai."

Margie made a *tsk*ing sound. "If you are not ruining a sixteen-year-old girl's life, you are not parenting her. That's not what I'm worried about. She regrets how she treated her mother, I think. Usually one grows out of that, but when your mom dies . . ."

Behind them, the airport's pneumatic doors whooshed opened and Tully came running toward them wearing a sundress, ridiculously high-heeled sandals, and a floppy white hat. She was rolling a Louis Vuitton duffel behind her.

She came to a breathless stop in front of them. "What? What's wrong? If it's the time, I did my best."

Johnny stared at Tully. What the hell was she doing here? Margie said something quietly, and then shook her head.

"Tully!" Marah cried out. "Thank God."

Johnny took Tully by the arm and pulled her aside.

"You aren't invited on this trip, Tul. It's just the four of us. I can't believe you thought—"

"Oh." The word was spoken quietly, barely above a breath. He could see how hurt she was. "You said 'we.' I thought you meant me, too."

He knew how often she'd been left behind in her life, abandoned by her mother, but he didn't have the strength to worry about Tully Hart right now. He was close to losing control of his life; all he could think about was his kids and not letting go. He mumbled something and turned away from her. "Come on, kids," he said harshly, giving them only a few minutes to say goodbye to Tully. He hugged his in-laws and whispered, "Goodbye."

"Let Tully come," Marah whined. "Please . . ."

Johnny kept moving. It was all he could think of to do.

✦

For the past six hours, both in the air and in the Honolulu airport, Johnny had been completely ignored by his daughter. On the airplane, she didn't eat or watch a movie or read. She sat across the aisle from him and the boys, her eyes closed, her head bobbing in time to music he couldn't hear.

He needed to let her know that even though she felt alone, she wasn't. He had to make sure she knew that he was still here for her, that they were still a family, as wobbly as that construct now felt.

But timing mattered. With teenage girls, one had to carefully pick the moment to reach out, or you'd draw back a bloody stump where your arm had been.

They landed in Kauai at four P.M. Hawaiian time, but it felt as if they'd been traveling for days. He moved down the jetway while the boys walked on ahead. Last week they would have been laughing; now they were quiet.

He fell into step beside Marah. "Hey."

"What?"

"Can't a guy just say hey to his daughter?"

She rolled her eyes and kept walking.

They walked past the baggage claim area, where women in muumuus handed out purple and white leis to people who'd come here on package deals.

Outside, the sun was shining brightly. Bougainvilleas in full pink bloom crawled over the parking area fence. Johnny led the way across the street to the rental car area. Within ten minutes they were in a silver convertible Mustang and headed north along the only highway on the island. They stopped at a Safeway store, loaded up on groceries, and then piled back into the car.

To their right, the coastline was an endless golden sandy beach lashed by crashing blue waves and rimmed in black lava rock outcroppings. As they drove north, the landscape became lusher, greener.

"Uh, it's pretty here," he said to Marah, who was beside him in the front passenger seat, hunched down, staring at her phone. Texting.

"Yeah," Marah said without looking up.

"Marah," he said in a warning tone. As in: *You're skating on thin ice.*

She looked over at him. "I am getting homework from Ashley. I *told* you I couldn't leave school."

"Marah—"

She glanced to her right. "Waves. Sand. Fat white people in Hawaiian shirts. Men who wear socks with their sandals. Great vacation, Dad. I totally forgot that Mom just died. Thanks." Then she went back to texting on her Motorola Razr.

He gave up. Ahead, the road snaked along the shoreline and spilled down into the verdant patchwork of the Hanalei Valley.

The town of Hanalei was a funky collection of wooden buildings and brightly colored signs and shave-ice stands. He turned onto the road indicated by MapQuest and immediately had to slow down to avoid the bikers and surfers crowded along either side of the street.

The house they'd rented was an old-fashioned Hawaiian cottage on Weke—pronounced *Veke,* apparently—Road. He pulled into the crushed-coral driveway and parked.

The boys were out of the car in an instant, too excited to be contained a second longer. Johnny carried two suitcases up the front steps and opened the door. The wooden-floored cottage was decorated in 1950s bamboo-framed furniture with thick floral cushions. A koa-wood kitchen and eating nook was on the left side of the main room, with a comfortable living room on the right side. A good-sized TV delighted the boys, who immediately ran through the house yelling, "Dibs!"

He went to the set of glass sliding doors that faced the bay. Beyond the grassy yard lay Hanalei Bay. He remembered the last time he and Kate had been here. *Take me to bed, Johnny Ryan. I'll make it worth your while . . .*

Wills bumped into him hard. "We're hungry, Dad." Lucas skidded up beside them. "Starving."

Of course. It was almost nine P.M. at home. How had he forgotten that his kids needed dinner? "Right. We'll go to a bar that your mom and I love."

Lucas giggled. "We can't go in a bar, Dad."

He ruffled Lucas's hair. "Not in Washington, maybe, but here it's A-okay."

"That's so cool," Wills said.

Johnny heard Marah in the kitchen behind him, putting groceries away. That seemed like a good sign. He hadn't had to beg or threaten her.

It took them less than thirty minutes to put their things away, claim their rooms, and change into shorts and T-shirts; then they walked along the quiet street to a ramshackle old wooden building near the center of town. The Tahiti Nui.

Kate had loved the retro Polynesian kitsch of the place, which was more than just a décor here. Rumor was that the interior had looked the same for more than forty years.

Inside the bar, which was filled with tourists and locals—easily separated by their dress—they found a small bamboo table near the "stage"—a three-foot-by-four-foot flat area with two stools and a pair of stand-up microphones.

"This is *great*!" Lucas said, bouncing on his seat so hard Johnny worried that he might fall through and hit the floor. Normally Johnny would have said something, tried to tame the boys, but their enthusiasm was exactly why they'd come here, so he nursed his Corona and said nothing. The tired-looking waitress had just delivered their pizza when the band—two Hawaiians with guitars—showed up. Their first song was Israel Kamakawiwo'ole's iconic ukulele version of "Somewhere Over the Rainbow."

Johnny felt Kate materialize on the bench seat beside him, singing quietly in her off-key voice, leaning against him, but when he turned, all he saw was Marah, frowning at him.

"What? I wasn't texting."

He didn't know what to say.

"Whatever," Marah said, but she looked disappointed.

Another song started. *When you see Hanalei by moonlight . . .*

A beautiful woman with sun-bleached blond hair and a bright smile went to the minuscule stage and danced a hula to the song. When the music stopped, she came over to their table. "I remember you," she said to Johnny. "Your wife wanted hula lessons the last time she was here."

Wills stared at the woman. "She's dead."

"Oh," the woman said. "I'm sorry."

God, but he was tired of those words. "It would mean a lot to her that you remembered," Johnny said tiredly.

"She had a beautiful smile," the woman said.

Johnny nodded.

"Well." She patted his shoulder as if they were friends. "I hope the island helps you. It can if you let it. Aloha."

Later, as they walked home in the fading light, the boys were so tired they started fighting. Johnny was too weary to care. In the house, he helped them get ready for bed and tucked them in, kissing them each good night.

"Dad?" Wills said sleepily. "Can we go in the water tomorrow?"

"Course, Conqueror. That's why we're here."

"I'll go in first, I bet. Luke's a chicken."

"Am not."

Johnny kissed them again and stood up. Pushing a hand through his hair and sighing, he walked through the house, looking for his daughter. He found her on the lanai, sitting in a beach chair. Moonlight bathed the bay. The air smelled of salt and sea and plumeria. Heady and sweet and seductive. Dotted along the two-mile curve of beach were fires, around which shadowy people danced and stood. The sound of laughter rose above the whooshing of the waves.

"We should have come here when she was alive," Marah said. She sounded young and sad and far away.

That stung. They'd meant to. How many times had they planned a trip, only to cancel for some now-forgotten reason? You think you have all the time in the world until you know you don't. "Maybe she's watching us."

"Yeah. Right."

"A lot of people believe in that."

"I wish I was one of them."

Johnny sighed. "Yeah. Me, too."

Marah got up. She looked at him, and the sadness he saw in her eyes was devastating. "You were wrong."

"About what?"

"The view doesn't change anything."

"I needed to get away. Can you understand that?"

"Yeah, well. I needed to stay."

On that, she turned and went back into the house. The door slid shut behind her. Johnny stood there, feeling shaken by her words. He hadn't thought of what his kids needed, not really. He'd folded their needs into his own and told himself they'd all be better off.

Kate would be disappointed in him. Already. Again. And even worse, he knew his daughter was right.

It wasn't paradise he wanted to see. It was his wife's smile, and that was gone forever.

This view didn't change a thing.

Four

✦

Even in paradise—or maybe especially in paradise—Johnny slept poorly, unaccustomed as he was to being alone, but each morning he woke to sunshine and blue skies and the sound of waves that seemed to be laughing as they rolled onto the sand. He was usually the first to waken. He started his day with a cup of coffee on the lanai. From there, he watched daylight come to the blue waters of the horseshoe-shaped bay. He often talked to Katie out here, saying things he wish he'd said before. In the end, as Kate lay dying, the mood in their house had been as somber as gray flannel, hushed and soft. He knew that Margie had let Katie talk about what scared her—leaving her children, knowing they would be sad, her pain—but Johnny had been unable to listen, even on that last day.

I'm ready, Johnny, she'd said in a voice as quiet as the brush of a feather. *I need you to be ready, too.*

I can't be, he'd said. What he should have said was, *I will always love you.* He should have held her hand and told her it was okay.

"I'm sorry, Katie," he said to her then—too late. He strained for a sign that she'd heard. A breeze in his hair, a flower falling in his lap. Something. But there was nothing. Just the sound of the waves whooshing coquettishly onto the sand.

The island had helped the boys, he thought. From dawn to dusk, they were on the go. They ran races in the yard, learned to bodysurf in the bubbling foam of the breaking waves, and buried each other in the sand. Lucas talked about Kate often, mentioning her in casual conversations almost every day. He made it sound as if she were at the store and would soon come home. At first it had disconcerted the rest of them, but in time, like the gentle, ceaseless roll of the waves, Lucas had brought Kate into their circle again, kept her present, shown them the way to remember her. *Mom would have loved this* became a common refrain, and it helped them all.

Well, perhaps that wasn't quite right. After a week in Kauai, Johnny still had no idea what would help Marah. She had become a pod version of herself—same elegant beauty and commitment to personal grooming, but with a flat look in her eyes and an automatronic way of moving. While he and the boys played in the surf, she sat on the beach, listening to music and tapping her cell phone as if it were a transponder that could get her rescued. She did everything that was asked of her, and more that wasn't, but she was a ghost version of herself. There and not there. When Kate was mentioned, Marah invariably said something like, *She's gone,* and walked away. She was always walking away. She didn't want to be on this vacation and she wanted to reiterate that point on a daily basis. Not once had she put so much as a toe in the water.

Like now. Johnny was standing waist-deep in the warm blue water, helping the boys catch waves on their Styrofoam boogie boards, while Marah sat in a bright pink beach chair on the sand, staring to her left.

As he watched her, a group of young men approached her.

"Keep walking, guys," he muttered.

"What, Dad?" Wills yelled. "Push me!"

Johnny gave Wills a push into the gathering wave and said, "Kick," but he wasn't watching his son.

On shore, the young men gathered around his daughter like bees to a blossom.

The boys were older, probably college-age. He was just about to get out of the water, march across the hot sand, and grab one of the kids by his surfer-dude hair when they walked away.

"Be right back, boys," he said, walking through the two-foot surf to the beach. He sat down next to his daughter. "So what did the Backstreet Boys want?" He tried to sound casual.

She didn't answer.

"They're too old for you, Marah."

She looked at him finally. Dark sunglasses shielded the expression in her eyes. "I was not having sex with them, Dad. We were just talking."

"About what?"

"Nothing." On that enlightening answer, she got up and walked back toward the house. The sliding door cracked shut behind her. They hadn't had a conversation that lasted longer than three sentences all week. Her anger was a Teflon shield. He could occasionally see glimpses of her pain and confusion and grief, but those seconds didn't last. She was hidden inside all that anger, a little girl crouched inside a teen with the perfect defense, and he didn't know how to break through the façade. That had always been Kate's job.

✦

That night, Johnny lay in bed, arms wishboned behind his head, staring at nothing. A ceiling fan whirred lazily overhead; the mechanism caught once each revolution, made a clicking sound between the *thwop-thwop-thwop* of the turning blades. The louvered shutters on his door clattered quietly, buffeted by the breeze.

It didn't surprise him that he was still awake on this last night of their vacation—if that was what a trip like this could reasonably be called—and he was pretty sure he wouldn't be able to go to sleep. He glanced at the digital clock: 2:15.

He threw back the sheets and got out of bed. He opened the louvered door and stepped out onto the lanai. A full moon hung in the night sky, impossibly bright. Black palm trees swayed in the plumeria-scented air. The beach looked like a curl of tarnished silver.

He stood there a long time, breathing in the sweet air, listening to the sound of the waves. It calmed him so much he thought maybe he could sleep.

He made a pass through the darkened house. It had become his habit in the past week to check on his kids during the night. He carefully opened the boys' bedroom door. They slept in twin beds, side by side. Lucas clutched his favorite toy—a stuffed orca whale. His brother had no time for such little-boy's toys.

He closed the door slowly and went down to Marah's room, opening the door quietly.

What he saw inside her room was so unexpected, it took him a second to comprehend.

Her bed was empty.

"What the hell . . . ?"

He turned on the light and looked more closely.

She was gone. So were her gold flip-flops. And her purse. Those were the only things he knew for sure, but it was enough to tell him that she hadn't been abducted. Well, that and the open window—which had been locked when she went to bed and could only be opened from the inside.

She had sneaked out.

"Son of a bitch." He went back to the kitchen and rummaged through the cupboards until he found a flashlight. Then he set off in search of his daughter.

The beach was mostly empty. Here and there he saw couples walking hand in hand along the silvery foam line left by the waves or coiled up together on beach towels. He didn't hesitate to bathe anyone he saw in the bright beam from the flashlight.

At the old concrete pier that jutted out into the surf, he paused, listening. He could hear laughter and smell smoke. There was a bonfire up ahead.

And he smelled marijuana.

He walked up onto the grass and around the start of the pier and headed into the big trees that grew in the area locals called Black Pot Beach.

There was a bonfire out on the point of land that separated Hanalei Bay from the Hanalei River. Even from here, he could hear the music—Usher, he was pretty sure—grinding out through cheap plastic speakers. Several cars had their headlights on.

He could see some kids dancing around a bonfire and more were gathered around a string of Styrofoam ice chests.

Marah was dancing with a long-haired, shirtless, cargo-shorted young man. She was downing the last of a beer as she moved her hips, swaying to the music. She was wearing a jeans skirt so small it could double as a cocktail napkin, and a tank top that she'd cut off to show her flat stomach.

No one even noticed him as he strode through the party. When he grabbed Marah by the wrist, she laughed at first and then gasped in recognition.

"Whoa, old guy," her dance partner said, frowning deeply, as if trying to focus.

"She's sixteen years old," Johnny said, thinking that he should get some kind of medal for not coldcocking the kid.

"Really?" The young man straightened and backed away, his hands lifted in the air. "Dude . . ."

"What is that supposed to mean? Is it a question or a statement or an admission of wrongdoing?"

The kid blinked in confusion. "Whoa. Huh?"

Johnny dragged Marah away from the party. At first she was complaining, but she went quiet just before she puked all over his flip-flops. Halfway down the beach, after she'd vomited twice more (with him holding her hair back), he put an arm around her to steady her.

In front of their cottage, he led her to a chair on the lanai.

"I feel like crap," she moaned as she slumped into the seat.

He sat down beside her. "Do you have any idea how much trouble a girl can get into in a situation like that? You could have been really hurt."

"Go ahead and yell at me. I don't care." She turned to him. There was a sorrow in her eyes that broke his heart, a new understanding of grief and unfairness. The loss of her mother would mold her life now.

He was in the weeds here. He knew what she needed: reassurance. She needed him to lie to her, to say that she could still be happy with her mom gone. But it wasn't true. No one would ever know Marah so well again, and they both knew it. He was a poor substitute.

"Whatever," Marah said, getting to her feet. "Don't worry, Dad. This won't happen again."

"Marah. I'm trying. Give me a—"

Ignoring him, she stomped back into the house. The door banged shut behind her.

He went back to his room, but there was no peace waiting for him in bed. He lay there, listening to the thwopping and clicking of the ceiling fan, trying to imagine life as it would be from tomorrow on.

He couldn't.

Neither could he imagine going home, standing in Kate's kitchen, sleeping on one side of the bed, waiting for her kiss to waken him every morning.

No way.

He needed a fresh start. They all did. It was the only way. And not a one-week vacation.

At seven A.M. Kauai time, he made a call. "Bill," he said when his friend answered. "Are you still looking for an executive producer for *Good Morning Los Angeles?*"

✦

September 3, 2010
6:21 A.M.

"Mr. Ryan?"

Johnny came back to the present. When he opened his eyes, bright lights surrounded him; the place smelled of disinfectant. He was sitting on a hard plastic chair in the hospital waiting area.

A man stood in front of him, wearing blue scrubs and a surgical cap. "I'm Dr. Reggie Bevan. Neurosurgeon. You're Tallulah Hart's family?"

"Yes," he said, after a pause. "How is she?"

"She's in critical condition. We've stabilized her enough for surgery, but—"

Code Blue, Trauma Nine blared through the hallway.

Johnny got to his feet. "Is that about her?"

"Yes," the doctor said. "Stay here. I'll be back." Without waiting for a reply, Dr. Bevan turned and ran toward the elevators.

Five

✦

Where am I?

Darkness.

I can't open my eyes, or maybe I can open them and there's nothing to see. Or maybe my eyes are ruined. Maybe I'm blind.

CLEAR.

Something hits me in the chest so hard I lose control of my body. I feel myself arch up and flop back down.

NOTHINGDRBEVAN.

There is a crush of pain, the kind I never even imagined, the kind that makes you want to give up, and then . . . nothing.

I am as still as a held breath; the darkness that cradles me is thick and quiet.

It takes no effort to open my eyes now. I am still in the dark, but it's different. Liquid, and as black as water on the seafloor. When I try to move, it resists. I push and push until I am sitting up.

The dark lessens in stages, turns gray and gloomy, and a light appears, diffuse, almost like a distant sunrise. And then suddenly it is bright.

I am in a room of some kind. I'm up high, looking down.

Below me, I see a crowd of people moving feverishly, calling out words I can't understand. There are machines in the room, and something red is spilling across the pale floor. The image is familiar; something I've seen before.

They are doctors and nurses. I am in a hospital room. They are trying to save someone's life. They are clustered around a body on a gurney. A woman's body. No. Wait.

My body.

I am the broken, bleeding, naked body on the gurney. It is my blood dripping onto the floor. I can see my bruised, bleeding, cut-up face . . .

The weird thing is that I feel nothing. It is *me,* Tully Hart. I am the body bleeding out in this room, but this is me, too; I'm floating in the corner, above it all.

White coats crowd in around my body. They are yelling to each other—I can see how worried they are by how widely they open their mouths and how red their cheeks become and how deeply they frown. They drag other machines into the room, wheels whining on the bloody floor, leaving white tracks in the red.

Their voices make sounds that mean nothing to me, like the adults in a Charlie Brown TV special. *Wa-WA-wa.*

SHESCODING.

I should care, but I don't. The drama down there is like a soap opera I've already seen. I turn suddenly and the walls are gone. In the distance, I see an effervescent, luminous light, and it beckons to me, warms me.

I think, *Go,* and as I think it, I am moving. I float into a world that is so sharp and clear it stings my eyes. Blue, blue sky, green, green grass, a snow-white flower falling from the cottony clouds. And light. Beautiful, incandescent light that is like nothing I've ever seen. For the first time in as long as I can remember, I feel at peace. As I move through the grass, a tree appears in front of me, a sapling at first, bending and knobby; it grows as I stand there, punching outward, widening until it takes up my entire field of vision. I wonder if I should go back, if this tree will grow over me, swallow me in its tangle of roots. As it grows, night falls around me.

When I look up, I see an array of stars. The Big Dipper. Orion's Belt. The same constellations I once studied from my yard as a girl, back when the world didn't seem big enough to hold all my dreams.

From somewhere far away, I hear the first tentative strains of music. *Billy, don't be a hero . . .*

The song opens me up in a way that makes it hard to breathe. It made me cry at thirteen, this song. Then, I'd thought it was a tragic love story, I think. Now I know it is a tragic life story.

Don't be a fool with your life.

A bicycle appears in front of me, an old-fashioned banana-seated girl's bike with a white basket. It is leaning against a hedge of roses. I go to it and climb on, pedaling . . . where? I don't know. A road appears beneath me, stretches as far as I can see. It is the middle of a starry night, and suddenly I am speeding downhill like a kid again, my hair is alive, whipping all around my face.

I know this place. Summer Hill. It is woven into my soul. Obviously I'm not *really* here. The real me is lying on a hospital bed, broken and bleeding. So I am imagining this, but I don't care.

I throw my arms open and let my speed pick up, remembering the first time I did this. We were in the eighth grade, Kate and me, and we were on these bikes, on this hill, riding into the start of a friendship that is the only true love story of my life. I forced her, of course. Threw rocks at her bedroom window and woke her up in the middle of the night and begged her to sneak out with me.

Did I know how our whole lives would be changed with that one choice? No. But I knew my life needed changing. How could I not? My mother had perfected the art of leaving me and I had spent my entire childhood pretending truth was fiction. Only with Kate had I ever really been honest. My BFF. The only person who had ever loved me for me.

The day we became friends is one I will never forget. It makes sense to me that I remember it now. We were fourteen-year-old girls, both friendless and as different as salt and pepper. On that first night, I'd told my stoned mom—who'd started calling herself Cloud in the seventies—that I was going to a high school party and she'd told me to have fun.

In a dark stand of trees, a boy I barely knew raped me and left me to walk home alone. On the way, I saw Katie sitting on the top rail of her fence. She spoke to me as I walked past.

"I love it out here at night. The stars are so bright. Sometimes, if you stare up at the sky long enough, you'll swear tiny white dots are falling all around you, like fireflies." A retainer drew the s's into a long lisp. "Maybe that's how this street got its name. You probably think I'm a nerd for even saying that. . . . Hey, you don't look good. And you reek like puke."

"I'm fine."

"Are you okay? Really?"

To my horror, I started to cry.

That was the beginning. Our beginning. I told her my secret shame and she held out her hand and I clung to her. From that day on, we were inseparable. Through high school and college, and forever after that, no experience was real until I told Katie about it, no day was quite right if we didn't talk. By the time we were eighteen, we were TullyandKate, the pair, impossible to separate. I was there at her wedding and at the birth of her babies, and when she tried to write a book, and I was there in 2006 when she took her last breath.

With my hands outstretched and the wind streaming through my hair and memories riding alongside me, I think: *This is how I should die.*

Die? Who says you get to die?

I would know that voice anywhere. I have missed it every single day for the last four years.

Kate.

I turn my head and see an impossible sight: Kate is on a bike beside me. The sight of her overwhelms me, and I think: *Of course.* This is my version of going into the light, and she has always been my light. For a brief, beautiful last second, we're TullyandKate again.

"Katie," I say in awe.

She gives me a smile that seems to sear through the years.

The next thing I know, we are sitting on the grassy, muddy bank of the Pilchuck River, just like we used to, back in the seventies. The air smells of rain and mud and deep green trees. A decaying, moss-furred log gives us something to rest against. The river's gurgling song swirls around us.

Hey, Tul, she says.

At the sound of her voice, happiness unfolds within me, a beautiful white bird opening its wings. Light is everywhere, bathing us. In it, I feel that beautiful peace again, and it soothes me. I have been in pain for so long, and lonely for even longer.

I turn to Kate, drink in the sight of her. She is translucent almost, shimmery. When she moves, even just a little, I can see a hint of the grass beneath her. When she looks at me, I see both sadness and joy in her eyes and I wonder how those two emotions can exist in such perfect balance within her. She sighs and I get a scent of lavender.

The river bubbles and slaps around us, sends up its rich, fecund scent of both new growth and decay. It turns into music, our music; the wave tops form notes and rise up and I can hear that old Terry Jacks song, *We had joy, we had fun, we had seasons in the sun*. How many nights had we hauled my little transistor radio down here and set it up and listened to our music while we talked? "Dancing Queen" . . . "You Make Me Feel Like Dancing" . . . "Hotel California" . . . "Da Do Run Run."

What happened? Kate asks quietly.

I know what she is asking. Why am I here—and in the hospital.

Talk to me, Tul.

God, how I have missed hearing her say that to me. I *want* to talk to my best friend, tell her how I screwed up. She always made everything okay. But the words don't come to me. I can't find them in my head; they dance away like fairies when I reach for them.

You don't need words. Just close your eyes and remember.

I remember when it started to go wrong. The one day that was worse than all the rest, the one day that changed everything.

October of 2006. The funeral. I close my eyes and remember being in the middle of the St. Cecilia's parking lot all . . .

alone. There are cars all around me, parked neatly in their spots. A lot of SUVs, I notice.

Kate has given me an iPod as her goodbye gift and a letter. I am supposed to listen to "Dancing Queen" and dance all by myself. I don't want to do it, but what choice do I have, and really, when I hear the words *you can dance,* for a brief, wondrous moment, the music takes me away from here.

And then it is over.

I see her family coming toward me. Johnny; Kate's parents, Margie and Bud; her kids; her brother, Sean. They look like prisoners of war freed at the end of a long death march—broken-spirited and surprised to be alive. We gather together and someone says something—what, I don't know. I answer. We pretend to be okay for each other. Johnny is angry—how could it be any other way?

"People are coming to the house," he says.

"It's what she wanted," Margie says. (How can she be standing? Her grief outweighs her by a hundred pounds.)

The thought of it—a so-called celebration of Kate's life—makes me feel sick.

I was not good at the whole making-death-a-positive-transition thing. How could I? I wanted her to fight to the last breath. It was a mistake. I should have listened to her fear, comforted her. Instead I'd promised her that everything would be okay, that she would heal.

But I'd made another promise, too. At the end. I'd sworn to take care of her family, to be there for her children, and I would not let her down again.

I follow Margie and Bud to their Volvo. Inside, the car smells like my childhood at the Mularkeys'—menthol cigarettes, Jean Nate perfume, and hair spray.

I imagine Katie beside me again, in the backseat of the car, with her dad driving, and her mom blowing smoke out the open window. I can almost hear John Denver singing about his Rocky Mountain high.

The four miles that stretch between the Catholic church and the Ryan house seem to take forever. Everywhere I look, I see Kate's life. The drive-through coffee stand she frequented, the ice-cream shop that made her favorite *dulce de leche,* the bookstore that was always her first stop at Christmastime.

And then we are there.

The yard has a wild, untended look to it. Overgrown. Katie had always been "going to" learn to garden.

We park and I get out. Kate's brother, Sean, comes up beside me. He is five years younger than Kate and me . . . or than *me,* I guess . . . but he is so slight and nerdy and hunched that he looks older. His hair is thinning and his glasses are out of date, but behind the lenses his green eyes are so like Katie's that I hug him.

Afterward, I step back, waiting for him to speak. He doesn't, and neither do I. We have never had much to say to each other and today is obviously not a day to begin a conversation. Tomorrow he will return to his tech job in the Silicon Valley, where I imagine him living alone, playing video games at night, and eating sandwiches for every meal. I don't know if this is even close to his life, but it's how I see it.

He steps away and I am left alone at the car, staring up at a house that has always felt like my home, too.

I can't go in.

I can't.

But I have to.

I draw in a deep breath. If there's one thing I know how to do, it's go on. I have perfected the art of denial, haven't I? I have always been able to ignore my pain, smile, and go on. That's what I have to do now.

For Kate.

I go inside and join Margie in the kitchen. Together, we go about the business of setting up for a party. I move fast, becoming one of those bustling women who flit like a hummingbird. It is the only way I can keep going. *Don't think about her. Don't remember.* Margie and I become a work crew, wordlessly readying this house for a party neither of us wants to attend. I set up easels throughout the house and place photographs on them, the pictures Kate had chosen to reflect her life. I can't look at any of them.

I am hanging on to my composure one indrawn breath at a time when I hear the doorbell ring. Behind me, footsteps thud on hardwood.

It is time.

I turn and do my best to smile, but it is uneven and impossible to maintain. I move through the crowd carefully, pouring wine and taking plates away. Every minute seems like a triumph of will. As I move, I hear snippets of conversation. People are talking about Kate, sharing memories. I don't listen—it hurts too much and I am close to losing it now—but the stories are everywhere. As I hear *her bid at the Rotary auction,* I realize that the people in this room are talking about a Kate I didn't know, and at that, sadness darts deep. And more. Jealousy.

A woman in an ill-fitting and outdated black dress comes up to me and says, "She talked about you a lot."

I smile at that, grateful. "We were best friends for more than thirty years."

"She was so brave during her chemo, wasn't she?"

I can't answer that. I wasn't there for her, not then. In the three decades of our friendship, there was a two-year blip when a fight escalated. I had known how depressed Kate was and I'd tried to help, but as is usual for me, I went about it all wrong. In the end, I hurt Kate deeply and I didn't apologize.

In my absence, my best friend battled cancer and had a double mastectomy. I was not there for her when her hair fell out or when her test results turned bad or when she decided to stop treatment. I will regret it for as long as I breathe.

"That second round was brutal," says another woman, who looks like she has just come from yoga, in black leggings, ballet flats, and an oversized black cardigan.

"I was there when she shaved her head," another woman says. "She was *laughing,* calling herself GI Kate. I never saw her cry."

I swallow hard.

"She brought lemon bars to Marah's play, remember?" someone else says. "Only Katie would bring treats when she was . . ."

"Dying," someone else says quietly, and finally the women stop talking.

I can't take any more of this. Kate had asked me to keep people smiling. *No one livens up a party like you, Tul. Be there for me.*

Always, girlfriend.

I break free of the women and go over to the CD player. This old-man jazz music isn't helping. "This is for you, Katie Scarlett," I say, and pop a CD into the slot. When the music starts, I crank up the volume.

I see Johnny across the room. The love of her life, and, sadly, the only man in my own. The only man I've ever been able to count on. When I look at him, I see how battered he is, how broken. Maybe if you didn't know him you wouldn't see it—the downward shoulders, the place he'd missed in his morning shave, the lines beneath his eyes that had been etched there by the string of nights when he hadn't slept. I know he has no comfort to offer me, that he has been scrubbed bare by grief.

I've known this man for most of my life, first as my boss and then as my best friend's husband. For all the big events of both our lives, we've been together, and that's a comfort to me. Just seeing him eases my loneliness a little. I need that, to feel less alone on this day when I've lost my best friend. Before I can go to him, he turns away.

The music, our music, pours like elixir into my veins, fills me. Without even thinking, I sway to the beat. I know I should smile, but my sadness is waking again, uncoiling. I see the way people are looking at me. Staring. As if I'm inappropriate somehow. But they are people who didn't know her. I was her best friend.

The music, our music, brings her back to me in a way no spoken words ever could.

"Katie," I murmur as if she were beside me.

I see people backing away from me.

I don't care what they think. I turn and there she is.

Kate.

I come to a stop in front of an easel. On it is a picture of Kate and me. In it, we are young and smiling, with our arms looped around each other. I can't remember when it was taken—the nineties, judging by my completely unflattering "Rachel" haircut and vest and cargo pants.

Grief pulls the legs out from underneath me and I fall to my knees. The tears I have been holding back all day burst out of me in great, wracking sobs. The music changes to Journey's *Don . . . n't stop bee-lieving* and I cry even harder.

How long am I there? Forever.

Finally, I feel a hand on my shoulder, and a gentle touch. I look up and see Margie through my tears. The tenderness in her gaze makes me cry again.

"Come on," she says, helping me to my feet. I cling to her, let her help me into the kitchen, which is busy with women doing dishes, and then into the laundry room, where it is quiet. We hold on to each other but say nothing. What is there to say? The woman we love is gone.

Gone.

And suddenly I am beyond tired. I am exhausted. I feel myself drooping like a fading tulip. Mascara stings my eyes; my vision is still watery with tears. I touch Margie's shoulder, noticing how thin and fragile she has become.

I follow her out of the shadowy laundry room and make my way back into the living room, but I know instantly that I can't be here anymore. To my shame, I can't do what Kate asked of me. I can't pretend to celebrate her life. Me, who has spent a lifetime pretending to be fine-good-great, can't do that now. It is too soon.

✦

The next thing I know, it's morning. Before I even open my eyes it hits me. *She's gone.*

I groan out loud. Is this my new life, this constant rediscovery of loss?

As I get out of bed, I feel a headache start. It gathers behind my eyes, pulses. I have cried in my sleep again. It is an old childhood habit that grief has reanimated. It reminds me that I am fragile.

It is a state of being that offends me, but I can't seem to find the strength to combat it.

My bedroom feels foreign to me, too. I have hardly been here in the last five months. In June, when I found out about Kate's cancer, I changed my life in an instant; I walked away from everything—my mega-successful TV talk show and my condominium—and dedicated my life to caring for my best friend.

My phone rings and I stumble toward it, grateful for any distraction. The caller ID says *Ryan* and my first thought is, *Kate's calling,* and I feel a spike of joy. Then I remember.

I pick up, hearing the strain in my voice as I say, "Hello?"

"What happened to you last night?" Johnny says without even bothering to say hi.

"I couldn't take it," I say, slumping onto the floor by my bed. "I tried."

"Yeah. Big surprise."

"What does *that* mean?" I sit up. "The music? It's what Kate wanted."

"Did you even talk to your goddaughter?"

"I tried," I say, stung. "She only wanted to be with her friends. And I read the boys a story before bed. But . . ." My voice cracks. "I couldn't stand it, Johnny. Being without her . . ."

"You were okay for the two years of your fight."

I draw in a sharp breath. He has never said anything like this before. In June, when Kate called and I came running to the hospital, Johnny welcomed me back into the family without a word. "She forgave me. And believe me, I was not okay."

"Yeah."

"Are you saying you didn't forgive me?"

He sighs. "None of this matters anymore," he says after a pause. "She loved you. That's that. And we're all hurting. Christ. How are we going to make it? Every time I look at the bed, or at her clothes in the closet . . ." He clears his throat. "We're going to Kauai today."

"What?"

"We need time together now. You said so yourself. Our flight is at two, on Hawaiian."

"That's not much time to get ready," I say. An image blossoms in my mind—the five of us on the beach, healing together. "It's perfect. Sunshine and—"

"Yeah. I gotta go."

He's right. We can talk later. Now, I need to hurry.

✦

I hang up and get moving. Packing for paradise takes no time at all, and in less than twenty minutes, I am packed and showered. I pull my damp hair into a stubby ponytail and dash on makeup as quickly as I can. Johnny hates it when I'm late. Tully-time, he calls it, and he's not smiling when he says it.

In my walk-in closet, I find a teal and white Lilly Pulitzer dress and pair it with silver high-heeled sandals and a white straw hat.

As I slip into the jersey dress, I imagine this vacation. It is something I need—this time away with the only family I have. We will grieve together, share memories, and keep Kate's spirit alive among us.

We need each other. God knows I need them.

I am ready at 11:20—only a few minutes later than optimal—and I call for a Town Car. I'm not that late. No one really needs two hours at the airport.

I grab my small rolling bag and leave the condo. Downstairs, a black Town Car is waiting in front of the building.

"SeaTac," I say, depositing my luggage at the curb by the trunk.

Surprisingly, the traffic is sluggish on this warm autumn morning. I look at my watch repeatedly.

"Go faster," I say to the driver, tapping my foot on the floor. At SeaTac, we pull up to the terminal and I am out of the car before the driver can even open his door. "Hurry up," I say, waiting for him to get my luggage, checking my watch. It is 11:47. I am late.

Finally, I get my bag and I run, holding my hat on my head and dragging the suitcase behind me. My big straw bag keeps slipping off my shoulder, scratching my bare arm. The terminal is crowded. It takes me a minute to find them in the crowd, but there they are, over by the Hawaiian Airlines ticket counter.

"I'm here!" I yell, waving like a game show contestant trying to get noticed. I run toward them. Johnny stares at me in confusion. Have I done something wrong?

I come to a breathless stop. "What? What's wrong? If it's the time, I did my best."

"You're always late," Margie says with a sad smile. "It's not that."

"Am I overdressed? I have shorts and flip-flops."

"Tully!" Marah says, grinning. "Thank God."

Johnny moves in closer to me. Margie eases away at the same time. Their movements feel staged, as choreographed as something from *Swan Lake,* and it bothers me. Johnny takes me by the arm and pulls me aside.

"You aren't invited on this trip, Tul. It's just the four of us. I can't believe you thought—"

I feel as if I've been punched in the stomach, hard. The only thing I can think of to say is, "Oh. You said 'we.' I thought you meant me, too."

"You understand," he says, phrasing it as a statement, not a question.

Apparently I am a fool for *not* understanding.

I feel like that abandoned ten-year-old again, sitting on a dirty city stoop, forgotten by my mother, wondering why I am so easy to leave behind.

The twins come up on either side of us, jubilant in their excitement, amped up on the idea of adventure. They have unruly brown hair that is too long and curling at the ends and bright blue eyes and smiles that have returned since yesterday.

"You comin' to Kauai with us, Tully?" Lucas says.

"We're gonna *surf,*" Wills says, and I can imagine how aggressive he will be in the water.

"I have to work," I say, even though everyone knows that I walked away from my show.

"Yeah," Marah says. "Cuz, like, having you come would make it fun, so natch you're not coming."

I untangle myself from the boys and go to Marah, who is standing by herself, doing something on her phone. "Cut your old man some slack. You're too young to know about true love, but they found it, and now she's gone."

"And, like, *sand* is going to help?"

"Marah—"

"Can I stay with you?"

I want it so badly I feel sick, and although I am notoriously self-centered—in fights, Kate often called me narcissistic—I know a bone-crushing fall when I see it. This is not about me. And Johnny is in no mood for this. I can see it. "No, Marah. Not this time. You need to be with your family."

"I thought you were part of the family."

Have fun is all I can manage.

"Whatever."

As I watch them walk away, I feel scaldingly, achingly alone. None of them looks back at me.

Margie moves closer and touches my face. Her soft, lined palm presses against my cheek. I smell the citrusy hand lotion she loves; that and the barest hint of menthol cigarettes.

"They need this," she says quietly. I hear the raspy sound of her voice and know how tired she is—to her bones. "Are you okay?"

Her daughter is dead and she is worried about me. I close my eyes, wishing I could be stronger.

Then I hear her crying; it is a sound as soft as a feather falling, almost lost in the airport noise. She has been strong for so long, strong for her daughter and everyone. I know there are no words, so I offer none. I just pull her into my arms and hold her close. Finally, she lets go and steps back.

"You want to come home with us?"

I don't want to be alone, but I can't go to the house on Firefly Lane. Not yet. "I can't," I say, and I see that she understands.

After that, we go our separate ways.

✦

At home, I pace the rooms of my high-rise condominium. It has never been a home, this place. No one has ever lived here except me, and I have really only resided here. There are few personal mementos or knickknacks. My designer pretty much chose everything and apparently she liked ivory. Everything is some shade of off-white: marble floors, nubby winter-white furniture, and stone and glass tables.

It is beautiful in its way, and looks like the home of a woman who has it all. But here I am, forty-six, and alone.

Work.

My career has been my choice, over and over. As far back as I can remember, I've had dreams with a capital *D*. It began in the house on Firefly Lane, with Kate, when we were fourteen years old. I remember the day as if it were yesterday; it is a story I've told in a dozen interviews over the years. How Katie and I were in her house, and Margie and Bud were watching the news and Margie turned to me and said, "Jean Enerson is changing the world. She's one of the first women to anchor the nightly news."

And I said, "I'm going to be a reporter."

It had been as natural as breathing, saying that. I wanted to become a woman the whole world admired. I did it by paring away every single dream except one: I needed success like a fish needed water. Without it, who would I be? Just a girl with no family who was easy to leave behind and put aside.

It is what I have in life—fame and money and success.

At that, I know. It is time for me to go back to work.

That's how I will get through this grief. I will do what I've always done. I'll look strong and pretend. I'll let the adoration of strangers soothe me.

I go into my walk-in closet and exchange the brightly colored jersey dress for a pair of black pants and a blouse. This is when I realize I have gained weight. The pants are so tight I can't get them zipped.

I frown. How is it that I didn't notice gaining weight in the last few months? I grab a knit skirt and put it on instead, noticing the bulge of my belly and the widening of my hips.

Great. Something else to worry about: weight gain in a high-def world. I grab my purse and head out, ignoring the pile of mail the building manager has placed on my kitchen counter.

It is only a handful of blocks to my studio, and usually I have a driver pick me up, but today, in honor of the widening of my ass, I decide to walk. It is a gorgeous fall day in Seattle, one of those sunshine masterpieces that turn this city into one of the prettiest in the country. The tourists have gone home and so the sidewalks are quiet, populated by locals who rush to and fro without making eye contact.

I come to the large, warehouse-type building that houses my production company. Firefly, Inc. The space is absurdly expensive, located as it is in Pioneer Square, less than a block from the blue shores of Elliott Bay, but what do I care about cost? The show I produce makes millions.

I unlock the door and go inside. The halls are dark and empty, a stark reminder that I walked away and never looked back. Shadows collect in corners and hide in hallways. As I walk toward the studio, I feel my heartbeat speed up. Sweat breaks out along my forehead, itches. My palms turn damp.

And then I am there, standing at the red curtain that separates backstage from my world. I push the curtain aside.

The last time I was on this stage, I'd told my audience about Katie, how she'd been diagnosed with inflammatory breast cancer, and I'd talked about the warning signs, and then I signed off. Now I would have to talk about what had happened, explain how it felt to sit by my best friend's bed and hold her hand and tell her it would be okay long past the time when that was true. Or how it felt to gather up her pills and pour out the last of the water in the pitcher by her empty bed.

I grab the stanchion beside me. It feels cold and unforgiving in my grip, but it keeps me standing.

I can't do it. Not yet. I can't talk about Katie, and if I can't talk about her, I can't stride back into my old life, onto my stage, and be the Tully Hart of daytime TV.

For the first time in forever, I don't know who I am. I need a little time to myself, so that I can find my balance again.

✦

When I step back out onto the street, it is raining. The weather in Seattle is like that: quicksilver. I clutch my handbag and lumber up the slick sidewalk, surprised to find that I am out of breath when I get to my building.

There, I come to a stop.

What now?

I go up to my penthouse and I walk idly into the kitchen, where mail is piled in a huge number of stacks. It's funny, in all my months away, I never really thought about the nuts and bolts of my other life. I didn't check messages or open my bills or even think much about any of it. I counted on the machinery of my life—agents, managers, accountants, stockbrokers—to keep me on track.

I know I need to dive back in, to take charge again and reclaim my life, but honestly, the thought of going through all this mail is daunting. Instead, I call my business manager, Frank. I will hand off the responsibility to him. It's what I pay him for: to pay my bills and invest my money and make my life easier. I need that now.

The number rings repeatedly and then goes to voice mail. I don't bother to leave a message. Is it Saturday?

Maybe a nap will help. Mrs. Mularkey used to say that a good night's sleep could change everything, and I need to be changed. So I go into my room, pull the curtains shut, and crawl into bed. For the next five days, I do almost nothing except eat too much and sleep poorly. Each morning when I wake up, I think this is it, this is the day I will be able to climb out of this grief and be me again, and each night I drink until I can't remember the sound of my best friend's voice.

And then it comes to me, on the sixth day after Kate's funeral. An idea so grand and perfect that I can't believe I haven't considered it before.

I need closure. That's how I will put all this dark sadness away and go on, that's how I will heal. I need to look this grief in the heart and say goodbye. I need to help Johnny and the kids, too.

Suddenly, I know how to do it.

✦

It is nightfall when I pull up into the Ryans' driveway and park. Stars litter the charcoal and purple sky, a faint autumn-scented breeze ruffles the green skirts of the cedar trees that line the property. I struggle to lift the flattened cardboard moving boxes out of my small, sleek Mercedes and carry them across the wild front yard, which is strewn with kids' toys and overrun with weeds. In the past year, yard work and maintenance have hardly been on anyone's list.

Inside, the house is dark and quieter than I can ever remember it being.

I come to a stop and think, *I can't do it.* What have I been thinking? *Closure.*

And there is more, something else. I remember our last night together, Katie's and mine. She had made up her mind; we all knew it. The decision had weighed us down, so that we moved more slowly, talked in whispers. We had one last hour alone, just the two of us. I'd wanted to climb into bed with her, to hold her matchstick body close, but even with her pain cocktail, the time for that had passed. Every breath hurt her, and by extension, me, too.

Take care of them, she'd whispered, clutching my hand in hers. *I've done everything for them.* At this she laughed; it was a crinkling, breathy release of air. *They won't know how to start without me. Help them.*

And I had said, *Who will help me?*

The shame of that washes over me, tightens my stomach.

I'll always be with you, she'd lied, and that had been the end of it. She'd asked for Johnny and the kids then.

And I'd known.

I tighten my hold on the boxes and trudge up the stairs, ignoring the way the cardboard edges bang into the worn, scuffed risers. In Kate and Johnny's bedroom, I pause, feeling reluctant suddenly to intrude.

Help them.

What had Johnny said to me the last time we spoke? *Every time I look at the clothes in her closet . . .*

I swallow hard and go into their walk-in closet, turning on the light. Johnny's clothes are on the right side, neatly organized. Kate's are on the left.

At the sight of her things, I almost lose my nerve; my knees buckle. Unsteady on my feet, I unfold one of the boxes and tape the ends and set it beside me. I grab an armful of hangered clothes and sit down on the cold hardwood floor.

Sweaters. Cardigans and turtlenecks and V-necks. I fold each one carefully, reverently, breathing in the last, lingering scent of her—lavender and citrus.

I do okay until I come to a worn, stretched-out-of-shape gray UW sweatshirt, soft from years of washing.

A memory washes over me: We are in Kate's bedroom, packing to go off to college together. A couple of eighteen-year-old girls who have imagined this moment for years, talked about it all summer, polished our dream until it is shiny. We are going to join the same sorority and become famous journalists.

They'll want you, Kate had said quietly. I'd known she was feeling afraid, the unpopular girl her classmates had called Kootie all those years ago.

You know I won't join a sorority unless we're in it together, right?

That was what Kate had never understood, or at least hadn't believed: of the two of us, I needed her more than she needed me.

I fold up the sweatshirt and set it aside. I will take it home with me.

For the rest of that night, I sit in my best friend's closet, remembering our friendship and boxing up her life. At first I try to be strong, and the trying gives me a terrible headache.

Her clothes are like a scrapbook of our lives.

At last, I come to a jacket that hasn't been in style since the late eighties. I bought it for her on her birthday, with the first big paycheck I ever earned. There are honest-to-God sparkles on the shoulder pads.

You can't afford this, she'd said when she pulled the purple double-breasted suit from the box.

I'm on my way.

She'd laughed. *Yeah. You. I'm knocked up and getting fat.*

You'll come to New York to see me after the baby is born and you'll need something totally rad to wear . . .

I get to my feet. Holding the jacket to my chest, I go downstairs and pour myself another glass of wine. Madonna's voice comes at me through the living room speakers. As I stop to listen, it occurs to me that I've left my lunch dishes on the counter and the takeout boxes from my dinner should really go in the garbage, but how can I think of that when the music is in me again, taking me back?

Vogue. We'd danced to the music in suits just like this one. I go to the CD player and crank the volume so I can hear it upstairs. For just a moment, I close my eyes and dance, holding her jacket, and I imagine her here, hip-bumping me and laughing. Then I go back to work.

✦

I wake up on the floor of her closet, wearing a pair of her black sweatpants and the old UW sweatshirt. The wineglass beside me has fallen on its side and broken into pieces. The bottle is empty. No wonder I feel terrible.

I struggle to sit up, pushing the hair out of my eyes. It is my second night here, and I am almost done packing Kate's things away. Her side of the closet is completely empty and there are six boxes stacked beneath the silver rod.

On the floor next to my broken wineglass is Kate's journal, the one she wrote in the last months of her life.

Marah will come looking for me one day, Kate had said, pressing the journal into my hands. *Be with her when she reads it. And my boys . . . show them these words when they can't remember me.*

The music is still blaring downstairs. I'd drunk too much wine and forgotten to turn it off last night. Prince. *Purple Rain.*

I get to my feet, feeling weak, but at least I have done *something.* This will make Johnny's life easier when he gets back. It is one difficult job he needn't do.

Downstairs, the music snaps off.

I frown, turn, but before I leave the closet, Johnny appears in the doorway.

"What the *fuck*?" he yells at me.

I am so taken aback, I just stare at him. Was it today they were returning from Kauai?

He glances past me, sees the boxes lining the wall with labels like *Kate's summer clothes,* and *Goodwill,* and *Kate, misc.*

I see his pain, how he is struggling for composure as his children come up behind him. I push my way into his embrace, waiting—waiting—for him to hold me. When he doesn't, I step back. I feel tears burn my eyes. "I knew you wouldn't want—"

"How *dare* you come into this house and go through her things and box them up as if they're garbage?" His voice breaks, words vibrate. "Is that her sweatshirt you're wearing?"

"I was trying to help."

"Help? Is it a *help* to leave empty wine bottles and food cartons on the counter? Is it a help to blast music at the edge of pain? Do you think it will *help* me to look into her empty closet?"

"Johnny—" I reach for him. He pushes me aside so hard I stumble and almost drop the journal.

"Give me that," he says in a voice that is trip-wire tight.

I hold it to my chest and back away. "She entrusted it to me. I'm supposed to be with Marah when she reads it. I promised Katie."

"She made a lot of mistakes when it came to you."

I shake my head. This is happening so fast I can't quite process it. "Did I make a mistake in cleaning out her closet? I thought you—"

"You *only* ever think about yourself, Tully."

"Dad," Marah says, pulling her brothers in close. "Mom wouldn't want—"

"She's gone," he says sharply. I see how the words hit him, how grief rearranges his face, and I whisper his name, not knowing what else to say. He's wrong. I meant to help.

Johnny backs away from me. He pushes a hand through his hair and looks at his children, who look scared now, and uncertain. "We're moving," he says.

Marah goes pale. "What?"

"We're moving," Johnny says, more in control this time. "To Los Angeles. I've taken a new job. We need a new start. I can't live here without her"—he indicates his bedroom. He can't even look at the bed. He looks at me instead.

"If this is because I tried to help—"

He laughs. It is a dry, scraping sound. "Of course you think it's about you. Did you *hear* me? I can't live in her house."

I reach for him.

He sidesteps me. "Just go, Tully."

"But—"

"Go," he says again, and I can see that he means it.

I clutch the journal and ease past him. I hug the boys together, holding them tightly and kissing their plump cheeks, trying to imprint their images on my soul. "You'll visit us, right?" Lucas says unevenly. This little boy has lost so much and the uncertainty in his voice kills me.

Marah grabs my arm. "Let me live with you."

Behind us, Johnny laughs bitterly.

"You belong with your family," I say quietly.

"This isn't a family anymore." Marah's eyes fill with tears. "You told her you'd be there for me."

I can't listen to any more. I pull my goddaughter into a fierce, desperate hug so tight she struggles to break free. When I pull away and leave the room, I can hardly see through my tears.

Six

✦

"Will you *please* stop humming?" I say to Kate. "How am I supposed to think with you making that racket? It's not like these are pleasant memories for me."

I am not humming.

"Okay. Quit beeping. What are you, the Road Runner?" The sound is soft at first, like a mosquito buzzing near my ear, but it amplifies steadily, becomes ridiculously loud. "Stop making that noise." I am starting to get a headache.

A *real* headache. Pain sparks to life behind my eyes, seeps out, turns into a hammer-pounding migraine.

I am as quiet as the grave over here.

"Very funny. Wait. That's not you. It sounds like a car alarm. What the fu—"

WELOSTHER, someone says, yells, really. Who?

Beside me, I hear Katie sigh. It is a sad sound, somehow, like the tearing of old lace. She whispers my name and then says: *Time*. It scares me, both the exhaustion I hear in her voice and the word itself. Have I used up all the time allotted to me? Why didn't I *say* more? Ask more questions? What happened to me? I know she knows. "Kate?"

Nothing.

Suddenly I am falling, tumbling.

I can hear voices, but the words make no sense and the pain is so pummeling, so brutalizing, that it takes everything I have not to scream.

ALLCLEAR.

I feel my spirit ebbing away, draining out of my body. I want to open my eyes—or maybe they are open—I can't tell. I just know that this darkness is ugly, cold, thick as coal dust. I scream for help, but it's all in my head and I know it. I can't open my mouth. The sound I imagine echoes and fades away, and I do the same . . .

✦

September 3, 2010
6:27 A.M.

Johnny stood outside Trauma Nine. It had taken him all of five seconds to decide to follow Dr. Bevan to this room, and it took him even less time to decide to open the door. He was a journalist, after all. He'd made a career out of going where he wasn't wanted.

As he opened the door, he was bumped into hard, pushed aside by a woman in scrubs.

He moved out of her way and slipped into the crowded room. It was glaringly bright and swarming with people in scrubs who had collected around a gurney. They were talking all at once, moving back and forth like piano keys in play. Because of their bodies, he couldn't see the patient—just bare toes sticking up from the end of a blue blanket.

An alarm sounded. Someone yelled, "We lost her. *Charge*."

A high humming sound thrummed through the room, riding above the voices. He felt the vibration of the sound to his bones.

"All clear."

He heard a high *wrrr* and then the body on the table arched up and thumped back down. An arm fell sideways, hung off the side of the gurney.

"She's back," someone said.

Johnny saw heartbeats move across the monitor. The swarm seemed to relax. A few of the nurses stepped away from the bed, and for the first time he saw the patient.

Tully.

It felt as if air rushed back into the room. Johnny finally took a breath of it. There was blood all over the floor. A nurse stepped in it and almost fell.

Johnny moved in closer to the bed. Tully lay unconscious, her face battered and bloodied; a bone stuck up through the ripped flesh of her arm.

He whispered her name; or maybe he just thought he did. He slipped in between two nurses—one who was starting an IV, and the other who had pulled a blue blanket up to cover Tully's bare chest.

Dr. Bevan materialized beside him. "You shouldn't be here."

Johnny waved the comment away but couldn't respond. He had so many questions for this man, and yet, as he stood there, shocked by the extent of her injuries, what he felt was shame. Somehow, some way, he had a part to play in this. He'd blamed Tully for something that wasn't her fault and cut her out of his life.

"We need to get her to the OR, Mr. Ryan."

"Will she live?"

"Her chances are not good," Dr. Bevan said. "Step out of the way."

"Save her," Johnny said, stumbling back as the gurney rolled past him.

Feeling numb, he walked out of the room and made his way down the hall and into the fourth-floor surgical waiting area, where a woman sat in the corner, knitting needles in hand, crying.

He checked in with the woman at the desk, told her he was waiting for word on Tully Hart, and then he took a seat beside the blank television. Feeling the first distant ping of a headache, he leaned back.

He tried not to remember all that had gone wrong in the Kateless years, all the mistakes he'd made—and there were some doozies. Instead, he prayed to a God he'd stopped believing in on the day of his wife's death and turned back to when his daughter disappeared.

For hours, he sat in the waiting room, watching people come and go. He hadn't called anyone yet. He was waiting for word on Tully's condition. There had been enough tragedy calls in their family. Bud and Margie lived in Arizona now; Johnny didn't want Margie to rush to the airport unless it was absolutely necessary. He would have called Tully's mom, even in this early hour, but he had no idea how to reach her.

And then there was Marah. He didn't know if she'd even take his call.

"Mr. Ryan?"

Johnny looked up sharply, saw the neurosurgeon coming toward him.

He wanted to stand, to meet the man halfway, but he felt weak.

The surgeon touched his shoulder. "Mr. Ryan?"

Johnny forced himself to stand. "How is she, Dr. Bevan?"

"She survived the surgeries. Come with me."

Johnny let himself be led out of the public waiting room and into a small, windowless conference room nearby. Instead of a floral arrangement in the middle of the table there was a box of tissue.

He sat down.

Dr. Bevan sat across from him. "Right now, the biggest concern is cerebral edema—the swelling in her brain. She sustained massive head trauma. We've put a shunt in to help with the swelling, but the efficacy of that is uncertain. We have lowered her body temperature and put her into a medically induced coma to help relieve the pressure, but her condition is critical. She's on a ventilator."

"May I see her?" Johnny asked.

The doctor nodded. "Of course. Come with me."

He led Johnny down one white corridor after another, into an elevator and out of it. At last they came to the ICU. Dr. Bevan walked over to a glass-walled private room, one of twelve placed in a U-shape around a busy nurses' station.

Tully lay in a narrow bed, surrounded by machines. Her hair had been shaved and a hole had been drilled into her skull. A catheter and pump were working to relieve the pressure on her brain. There were several tubes going into her—a breathing tube, a feeding tube, a tube into her head. A black screen behind the bed showed the intracranial pressure; another tracked her heartbeat. Her left arm was in a cast. Cold radiated off her pale, bluish skin.

"Brain injuries are impossible to predict," Dr. Bevan said. "We don't really know the extent of her injuries yet. We hope to know more in twenty-four hours. I wish I could be more definitive, but this is uncertain territory."

Johnny knew about brain injuries. He'd suffered one as a reporter covering the first war in Iraq. It had taken him months of therapy to become himself again, and still he couldn't remember the explosion. "Will she be herself when she wakes up?"

"*If* she wakes up is really the question. Her brain is functioning, although we don't know how well because of the medications we have her on. Her pupils are responsive, and that's a good sign. The coma will give her body time, we hope. But if a bleed develops or the swelling continues . . ."

He didn't have to finish the sentence. Johnny knew.

The ventilator's *thunk-whoosh* reminded him with every sound that she wasn't breathing on her own.

This was what it sounded like to play God and keep someone alive—a cacophony of beeping monitors, droning indicators, and the whooshing ventilator. "What happened to her?" Johnny finally asked.

"Car accident, from what I've heard, but I don't have any details." Dr. Bevan turned to him. "Is she a spiritual woman?"

"No. I wouldn't say so."

"That's too bad. Faith can be a comfort at times like this."

"Yes," Johnny said tightly.

"We believe it helps to talk to comatose patients," Dr. Bevan said.

The doctor patted his shoulder again and then headed out of the room.

Johnny sat down beside the bed. How long did he sit there, staring at her, thinking, *Fight, Tully,* whispering words he couldn't say out loud? Long enough for guilt and regret to turn into a knot in his throat.

Why did it take a tragedy to see life clearly?

He didn't know what to say to her, not now, after all that had been said—and left unsaid—between them. The one thing he knew for sure was this: if Kate were here, she'd kick his ass for how he'd unraveled after her death and how he'd treated her best friend.

He did the only thing he could think of to reach Tully. Quietly, feeling stupid but doing it anyway, he started to sing the song that came to him, the one that had always reminded him of Tully. "Just a small town girl, living in a lo-nely wor-ld . . ."

✦

Where am I? Dead? Alive? Somewhere in between?

"Kate?"

I feel a whoosh of warmth come up beside me and my relief is enormous.

"Katie," I say, turning. "Where were you?"

Gone, she says simply. *Now I'm back. Open your eyes.*

My eyes are closed? That's why it's so dark? I open my eyes slowly, and it's like waking up on the face of the sun. The light and heat are so intense I gasp. It takes seconds for my eyes to adjust to the brightness, and when they do I see that I am back in the hospital room with my body. Below me, an operation is going on. Several people in scrubs stand around an operating table. Scalpels and instruments glitter on silver trays. There are machines everywhere, beeping, droning, buzzing.

Look, Tully.

I don't want to.

Look.

I am moving in spite of my intention not to. A cold dread has taken hold of me. It is worse than the pain. I know what I am going to see on that sleek table.

Me. And not me, somehow.

My body is on the table, draped in blue, bloodied. The nurses and the surgeon are talking; someone is shaving my head.

I look so small and pale without hair, childlike. Someone in scrubs paints a brown liquid on my bald head.

I hear a sound like a buzz saw starting up and I feel sick to my stomach.

"I don't like it here," I say to Kate. "Take me somewhere."

We'll always be here, but close your eyes.

"Gladly."

The sudden darkness scares me this time. I don't know why. It's weird, really, because I harbor a lot of dark emotions in my soul, but fear isn't one of them. I'm not afraid of anything.

Ha. You are more afraid of love than any person I've ever met. It's why you keep testing people and pushing them away. Open your eyes.

I open my eyes and, for a second it is still dark, then color bleeds down from the impenetrable blackness above, falling like those computer codes in *The Matrix,* solidifying in strands. First comes the sky, a perfect, cloudless blue, and then the cherry trees in bloom—tufts of pink blossoms clinging to branches and floating in the sweet air. Buildings sketch themselves into place, pink gothic structures with elegant wings and towers, and finally the green, green grass, inlaid with concrete walkways going this way and that. We are at the University of Washington. The colors are painfully vivid. There are young men and women everywhere—kids—carrying backpacks and playing hacky sack and lying on the grass with books open in front of them. Somewhere a boom box is turned on as high as it will go and a scratchy version of "I've Never Been to Me" comes through the speakers. God, I hated that song.

"None of this is real," I say, "right?"

Real is relative.

Not far from where we are sitting in the grass, a pair of girls are stretched out side by side; one is brunette, the other is blond. The blonde is wearing parachute pants and a T-shirt and has a Trapper Keeper notebook open in front of her. The other girl—okay, it's me, I know it, I can remember when I wore my hair all ratted up like that and pulled back from my face in a huge metallic bow, and I remember the cropped, off-the-shoulder white sweater. It had been my favorite. They—we—look so young I can't help smiling.

I lie back, feeling the grass prickling beneath my bare arms, smelling its sweet, familiar scent. Kate does the same. We are together again, both staring up at the same blue sky. How many times in our four years at the UW did we do exactly this? The light around us is magical, as clear and sparkly as champagne glimpsed in sunlight. In its glow I feel so peaceful. My pain is a distant memory here, especially with Kate beside me again.

What happened tonight? she asks, ripping a little of that peace away.

"I can't remember." It's true, strangely. I can't remember.

You can remember. You don't want to.

"Maybe there's a good reason for that."

Maybe.

"Why are you here, Kate?"

You called for me, remember? I came because you need me. And to remind you.

"Of what?"

Memories are who we are, Tul. In the end, that's all the luggage you take with you. Love and memories are what last. That's why your life flashes before your eyes when you die—you're picking the memories you want. It's like packing.

"Love and memories? Then I am double-Oreo fucked. I don't remember anything, and love—"

Listen.

A voice is speaking. "Will she be herself when she wakes up?"

"Hey," I say. "That's—"

Johnny. The way she says her husband's name is full of love and pain.

". . . *if* she wakes up is really the question . . ." A male voice.

Wait. They are talking about my *death.* And the chance of something worse—a brain-damaged life. An image flashes through my mind—me, confined to bed, held together by tubes, unable to think or speak or move.

I concentrate hard and I am in the hospital room again.

Johnny is standing by my bed, looking down at me. A stranger in blue scrubs is beside him.

"Is she a spiritual woman?" This from the stranger.

"No. I wouldn't say so," Johnny says tiredly. He sounds so sad I want to take his hand, even after all that has happened between us, or maybe because of it.

He sits down by the bed where my body is. "I'm sorry," he says to the me that can't hear.

I have waited so long to hear those words from him, but why? I can see now that he loves me. I can see it in his moist eyes, in his shaking hands, in the way he bows his head to pray. He doesn't pray—I know him better than that; it is defeat, that lowering of his chin to his chest.

He will miss me, even after all of it.

And I will miss him.

"Fight, Tully."

I want to answer him, to let him know that he has reached me, that I am *here,* but nothing works. "Open your eyes," I say to my body. "Open your eyes. Tell him you're sorry, too."

And then he starts to sing in a cracked, croaking voice. "Just a small town girl . . ."

God, I love that man, Kate says.

He is halfway through the song when someone else walks into the room. A beefy man in a cheap brown sport coat and blue slacks. "I'm Detective Gates," the man says.

I hear the words *car accident* and images flash through my mind—a rainy night, a concrete stanchion, my hands on the steering wheel. It almost becomes a memory. I can feel it coming together, meaning something, but before I can put it together, I am hit in the chest so hard I fall back against the wall. The pain is crushing, excruciating.

CODEBLUECALLDRBEVAN.

"Kate!" I scream, but she is gone.

The noises are thunderous now, echoing and banging and beeping. I can't breathe. The pain in my chest is killing me.

ALLCLEAR.

I am thrown into the air like a kid's rag doll, and up there, I burst into flames. When it's over, I'm floating again, falling alongside the starlight.

Kate takes my hand in the darkness, and instead of falling, we are flying. We touch down, soft as a butterfly landing, in a pair of worn wooden chairs that face the beach. The world is dark but somehow electrically bright: white, white moon, endless stars, candles flickering in Mason jars from the branches of an old maple tree.

Her back deck. Kate's.

Here, the pain is an echo, not the beat. Thank God for that.

I hear Kate breathing beside me. In each exhalation I smell lavender and something else, snow, maybe. *Johnny fell apart,* she says, reminding me of where we were before—talking about my life. *I didn't think he would.*

"We all did." That's the sad, sorry truth of it. "You were the glue that held us together. Without you . . ."

There is a long silence; in it, I wonder if she is remembering her life, her loves. How does it feel to know that people couldn't handle living without you? How does it feel to know you were loved by so many people?

What happened to you after he moved to Los Angeles?

I sigh. "Can't I just walk into the damned light and be done with all this?"

You yelled for me, remember? You said you needed me. I'm here. And this is why: you need to remember. This is it. So, talk.

I lean back in the chair, staring up at a votive candle burning within the rounded glass sides of the Mason jar. Rough twine holds the jar in place; an impossible breeze touches it every now and then, splashing light into the dark lower branches of the tree. "After you died, Johnny and the kids moved to Los Angeles. It happened fast, that moving. Your husband just up and decided he was going to Los Angeles, and the next thing I knew, he and the kids were gone. I remember saying goodbye in November of 2006, standing with your mom and dad in the driveway, waving goodbye. After that, I went home and crawled . . .

into bed. I know I need to go back to work, but I can't do it. Honestly, the very idea is overwhelming. I can't summon the strength to begin the process of starting my life over without a best friend. At that, loss weighs me down and I close my eyes. It's okay to be depressed for a while, who wouldn't be?

Somehow I lose two weeks. I mean, I don't really *lose* them. I know where they are, and where I am. I am like some wounded animal in a darkened lair, nursing the thorn in my paw, unable to find anyone to pull it out. I call Marah every night at eleven o'clock. I know that she can't sleep, either. I lie in my bed, listening to her complain about her father's decision to move, and I tell her that it will be okay, but neither of us believes it. I promise to visit soon.

Finally, I can't stand it anymore. I throw the covers off me and go through my condo, turning on lights and opening containers. Light fills the rooms, and in its glare I see myself for the first time: my hair is tangled and dirty, my eyes are glazed-looking, and my clothes are a wrinkled mess.

I look like my mother. I am ashamed and embarrassed that I have fallen so far and so fast.

It is time to recover.

There it is. My goal. I can't just lie around missing my best friend and grieving for what is gone. I have to put all of this behind me and go on.

I know how to do that. I've been doing it all my life. I call my agent, make an appointment to see him. He is in Los Angeles: I will see my agent, get back to work, and surprise Johnny and the kids with a visit.

Yes. Perfect. A plan.

With an appointment made, I feel better. I take a shower and style my hair with care. I notice that I am gray at the roots.

When did that happen?

Frowning, I try to hide it by pulling my hair back into a ponytail. I apply makeup with a heavy hand. I'm going out into the world, after all, and there are cameras everywhere these days. I dress in the only thing that fits comfortably over my widening hips—a black knit pencil skirt, knee-length boots, and a black silk fitted blouse with an asymmetrical collar.

I do well—I mean, I call my travel agent and make reservations and get dressed, and all the while I am smiling, thinking, *I can do this, of course I can*—and then I open the door of my condo and I feel a flash of panic. My throat goes dry, my forehead prickles with sweat, my heartbeat speeds up.

I am *afraid* to leave my house.

I don't know what in the hell is wrong with me, but I won't stand for it. I take a deep breath and plunge forward. All the way to the elevator, and down to my car, and into the driver's seat. I can feel my heart thudding in my chest.

I start the car and drive out into the busy, bustling Seattle street. A heavy rain is falling, clattering drops on my windshield, obscuring my view. Every single second, I want to turn back, but I don't. I force myself to keep going, until I am on the plane, seated in first class.

"Martini," I say to the flight attendant. The look on her face reminds me that it is not yet noon. Still, a drink is all I can think of to help get me through this embarrassing episode.

Softened by two martinis, I finally am able to lean back in my seat and close my eyes. I will be better once I am back to work. It has always been my salvation.

In Los Angeles, I see a driver, dressed in black, holding up a sign. HART. I hand him my small calfskin overnight bag and follow him out to a waiting Town Car. On the drive from LAX to Century City, the traffic is bumper-to-bumper. People on these freeways honk constantly, as if it will make a difference, and motorcycles zip dangerously between lanes.

I lean into the cushy seat and close my eyes, taking a moment to collect my thoughts and organize my ideas. Now that I am here, moving forward, taking my life back, I feel a little calmer. Or maybe it is the martinis. Either way, I am ready for my comeback.

The car pulls up to the imposing white building identified only by a discreet carved sign: CREATIVE ARTISTS AGENCY.

Inside, the building is an endless stretch of white marble and glass, like a giant icehouse, and equally as cold. Everyone is dressed well, in expensive suits. Beautiful women and gorgeous men move through what looks like a magazine shoot.

The girl at the front desk doesn't recognize me. Not even when I say my name.

"Oh," she says, her gaze disinterested. "Is Mr. Davison expecting you?"

"Yes," I say, trying to maintain a smile.

"Take a seat, please."

Honestly, I feel like putting this girl in her place, but I know I need to be careful in the hallowed halls of CAA, so I bite my tongue and take a seat in the modernly decorated waiting room.

Where I wait.

And wait.

At least twenty minutes after my scheduled appointment time, a young man in an Italian suit comes for me. Wordlessly, like a drone, he leads me up to the third floor and into a corner office.

My agent, George Davison, is seated behind a huge desk. He stands at my entrance. We hug, a little awkwardly, and I step back.

"Well. Well," he says, indicating a chair for me.

I sit down. "You look good," I say.

He glances at me. I see the way he notices my weight gain, and my ponytail doesn't fool him. He sees the gray in my hair. I shift uncomfortably in my seat.

"Your call surprised me," he says.

"It hasn't been that long."

"Six months. I left at least a dozen messages for you. None of which were returned."

"You know what happened, George. I found out that my best friend had cancer. I wanted to be with her."

"And now?"

"She died." It's the first time I've said it out loud.

"I'm sorry."

I wipe my eyes. "Yes. Well. I'm ready to go back to work now. I'd like to start taping on Monday."

"Tell me you're joking."

"You think Monday is too soon?" I don't like the way George is looking at me.

"Come on, Tully. You're smarter than this."

"I don't know what you mean, George."

He shifts in his chair. The expensive leather makes a whispering sound. "Your show, *The Girlfriend Hour,* was number one in its time slot last year. Advertisers were clamoring to buy time. Manufacturers loved to give away products to your audience, many of whom drove hundreds of miles and stood in line for hours to see you."

"I am aware of all of this, George. That's why I'm here."

"You walked off set, Tully. Took off your mic, said goodbye to your audience, and left."

I lean forward. "My friend—"

"Who gives a shit?"

I sit back, stunned.

"How do you think the network felt about your exit? Or your employees, all of whom were suddenly unemployed?"

"I . . . I . . ."

"That's right. You didn't think about them, did you? The network wanted to sue you."

"I had no idea—"

"Unreturned phone calls," he snaps. "I fought like a tiger to protect you. They decided not to sue—thought it would be a public relations nightmare because of the cancer card. But they pulled the show, no reruns, and replaced you."

How do I not know this? "They *replaced* me? With whom?"

"*The Rachael Ray Show*. It's kicking ass in the ratings. Growing fast. And *Ellen* and *Judge Judy* are still pulling huge numbers. And *Oprah,* of course."

"Wait. What are you saying exactly? I *own* my show, George. I produce it."

"Too bad you don't own a network. And they have the right to air reruns exclusively for now. They aren't running them, either. That's how pissed they are."

I can't even process this information. I have been successful *forever.* "You're saying *The Girlfriend Hour* is done."

"No, Tully. I'm saying *you're* done. Who is going to hire someone who walks away without a conversation?"

Okay, so this is bad. "I'll produce another show. On spec. We'll sell it ourselves."

"Have you spoken to your business manager recently?"

"No. Why?"

"Do you remember donating a substantial sum to Stand Up 2 Cancer four months ago?"

"It was a gift for Kate. And it was great publicity. They reported it on *Entertainment Tonight.*"

"A lovely, beautiful gesture, yes. Except you have no money coming in, Tully. Not since you walked. You had to pay off a lot of employee contracts when you stopped taping the show. It cost you a small fortune. And let's face it, saving money was never your strong point."

"Are you saying I'm broke?"

"Broke? No. You're still more than comfortable. But I've spoken to Frank. You don't have enough to bankroll production. And no one is going to want to invest in you right now."

I feel an edgy panic; my foot taps on the floor, my fingers curl tightly around the armrests. "So I need a job."

The look George gives me is sad. In his eyes, I see the whole arc of our relationship. He became my agent almost two decades ago, when I was low man on the totem pole at the network morning show. We'd been drawn together by our mutual ambition. He'd brokered every major contract of my career and helped me make millions, most of which I'd pissed away on extravagant travel and gifts. "It won't be easy. You're kryptonite, Tul."

"You're saying I can only work at the local level?"

"I'm saying you'll be *lucky* to work at the local level."

"No top ten."

"I don't think so."

The pity and compassion in his gaze is more than I can bear. "I've worked since I was fourteen, George. I got a job at the *Queen Anne Bee* newspaper in high school, and I was on air before my twenty-second birthday. I have built this career from *scratch*. No one gave me anything." My voice breaks. "I put everything into my work. Everything. I don't have kids or a husband or a family. I have . . . work."

"I guess you should have thought about that before," he says, and the gentleness of his voice takes none of the sting out of his observation.

He's right. I know the journalism business, and, worse, TV. I know "out of sight, out of mind." I know you can't do what I did and come back from it.

So why didn't I know it in June?

I did.

I must have. I chose Kate instead. "Find me a job, George. I'm begging you." I turn away before he can see what this last bit has cost me. I don't beg. I've never begged, not for anything . . . except my mother's love. And that was a useless waste of time.

I walk quickly through the hallowed white halls, making eye contact with no one, my heels clicking on the marble floor. Outside, the sun is shining so brightly it hurts my eyes. The sweat on my forehead prickles along my scalp.

I will solve this.

I will.

It is a setback, to be sure, but I am a survivor and always have been.

I flag down my driver and get into the back of the Town Car, grateful for the dark, quiet interior. I have a pounding headache.

"Beverly Hills, ma'am?"

Johnny and the kids.

I want to go to them now. I want to spill these troubles to Johnny and have him tell me I will be all right.

But I can't do it. My shame is overwhelming and pride stops me.

I put on my sunglasses. "LAX."

"But—"

"LAX."

"Yes, ma'am."

I hold myself together one second at a time. I squeeze my eyes shut and say silently: *You will be okay.* Over and over again.

But for the first time in my life, I can't make myself believe it. Panic and fear and anger and loss are running headlong inside of me, filling me up, spilling over. Twice on the flight home I burst into tears and have to clamp a hand over my mouth to silence my sobs.

When the flight is over, I walk off the plane like a zombie, my red eyes hidden behind sunglasses.

I have always prided myself on my professionalism, and my work ethic is legendary. This is what I tell myself, pretending I don't feel as fragile and thin as a strand of hair.

On my show, I used to tell my viewers that you could have it all in life. I told them to ask for help, to take time for yourself, know what you want. Be selfish. Be selfless.

The truth is I have no idea how to have it all. I've never had anything except my career. With Kate and the Ryans, it was enough, but now I see the void in my life.

I am shaking as I pull up in front of my building. Control feels far, far away.

I open the door and go into the lobby.

My heart is pounding hard, my breathing is shallow. People are looking at me. They know what a failure I am.

Someone touches me. It startles me so much that I almost fall.

"Ms. Hart?"

It is my doorman. Stanley.

"Are you okay?"

I shake my head slightly to clear it. I need to ask him to park my car, but I feel . . . buzzed somehow, electrified. My laugh sounds high-pitched and nervous, even to my own ears.

Stanley frowns. "Ms. Hart? Do you need help home?"

Home.

"You're crying, Ms. Hart," my doorman says tenderly.

I look up at him. My heart is racing so fast I feel sick and out of breath.

What is wrong with me?

It feels suddenly as if a semi has driven into my chest. I gasp at the pain of it.

I reach for Stanley, chirp, *Help,* as I trip over something and crash to the cold concrete floor.

✦

"Ms. Hart?"

I open my eyes and discover that I'm in a hospital bed.

There's a man in a white coat standing beside me. He is tall and a little disreputable-looking, with black hair that is too long in this buttoned-down era. His face is sharply planed, his nose a little hawk-like. His skin is the color of creamed coffee. He's part Hawaiian, maybe, or Asian and African-American. It's hard to tell. I see tattoos along his wrists—tribal ones.

"I'm Dr. Grant," he says. "You're in the ER. Do you remember what happened?"

I remember all of it; amnesia would be a gift. But I don't want to talk about it, especially not with this man, who looks at me as if I'm damaged goods. "I remember," I answer.

"That's good." He glances down at my chart. "Tallulah."

He has no idea who I am. That depresses me. "So when can I get out of here? My heart is doing its job now." I want to go home and pretend I didn't have a heart attack. Which reminds me: I'm forty-six years old. How could I have had a heart attack?

He puts on a pair of ridiculously out-of-date reading glasses. "Well, Tallulah—"

"Tully, please. Only my brain-damaged mother calls me Tallulah."

He looks at me over the rim of his reading glasses. "Your mother is brain-damaged?"

"It was a joke."

He is not impressed by my humor. He probably lives in a world where people grow their own food and read philosophy before bed. He is as much an alien to my world as I am to his. "I see. Well. The point is that you didn't have what's commonly referred to as a heart attack."

"Stroke?"

"A panic attack often mirrors the symptoms—"

I sit up. "Oh, no. I did *not* have a panic attack."

"Did you take any drugs prior to the panic attack?"

"I did *not* have a panic attack. And of course I didn't take drugs. Do I look like a drug addict?"

He seems not to know what to make of me. "I've taken liberty of contacting a colleague for a consult—"

Before he can finish, the curtains part and Dr. Harriet Bloom walks toward my bed. She is tall and thin; severe is the word that comes to mind—until you see the softness in her eyes. I have known Harriet for years. She is a prominent psychiatrist and has been a guest on my show many times. It's good to see a friendly face.

"Harriet. Thank God."

"Hello, Tully. I'm glad I was on call." Harriet smiles at me and then looks at the doctor. "So, Desmond, how is our patient?"

"Not pleased to have had a panic attack. Apparently she'd prefer a heart attack."

"Call me a car service, Harriet," I say. "I'm getting the hell out of here."

"She's a board-certified psychiatrist," Desmond says to me. "She doesn't call car services."

Harriet gives me an apologetic smile. "Des doesn't watch TV. He probably wouldn't recognize Oprah, either."

I am not surprised my doctor considers himself above TV. He has that too-cool-for-school look about him. I'll bet he was a hell-raiser at some point, but middle-aged men with tattoos are not exactly my demographic. I imagine there's a Harley-Davidson in his garage, along with an electric guitar. But really, you'd have to live under a rock not to know Oprah.

Harriet takes my chart from Desmond.

"I've ordered an MRI. The paramedics say she hit the ground pretty hard." He looks down at me, and again I see that he is judging me, finding me lacking, maybe. A white middle-aged woman in expensive clothes who face-plants for no good reason. "Be well, Ms. Hart." The smile he gives me is irritatingly kind, and then he leaves.

"Thank God," I say with a sigh.

"You had a panic attack," Harriet says when we are alone.

"Says Dr. Granola."

"You had a panic attack," Harriet says, more gently this time. She puts down the chart and moves closer to the bed. Her angular face, too sharp to be quite beautiful, has a regal, detached coolness, but her eyes reveal a woman who, in spite of her austere face and buttoned-down demeanor, cares deeply about people.

"You've been depressed, I take it?" Harriet asks.

I want to lie, to smile, to laugh. Instead, I nod, humiliated by this weakness. In a way, I *would* rather have had a heart attack.

"I'm tired," I say softly. "And I never sleep."

"I am going to prescribe Xanax for your anxiety," Harriet says. "We'll start with point-five milligrams three times a day. And I think a few therapy sessions could really help. If you're ready to do some work, maybe we can help you feel in more control of your life."

"The Tully Hart life tour? Thanks, but no, thanks. Why think about what hurts? has always been my motto."

"I know about depression," she says, and in her voice I hear a poignant sadness. I think suddenly that Harriet Bloom knows about sorrow and despair and loneliness. "Depression is nothing to be ashamed of, Tully, and it's nothing to ignore. It can get worse."

"Worse than today? How is that possible?"

"Oh, it's possible, believe me."

I am too exhausted to question her, and honestly, I don't want to know what she has to say. The pain in my neck is increasing.

Harriet writes two prescriptions and tears off the pages, handing them to me. I look down at them. Xanax for panic attacks, and Ambien for sleeping.

All of my life I have avoided narcotics. It doesn't take a rocket scientist to know why. When you grow up watching your mother get high and stumble around and puke, you see the unglamorous side of drugs.

I look up at Harriet. "My mom—"

"I know," Harriet says. It is one of the truths that come with life in the fishbowl of fame. Everyone knows my sad story. Poor Tully, abandoned and unloved by her hippie/addict mom. "Your mom has an issue with substance abuse. You're right to be careful, but just follow the prescription."

"It would be nice to sleep."

"May I ask you something?"

"Sure."

"How long have you been pretending not to be in pain?"

The question hits me hard. "Why do you ask me that?"

"Because, Tully, sometimes the well just fills up with our tears. And water starts to spill over."

"My best friend died last month."

"Ah," Harriet says. Just that. Then she nods and says, "Come see me, Tully. Make an appointment. I can help."

After she leaves, I sink back into the pillows and sigh. The truth of my circumstance climbs into the bed with me and takes up too much room.

A nice older woman takes me down for an MRI, and then a gorgeous young doctor calls me ma'am and tells me that at my age, falls like mine often cause neck trauma and that the pain will diminish. He writes me a prescription for pain pills and tells me that physical therapy will help.

By the time I am wheeled back into my room, I am beyond tired. I let the nurse tell me about how my show on autistic children saved her cousin's best friend's life, and even manage to smile and thank her when the long story finally ends. The nurse gives me Ambien. Afterward, I lie back in bed, closing my eyes.

For the first time in months, I sleep through the night.

Seven

✦

The Xanax helps. On it, I feel less edgy and anxious. By the time Dr. Granola discharges me, I have come up with a plan. No more whining. No more waiting.

At home, I immediately start making phone calls. I have been in the business for decades; surely someone needs a prime-time anchor.

An old friend, Jane Rice, is my first call. "Of course," she says. "Come in and see me."

I almost laugh. That's how relieved I feel. George was wrong. I am not Arsenio Hall. I am Tully Hart.

I prepare for my interview with care. I know how important first impressions are. I get my hair cut and colored.

"Oh, my," Charles—my longtime hairdresser—says when I climb into his chair. "Someone has been going native." He wraps the turquoise cape around my neck and gets to work.

On the day of my meeting with Jane, I dress carefully in conservative clothes—a black suit and pale lavender blouse. I have not been in the KING-TV building in years, but I immediately feel comfortable. This is my world. At the reception desk, I am greeted like a heroine and I don't have to give my name and relief eases the tightness of my shoulders. Behind the receptionists are large photographs of Jean Enerson and Dennis Bounds, the nightly news anchors.

An assistant leads me up the stairs, past several closed doors, to a small office on the second floor, where Jane Rice is standing by the window, obviously waiting for me. "Tully," she says, striding forward, her hand outstretched.

We shake hands. "Hello, Jane. Thanks for seeing me."

"Of course. Of course. Sit down."

I take the seat she has indicated.

She sits behind her desk and scoots in close, looking at me.

And I know. Just like that. "You can't hire me." It isn't even a question, not the way I say it. I may have been a talk show host for the last few years, but I am still a journalist. I read people well. That's one of my skills.

She sighs heavily. "I tried. I guess you really burned some bridges."

"Nothing?" I say quietly, hoping my voice doesn't betray my desperation. "How about a reporting job, not on camera? I'm no stranger to hard work."

"I'm sorry, Tully."

"Why did you agree to see me?"

"You were a hero to me," she says. "I used to dream of being like you."

Were a hero.

Suddenly I feel old. I get to my feet. "Thank you, Jane," I say quietly as I leave her office.

A Xanax calms me down. I know I shouldn't take it—not an extra one—but I need it.

✦

At home, I ignore my mounting panic and get to work. I sit down at my desk and start making calls to everyone I know in the business, especially anyone for whom I have ever done a favor.

By six o'clock, I am exhausted and defeated. I have called all my contacts in the top ten markets and on the major cable channels, and my agent. No one has an offer for me. I don't get it: six months ago I was on top of the world. How can I have fallen so far so fast?

My condo suddenly feels smaller than a shoe box and I am starting to hyperventilate again. I dress in whatever I can find—jeans that are too tight and a tunic-length sweater that hides my strained waistband.

It is past six-thirty when I leave my building. The streets and sidewalks are full of commuters coming home from work. I blend into the Gore-Tex garbed crowd, ignoring the rain that spits down on us. I don't even know where I'm going until I see the outdoor seating area in front of the Virginia Inn restaurant and bar.

I sidle through the outdoor tables and go inside. The dark interior is exactly what I need right now. I can disappear in here. I go to the bar and order a dirty martini.

"Tallulah, right?"

I glance sideways. Dr. Granola is beside me. Just my luck to run into a man who has seen me at my worst. In the gloom, his face looks sharp, maybe a little angry. His long hair is unbound and falls forward. Cufflike tattoos cover his forearm. "Tully," I say. "What are you doing in a place like this?"

"Collecting for the widows and orphans fund."

It figures.

He laughs. "I'm having a drink, Tully. Same as you. How are you doing?"

I know what he is asking and I don't like it. I certainly don't want to talk about how vulnerable I feel. "Fine. Thanks."

The bartender hands me my drink. It is all I can do not to pounce on it. "Later, Doc," I say, carrying my drink to a small table in the back corner of the bar. I slump onto the hard seat.

"May I join you?"

I look up. "Would it make an impact if I said no?"

"An impact? Of course." He sits down in the chair opposite me. "I thought about calling you," he says after a long, awkward silence.

"And?"

"I hadn't decided."

"Be still my heart."

Through speakers hidden somewhere in the walls, Norah Jones's husky, jazzy voice urges people to *come away with me.*

"Do you date much?"

It surprises me enough that I laugh. Apparently he's a man who says what is on his mind. "No. Do you?"

"I'm a single doctor. I get set up more often than a set of bowling pins. You want me to tell you how it works these days?"

"Blood tests and background checks? Condoms by Rubbermaid?"

He stares at me as if I belong in a display case for Ripley's Believe It or Not.

"Fine," I say. "How does the dating game work these days?"

"At our age, we all have stories. They matter more than you'd think. Sharing them and hearing them is the start of it. The way I see it, there are two ways to go: tell your story up front and let the chips fall where they may, or stretch them out over a bunch of dinners. Wine helps in this second tack, especially if one's story is long and boring and self-aggrandizing."

"Why do I think you put me in the last category?"

"Should I?"

I smile, surprising myself. "Maybe."

"So, here's my plan. Why don't you tell me your story, and I'll tell you mine, and we'll see if this is a date or if we're ships passing in the night?"

"It's not a date. I bought my own drink and I didn't shave my legs."

He smiles and leans back in his chair.

There is something about him that intrigues me, a charm I didn't see the first time. And really, what better thing do I have to do? "You first."

"My story is simple. I was born in Maine, in a farmhouse, on land that had been in my family for generations. Janie Traynor was my neighbor down the road. We fell in love somewhere around eighth grade, right after she stopped throwing spitballs at me. For twenty-some years, we did everything together. We went to NYU, got married in the church in town, and had a beautiful daughter." His smile starts to fall, but he hikes it back up and squares his shoulders. "Drunk driver," he says. "Crossed the median and hit the car. Janie and Emily died at the scene. That's when my story veers west, you might say. Since then, it's just me. I moved to Seattle, thinking a new view would help. I'm forty-three, in case you were wondering. You seem like a woman who wants details." He leans forward. "Your turn."

"I'm forty-six—I'll lead with that, although I don't like to. Unfortunately, you can get my entire life story off of Wikipedia, so there's no point in my lying. I have a degree in journalism from the UW. I worked my way up the network news ranks and became famous. I started a successful talk show, *The Girlfriend Hour.* Work has been my life, but . . . a few months ago, I learned that my best friend had been diagnosed with breast cancer. I walked away from my career to be with her. Apparently this is an unforgivable breach and I am now a cautionary tale instead of a shining star. I have never been married and have no children and my only living relative—my mother—calls herself Cloud. That pretty much sums her up."

"You didn't say anything about love," he says quietly.

"No. I didn't."

"Never?"

"Once," I say. Then, more softly. "Maybe. It was a lifetime ago."

"And . . ."

"I picked my career."

"Hmmm."

"Hmmm, what?"

"This is just a first for me, that's all."

"A first. How?"

"Your story is sadder than mine."

I don't like the way he's looking at me, as if I am somehow vulnerable. I toss back the rest of my martini and get to my feet. Whatever he is going to say next, I don't want to hear. "Thanks for the dating matrix," I say. "'Bye, Dr. Granola."

"Desmond," I hear him say, but I am already moving away from him, heading for the door.

At home, I take two Ambien, and crawl into bed.

✦

I don't like what I'm hearing. Xanax. Ambien, Kate says, interrupting my story.

That's the thing about your best friend. She knows you. Inside and out, down to the studs, as they say. Even worse, you see your own life through her eyes. It has always been true: Kate's is the voice in my head. My Jiminy Cricket.

"Yeah," I say. "I made a few mistakes. The worst wasn't the meds, though."

What was the worst?

I whisper her daughter's name.

✦

September 3, 2010
8:10 A.M.

Time slowed to a crawl in hospitals. Johnny sat in the uncomfortable chair, tucked in close to Tully's bed.

He pulled the cell phone out of his pocket and stared down at it. Finally he pulled up his contact list and called Margie and Bud. They lived in Arizona now, near Margie's widowed sister, Georgia.

Margie answered on the third ring, sounding a little out of breath. "Johnny!" she said, and he could hear the smile in her voice. "How good to hear from you."

"Hey, Margie."

There was a pause, then: "What's wrong?"

"It's Tully. She's been in a car accident. I don't have all the details, but she's here in Sacred Heart." He paused. "It's bad, Margie. She's in a coma—"

"We'll be on the next flight out. I'll send Bud straight to Bainbridge to be with the boys when they get home from school."

"Thanks, Margie. Do you know how to reach her mother?"

"No worries. I'll get ahold of Dorothy. Does Marah know yet?"

He sighed at the very thought of calling his daughter. "Not yet. Honestly, I have no idea if I'll be able to get ahold of her. Or if she'll care."

"Call her," Margie said gently.

Johnny said goodbye and disconnected the call. He closed his eyes for a moment, readying himself. The edge his daughter lived in these days was narrow; a whisper could push her off.

Beside him, a machine beeped steadily, reminding him with every chirp that it was keeping Tully alive, breathing for her, giving her a chance.

A chance that Dr. Bevan reported was *not good*.

He didn't need the doctor's report to know that. He could see how gray she was, how broken and fragile.

Reluctantly, he pulled up his contact list again and made another call.

Marah.

Eight

✦

September 3, 2010
10:17 A.M.

The Dark Magick Bookstore in Portland, Oregon, prided itself on an ambience created by dim lighting, burning incense, and black curtains. Used books were crowded together on dusty shelves; there were sections devoted to subjects like spiritual healing, Wiccan practices, pagan rituals, and meditation. There was no doubt to even the most casual observer that this was a store that wanted to be spooky and spiritual at the same time. The only problem was shoplifters. In the muddy lighting and smoke-filled air, it was tough to keep track of the merchandise. Too much of it left in pockets and backpacks.

Marah Ryan had told her boss this on several occasions, but the woman refused to be bothered with worldly concerns.

So Marah let it go. It wasn't as if she really cared, anyway. This was just another stupid job in a long line of stupid jobs she'd had in the two years since she graduated from high school. The only good thing about it was that no one hassled her for the way she looked. Oh, and usually the hours were good. But this week was inventory, so Marah had had to come in super early, which blew as far as she was concerned, especially because she just counted items that never sold anyway. Most stores took inventory after work. Not the Dark

Magick. Here, they did inventory in the predawn hours. Why? Marah had no fricking clue.

Now, as she stood in the Voodoo section, counting and recording black skull candles, she toyed with the idea of quitting this dead-end job, but the idea of looking for work again, of moving on, depressed her.

Then again, everything depressed her. She wasn't supposed to look to the future; she was supposed to accept the present. That was what the shrink had told her years ago, the shark-eyed woman in a plaid suit who'd lied to Marah about almost everything. Dr. Harriet Bloom.

Time heals all wounds.

It will get better.

Give yourself permission to grieve.

Whatever you feel is okay.

Horseshit piled upon horseshit. It did no good to look away from the pain in your soul. Quite the opposite was true.

Examination was the only solace. Instead of looking away from heartache, you needed to crawl inside of it, wear it like a warm coat on a cold day. There was peace in loss, beauty in death, freedom in regret. She had learned that the hard way.

She finished counting the skull candles and left her tally sheet in the bookcase. She was pretty sure she'd forget where it was, but who cared? It was time for her break. Well, she was early, but rules like that didn't matter around here.

"I'm going to lunch, Star," she called out.

From somewhere, she heard, "All right. Tell the coven I said hello."

Marah rolled her eyes. No matter how often she told her boss that she wasn't a witch and that her friends weren't a coven, Starla never believed her. "What-ever," she said, and walked through the shadowy bookstore to the cash register, where she retrieved her phone from the drawerful of junk. One of the few enforced store rules was no cell phones at work. Starla said that nothing broke a buying spell like a chirping phone.

Marah grabbed her phone and walked out of the store. As the door opened, a cat's screech sounded—the store's version of a welcome bell. Ignoring it, she stepped out into the light. Literally.

A text notice blipped on her phone. She looked down at it. Her dad had called four times in the last two hours.

Marah shoved her phone in her back pocket and started walking.

It was a gorgeous September day in downtown Portland. Sunlight bathed this historic section of the city, made the squatty brick buildings look well kept. She tucked her chin in close. She'd learned a long time ago not to make eye contact with "normal" people when she walked. They dismissed kids like her in a sour glance. There weren't really "normal" people anyway. Most were like her on the inside, fruit slowly going bad.

As she walked toward her apartment, the view degenerated around her. Only a few blocks in, the city became uglier, darker. Garbage collected in gutters and posters for lost kids were hammered onto wooden poles and taped in dirty windows. In the park across the street, homeless teens slept beneath trees, in faded sleeping bags, their dogs beside them. In this part of town, you couldn't go five feet without a homeless kid begging you for money.

Not that they asked her.

"Hey, Marah," some kid in all black said. He was sitting in a doorway, smoking a cigarette, feeding M&M's to a scrawny Doberman.

"Hey, Adam." She went a few more blocks and paused, glancing left to right.

No one was watching her. She stepped up the concrete riser and went into the Light of God Mission.

The quiet was unnerving, given the number of people in the place. Marah kept her gaze down, moved through the maze of check-in, and went into the main space.

Homeless people sat together on long benches, their arms coiled protectively around the yellow plastic food trays in front of them. There were rows and rows of people seated at Formica tables, dressed in layers, even on this nice day. Knit caps, most sporting holes, covered dirty hair.

There were more young people in here than usual. Must be the economy. Marah felt sorry for them. At twenty, she already knew about carrying everything you owned into a gas station bathroom because, even as little as it was, it was all you had.

She got into the slow-moving line, listening idly to the shuffle of feet around her.

The breakfast they served her was a watery oatmeal, with a piece of dry toast. As tasteless as it was, it filled her up and she was grateful for it. Her roommates hated it when she came here. Paxton called it takin' from The Man—but she was hungry. Sometimes you had to choose between food and rent; especially lately. She took her empty bowl and spoon to the window, where she set it in the gray rubber bin that was already overflowing with dirty bowls and spoons—no knives—and cups.

She hurried out of the mission and turned onto the street. Climbing the hill slowly, she went to the sagging old brick building with the cracked windows and lopsided stoop. Dirty sheets hung as drapes in several of the windows.

Home.

Marah picked her way around an overflowing garbage can and past a motley-looking cat. Inside, it took her eyes a moment to adjust to the gloom. The bulb in the hallway's light fixture had gone out two months ago and no one had the money to replace it. The so-called super couldn't care less.

She climbed four flights of stairs. On the front door of the apartment, half of an eviction notice hung from a rusty nail. She ripped the rest of it away and tossed it to the floor, and then opened the door. The small studio apartment, with its sloping, water-damaged floors and putty-colored walls, was thick with smoke and smelled of marijuana and clove cigarettes. Her roommates sat in mismatched chairs and on the floor, most of them sprawled comfortably. Leif was strumming his guitar in a half-assed, high kind of way, and dread-locked Sabrina was smoking dope from a bong. The boy who called himself Mouse was asleep on a mound of sleeping bags. Paxton sat in the La-Z-Boy chair she'd rescued from the trash near her work.

As usual, he was dressed all in black—skinny jeans, unlaced antique-looking boots, and a ripped Nine Inch Nails T-shirt. The pallor of his skin was emphasized by shoulder-length blue-streaked black hair and whiskey-colored eyes.

She stepped over clothes and pizza boxes and Leif's old shoes. Paxton looked up at her, gave her a stoned smile. He showed her a piece of paper with scribbles written across it. She could tell by the handwriting how high he was.

"My latest," he said.

She read the poem aloud, in a voice too quiet for anyone else to hear. "It is us . . . we two . . . alone in the dark, waiting, knowing . . . love is our salvation and our demise . . . no one sees us save each other."

"Get it?" he said, smiling languidly. "It's a double meaning."

His romanticism spoke to her damaged soul. She took the piece of paper from him, studying the words as she had once studied Shakespeare in high school lit class, a lifetime ago. As he reached up, she saw the beautiful white scars on his wrist. He was the only person she'd ever met who understood her pain; he'd shown her how to transform it, to cherish it, to become one with it. Each of the people in this room knew about the fine lines a knife could leave behind.

On the floor, Sabrina lolled sideways, holding out the still-smoking bong. "Hey, Mar. You want a hit?"

"Yeah, sure." She needed to draw the sweet smoke into her lungs and let it do its magic, but before she could cross the room, her cell phone bleated.

She reached into her pocket and pulled out the small purple Motorola Razr she'd had for years.

"My dad's calling," she said. "Again."

"It drives him crazy that you're your own person. Of course he's going to check up on you," Leif said. "It's why he keeps payin' your phone bill."

Paxton stared up at her. "Hey, Sabrina, pass me the bong. The princess is getting a call."

Marah immediately felt ashamed of the way she'd grown up, the luxuries that she'd been given. Pax was right; she had been like a princess until the queen's death. Then the whole fairy tale had collapsed. The bleating stopped. Immediately a text came in. It read: *Emergency. Call me.* She frowned. She hadn't spoken to her father in, what? A year?

No. That wasn't right. She knew precisely when she'd spoken to him last. How could she forget?

December 2009. Nine months ago.

She knew he missed her, and that he regretted their last conversation. The trail of his messages and texts attested to his regret. How many times had he left messages begging for her to come home?

But he'd never claimed that there was an emergency. He'd never tried to trick her into calling.

She picked her way over Sabrina and around Leif, who had passed out with his guitar on his chest, and went into a kitchen that smelled of slowly rotting wood and mildew. There, she called her dad's cell. He answered so quickly, she knew he'd been waiting.

"Marah, it's Dad," he said.

"Yeah. I got that." She went into the corner of the kitchen, where a broken stove and rusted sink bookended a 1960s green fridge.

"How are you, Munchkin?"

"Don't call me that." She leaned against the fridge, blaming it for her sudden cold.

He sighed. "Are you ready to tell me where you are yet? I didn't know even what time zone to count on. Dr. Bloom says this phase—"

"It's not a phase, Dad. It's my life." She pulled away from the fridge. Behind her, in the main room, she could hear the bong bubbling and Pax and Sabrina laughing. The sweet smoke drifted her way. "I'm aging, Dad. What's the emergency?"

"Tully has been in a car accident," he said. "It's bad. We don't know if she's going to make it."

Marah drew in a small, desperate breath. *Not Tully, too.* "Oh, my God . . ."

"Where are you? I could come get you—"

"Portland," she said quietly.

"Oregon? I'll get you a plane ticket." There was a pause. "There are flights every hour. I can have an open ticket waiting for you at the Alaska counter."

"Two tickets," she said.

He paused again. "Fine. Two. What flight—"

She snapped the phone shut without saying goodbye.

Paxton strolled into the kitchen. "What's up? You look freaked."

"My godmother might be dying," she said.

"We're all dying, Marah."

"I need to see her."

"After what she did?"

"Come with me. Please? I can't go alone," she said. "*Please.*"

His gaze narrowed; she felt sliced by the sharpness of it. Exposed.

He tucked his long hair behind one silver-beaded ear. "It's a bad idea."

"We won't stay long. Please, Pax. I'll get some money from my dad."

"Sure," he said finally. "I'll go."

✦

Marah felt people staring at her and Pax as they walked through the small Portland airport.

She liked that so-called normal people were offended by Pax's goth look and the safety pins in his ears and the tattoo on his neck and collarbone. They didn't see the beauty of the scrollwork around the tattooed words or the ironic humor.

Marah boarded the plane, took her seat in the back, and connected her seat belt.

She stared into the window, seeing a shadowy reflection of her pale face: heavily lined brown eyes, purplish lips, and spiked pink hair.

A *ping* sounded through the aircraft and they were off, rocketing down the runway, rising into the cloudless sky.

She closed her eyes. Memories tapped on her consciousness like the raven from Pax's favorite poem. Tap. Tap. Tap.

She didn't want to remember the past, not ever. For years she had buried all of it—the diagnosis, the cancer, the goodbyes, the funeral, and the long gray months that followed—but it was all coming up again, clawing its way to the surface.

She closed her eyes and saw herself as she'd been on the last ordinary day: a fifteen-year-old girl on her way to school.

"Surely you don't think you're wearing that to school?" Mom said, coming into the kitchen.

Across the breakfast table, the twins went suddenly silent and stared at Marah like a pair of bobbleheads.

"Uh-oh," Wills said.

Lucas nodded so fast his mop of hair shimmied.

"There's nothing *wrong with my clothes." Marah got up from the table. "This is* fashion, *Mom." She let her gaze sweep her mom's outfit—cheap, pilly flannel pajamas, tired hair, out-of-date slippers—and frowned. "You should trust me on this."*

"Your outfit is perfect for Pioneer Square at midnight with your pimp. Unfortunately, it's a Tuesday morning in November and you're a sophomore in high school, not a guest on Jerry Springer. *Let me be more specific: that jean skirt is so short I can see your underwear—pink with flowers—and the T-shirt clearly came from the toddler department. You are not showing your stomach at school."*

Marah stomped her foot in frustration. This was exactly *what she wanted Tyler to see her in today. He would look at her and think* cool *instead of* young.

Mom reached for the chair in front of her and clutched it as if she were an old, old lady. With a sigh, she sat down. Then she picked up her coffee cup—the one that said WORLD'S BEST MOM—and held it in both of her hands, as if she needed to be warmed. "I don't feel good enough to fight with you today, Marah. Please."

"So don't."

"Exactly. I'm not fighting. You are not going to high school looking like Britney Spears on crack. Or showing your crack. Period. The cool thing is that I'm your mother. That makes me the CEO of this house. Or the warden. Point is, my house, my rules. Change your clothes or face the consequences. Consequences, I might add, which begin with being late for school and losing your precious new phone, and go downhill from there." Mom put down her coffee cup.

"You're trying *to ruin my life."*

"Ah, you have uncovered my master plan. Rats." Mom leaned over and ruffled Wills's mop of hair. "You guys are still little. I won't ruin your lives for years. No need to worry."

"We know that, Mommy," Wills said earnestly.

"Marah's face is all red," Lucas observed, then went back to building a Cheerios tower.

"The Ryan family school bus leaves in ten minutes," Mom said. She placed her palms on the table and pushed slowly to her feet.

I don't feel good enough to fight with you today.

That had been state's evidence #1. Not that Marah had collected it or even cared. She'd gone on doing what she did—working it at school, being popular, making sure that everyone who was anyone wanted to be her friend. Until that first family meeting.

"I had a doctor's appointment today," Mom said. "There's nothing for you to worry about, but I'm sick."

Marah could hear the boys talking, asking stupid questions, not getting it. Lucas—the mama's boy—ran up and hugged Mom.

Dad herded the boys out of the room. As he passed Marah, he looked down at her and there were tears in his eyes and she felt her knees give out. There was only one reason he would cry.

She looked at her mother and saw her in detail—the pale, pale skin, the dark circles under her eyes, the chapped, colorless lips. It was as if her mom had been dunked in bleach and come out as this colorless version of herself. Sick. *"It's cancer, isn't it?"*

"Yes."

Marah was shaking so hard she clasped her hands together to try to still them. How was it she hadn't known this was possible, that your whole life could tilt sideways in a split second? "You'll be fine. Right?"

"The doctors say I'm young and healthy, so I should be fine."

Should be.

"I'm going to the very best doctors," Mom said. "I'll beat this thing."

Marah released her breath. "Okay, then," she said at last, feeling that terrible tightness in her chest ease up. Her mom never lied.

But she had. She'd lied and she'd died, and without her, Marah's life had lost its shape. In the years afterward, she'd tried to get to know a woman who'd disappeared, but all she could remember was cancerville Mom—the pale, frail, birdlike woman with no hair and no eyebrows and thin white arms.

The horrible "celebration of Mom's life" had been unbearable. Marah had known what was expected of her that night. Everyone had told her. Dad had said tiredly, *It blows, I know, but this is what she wanted;* Grandma had said you can help me in the kitchen—*it will be easier that way.* Only Tully had been honest and real. All she'd said was, *Good God, I'd rather poke my eye out than do this. Marah, can you hand me a serving fork?*

October of 2006. Marah closed her eyes and remembered. It was when everything had started to go so wrong. The night of the funeral. She'd been sitting at the top of the stairs at home, staring down at a room full of people . . .

dressed in black. Every few minutes the doorbell rang and another woman carrying a foil-covered casserole dish came inside (because, really, nothing made you hungrier than burying someone you loved). The music was a version of death, too—jazzy stuff that made sixteen-year-old Marah think of old men with skinny ties and women with beehive hairdos.

She knew she should go down there, mingle, offer drinks and take plates, but she couldn't stand all those pictures of her mom. Besides, when she did accidentally glance at someone—a soccer mom, a dance mom, Mrs. Baakie from the grocery store—all she got was that poor-Marah look that ripped out a piece of her heart and reminded her that this loss was Forever. It had been two days—two days—and already the vibrant, laughing woman in the photos was fading from memory. All Marah could picture in her mind was the colorless, dying version of her mother.

The doorbell rang again.

Her friends came through the front door like warriors ready to save the princess, shoulder to shoulder, their makeup smeared by tears, their eyes wide with sorrow.

Marah had never needed them more. She stood up, feeling unsteady on her feet. Ashley and Coral and Lindsey rushed up the stairs and hugged her, all of them at once. They held her so tightly her feet practically came up off the floor, and the tears she'd been holding back burst out.

"We don't know what to say," Coral said when Marah finally stepped back.

"Your mom was way cool," Ashley said earnestly, and Lindsey nodded.

Marah wiped her eyes. "I wish I'd told her that."

"She totally, like, *knows,*" Ash said. "My mom says to tell you that."

"Remember when she brought cupcakes to Ms. Robbins's classroom? She'd decorated them just like that book we were reading. What was it?" Lindsey frowned, trying to remember.

"*Mrs. Frisby and the Rats of NIMH.* She put whiskers on the cupcakes," Coral said. "It was, like, so amazing."

They nodded together; tears filled their eyes.

Marah remembered, too: *You came into my class! OH, MY GOD. And what are you wearing?*

"The Pavilion is showing a midnighter of *Nightmare Before Christmas*. I think we should go," Lindsey said. "We could chill at Jason's until it starts."

Marah almost said, *My mom would never let me.* At the thought, her eyes glazed with tears. She could feel her emotions spinning out of control. She felt as unsteady as a collapsing building. Thank God her friends were here. "Let's go," she said, leading them down the stairs and through the living room. As she reached for the front door, she would have sworn she heard her mother's voice. *Come back here, young lady. You four are not going to a midnight show. Nothing good happens on this island after eleven.*

Marah stopped. Her friends gathered around her.

"Don't you have to, like, tell your dad we're going?" Lindsey asked.

Marah turned, looked back at the crowd of black-clad mourners in the living room. It looked a little like one of her parents' Halloween parties.

"No," she said softly. Her dad hadn't come looking for her once tonight, and Tully cried every time she looked at her. "No one will even notice I'm gone."

That was a mom's job, keeping track of her children. And Mom was gone.

✦

The next morning, her dad decided they needed a vacation. Why her father thought sand and surf would help, Marah had no idea. She tried to talk him out of it, but she had no vote in the things that mattered. So she went on stupid vacation #1 AM (After Mom—the way life was calculated now, before and after) and didn't even try to make the best of it.

She wanted her dad to know how pissed off she was. All she had was her friends, and they were three thousand miles away when she needed them most.

She hated paradise. The sunshine pissed her off, and so did the smell of burgers on the grill, and seeing her dad's sad face made her want to cry. They didn't talk about anything that mattered that week. He tried—now and then—to make contact, but the pain in his eyes just sucked her in and made it worse, so she stopped looking at him.

She called her friends at least ten times a day until the vacation from hell was finally over.

When they landed back in Seattle, Marah felt herself relaxing for the first time, breathing easily. She'd thought the worst was over.

How wrong she'd been.

They'd come home to find music blaring through the house, empty food containers on the kitchen counter, and Tully in the closet, with Mom's clothes all boxed up. Dad had blown a gasket and said terrible things to Tully and made her cry, but nothing he said was as bad as: "We're moving."

Nine

✦

In November of 2006, less than a month after Mom's funeral, they moved to California. The two weeks before their departure were terrible. Horrible. Marah spent every waking hour either pissed at her dad or inconsolable. She stopped eating, stopped sleeping. All she cared about was talking to her friends, and when the four best friends got together it was just one endless goodbye, broken down into parts. Every sentence began with, *Remember when.*

Marah's anger could hardly be contained. It was a *thing* inside of her, pushing against her ribs, making her blood boil. Even her grief had been consumed by it. She stomped around the house and slammed doors and burst into tears at every memento that had to be packed. She couldn't stomach the idea of just locking up the house—their home—and driving away. The only slightly good news was that they weren't selling it. Someday, Dad promised, they'd return. The big things—furniture, art, rugs—they left behind. They were renting a furnished house. As if different furniture would make them all forget losing Mom.

When the day finally came to move, she'd clung to her friends and sobbed in their arms and told her dad she hated him.

None of it mattered. *She* didn't matter. That was the dark truth. Mom had been a reed; she would have bent to Marah's will. Dad was a wall of steel, cold and implacable. She knew because she'd hurled herself against him and fallen in a heap at his feet.

On the two-day drive to Los Angeles, Marah said nothing. Not one word. She put her earbuds in and listened to music, texting one message after another to her friends.

They left green and blue Washington and drove south. By Central California, everything was brown. Stubby brown hills huddled beneath a bright autumnal sun. There wasn't a decent tree for miles. Los Angeles was even worse: flat and endless. One freeway after another, every lane jam-packed with cars. By the time they pulled up to the house Dad had rented in Beverly Hills, Marah had a splitting headache.

"Wow," Lucas said, drawing at least three syllables out of the word.

"What do you think, Marah?" Dad said, turning in his seat to look at her.

"Yeah," she said. "You care about what I think." She opened the car door and got out. Ignoring everything, she texted Ashley, *Home Sweet Home,* as she walked from the driveway to the house's front door.

It was a house that had obviously been remodeled sometime recently—an old seventies rambler had been punched up to look modern and boxy. The yard out front was flawlessly clipped and carefully manicured. Flowers grew where they were supposed to; their blossoms were supersized because of the sun and the sprinklers.

This wasn't a home. Not for the Ryans, anyway. Inside, everything was sleek and cold, with floor-to-ceiling windows and a stainless steel kitchen and gray stone floors. The furniture was defiantly modern, with sharp edges and chrome accents.

She looked at her dad. "Mom would have hated this." She saw how her words hurt him, and she thought, *Good,* and went upstairs to claim her room.

✦

On her first day at Beverly Hills High School, Marah knew that she would never fit in here. The kids were like beings from another planet. The student parking lot was filled with Mercedes-Benzes and Porsches and BMWs. The carpool lane actually had a few limousines in between the luxury cars and Range Rovers. Not every kid was dropped off by a driver, of course, but the point was that *some* were. Marah couldn't believe it. The girls were gorgeous, with expertly colored hair and purses that cost more than some cars. They clung together in well-dressed pods. No one even said hi to Marah.

On her first day, she moved through her classes on autopilot. None of her teachers called on her or asked her questions. She sat alone at lunch, barely listening to the commotion going on around her, not caring about anything.

In fifth period, she took a seat in the back and put her head down while the other students took a test. The loneliness she felt was epic, overwhelming. She kept thinking how much she needed her friends—and her mom—to talk to. It hurt so much she felt herself start to shake.

"Marah?"

She looked up through the curtain of her hair.

The teacher—Ms. Appleby—had stopped at her desk. "Come see me if you need help getting up to speed. I'm always available." She set a syllabus on the desk. "We all know how hard it is, with your mom . . ."

"Dead," Marah said flatly. If adults were going to talk to her, they might as well say the word. She hated all those pauses and sighs.

Ms. Appleby couldn't move away fast enough.

Marah smiled grimly. It wasn't much of a defense, having to say the word, but it was effective.

The bell rang.

The other kids jumped up and immediately started talking. Marah didn't make eye contact with any of them, and no one made eye contact with her. She was dressed all wrong; she'd known that when she stepped onto the bus. This wasn't a school where Macy's jeans and a fitted blouse were going to cut it.

She loaded up her backpack, making sure that her books were in order and facing the right way. It was a new obsession, one she couldn't shake. She needed her things to be orderly.

Alone, she walked out into the hallway. A few kids were still out here, roughhousing and laughing. Overhead, a big yellow banner hung limply, pulled loose from one of its moorings. It read: GO NORMANS. Someone had scratched out NORMANS, written TROJANS, and drawn a penis beneath the words.

It was the sort of thing she would have told her mom about. They would have laughed together, and when they were done, Mom would have launched into one of her serious talks about sex and teenage girls and appropriateness.

"You do realize you're standing in the middle of the hallway, staring at a penis, and crying, right?"

Marah turned and saw a girl beside her. She had on enough makeup for a photo shoot, and boobs that looked like footballs.

"Leave me the hell alone," Marah said, pushing past the girl. She knew she should have made a smart-ass comment, loudly enough to be overheard. That was how to get some cool cred, but she didn't care. She didn't want new friends.

She skipped last period and left campus early. Maybe *that* would get her dad's attention. She walked all the way home, but it didn't help to be in this cold house that sounded echoey when she walked through it. The boys were with Irena—the older woman her dad had hired to be a part-time nanny—and Dad was still at work. She walked through the big, impersonal house, but it wasn't until she got to her room that her resolve started to crack.

This wasn't her room.

Her room had pale, striped wallpaper and wooden floors and lamps instead of an interrogation-bright overhead light fixture. She walked over to the sleek black dresser, imagining the one that should be there—her dresser, the one her mom had hand-painted all those years ago. (*More colors, Mommy; more stars.*) It would look absurdly out of place in this austere room, as peculiar as Marah at Beverly Hills High.

She reached for the small Shrek jewelry box she'd packed so carefully and brought down here. She'd gotten it from Tully on her twelfth birthday.

It seemed smaller than she remembered, and greener. She turned the key to wind it and lifted the hinged lid. A plastic Fiona snapped erect, spinning in time to the music: *Hey, now, you're an all-star.*

Inside was a tangled collection of her favorite things—an agate from Kalaloch Beach, an arrowhead she'd found in her own backyard, an old plastic dinosaur, a Frodo action figure, the garnet earrings Tully had bought her for her thirteenth birthday, and at the bottom, the pink Space Needle pocketknife she'd gotten at the Seattle Center.

She opened the knife, stared down at the small blade.

Johnny, I don't think she's old enough.

She's old enough, Kate. My girl is smart enough not to cut herself. Right, Marah?

Be careful, baby girl, don't stab yourself.

She pressed the squat silver blade against the flesh of her left palm.

A tingle moved through her. A *feeling*. She moved the blade just a little and accidentally cut her hand.

Blood bubbled up. The color of it mesmerized her. It was unexpectedly bright and beautiful. She couldn't remember ever seeing such a perfect color, like Snow White's red lips.

She couldn't look away. There was pain, of course; it was sharp and sweet and bitter all at the same time. Better somehow than the vague sense of losing what mattered, of being left behind.

This *hurt,* and she welcomed the honesty of that, the clarity. She watched blood slide down the side of her hand and plop onto her black shoe, where it almost disappeared, but not quite.

For the first time in months, she felt better.

✦

In the weeks that followed, Marah lost weight and marked her grief in small red slices on the inside of her upper arm and at the tops of her thighs. Every time she felt overwhelmed or lost or mad at God, she cut herself. She knew she was doing something bad and sick, but she couldn't stop. When she opened her pink pocketknife with its now reddish black crusted blade, she felt a rush of empowerment.

As impossible as it sounded, when she was most depressed, the only thing that helped was hurting herself. She didn't know why that was; she didn't care. Bleeding was better than crying or screaming. Cutting allowed her to carry on.

On Christmas morning, Marah woke early. Her first dreamy thought was, *It's Christmas, Mom,* and then she remembered. Mom was gone. She closed her eyes again, wishing for sleep, wishing for a lot of things.

Downstairs, she heard the sounds of her family coming together. Footsteps thudded on the stairs; doors banged shut. Her brothers screamed for her. They were probably already running around like crazy, grabbing for Grandma's hand, pulling presents out from under the tree, shaking them so hard they rattled. And Mom wasn't here to calm them down. How would they all make it through today?

It helps. You know it does, and it only hurts for a second. No one will know.

She got out of bed and went to her dresser, to the pretty Shrek box. Her hands were shaking as she opened it.

There it was, her knife. She eased it open.

The tip was so sharp, so pretty.

She stuck the tip into the pad of her fingertip and felt her skin slice. Blood oozed up, a perfect red droplet, and the sight of it sent that thrill moving through her again. The pressure that had been building in her chest disappeared, like steam released with the turn of a wheel. A few drops slid down the back of her hand and plopped onto the hardwood floor.

She watched the red stream form and fall in awe.

Her cell phone rang. She backed away, looked around, found her phone by her bed. Picking it up, she answered. "Hello?"

"Hey, Marah. It's me. Tully. I wanted to call you before your big present-opening day started. I know how much time that takes your household, with all that opening one at a time."

Marah grabbed a sock from her top drawer and wrapped it around her finger.

"What's the matter?" Tully said.

Marah squeezed her bleeding finger. The cut throbbed. It should have comforted her, that pain, but with Tully listening to her every breath, all Marah felt was shame. "Nothing. You know . . . Christmas without her."

"Yeah."

Marah sat down on the edge of her bed. She wondered idly what would happen if she told someone about her cutting. She wanted to stop doing it; she really did.

"Have you made any friends yet?" Tully asked.

Marah hated this question. "Lots."

"They're mean girls, aren't they?" Tully said. "The Beverly Hills crowd."

Marah didn't know how to answer. She hadn't made any friends at BHHS, but she hadn't really tried to, either.

"You don't need tons of friends, Marah. You just need one."

"TullyandKate," she said dully. The mythic friendship story.

"I'm here for you, you know that, right?"

"So help me. Tell me how to be happy."

Tully sighed. "Your mom would be better at a time like this. She believed in happy endings and life getting better. Me, I pretty much go in for the life-blows-and-then-you-die school of thought."

"Believe me, life *does* blow. And then you die."

"Talk to me, Marah."

"I don't like it here," she said quietly. "I miss her every day."

"Me, too."

After that, there was nothing to say. Gone was gone. They had both learned that lesson.

"I love you, Marah."

"What are you doing for Christmas?"

There was a pause. In it, Marah thought she heard her godmother draw in a breath. "Oh, you know."

"It's all changed," Marah said.

"Yeah," Tully said. "It's all changed, and I hate it. Especially on days like today."

That was what Marah loved about her godmother. Tully was the only one who never lied and told her it would get better.

✦

The first few months at Beverly Hills High were a nightmare. Marah stumbled in all of her classes; her grades dropped. The curriculum was difficult and competitive, but that wasn't the problem. She couldn't concentrate in class and didn't care. In early 2007, she and her dad had a meeting with the principal and a counselor. There were sad looks all around, and an excess of clucking noises, and the words *grief* and *therapy* were offered repeatedly. By the close of the meeting, Marah understood what was expected of her in this new, motherless, irrigated world of hers. She almost said she didn't care.

Until she looked in her father's eyes and saw how deeply she'd disappointed him. *How can I help you?* he'd asked quietly. Before, she'd thought that was what she was waiting for—that offer—but when he said it, she felt even worse. She'd known then what she hadn't known before: She didn't want help. She wanted to disappear. And she knew how to do it now.

Make no waves.

After that, Marah pretended to be fine. At least fine enough to pass muster for her dad, which was depressingly easy to do. As long as she brought her grades up and smiled at dinner, he looked right through her. He was too busy working. She had learned her lesson: she needed to act normal. The boys' nanny, Irena (a sad-eyed woman who never missed an opportunity to say that her own kids had grown up and moved away, leaving her with too many empty hours on her hands), barely spent any time with Marah, either. All she had to do was pretend she was on some sports team, and she could be gone as much as she wanted, and no one ever asked to come to one of her games or asked her if she was okay.

By senior year, she had it down to a science: She woke on time every morning, bleary-eyed from bad dreams, and stumbled into her bathroom. Rarely did she bother showering or washing her hair, even on school days. It was too exhausting. And it wasn't like it mattered if she was clean or dirty.

She'd given up all hope of making friends at BHHS—and good riddance to the shallow, hair-tossing set who thought the right car proved your worth.

Finally, it was June of 2008. Her graduation from Beverly Hills High. Everyone was downstairs, waiting for her. Grandma and Grandpa and Tully had flown in for the Big Event. They were buzzing with enthusiasm, playing Ping-Pong with words like *exciting* and *accomplishment* and *pride*.

Marah didn't feel any of it. As she reached for her graduation robe, she felt a cold dread descend. The cheap polyester fabric rustled in her grasp. She put on the robe and zipped it up and then went to the mirror.

She was pale and thin and had puffy lavender-colored shadows beneath her eyes. How was it that none of the people who supposedly loved her had noticed how bad she looked?

As long as she did what was expected of her—did her homework, applied to colleges, and pretended to have friends—no one really looked at her. That was what she'd wanted, what she'd chosen, and yet it hurt. Mom would have seen how unhappy she was. That was one of the truths Marah had learned: no one knew you as well as your mom. She would give anything for one of the oh-no-you-don't-young-lady looks she used to hate.

Her dad yelled up from downstairs, "Time to go, Marah."

She walked to her dresser and stared longingly at the Shrek music box. Anticipation quickened her heartbeat.

She opened the lid. Inside, she found the knife and dozens of tiny pieces of gauze, stained brown with old blood; relics she couldn't release. Slowly, she opened the knife and pulled up her sleeve and made a quick, pretty slice on the inside of her forearm, where it wouldn't be seen.

She cut too deep. She knew it instantly.

Blood rushed down her arm, splatted on the floor. She needed help. And not just to stop the bleeding. She was out of control somehow.

She went downstairs. In the living room, blood splattered the stone floor at her feet.

"I need help," Marah said quietly.

Tully was the first to respond.

"Jesus, Marah," her godmother said, tossing her camera onto the sofa. She swooped forward and grabbed Marah's other wrist and dragged her into the nearest bathroom, forcing her to sit on the closed toilet.

Dad rushed into the bathroom behind them as Tully burrowed through drawers, throwing out bars of hand soap and hairbrushes and tubes of hand cream.

"What the hell happened?" her dad yelled.

"Bandages," Tully snapped, kneeling beside Marah. *"Now!"*

Dad left them. He was back in no time with gauze and adhesive tape. He stood back, looking confused and angry, while Tully applied pressure to stop the bleeding and then bandaged the wound. "There," Tully said. "But I think she'll need stitches." Tully stepped back, allowed Dad to move in. "Jesus . . ." he said, shaking his head. He bent down to be eye level with Marah.

He tried to smile, and she thought: *This isn't my dad, not this man who can't straighten his shoulders and rarely laughs anymore.* He wasn't himself any more than she was the daughter he remembered. He was even going gray—when had that started?

"Marah?" he said. "What happened?"

She was too ashamed to answer. She'd already disappointed him so much.

"Don't be afraid," Tully said. "You asked for help. You mean therapy, don't you?"

Marah stared up into her godmother's warm brown gaze. "Yes," she said softly.

"I don't understand," Dad said, looking from Tully to Marah.

"She did it on purpose," Tully said.

Marah could see how confused her father was. It made no sense to him that cutting herself *helped*. "How could I not know that you were hurting yourself?"

"I know someone who can help her," Tully said.

"Here in L.A.?" Dad asked, turning to look up at Tully.

"In Seattle. Remember Dr. Harriet Bloom? From my show? I bet I could get Marah in to see her on Monday."

"Seattle," Marah said. It was a lifeline being thrown to her. How often had she dreamed of going back to see her friends? But now that the opportunity was here, she found that she didn't care. It was more proof that she was sick. Disturbed. Depressed.

Dad shook his head. "I don't know . . ."

"She did it down here, Johnny, in Los Angeles," Tully said. "Today of all days. I may not be Freud, but I can tell you this is a cry for help. Let me help her."

"You?" he said sharply.

"You're still angry with me? What the hell for? No, don't answer that. I don't care. I am not going to back down this time, Johnny Ryan. I'm not giving you space or cutting you slack. If I didn't fight you right now, Katie would kick my ass. I promised her I would take care of Marah. You obviously haven't done a great job."

"Tully." The warning in his voice was unmistakable.

"Let me take her home and get her in to see Harriet on Monday, or Tuesday at the latest. Then we can decide what comes next."

Dad looked at Marah. "Do you want to see Dr. Bloom in Seattle?"

The truth was, Marah didn't care about Dr. Bloom. She didn't want anything except to be left alone. And to leave Los Angeles. "Yeah," she said tiredly.

Dad turned to Tully. "I'll come up as soon as I can."

Tully nodded.

Dad didn't look convinced. He stood up and faced Tully. "I can trust you to take care of her for a few days?"

"I'll be like a mama hen sitting on precious eggs."

"I will want a full report."

Tully nodded. "You'll have one."

Ten

Marah didn't go to her high school graduation after all, and it was a relief. Instead, she boarded a plane with Tully and flew back to Seattle. True to her word, Tully got Marah a two o'clock appointment with Dr. Harriet Bloom on the following Monday.

Today.

Marah didn't want to get out of bed. She hadn't slept well last night and now she was exhausted. Still, she did what was expected of her. She took a shower and washed her hair and even bothered to dry it. Although it took a lot of effort, she picked her clothes from her suitcase instead of from the pile she'd left on the floor last night.

When she put on her 7 for All Mankind jeans—once one of her favorite possessions, in that other life—she was horrified at how much weight she'd lost. The jeans hung on her, exposed the sharp knobs of her hip bones. She chose a heavy Abercrombie sweatshirt to give her slight frame a little bulk—and to hide the scars on her upper arms.

Zipping the hoodie up to her throat, she started to leave the bedroom. She meant to just walk out, slam the door shut behind her, and get started.

But as she passed her open suitcase, her gaze landed on the pocket sewn into the side, where her pocketknife was hidden. For a second, the world seemed to blur and slow down. She heard her heartbeat thudding and felt the blood flowing through her veins. She imagined it: bright red, beautiful. The thought of hurting herself for a second, just once so that this terrible pressure in her chest would ease, was so tempting she actually took a step forward, reached out.

"Marah!"

She yanked her hand back and glanced quickly around.

She was alone.

"Marah!"

It was Tully. She'd yelled twice. That meant she could be on her way down the hall.

Marah fisted her hands, felt the pinch of fingernails in the fleshy middle of her palms. "Coming," she said, although her voice was dry and small, barely audible even to her.

She left the bedroom and shut the door with a little click.

In no time, Tully was beside her, holding her by the arm, guiding Marah out of the condominium, as if she were blind.

As they walked uptown, Tully talked.

Marah tried to listen, but her heart was beating so fast it deafened her to anything else. Her hands were sweating. She didn't want to sit down with some stranger and talk about cutting herself.

"Here we are," Tully said at last, and Marah came out of the gray fog and found herself standing in front of a tall glass building. When had they passed the park where the homeless people gathered beneath the totem pole? She didn't remember. That scared her.

She followed Tully into the elevator and up to the doctor's office, where a serious young woman with a lot of freckles offered them seats in the waiting room.

Marah perched uncomfortably on an overstuffed blue chair by an aquarium.

"I guess fish are supposed to be calming," Tully said. She sat down beside Marah and took hold of her hand. "Marah?"

"What?"

"Look at me."

She didn't want to, but one thing she knew: it was a waste of time to ignore Tully. Slowly she turned. "Uh-huh?"

"There's nothing wrong with how you feel," she said gently. "Sometimes missing her hurts more than I can stand, too."

No one *ever* said stuff like this anymore. Oh, they'd talked about Mom all the time eighteen months ago, but apparently there was an expiration date on grief. It was like an exterior door closing; once it shut and you were in the dark, you were supposed to forget how much you missed the light. "What do you do when it, you know, hurts to remember?"

"If I told you, your mom would come down from heaven and kick my ass. I'm supposed to be the responsible adult here."

"Fine," Marah said. "Don't fricking tell me how you handle it. No one ever does." She glanced sideways to see if the receptionist was eavesdropping, but the woman wasn't paying attention to them.

Tully didn't respond for a minute, which seemed to go on too long. Finally, she nodded and said, "I started having panic attacks after her death, so I take Xanax. And I can't sleep for shit anymore. And sometimes I drink too much. What do you do?"

"I cut myself," Marah said quietly. It felt surprisingly good to admit.

"We are quite a pair," Tully said with a wan smile.

Behind them, a door opened and a slim woman emerged from the office. She was beautiful, in a gritted-teeth, angry kind of way that Marah recognized as pain. The woman wore a heavy plaid scarf wrapped around her upper body and held it closed with a gloved hand, as if she were heading out into a snowstorm instead of a Seattle day in June.

"See you next week, Jude," said the receptionist.

The woman nodded and put on sunglasses. She didn't glance at either Marah or Tully as she left the office.

"You must be Marah Ryan."

Marah hadn't even noticed the other woman who'd come into the waiting room.

"I'm Dr. Harriet Bloom," the woman said, extending a hand.

Marah stood up reluctantly. Now she really wanted to bolt. "Hi."

Tully got to her feet. "Hi, Harriet. Thanks for agreeing to help us on such short notice. I know you had to change your schedule. You'll need some background information, of course. I'll come in for—"

"No," the doctor said.

Tully looked nonplussed. "But—"

"I'll take good care of her, Tully, but this is between Marah and me. She's in good hands. I promise."

Marah didn't think so. In fact, she thought she was in weird hands, bony hands with age-spotted skin. The opposite of good hands. Still, she played her good-girl role and followed the doctor into her sleek, grown-up office.

A wall of windows looked out over the Pike Place Market and the sparkling blue Sound. A polished wooden desk cut the room in half; behind it was a big black leather chair. Two comfortable-looking chairs sat facing the desk and a black sofa was pushed against the back wall. Above it was a soothing picture of a beach in the summer. Hawaii, maybe. Or Florida. There were palm trees anyway.

"I suppose you want me to lie down," Marah said, hugging herself. She was cold in here, too. Maybe that was why the other lady was so layered up. The weird thing was that there was a gas fireplace in the wall, and bright orange and blue flames sent heat splashing toward her. She could feel it and she couldn't.

Dr. Bloom sat down behind her desk and uncapped a pen. "You may sit wherever you like."

Marah flopped into a chair and stared at the plant in the corner, counting its leaves. One . . . two . . . three . . . She really didn't want to be here. Four . . . five . . .

She heard a clock ticking through the minutes, and the even in and out of the doctor's breathing, and the rough hiss of her black nylons as she crossed and uncrossed her legs.

"Do you think there's something you'd like to talk about?" the doctor asked after at least ten minutes had passed.

Marah shrugged. "Not really." Fifty-two . . . fifty-three . . . fifty-four. The room was getting hot now. That little fireplace was a real dynamo. She felt sweat crawling across her forehead. A drop slid down the side of her face. She tapped her foot nervously on the floor.

Sixty-six . . . sixty-seven.

"How do you know Tully?"

"She's a friend of—"

"Your mother's?"

The way she said it was all wrong, clinical, the way you'd ask about a car or a vacuum, but still Marah felt her stomach tightening. She did not want to talk about her mom with a stranger. She shrugged and kept counting.

"She's gone, right?"

Marah paused. "She's in my dad's closet, actually."

"Excuse me?"

Marah smiled. Score one for the home team. "We rented a casket for the funeral—which was way weird, if you ask me. Anyway, we cremated her and put her in this rosewood box. When Tully wanted to scatter her ashes, Dad wasn't ready, and when Dad was ready, Tully wasn't. So Mom's in the closet behind my dad's sweaters."

"What about when you were ready?"

Marah blinked. "What do you mean?"

"When would you like to scatter your mother's ashes?"

"No one's asked me that."

"Why do you think that is?"

Marah shrugged and looked away again. She didn't like where this was going.

"Why do you think you're here, Marah?" the doctor said.

"You know why."

"I know what you did to yourself. The cutting."

Marah looked at the plant again. The leaves were really waxy-looking. Seventy-five . . . seventy-six . . . seventy-seven.

"I know it makes you feel better when you do it."

Marah glanced at Dr. Bloom, who sat perfectly still, her sharp nose hooked out over her thin lips. "But when you're done, and your razor blade or knife is full of dried blood, I bet you feel worse. Ashamed, maybe, or afraid."

Seventy-eight . . . seventy-nine.

"I can help you with those feelings, if you'll talk to me about how you feel. It's not uncommon, how you're feeling."

Marah rolled her eyes. That was one of those tarry lies adults told kids to make the world prettier.

"Well," Dr. Bloom said later, closing her notebook. Marah wondered what she'd written in it. Probably, *Whack job, loves plants*. "That's all the time we have for today."

Marah shot to her feet and turned for the door. As she reached for the knob, Dr. Bloom said:

"I have a teen grief group meeting that might help you, Marah. Would you like to join us? It's Wednesday night."

"Whatever." Marah opened the office door.

Tully lurched to her feet. "How was it?"

Marah didn't know what to say. She glanced away from Tully and saw that there was someone else in the waiting room: a young man dressed in skin-tight, torn black jeans that disappeared into scuffed black boots with the laces falling slack. He was thin, almost femininely so, and wearing a black T-shirt that read BITE ME beneath a smoke-colored jacket. At his throat, a collection of pewter skulls hung like keys on a chain, and his shoulder-length hair was unnaturally black, tinged here and there in peacock streaks of magenta and green. When he looked up, Marah saw that his eyes were strange, almost golden, and heavy black guyliner accentuated the color. His skin was pale. Like maybe he was sick.

Dr. Bloom came up beside Marah. "Paxton, perhaps you'd tell Marah that our therapy group isn't such a bad little gathering."

The young man—Paxton—stood up and moved toward Marah with the kind of grace that seemed staged.

"Tully?" Dr. Bloom said. "May I speak to you for a moment?"

Marah was aware of the two older women moving away from her, whispering to each other.

Marah knew she should care what they were saying, but she couldn't think of anything except the boy coming toward her.

"You're afraid of me," he said when he was close to her. She could smell spearmint gum on his breath. "Most people are."

"You think I'm scared of a little black clothing?"

He lifted a pale hand and tucked his hair behind one ear. "Nice girls like you should stay in suburbia where it's safe. The group isn't for you."

"You don't know anything about me. But maybe you should stop playing in your mom's makeup."

His laugh surprised her. "Fire. I like that."

"Hey, Marah," Tully said. "It's time to go." She strode across the waiting room and took Marah by the arm and led her out of the office.

✦

All the way home, Tully kept up a stream of conversation. She kept asking Marah if she wanted to go to Bainbridge Island to see her friends, and Marah wanted to say yes, but she didn't belong there anymore. In the year and a half of her absence, the old friendships had degraded like moth wings; now they were tattered bits of white that couldn't possibly fly again. She had nothing in common with those girls.

Tully led Marah into the bright, elegant condo and turned on the fireplace in the living room. Flames flowered up, zipped along a fake log. "So. How was it?"

Marah shrugged.

Tully sat down on the sofa. "Don't shut me out, Marah. I want to help."

God, she was tired of disappointing people. She wished there were a handbook for children of the deceased, like in *Beetlejuice,* so that she would know what to do and say so that people would leave her alone. "I know."

She sat down on the stone hearth, facing Tully. The fire warmed her back, made her shiver. She hadn't even realized that she was cold.

"I should have made your dad put you in counseling when Kate died. But we fell apart, your dad and me. I asked about you, though, and talked to you every week. You never said a thing. I never heard you cry. Your grandma said you were handling it."

"Why should you have known?"

"I know about abandonment and grief. I know about shutting down. When my gran died, I barely let myself grieve. When my mom left me—every time—I told myself it didn't hurt and went on."

"And with Mom's death?"

"It's been harder. I'm not bouncing back well."

"Yeah. Me, either."

"Dr. Bloom thinks you should attend that teen grief therapy session Wednesday night."

"Yeah. Like that will help."

She saw how her answer wounded Tully. Marah sighed. She had too much of her own pain. She couldn't bear Tully's, too.

"Fine," Marah said. "I'll go."

Tully got up and pulled Marah into a hug.

She drew back as quickly as she could, smiling shakily. If her godmother knew how alone and desperate she felt, it would break her heart, and God knew none of them could handle more heartbreak. She just needed to do what she'd done for months—get through this. She could handle a few therapy sessions if it would get everyone off her back. In September, she'd be a college freshman at the UW and she could live however she wanted and she wouldn't be constantly hurting or disappointing people.

"Thanks," she said tightly. "Now I'm going to lie down. I'm tired."

"I'll call your dad and tell him how it went. He'll be here on Thursday to meet Dr. Bloom after your next appointment."

Great.

Marah nodded and headed down the hall toward the guest bedroom, which looked like a suite in some elegant hotel.

She couldn't believe she'd agreed to go to a teen grief therapy meeting. What in the hell would she say to strangers? Would they make her talk about her mom?

Anxiety seeped through her, turning into a physical presence, like bugs crawling on her skin.

Skin.

She didn't mean to go to the closet, didn't want to, but this buzzing in her blood was making her crazy. It was like listening to some staticky overseas line where a dozen conversations tumbled over each other and, no matter how hard you listened, you couldn't hear anything that made sense.

Her hands were shaking as she opened her suitcase and reached inside the interior pocket.

Opening it, she found the small Space Needle knife and several squares of bloodstained gauze.

She pushed her sleeve up, until her bicep was revealed, so thin it was just a knot of muscle, pale in the darkness, as soft and white as the inside of a pear. Dozens of scar lines crisscrossed her skin, like spiderwebs.

She touched the sharp tip of the blade to her skin and poked hard, then cut. Blood bubbled up. It was beautiful, rich, red. She watched her blood well and fall, like tears, into her waiting palm. Every bad emotion filled those drops of blood and fell away, left her body.

"I'm fine," she whispered.

I am the only one who can hurt me. Only me.

✦

Unable to sleep that night, as Marah lay in the bed that wasn't hers, in a city that used to feel like home, listening to the nothingness that came from being perched in a jewel box high above the city, she replayed tonight's conversation with her dad.

Fine, she'd said when he asked how the meeting with Dr. Bloom had gone. But even as she said it, she thought: *How come no one asks me how I can be so fine all the time?*

You can talk to me, he'd said.

Really? she'd snapped. *Now you want to talk.* But when she heard him sigh she wanted to take it back.

Marah, how the hell did we get here?

She'd hated the disappointment in his voice; it made her feel both guilty and ashamed.

I'm going to a teen grief support meeting Wednesday night. Doesn't that sound fun?

I'll be there on Thursday. I promise.

Sure.

I'm proud of you, Marah. It's hard to face pain.

She'd fought for composure, felt the sting of tears. Memories had besieged her—times she'd fallen or been hurt and run to her daddy for a hug. His arms had been so strong and protective.

When had he held her last? She couldn't remember. In the past year, she'd pulled back from the people who loved her, and grown fragile in their absence, but she didn't know how to change. She was always afraid of bursting into tears and revealing her pain.

The next morning, she woke feeling sluggish and headachy. Needing coffee, she put on a robe that belonged to Tully and wandered out of her room.

She found Tully asleep on the sofa, one arm flung onto the coffee table. An empty wineglass lay on its side on the table, a pile of papers beside it. There was a small orange prescription pill container near it.

"Tully?"

Tully sat up slowly, looking a little pale. "Oh. Marah." She rubbed her eyes and shook her head as if to clear it. "What time is it?" Her speech was slow.

"Almost ten."

"Ten! Shit. Get dressed."

Marah frowned. "Are we going somewhere?"

"I have a surprise planned for you."

"I don't want to be surprised."

"Of course you do. Go. Take a shower." Tully shooed her down the hall. "Meet me in twenty."

Marah took a shower and put on a pair of baggy jeans and an oversized T-shirt. Without bothering to dry her hair, she pulled it back in a ponytail and went out into the kitchen.

Tully was already there, dressed in a blue suit that was at least a size too small. She was taking a pill and washing it down with coffee when Marah came up beside her.

Tully yelped when Marah touched her, as if surprised. Then she laughed. "Sorry. Didn't hear you come up."

"You're acting weird," Marah said.

"I'm excited. About my surprise."

"I told you. No surprises." Marah eyed her. "What are you taking?"

"The pill? It's a vitamin. At my age, you can't forget vitamins." She studied Marah, frowned. "Is that what you're wearing?"

"Yeah. Why?"

"No makeup, even?"

Marah rolled her eyes. "What am I doing, trying out for *America's Next Top Model*?" The doorbell rang. Marah was instantly suspicious. "Who's that?"

"Come on," Tully said, smiling now, herding her toward the door. "Open it," she said.

Marah opened the door cautiously.

Ashley, Lindsey, and Coral stood there, clustered together. When they saw Marah they screamed—really, it was this ear-piercing shriek—and surged toward her, pulling her into a group hug.

Marah felt as if she were experiencing it all from some great distance. She heard their voices but couldn't quite make out what they were saying. Before she knew it, she was being swept out of the condo on the tide of her three best friends' enthusiasm. They were all talking to her at once as they climbed into Coral's Honda and drove down to the ferry terminal, where a boat was waiting. They drove right on and parked.

"It's *so* cool that you're back," Lindsey said, bouncing in the backseat, leaning forward.

"Yeah. We, like, couldn't believe when Tully called. Were you going to surprise us?" Ashley asked.

"Of course she was," Coral said from the driver's seat. "Now, we have to tell you *everything*!"

"Start with Tyler Britt," Lindsey said.

"Right. Totally." Coral turned to Marah and launched into a long, laughing story about Tyler Britt dating some skanky girl from North Kitsap and getting caught by the cops in his underwear and getting a minor-in-possession ticket and being banned from the homecoming football game.

Marah kept a smile on her face the whole time, but what she was thinking was, *I can hardly remember my crush on Tyler Britt*. It felt like a lifetime ago. She forced herself to nod and smile; sometimes she remembered to laugh when they told her funny stories about the grad party.

Later, when they were at Lytle Beach, stretched out on brightly colored towels, drinking Cokes and noshing on Doritos, Marah didn't know what to say.

She felt oddly separate, even though they lay close enough together that their shoulders touched. Coral was talking about college and how glad she was that she and Ashley were going to be roommates at Western Washington University, and Lindsey was whining that she didn't want to go off to Santa Clara alone.

"Where are you going?" Coral asked Marah.

Honestly, she was so out of it, barely listening in fact, that Marah didn't hear the question the first time it was asked.

"Mar?"

"Where are you going to college?"

"UW," Marah said, trying to concentrate. It felt as if a warm gray fog had fallen around her—just her.

She didn't belong with these girls who giggled all the time and dreamed of falling in love and starting college and thought their moms were too strict.

She wasn't like them anymore, and by the time their day was over, and they drove her back to Seattle, the awkward silences in the car attested to their understanding of this truth. They walked her up to the condo and gathered around her at the door, but now they all knew there was nothing to say. Marah hadn't known it before, but friendships could die, too, just wither away. She didn't have the strength to pretend to be the girl they used to know.

"We missed you," Coral said quietly, and this time it sounded like goodbye.

"I missed you, too," Marah said, and it was true. She would give anything to make it still true.

When they left, Marah walked back into Tully's condo. She found Tully in the kitchen, putting dishes away.

"How was it?"

Marah heard something in Tully's voice, a slurring of words that didn't quite make sense. If she didn't know better, she'd think Tully had had a few drinks, but it was way early for that.

And really, Marah didn't care. She just wanted to climb into bed and pull the covers up over her head and go to sleep. "It was great," she said dully. "Better than great. I'm tired, though, so I'm going to take a nap."

"Not too long," Tully said. "I rented *Young Frankenstein*."

One of Mom's favorite movies. How many times had Mom said, "Valk ziss vay," and pretended to hunch over like Marty Feldman? And how many times had Marah rolled her eyes in impatience at the old joke?

"Great. Yeah," she said, and headed for her room.

Eleven

✦

"Tell me that's not what you're wearing," Tully said when Marah walked into the living room on Wednesday night, wearing torn, low-rise flared jeans and an oversized gray sweatshirt.

"Huh? It's teen grief therapy," Marah said. "Let's face it, if you're invited, fashion isn't your biggest problem."

"You have pretty much dressed like a bag lady since you got here. Don't you want to make a good impression?"

"On depressed teens? Not really."

Tully got to her feet and crossed the room to stand in front of Marah. She reached up slowly, placed her palm against Marah's cheek. "I have a lot of really great personality traits. I have a few flaws, I'll admit—gaping holes in the fabric—but mostly I am an amazing person. I don't judge people on anything except their actions, even when they do bad things; I know how hard it is to be human. The point is, I love you, and I'm not your mom or dad. It's not my job to see that you grow up to be a smart, successful, well-adjusted adult. My job is to tell you stories about your mom when you're ready and to love you no matter what. I'm supposed to say what your mother would say—when I can figure out what that would be. Usually I'm in the mud on that, but this time it's easy." She smiled tenderly. "You're hiding, baby girl. Behind dirty hair and baggy clothes. But I see you, and it's time for you to come back to us."

Tully didn't give Marah time to answer. Instead, she took Marah by the hand and led her down the hallway and through the master bedroom and into Tully's huge walk-in closet (it used to be a bedroom—that was how big it was). There, Tully chose a white crinkly fitted blouse with a deep V-neck and lace around the collar. "You're wearing this."

"Who cares?"

Tully ignored the comment and took the blouse off the hanger. "The sad thing is that I thought I was fat when I wore this blouse. Now I couldn't button it. Here."

Marah yanked the blouse from Tully and went into the bathroom. She didn't want Tully to see her scars; it was one thing to hear that Marah was a cutter. It was something else to see the web of white scars on her skin. The patterned white fabric was deceptive; it seemed to show skin, but there was a flesh-colored liner beneath. When she walked over to the mirror, Marah barely recognized herself. Her thinness was accentuated by the fitted blouse; it made her look fragile and feminine. The jeans hugged her slim hips. She felt strangely nervous as she walked back into the bedroom. Tully was right: Marah had been hiding, although she hadn't known it. Now she felt exposed.

Tully pulled the elastic band from Marah's long black hair, let it fall free. "You are gorgeous. Every boy in the meeting will be driven crazy by you. Trust me."

"Thanks."

"Not that we care what therapy boys think. I'm just saying."

"I'm a therapy girl," she said quietly. "Crazy."

"You're sad, not crazy. Sad makes sense. Come on, it's time to go."

Marah followed Tully out of the condo and down to the lobby. Together they walked down First Street to the oldest part of the city. Pioneer Square. Tully came to a stop in front of a squat, blank-faced brick building that dated from before the Great Seattle Fire. "Do you want me to walk you inside?"

"Oh, my God. No. That guy with the eyeliner already thinks I'm Miss Suburbia. All I need is a chaperone."

"The guy from the waiting room? Edward Scissorhands? And I care what he thinks why?"

"I'm just saying it would be embarrassing. I'm eighteen years old."

"I get it. Okay. Maybe he's Johnny Depp under all that makeup." Tully turned to her. "So, you know how to get back to my place? It's eight blocks up First. The doorman's name is Stanley."

Marah nodded. Her mother would never have let her be alone in this part of town after dark.

Slinging her fringed leather purse strap over her shoulder, Marah walked away. The building in front of her was like many of the early brick structures in Pioneer Square; the interior was dark and the hallway was narrow and windowless. A single lightbulb hung overhead, casting a meager light below. In the foyer, a huge board was cluttered with scraps of paper and notices for AA meetings, lost dogs, cars for sale, and the like.

Marah followed the stairs down into a vaguely musty-smelling basement.

At the closed door, upon which had been tacked a notice for TEEN GRIEF GROUP, she paused and almost turned around. Who the hell wanted to be a part of *this* group?

She opened the door and went inside.

It was a big room, fluorescently well lit, with a long table at one end that held a coffeemaker, cups, and what looked like a high school bake sale array of treats. Several metal chairs formed a large circle in the center of the room. A box of Kleenex was positioned on the floor by each chair.

Great.

There were already four kids here, seated in the chairs. Marah looked at the other . . . patients? participants? nutcases? . . . through the black hair falling in front of her eyes. There was a very large girl with pimply skin and greasy hair who was chewing so hard on her thumbnail she looked like an otter trying to open an oyster. Beside her was a girl so thin that if she turned sideways, she'd vanish. She had a bald spot on the side of her head. Next to her sat a girl dressed all in black, with magenta-colored hair and enough facial piercings to play tic-tac-toe. She slouched away from a plump boy in horn-rimmed glasses beside her who was playing with his phone.

Dr. Bloom sat in the circle, too, wearing fitted navy pants and a gray turtleneck. As neutral as Switzerland. Marah wasn't fooled: there was nothing casual about the eagle-eyed way Dr. Bloom looked at her.

"We're glad you could join us, Marah. Aren't we, group?" Dr. Bloom said.

A few of the kids shrugged. Most didn't bother to even look up.

Marah took a seat by the heavy girl. She had barely taken her place when the door creaked open and Paxton walked in. As before, he was dressed like a goth, in black jeans and unlaced boots and a poorly fitted black T-shirt. A tattoo of words snaked over the ridge of his collarbone and curled up his throat. Marah looked away quickly.

He sat down across from Marah, next to the girl with the magenta hair.

Marah waited to the count of fifty to look at him again.

He was staring at her, smiling like he thought she was hot for him. She rolled her eyes and looked away.

"Well, it's seven o'clock, so we can get started," Dr. Bloom said. "As you can see, we have a new member: Marah. Who would like to make the introductions?"

There was a lot of looking away and chewing on nails and shrugging. Finally, Magenta Hair said, "Oh, hell. I'm Ricki. Dead mom. The fat chick's Denise. Her grandma has Parkinson's. Todd hasn't spoken in four months, so we don't know what his problem is. Elisa stopped eating when her dad killed himself. And Pax is here by court order. Dead sister." She looked at Marah. "What's your story?"

Marah felt everyone looking at her.

"I . . . I . . ."

"Mr. Football didn't ask her to the prom," the heavy girl said, giggling nervously at her own joke.

A few of the other kids snickered.

"We're not here to judge each other," Dr. Bloom said. "You all know how much that hurts, don't you?"

That shut them up.

"Cutter," Pax said quietly. He sat slouched in his chair, one arm draped across Magenta Hair's chair and one leg crossed over the other. "But why?"

Marah looked up sharply.

"Paxton," Dr. Bloom said. "This is a *support* group. Life is hard. You've all learned that at an early age. Each of you has experienced a profound loss and you know how hard it can be to keep going when a loved one has died or someone charged with caring for you has betrayed that sacred trust."

"My mother died," Marah said evenly.

"Would you like to talk about her?" Dr. Bloom asked gently.

Marah couldn't look away from Paxton. His golden gaze mesmerized her. "No."

"Who would?" he said quietly.

"How about you, Paxton?" Dr. Bloom said. "Do you have something you'd like to share with the group?"

"Never to suffer would never to have been blessed," he said with a negligent shrug.

"Now, Paxton," Dr. Bloom said, "we've talked about hiding behind other people's words. You're almost twenty-two years old. It's time to find your own voice."

Twenty-two.

"You don't want to hear what I have to say," Paxton said. Although he was slumped down and appeared uninterested in everyone around him, his eyes held an intensity that was unnerving, almost scary.

Court order.

Why would the court order someone to grief therapy?

"On the contrary, Paxton," Dr. Bloom said evenly, "you've been coming here for months and you haven't talked about your sister once."

"And I won't," he said, looking now at his black fingernails.

"The court—"

"Can order me to come, but it can't make me talk."

Dr. Bloom pursed her lips in disapproval. She stared at Paxton for a long moment and then smiled again, turning slightly so that her attention was on Stick Girl. "Elisa, perhaps you'd like to tell us more about how eating went this week . . ."

An hour later, as if by some secret alarm, the kids lurched out of their seats and rushed from the room. Marah hadn't been prepared. By the time she bent down to retrieve her purse from the floor and stood up, only Dr. Bloom was still there.

"I hope that wasn't too painful," the doctor said, walking over to her. "Beginnings can be difficult."

Marah looked past her to the open door. "No. Fine. I mean yes. Thanks. It was great."

Marah couldn't wait to get out of this room that smelled of stale cookies and burnt coffee. She ran outside and came to a sudden stop. The streets were crowded. On this Wednesday night in June, Pioneer Square was full of tourists and locals. Music spilled out of the taverns and bars.

Paxton appeared out of the darkness beside her; she heard him breathing a split second before she saw him. "You're waiting for me," he said.

She laughed. "Yeah, because guys in makeup really rev my engines." She turned to face him. "You were waiting for me."

"What if I was?"

"Why?"

"You'll have to come with me to find out." He held out his hand.

In the yellowy light from the streetlamp, she saw his pale hand and long fingers . . . and the scars that ran like an equal sign across his wrist.

Cut marks.

"Now you're scared," he said quietly.

She shook her head.

"But you're a good girl from the suburbs."

"I used to be." As she said the words, she felt the tightness in her chest ease up a little. Maybe she could change herself somehow, become a different version of herself, and maybe if she did, it wouldn't hurt so much to look in the mirror and see her mother's smile.

"Marah? Paxton?" Dr. Bloom walked up the sidewalk behind them. Marah felt a strange sadness, as if a beautiful opportunity had just been lost.

Marah smiled at the doctor. When she turned back, Paxton was gone.

"Be careful," Dr. Bloom said, following Marah's gaze across the street, to where Paxton stood in the shadows between two buildings, smoking a cigarette.

"Is he dangerous?"

It was a moment before Dr. Bloom said, "I can't answer that, Marah. Just as I wouldn't answer a similar question about you. But I would ask you this: Are you looking at him *because* you think he's dangerous? That kind of behavior can be risky for a girl in a vulnerable situation."

"I'm not looking at him at all," Marah said.

"No," Dr. Bloom said. "Of course you're not."

At that, Marah resettled her bag over her shoulder and headed up the dark street for home. All the way back to Tully's she thought she heard footsteps behind her, but every time she turned around, the sidewalk was empty.

✦

On the way up to the penthouse, Marah stared at her reflection in the elevator's mirrored walls. All her life she'd been told that she was beautiful, and for most of her teen years, that had been what she wanted to hear. In the years BC—before cancer—she'd spent hours studying her face, making it up, fixing her hair so that boys like Tyler Britt would notice her. But AC, it had changed. Now all she saw was her mother's smile and her father's eyes and it turned every glance in a mirror into something painful.

Now, though, she saw how thin she'd become, how pale, in the twenty months since her mother's death. The bleak look in her eyes depressed her. Then again, everything depressed her these days.

On the top floor, she exited the elevator and went to Tully's condo. Unlocking the door, she stepped into the bright apartment and went into the living room.

Tully was there, pacing in front of the wall of windows that overlooked the city at night. She had a glass of wine in her hand and she was talking on the phone, yelling, actually, saying, "*Celebrity Apprentice*? Are you *kidding* me? I can't be that far gone." She turned, saw Marah, and flashed a brittle smile. "Oh. Marah." She laughed and said, "I have to go, George," and hung up the phone. Tossing it onto the couch, she met Marah with open arms and hugged her tightly.

"Well, how was it?" she said at last, stepping back.

Marah knew what was expected of her. She was supposed to say, *It was great, wonderful, perfect. I feel better now,* but she couldn't do it. She opened her mouth and nothing came out.

Tully's gaze narrowed, became that journalist-on-a-story look Marah had seen before. "Hot cocoa," she said, and led Marah into the kitchen. Tully made two cups of hot cocoa with whipped cream and carried them into the guest bedroom. Just like when she was little, Marah climbed up onto the bed. Tully did the same. They leaned side by side against the tufted gray silk headboard. A large window framed the Seattle skyline, which glittered in vibrant neon against a starlit sky.

"So, tell me everything," Tully said.

Marah shrugged. "The kids in the group are pretty messed up."

"You think it's going to help you?"

"No. And I don't want to see Dr. Bloom again, either. Can we cancel tomorrow's appointment? I mean, what's the point?"

Tully took a sip of her hot cocoa and then leaned over and set her cup on the nightstand. "I'm not going to lie to you, Marah," she said at last. "Real-world relationship advice has never been my strong suit, but maybe if I had learned how to deal with things at your age I wouldn't be as screwed up as I am now."

"You really think talking to a stranger and sitting around with a bunch of crazies in a moldy basement will help me?" The minute she said *crazies,* she thought about the guy, Paxton, and the way he looked at her.

"Maybe."

Marah looked at Tully. "But it's therapy, Tully. Therapy. And I . . . can't talk about her."

"Yeah," Tully said quietly. "But here's the thing, kiddo. Your mom asked me to watch out for you and that's what I'm going to do. I was her best friend from the David Cassidy years to the second George Bush years. She's the voice in my head. And I know what she would say now."

"What's that?"

"Don't give up, baby girl."

Marah heard her mother's voice in those few words. She knew Tully was right—that was what her mom would say now—but she wasn't strong enough to try. What if she tried and failed? What then?

✦

The next day, her dad was set to arrive. Marah couldn't stop pacing. She chewed her fingernails until they bled. And then, finally, he was there, walking into Tully's beautiful condominium, giving Marah an uncertain smile.

"Hey, Dad." She should have been happy, but seeing him made her think of her mom and all that had been lost. No wonder she'd been unhappy for so long.

"How are you?" he said, approaching her warily, pulling her into an awkward hug.

What should she say? He wanted a lie. *I'm fine.* She glanced at Tully, who was uncharacteristically quiet. "Better," she said at last.

"I've found someone in Los Angeles, a doctor who specializes in teens who are in trouble," Dad said. "He can see you on Monday."

"But I have my second appointment with Dr. Bloom today," Marah said.

"I know, and I'm glad she could step in, but you need to see someone regularly," he said. "At home."

Marah smiled shakily. If he guessed how vulnerable she felt right now it would only hurt him more. But one thing she knew now for sure: she couldn't go back to Los Angeles with him.

"I like Dr. Bloom," she said. "And the group is kind of lame, but I don't mind."

Dad frowned. "But she's in Seattle. This doctor in L.A.—"

"I want to stay here for the summer, Dad. Live with Tully. I like Dr. Bloom." She turned to Tully, who looked thunderstruck. "Can I live here for the summer? I'll keep seeing Dr. Bloom twice a week. Maybe it will help."

"Are you kidding me?" Dad said. "Tully is no chaperone."

Marah dug in her heels. Suddenly she was certain: this was what she wanted. "I'm not eleven anymore, Dad. I'm eighteen and I'll be starting the UW in September anyway. This way I'll be able to make new friends and see my old ones." She went to him. "Please?"

Tully said, "I think—"

"I know what you think," Dad snapped. "You were the one who thought it was perfectly okay for her to go to a Nine Inch Nails concert when she was fourteen. You also encouraged modeling in New York when she was in eighth grade."

Marah looked up at him. "I need some distance, Dad."

She saw the war going on within him—he wasn't ready to let her go, but he saw that she wanted this. Maybe even that she needed it.

"This is a bad idea," he said to Tully. "You can't even keep plants alive. And you know jack shit about kids."

"She's an adult," Tully said.

"Please, Dad? *Please?*"

He sighed. "Shit."

She knew then. It was done. He looked down at her. "I've given my notice in L.A. We'll be moving back into the house on Bainbridge Island in September. It was going to be a surprise. We want to be living here when you're at the UW."

"That's great," she said, not really caring.

He looked past Marah to Tully. "You better take good care of my girl, Tully."

"Like she was my own daughter, Johnny," Tully said solemnly.

It was done.

✦

An hour later, Marah sat slouched in a chair in Dr. Bloom's office. She'd been staring at the ficus plant in the corner for at least ten minutes while Dr. Bloom scribbled something on paper.

"What are you writing? A grocery list?" Marah asked, staring at her hands.

"It's not a grocery list. What do you think I'm writing?"

"I don't know. But if you aren't going to say anything, why am I here?"

"Yours is the voice that matters in here, Marah. And you know you're welcome to leave."

"Tully and my dad are out there."

"And you don't want them to know you aren't committed to therapy. Why is that?"

"Do you *only* ask questions?"

"I ask a lot of them. It can help guide your thoughts. You're depressed, Marah. You're smart enough to know that, and you're cutting yourself. I don't think it's a bad idea for you to consider why you do it."

Marah looked up.

Dr. Bloom's gaze was steady. "I'd really like to help you, if you'll let me." She paused. "Do you want to be happy again?"

Marah wanted it so badly she felt sick. She wanted to be the girl she used to be.

"Let me help you."

Marah thought about the network of scars on her thighs and arms, and the way pain fascinated her, and the beautiful red of her blood.

Don't give up, baby girl.

"Yeah," she said. As soon as the word fell from her mouth, she felt a tightening of anxiety in her stomach.

"That's a start," Dr. Bloom said. "And now our time is up."

Marah got to her feet and followed Dr. Bloom out of the office. In the waiting room, she saw her dad first. He was sitting on the sofa by Tully, flipping through a magazine without looking at the printed pages. At her entrance, he got to his feet.

Before he could say anything, Dr. Bloom said: "Can we talk, Mr. Ryan? In my office?"

Tully said, "I'm coming in, too," and in a blink, they were gone, and Marah was alone in the waiting room. She looked back at the closed door. What was the doctor telling them? Dr. Bloom had promised Marah that their sessions were private. *You're eighteen,* she'd said, *an adult. Our sessions are ours alone.*

"Well, well, well."

She turned slowly.

Paxton leaned against the wall, with his arms crossed. He was dressed all in black again, and the sleeveless vintage vest hung on his pale chest, its V-neck revealing a tattoo that curled up from his collarbone and around his throat. It read: *Won't you join me in my slow descent into madness?* She stared at the scripty black words as he moved toward her.

"I've been thinking about you." He touched the back of her hand, barely, a sweeping little caress. "Do you know how to have fun, suburb girl?"

"Like what, animal sacrifice?"

The smile he gave her was slow and seductive. No one had ever stared at her so intently, as if she were edible. "Meet me tomorrow night at midnight."

"Midnight?"

"The witching hour. I bet you've only met nice boys for movie dates and pool parties."

"You don't know anything about me."

He smiled slowly, gazing directly at her. She could feel how sure he was of himself, of her. "Meet me."

"No."

"Curfew, huh? Poor little rich girl. Okay, then. But I'll wait for you at the pergola in Pioneer Square."

The pergola in Pioneer Square? Where the homeless people slept at night and bummed cigarettes from tourists?

She heard the door opening behind her. Her dad was saying, "Thank you, Dr. Bloom."

Marah pulled away from Paxton. He laughed quietly, a little cruelly, at her movement, so she stilled.

"Marah," Dad said sharply. She knew what he was seeing: his once-perfect, once-beautiful daughter talking to a young man wearing makeup and chains. The streaks in Paxton's hair were almost neon in the office's strong light.

"This is Paxton," Marah said to her dad. "He's in my therapy group."

Dad barely made eye contact with Paxton. "Let's go," Dad said, taking her hand, leading her out of the office.

Twelve

✦

That night, after a long and trying day in which her father had tried in a dozen subtle ways to change Marah's mind about staying in Seattle, she lay in bed, staring up at the ceiling. She had finally convinced him to let her stay with Tully for the summer, but he had laid down a matrix of behavioral rules. Just thinking about it gave Marah a headache. She couldn't help being relieved when he left.

The next day, she and Tully acted like tourists, enjoying the beautiful summer afternoon along the waterfront. But when night fell, and Marah went to bed alone, she found herself thinking about Paxton.

Meet me. Midnight.

Beside her, the digital alarm clock flipped through the minutes with a hushed *thwick-thwick-thwick*. She glanced sideways.

11:39.

11:40.

11:41.

I'll be waiting for you by the pergola.

She couldn't seem to banish that promise from her mind.

She was intrigued by Paxton. Why not admit it? He was unlike any guy she'd ever known. In his presence, she felt challenged somehow, *seen*; alive.

It was crazy.

He was crazy. And probably dangerous. And God knew she was screwed up enough, she didn't need to take a walk on the wild side. Mom would hate him.

11:42.

Who asked you to meet them at midnight? Goths and druggies and maybe rock stars. He was no rock star, although he looked like he could be one.

11:43.

Marah sat up.

She was going to meet him. When the decision settled in place, she knew it had been there all along, maybe from the moment he'd asked her to meet him. She eased out of bed and changed back into her clothes. She brushed her teeth and put on makeup for the first time in forever. Then she crept out of her room, turning off the lights and closing the door quietly behind her.

Shadows crouched along the furniture in the dark; beyond them, Seattle at night was a kaleidoscope of colored lights and black night sky. Tully's bedroom door was closed; there was a light on underneath.

11:49.

Grabbing her purse and sticking her phone in her back pocket, she started to leave. At the last minute, she stopped and dashed off a quick note—*Meeting Paxton in Pioneer Square*—and ran back to place it under her pillow. Just in case the police needed somewhere to start looking.

She tiptoed out of the apartment and slipped into the elevator. In the lobby, she tucked her chin into her chest and strode quickly across the marble floor. In no time, she was outside, standing alone on the busy sidewalk. She started walking.

Pioneer Square was full of action even this late. Taverns and bars pulled people in and spit them out. Every now and then music drifted on the night air. This was the original skid row, named back in the days when giant logs slid down Yesler Street toward the water. Now it was a haven for both the homeless and those drawn to nightclubs and jazz bars—life in the dark.

The pergola was a local landmark, a black, ornate ironwork fixture on the corner of First and James. Beneath it, homeless people lay on benches, covered in newspapers, and gathered in pods to smoke and talk.

She saw Paxton before he saw her. He was leaning against one of the stanchions, with a pad of paper in his hand. He was writing something down when she said, "Hey."

He looked up. "You came," he said, and something about his voice—or the look in his eyes—made her realize how much he'd wanted her here. He hadn't been as certain of her as she'd thought.

"I'm not afraid of you," she said firmly.

"I'm afraid of you," he answered matter-of-factly.

Marah had no idea what that meant, but she remembered her mom telling her about the first time she'd kissed Dad. *He said he was afraid of me,* Mom had said. *He didn't know it, but he was already in love with me.*

Paxton reached out his hand. "You ready, suburb girl?"

She took his hand. "I am, guyliner boy."

He led her down the street and onto a dirty, wheezing city bus. The truth—which she'd never tell him—was that she'd never been on a city bus before. In the crowded, brightly lit interior, they stood close together, staring at each other. He mesmerized her, electrified her in a way that had never happened before. She tried to think of something flip to say, but she couldn't think straight. When they got off the bus, he led her deep into the glittering world of Broadway at night. She'd been born in Seattle and raised on an island you could see from the city, and yet here was a world she knew nothing about, a shiny, neon-glazed fun-house version that crouched in the shadows and cracks of Seattle after dark. In Paxton's universe, there were black hallways and clubs without windows and drinks that puffed steam when you held them in your hands and kids who lived on the street.

From there, they took another bus, and this time, when they got off, Seattle was in the distance, a glittering diadem set against the night sky, across a body of black water. There were only a few streetlamps to illuminate the landscape.

The land in front of her rolled downhill; at its end, a rusted behemoth lurked by dark shores. Gas Works Park. She recognized it now. The centerpiece of this waterfront park was the old rusted gasification plant from the turn of the century. They'd come here once on a grade school field trip. Paxton held her hand and led her down the grassy lawn to a secret cavelike part of the structure.

"Are we committing a crime?" Marah asked.

"Do you care?" he asked.

"No." A tiny thrill went through her. She had never done anything wrong. It was time, maybe, to change that.

He led her deep into a hidden place within the rusted metal structure, then pulled a cardboard box out from a hiding place and made them a place to sit.

"Is that always there?" she asked.

"No. I put it here for us."

"How did—"

"I knew," he said, staring at her in a way that made her blood turn hot. "Have you ever had absinthe?" He pulled out enough supplies for a science experiment.

She shivered. Fear danced around her, poked and prodded, and she thought, *He's dangerous,* and she knew she should leave now, before it was too late. But she couldn't. "No. What is it?"

"Magic in a bottle."

He set out glasses and several bottles, then he performed a ritual of sorts, with spoons and sugar cubes and water. As a sugar cube melted into the liquid, the absinthe changed color, becoming a foamy, milky green.

He handed her the glass.

She stared at him.

"Trust me."

She shouldn't. Still, she brought the glass slowly to her lips, took a small sip. "Oh," she said in surprise. "It tastes like black licorice. Sweet."

As she drank, the night seemed to waken. Breezes blew the hair across her eyes, waves slapped against the shore, the rusted metal of the abandoned plant creaked and moaned.

She was well into her second glass of absinthe when Paxton took hold of her hand, turned her palm up. Tracing the lines in her palm, he let his fingers move up, along the sensitive flesh of her inner arm, to the first silvery scar.

"Blood can be so beautiful, so cleansing. And the pain only lasts for a second—a beautiful second—then it's gone."

Marah drew in a breath. The absinthe was relaxing her, making her light-headed, and she wasn't quite sure what was real until she looked at Paxton and stared into his golden eyes and thought, *He knows.* At last, here was someone who understood her. "When did you start?"

"After my sister died."

"What happened?" she asked quietly.

"How doesn't matter," he said, and it struck a chord with her, deep and clear. People always asked what had happened to her mother, as if it mattered whether she'd died of cancer or a car accident or a heart attack. "I held her as she died, that's what matters, and I watched them put her in the ground."

Marah reached over and held his hand.

He looked at her in surprise, as if he'd forgotten she was there. "Her last words on this earth were, 'Don't let go of me, Pax.' But I had to." He took a breath and let it go. Then he downed his absinthe in one drink. "It was drugs that killed her. My drugs. That's why the court ordered therapy. It was that or jail."

"Your parents?"

"They divorced because of it. Neither can forgive me, and why should they?"

"Do you miss them?"

He shrugged. "What difference would it make?"

"So you didn't used to be like . . ." She nodded at his look, embarrassed by her question but intrigued. It had never occurred to her that he had been different once, a normal high school kid.

"I needed a change," he said.

"Did it help?"

"No one asks how I'm doing except Dr. Bloom, and she doesn't really care."

"You're lucky. Everyone asks me how I'm doing, but they don't really want to know."

"Sometimes you just want to be left alone with it."

"Exactly," she said, feeling a heady sense of connection. He *knew* her, saw her. He understood.

"I've never told anyone that before," he said, gazing at her with a beautiful vulnerability. Was she the only one who could see how broken he was? "Are you here to piss off your dad? Because—"

"No." She wanted to add, *I want to be someone else, too,* but it sounded stupid and too young.

He touched her face, and his touch was the softest she'd ever known. "Do you believe in love at first sight?"

"I do now," she said.

It felt desperately solemn, this moment. He leaned forward slowly, so slowly she knew he expected her to push him away, but she couldn't. Right now, nothing mattered except the way he looked at her. She'd been cold and dead until this second; he'd brought her back to life. She didn't care if he was dangerous or did drugs or couldn't be trusted. This feeling, this coming alive, was worth any risk.

His kiss was everything she'd dreamed a kiss could be.

"Let's get high," he murmured softly, his lips against hers. "It'll make you forget it all."

She wanted that. Needed it. All it took was the smallest of nods.

✦

September 3, 2010
1:16 P.M.

Ping. "Flight attendants, please take your seats."

Marah let go of the memory and opened her eyes. Real life came back with a vengeance: it was 2010. She was twenty years old and sitting in an airplane, flying to Seattle to see Tully, who had been in a car accident and might not make it.

"Are you all right?"

Pax.

"They don't love you, Marah. Not like I do. If they did, they would respect your choices."

She stared out the small window as the plane touched down and taxied to the terminal. A man in an orange vest guided the plane to its parking place. She spaced out watching him, her vision blurred, until what she saw was a ghostly image of her own face in the window. Pale skin, pink hair, cut with a razor and gelled in place along her ears, and black-rimmed eyes. A pierced eyebrow.

"Thank God," Paxton said when the seat belt sign clicked off. He unhooked his seat belt and grabbed his brown paper bag out from under the seat in front of him. Marah did the same.

As she walked through the terminal, Marah clutched the wrinkled, stained bag that held all of her possessions. People glanced at them and quickly looked away, as if whatever had turned two kids into goths might be contagious.

Outside the terminal, smokers clustered beneath the overhang, puffing away, while the loudspeaker reminded them that it was a nonsmoking zone.

Marah wished now she'd told her dad what flight they'd be on.

"Let's get a cab," Paxton said. "You just got paid, right?"

Marah hesitated. Paxton never seemed to quite grasp the truth of their finances. Her minimum-wage job didn't exactly afford them the money for luxuries like a cab ride to Seattle from SeaTac. Hell, she'd had to sell her soul for the money to stop an eviction this month (*Don't think about that, not now*), and she was the only one of the roommates who even had a real job. Leif sold pot for a living, and Mouse panhandled. No one wanted to know what Sabrina did, but she was the only other one who seemed to ever have money. Paxton was too creative to hold down a steady job—it cut into his poetry-writing time, and that was their future.

But when he sold his poetry, they'd be rich.

She could have said no to the cab, but lately it was too easy to make him angry. It wasn't as easy to sell his poetry as he'd thought and the truth of that bothered him. She had to constantly reassure him about his talent.

"Yeah," she said.

"Besides, Daddy will give you money," he said, and he didn't sound unhappy about the prospect. It confused her. He wanted them to have nothing to do with her family. So why was it okay to take money from them?

They climbed into a cab and settled into the brown backseat.

Marah named the hospital and then leaned back against Pax, who put an arm around her. He immediately opened his worn, dog-eared copy of Lovecraft's *At the Mountains of Madness* and began to read.

Twenty-five minutes later, the car came to an abrupt stop in front of the hospital.

It was raining now, one of those nibbling, inconsistent September rains that came and went. In front of her, the hospital was a sprawling structure crouched beneath the battleship-gray sky.

They walked into the brightly lit lobby and Marah came to an abrupt stop. How many trips through this lobby had she made in her life?

Too many. And none had been happy.

Sit with me during chemo, baby girl. Tell me about Tyler . . .

"You don't have to do this," Pax said, sounding a little irritated. "It's your life, not theirs."

She reached for his hand, but he pulled away. She understood: he wanted her to know that he didn't want to be here. When it came to her family, he might be beside her, but she was alone.

On the fourth floor, they exited the elevator and walked down a beige, brightly lit lobby toward the ICU. A place she knew all too well.

She saw her father and grandmother in the waiting room. Dad looked up, saw her. She slowed, feeling both fragile and defiant in his presence.

He stood slowly. His movement must have alerted Grandma Margie, because she got to her feet, too. Grandma frowned—no doubt at Marah's heavy makeup and pink hair.

Marah had to force herself to keep walking. She hadn't seen her dad in so long; she was surprised by how much older he looked.

Grandma Margie limped forward and pulled Marah into a fierce hug. "It can be hard to come home. Good for you." Grandma drew back, looked at Marah through teary eyes. She looked thinner since the last time Marah had seen her, skinny enough to blow away. "Grandpa's at home, waiting for your brothers. He sends his love."

Her brothers. Marah's throat tightened at the thought of them. She hadn't realized how much she'd missed them until right now.

Dad's hair was grayer than she remembered. A day's growth of beard shadowed his jawline. He was dressed like an old rock star, in a faded Van Halen T-shirt and worn Levi's.

He came closer, moving a little awkwardly, and pulled her into a hug. When he let go and stepped back, she knew they were both thinking about the last time they'd been together. She and Dad and Tully and Paxton.

"I can't stay long," Marah said.

"Do you have something more important to do?"

"Still judging us, I see," Pax said lazily. "Big surprise."

Dad seemed determined not to look at Pax, as if ignoring her boyfriend could change the fact of his existence. "I don't want to jump into this again. You're here to see your godmother. Do you want to see her?"

"Yes," Marah said.

Behind her Paxton made a sound she knew well, that little snort of derision. How many times had he reminded her that her family didn't really accept her unless she was Good Girl Marah, who did what they wanted and looked a certain way? And hadn't Dad proved the truth of it last December?

That's not love, Pax had said. *They don't love the real you, and what's the use of anything else? I'm the one who loves you for you.*

"Come on," Dad said. "I'll take you to her."

Marah turned to Paxton. "Will you—"

He shook his head. Of course he didn't want to go. He hated pretense of any kind. He couldn't pretend to care about Tully's health. That would be dishonest. It was too bad; she could have used a hand to hold right now.

She and Dad walked down the hallway. There were people all around them, coming and going. Nurses and doctors and orderlies and visitors, all speaking in hushed tones. The muted conversations underscored the silence between her and her father.

Outside a glass-walled room in the ICU, he stopped and turned to her.

"She's in bad shape. You need to prepare yourself."

"You can't prepare for the shit life throws at you."

"Words of wisdom from Paxton Conrath, I'll bet."

"Dad—"

He held up his hand. "Sorry. But you *can* prepare yourself. She doesn't look good. The doctors have lowered her body temperature and put her into a medically induced coma in hopes that her brain swelling will go down. A shunt is supposed to help with that. They've shaved her head and she's bandaged up, so be ready. The doctors think she can hear us, though. Your grandma spent two hours today talking about when Tully and your mom were kids."

Marah nodded and reached for the door.

"Baby?"

She paused, turned.

"I'm sorry about what happened in December."

She stared up at him, seeing remorse in his eyes—and love—and it affected her so profoundly that it was all she could do to mutter, "Shit happens." She couldn't think about him—and them—now. Turning away, she went into the ICU room and closed the door behind her.

The click of the door sent her back in time. Suddenly she was sixteen again, coming into her mom's hospital room. *Come here, baby girl, I won't break. You can hold my hand . . .*

Marah shook the memory free and approached the bed. The room was sleek and boxy and filled with machines that plunked and whooshed and beeped. But all she saw was Tully.

Her godmother looked . . . ruined—crushed, almost—pierced by needles and hooked up to machines. Her face was bruised and cut and bandaged in places; her nose looked broken. Without hair, she looked small and vulnerable, and the tube going into her head was terrifying.

It's my job to love you.

Marah drew in a sharp, ragged breath. She was responsible for this; she knew it. Her betrayal of Tully had to be part of why her godmother was here, fighting for life.

"What's wrong with me?"

She'd never voiced this query before, not when she'd started smoking pot or sleeping with Pax, not when she'd cut her hair with a razor or pierced her eyebrow with a safety pin or when she'd gotten a small Celtic cross tattooed on the back of her wrist, not when she'd run away with Pax and lived on food they found in Dumpsters. Not even when she sold the story to *Star* magazine.

But she asked it now. She'd betrayed her godmother and run away from her family and ruined everything, broken the only hearts that mattered. Something must be wrong with her.

But what? Why had she turned her back so completely on everyone who loved her? And worse, why had she chosen to do that terrible, unforgivable thing to Tully?

"I know you'll never forgive me," she said, wishing now, for the first time, that she knew how to forgive herself.

✦

I waken in a darkness so complete I wonder if I have been buried alive. Or maybe I am dead.

I wonder if a lot of people came to my funeral.

Oh, for God's sake.

"Katie?" This time, I think I make a sound. It is her name, but it's enough.

Close your eyes.

"They are closed. It's dark. Where am I? Can you—"

Shhh. Relax. I need you to listen.

"I'm listening. Can you get us out of here?"

Focus. Listen. You can hear her.

There is a break in her voice when she says *her*.

". . . up. Sorry . . . Please . . ."

"Marah." When I say her name, lights come on. I see that I am in the hospital room again. Have I always been here? Is this the only here for me? Around me are walls of glass, through which I see other, similar rooms beyond. Inside here, there is a bed surrounded by machines that are hooked up to my broken body: tubes and electrodes and casts and bandages.

Marah is sitting beside that other me.

My goddaughter is in soft focus, her face is blurred a little. Her hair is cotton-candy-pink, razor-cut, and unattractive as hell, a little roosterlike the way she's gelled it, and she has on more makeup than Alice Cooper in his heyday. A big black coat makes her look like a kid playing dress-up for Halloween.

She is saying my name and trying not to cry. I love this girl, and her sadness scalds my soul. She needs me to wake up. I can tell. I will open my eyes and smile at her and tell her it is okay.

I concentrate hard, say, "Marah, don't cry."

Nothing.

My body just lies there, inert, breathing through a tube, eyes swollen and shut.

"How can I help her?" I ask Kate.

You'd have to wake up.

"I tried."

". . . Tully . . . I'm so sorry . . . for what I did."

The light in this room flickers. Kate pulls away from me and floats around the bed to stand by her daughter.

Marah looks small and dark next to the glowing image of her mother. Kate whispers: *Feel me, baby girl.*

Marah gasps and looks up. "M-mom?"

All of the air seems to go out of the room. There is an exquisite second in which I can see that Marah believes.

Then she slumps forward in defeat. "When will I learn? You're *gone.*"

"Can it be undone?" I ask Kate quietly. It scares me to ask, and the silence between my question and her answer feels like an eternity. At last, Kate looks away from her daughter and at me.

Can what be undone?

I indicate the woman in the bed—the other me. "Can I wake up?"

You tell me. What happened?

"I tried to help Marah, but . . . really. When have I ever been the person you want beside you in a foxhole?"

Always, Tul. You were the only one who didn't know that. She looks down at Marah again, and sighs quietly, sadly.

Had I even thought about Marah last night? I can't remember. I can't remember anything about what happened to me, and when I try, some dark truth presses in and I push it away. "I'm afraid to remember what happened."

I know, but it's time. Talk to me. Remember.

I take a deep breath and scroll through memories. Where to pick up the story? I think about the months after her death, and all the changes that happened. The Ryans moved to Los Angeles and we lost touch in the way that happens with distance and grief. By early 2007, everything had changed. Oh, I still saw Margie. I had lunch with her once a month. She always said she looked forward to her days in the city, but I saw the sadness in her eyes, and the way her hands had begun to tremble, and so I wasn't surprised when she told me that she and Bud were moving to Arizona. When they were gone, I tried like hell to get my life back on track. I applied for every broadcasting job I could find. I started with the top ten markets and worked my way down. But every single road came to a dead end. I was either overqualified or underqualified; some stations didn't want to piss off the networks by hiring me. Some had heard I was a diva. The reasons didn't really matter: the result was the same. I was unemployable. That's how I came to be back where I started.

I close my eyes and remember it in detail. June of 2008, less than a week before Marah's high school graduation and twenty months after the funeral, I . . .

am in the waiting room of KCPO, the small local TV station in Seattle where I first worked for Johnny, all those years ago.

The offices have moved—the station has grown—but it is still a little shabby and second-rate. Two years ago I would have considered local news beneath me.

I am not the woman I was before. I am like a leaf in the deep midwinter, curling up, turning black, becoming transparent and dry, afraid of a strong wind.

I am literally back where I began. I have begged for an interview with Fred Rorback, whom I've known for years. He is the station manager here now.

"Ms. Hart? Mr. Rorback will see you now."

I get to my feet, smiling with more confidence than I feel.

Today I am starting over. This is what I tell myself as I walk into Fred's office.

It is small and ugly, paneled in fake wood with a gunmetal-gray desk and two computers on the desk. Fred looks smaller than I remember, and—surprisingly—younger. When I first interviewed with him—in the summer before my senior year of high school—I thought he was older than dirt. I see now that he's probably only twenty years older than I am. He is bald now, and smiling at me in a way I don't like. There is sympathy in his eyes as he stands to greet me.

"Hi, Fred," I say, shaking his hand. "It's good of you to see me."

"Of course," he says, sitting back down. On his desk is a stack of paper. He points to it. "Do you know what those are?"

"No."

"The letters you wrote me in 1977. One hundred and twelve letters from a seventeen-year-old girl, asking for a job at the ABC affiliate station. I knew you'd be someone."

"Maybe I wouldn't have been if you hadn't given me that break in '85."

"You didn't need me. You were destined for greatness. Everyone saw it. Whenever I saw you on the networks, I was proud."

I feel a strange sadness at this. I never really thought about Fred after I left KLUE for New York. How hard would it have been to look back just once, instead of forward?

"I was sorry to hear about your show," he says.

And there we are; facing why I am here. "I guess I screwed up," I say quietly.

He stares at me, waiting.

"I need a job, Fred," I say. "I'll do anything."

"I don't have any anchor spots open, Tully, and even if I did, you wouldn't be happy—"

"Anything," I say again, fisting my hands. Shame burns my cheeks.

"I can't pay—"

"Money isn't my priority. I need a chance, Fred. I need to prove that I'm a team player."

He smiles sadly. "You've never been a team player, Tully. That's why you are a superstar. Do you remember how much notice you gave me when you got the network job in New York? None, that's how much. You came to my office, thanked me for the opportunity, and said goodbye. This is the first time I've seen you since."

I feel hopelessness well up. I refuse to let him see how deeply his words affect me, though. Pride is all I have left.

He leans forward, rests his elbows on his desk, and steeples his fingers. Through the vee, he stares at me. "I have a show."

I straighten.

"It's called *Teen Beat with Kendra*. It's thirty minutes of nothing much, really. But Kendra's a mover and shaker like you were. She's a senior at Blanchet and her father owns the station, which is how she got a show for teens. Because of her school schedule, it tapes in the early morning." He pauses. "Kendra needs a cohost, kind of a straight man to keep her from overemoting. Can you play second banana to a nobody on a fourth-rate show?"

Can I?

I want to be grateful for this offer—and I *am* grateful, honestly—but I am also hurt and offended. I should say no. In the great reformation of my image quest, this will do almost nothing for me.

I should say no and wait for something more worthy of me.

But it has been so long. Being out of work, being *nothing,* is killing me. I can't live this un-life anymore. And it can't hurt to do a favor for this station's owner.

And maybe I can mentor Kendra the way Edna Guber mentored me all those years ago.

"I'll take it," I say, and as I agree, I feel this huge weight sliding off my shoulders. A genuine smile tugs at my mouth. "Thank you, Fred."

"You're better than this, Tully."

I sigh. "I used to think so, too, Fred. I guess that's part of my problem. I'll succeed here. You'll see. Thank you."

Thirteen

✦

That night, I stay up late, surfing the Internet, finding out all that I can about my new cohost, Kendra Ladd. There is precious little. She is eighteen years old, a reasonably good athlete with stellar grades and a full-ride scholarship to the UW in the fall. She apparently came up with her show idea because kids are disenfranchised and confused these days. Her goal is to "bring teens together." At least this was her answer in the Miss Seafair competition last year, in which she was first runner-up. A "disappointing finish," apparently, which she wouldn't let "derail" her.

At that, I roll my eyes and think: *Listen to this, Katie.* Hours later, when I go to bed, I am exhausted but I can't sleep. The night sweats are so unbearable I get up at two and take a sleeping pill, which knocks me out; the next thing I know, my alarm is bleating.

I am so wrung out and medicated, it takes me a second to figure out why my alarm is ringing.

Then I remember. I throw the covers back and stumble out of bed, bleary-eyed. It is five o'clock and I look like something a gill-netter has dragged in with the day's catch. I don't suppose a show like *Teen Beat* has a makeup person, so I ready myself as best I can. I put on a black suit that is too tight, with a white blouse, and leave my condo. In no time, I am pulling up to the studio.

It is a nice Seattle predawn morning. I check in at the desk (security since 9/11 has changed everything about my profession—even on a nothing show like this) and go to the studio. A producer, who is young enough to be my son, greets me, mumbles something that might be recognition, and leads me to the set.

"Kendra is pretty green," he says as we stand behind the camera. "And challenging. Maybe you can help her." He sounds doubtful.

The moment I see the set, I know I am in trouble. It looks like a stuck-up teenage girl's bedroom, complete with enough sports trophies to sink a small yacht.

And then there is Kendra herself. She is tall, and Q-tip-thin, wearing tiny denim shorts, a plaid shirt with ruffles around the collar, a fedora with a gold lamé hatband, and what we used to call come-fuck-me pumps in the old days. Her hair is long and curly and makeup enhances her spectacular natural beauty.

She is leaning back against her dresser, talking to the camera as if it is her closest confidant. ". . . Time to talk about texting rules. Some of the kids I know are, like, making Herculean mistakes. In the old days, there were, like, books to tell you what to say and how to act, but we, like, don't have time for old school now, do we? Teens today are on the go-go-go. So Kendra is going to step in to the rescue." She smiles and moves away from the dresser, walking casually toward the bed. There is a blue X on the floor—her mark—which she misses. "I've come up with a list of five things that should never be texted." She moves across the room, misses her mark again. Tully hears the cameraman curse under his breath. "Let's start with sexting. Face it, girls, boob shots to your guy are a no-no—"

"Cut," the director says, and the cameraman breathes a sigh of relief.

"Kendra," the director says. "Can you stay on script?"

Kendra rolls her eyes and starts playing with her phone.

"Go on," the producer says, giving me a shoulder pat that might have been meant to be reassuring but feels more like a shove.

I square my shoulders and walk onto the set, smiling.

Kendra frowns at me. "Who are you?" she says to me. Into her mic, she says, "I have a stalker."

"I am hardly a stalker," I say, fighting the urge to roll my eyes.

She pops her gum. "You look like a waiter in that suit." She frowns. "No. Wait. You look kinda like someone."

"Tully Hart," I say.

"Yeah! You look like her, only fatter."

I clench my jaw. Unfortunately, my body picks this exact moment to overheat. A hot flash tingles uncomfortably across my flesh. Pins and needles. My face turns beet-red, I'm sure. I can feel myself sweating.

"Are you okay?"

"I'm fine," I snap. "I'm Tully Hart, your new cohost. There's nothing for me to do on today's script, but we can talk about tomorrow. In the meantime, you need to hit your mark. It's the sign of a professional."

Kendra stares at me as if I have just sprouted a beard and begun braying. "I don't have a cohost. *Carl!*"

The young producer is beside me in an instant, pulling me back into the shadows.

"And Carl is?" I ask.

"The director," the producer sighs. "But it really means she's going to call daddy. Did they tell you she's already had four cohosts fired?"

"No," I say quietly.

"We call her Veruca Salt."

I look at him blankly.

"The spoiled brat in *Charlie and the Chocolate Factory.*"

"You're fired," Kendra yells at me.

Beside me, the cameraman takes his place. The red light comes on and Kendra smiles brightly. "We were talking about sexting before the break. If you don't know what that is, I don't think you need to worry about it, but if you do . . ."

I back out of the studio. My hot flash is abating somewhat. I can feel the drizzle of sweat on my forehead drying up and my cheeks are cooling down, but my shame is not so easily retracted; neither is my anger. As I leave the studio and step back out onto the Seattle sidewalk, I am consumed by a sense of failure. *This* is what I have fallen to? Getting called fat and being fired by a talentless teen?

More than anything I want to call my best friend and have her tell me it will get better.

I can't breathe.

I can't *breathe.*

Calm down, I tell myself, but I feel sick to my stomach and feverishly hot and I can't catch my breath. Pain squeezes my chest.

My legs give out from underneath me and I fall to the sidewalk hard.

I get up, stumble forward, flag down a cab, and get in. "Sacred Heart," I gasp, fumbling through my purse for a baby aspirin, which I chew and swallow, just in case.

At the hospital, I throw a twenty-dollar bill at the cabbie and stagger into the emergency room. "Heart attack!" I scream at the woman at the front desk.

It gets her attention.

✦

Dr. Grant peers down at me. He is wearing the kind of cheater glasses Costco sells in a multipack. Behind him, a lackluster blue and white curtain gives us what little privacy exists in a big-city ER. "You know, Tully, you don't have to go to such lengths to see me. I gave you my number. You could have just called."

I am in no mood for humor. I flop back into the pillows behind me. "Are you the only doctor in this hospital?"

He moves toward the bed. "All kidding aside, Tully, panic attacks are a common experience during perimenopause and menopause. It's the hormonal imbalance."

And just like that, it gets worse. I'm unemployed, apparently unemployable; I am fat. I have no real family, and my best friend is gone, and Dr. Granola here can take one look at me and know I'm drying up from the inside.

"I'd like to test your thyroid."

"I'd like to host *The Today Show.*"

"What?"

I throw the flimsy sheet back and climb out of bed, not realizing that my hospital gown has flashed the doctor a shot of my middle-aged ass. I turn quickly, but it's too late. He has seen. "There's no proof I'm in menopause," I say.

"There are tests—"

"Exactly. I don't want them." I smile grimly. "Some people see a glass as half empty; some see it as half full. I put the glass in a cupboard and forget it's there. You get my point?"

He puts down my chart. "Ignoring bad news. I get it." He comes toward me. "And how's that working for you?"

God, I hate feeling stupid or pathetic, and something about this man and the way he looks at me makes me feel both. "I need Xanax. And Ambien. They helped before." I look up at him. "My prescription ran out a long time ago." This is a lie. I know I should tell him that in the past year, I've gotten these prescriptions from several doctors and that I am taking higher dosages, but I don't.

"I'm not sure that's a good idea. With your personality—"

"You don't know me. Let's be clear on that."

"No," he says. "I don't." He moves closer. I fight the urge to step back. "But I know how depressed sounds and how broken looks."

That's when I remember about his wife and daughter who were killed. He is thinking about them as well, I think. I see a deep sadness in him suddenly.

He writes a prescription and tears it off for me. "This won't last long. Get some help, Tully. See someone about your menopausal symptoms and your depression."

"I haven't confirmed either one of your diagnoses, you know."

"I know."

"So, where are my clothes?"

As an exit line, it pretty much blows, but it's all I can think of. I stand there, staring at him until he leaves. Then I get dressed and walk out of the hospital. In the pharmacy downstairs, I fill the prescription, take two Xanax, and start the long walk home.

The prescription does what it's supposed to: it calms me down, makes me feel bubble-wrapped and protected. My heart is beating normally. I take my phone out of my handbag and call Fred Rorback.

"Tully," he says, and I can tell by the tone of his voice that word of my departure has reached him. "I should have warned you."

"I'm sorry, Fred," I say.

"Don't be."

"Thanks, Fred," I say. I am about to do more, maybe even grovel a little, when I pass a Barnes & Noble bookstore. The book in the window catches my eye.

I stop dead. *Of course.* I should have thought of this before. "I have to go, Fred. Thanks again." Before he has even answered, I hang up. The Xanax is making me light-headed. So much so that it takes several tries to call my agent.

"George," I snap when he finally answers. "Guess where I am?"

"Well, you're not cohosting a low-rent TV show on an also-ran local station."

"You heard about that?"

He sighs. "I heard. You should vet these choices with me, Tully."

"Forget Kooky Kendra, who's an idiot. Guess where I am?"

"Where?"

"Outside a bookstore."

"And I care, why?"

"Because I'm looking at Barbara Walters's new memoir, *Audition.* It's in stores now. If I remember correctly, she got five million for it. And DeGeneres scored a huge deal. Hell, didn't she get a million for her book of essays?" This may be the best idea I've ever had. "I want a book deal."

"Have you written any pages of a memoir?"

"No. But how hard can it be? I'll start tonight. What do you say?"

George says nothing for so long, I prompt him again. "Well?"

He sighs. "Let me throw out a line and see if anyone bites. But let me ask you this, Tully: Are you sure about this? You've got some dark things in your past."

"I'm sure, George. Find me a deal."

✦

How hard can it be? I am a journalist. I'll write the story of my life. It will be a bestseller—inspirational and heartfelt.

By the time I get home, I am excited for the first time in forever. I change out of my black suit and put on sweats and pull out my laptop. Then I curl up on my sofa with a cup of tea and begin. I type: *Second Act.*

Then I scroll down, indent for the paragraph, and stare at the blank screen.

Maybe the title is a problem.

I stare at the blank screen for a while longer. A long while, long enough to decide that tea is the problem. Maybe wine will help.

I pour myself a glass and return to the sofa.

The blank screen again.

I push the laptop aside and check my watch. I have been "writing" for hours and have nothing to show for it. That depresses me, but I push it aside.

Research.

Any writer has to begin with research. I know that from my days in journalism. Once I was a cub reporter. I know about digging for a story.

And my life story is no exception. I have been the subject of several magazine articles and TV news shows, but I have carefully managed all of it. I have spoon-fed people my past. Through the magic of TV I have turned a bad childhood into a Cinderella fairy tale. *Poor Tully, abandoned by her evil mother, becomes an American success story.*

My audience wanted the fairy tale, so I gave it to them, and ours is an age of Disney tales, not Grimm's; evil has become animated lions and singing octopi.

These new fairy tales are perfect for me. How many times did I say that it had been a blessing of sorts, how often I'd been abandoned? The lack of a mother's love made me try harder; this was the truth as I packaged it. Ambition, I say, saved me.

In a memoir, for once I will have to tell the truth. That is what George asked me. I blithely said yes, but can I? Really?

I have to. Maybe I even need to.

A bestselling memoir could give me my life back.

I don't have much from my early years, but what I do have is in my storage unit downstairs in the parking garage. I haven't been in the unit for years, let alone looked into the boxes within. It has not been an oversight, either. I have made a point of not looking through the boxes.

I am going to do it.

But the decision is a weak one, like all made-in-desperation decisions are, and I can't make myself begin. Instead, I go to my window and stand there, drinking one glass of wine after another until the sky begins to cloud over and darken.

"Do it," I say to my reflection. I force myself to turn away from the window. On my way out of the condo, I grab a pen, a pad of paper, and, of course, a glass of wine.

In the parking garage, it takes longer than expected to find my unit.

I unlock the metal door, flick on the interior lights, and step inside.

It is about twelve feet square. I have never been in any of the other tenants' storage units, but I am pretty sure that most of them would be full from floor to ceiling with stacked plastic bins and cardboard boxes marked with words like *Xmas, Holiday, Winter, Summer, Baby Clothes,* etc. In those boxes would be evidence of lives, the boxed trail that leads one back to the beginning.

My unit is practically empty. There are my skis and tennis rackets and golf clubs—equipment for sports I have tried and given up but hope I might someday try again—and my extra luggage and an antique mirror I'd bought in France and forgotten all about.

And two boxes. Two. The evidence of my life doesn't take up much room.

I reach for the first box. Across it is written: *Firefly Lane.* The second box says: *Queen Anne.*

I feel a shiver of dread. These two boxes represent the two halves of my former life, my grandmother and my mother. Whatever is hidden within, I haven't seen for decades. At seventeen, I'd become the executrix of my grandmother's estate. She'd left me everything—the house on Queen Anne and the rental property on Firefly Lane. Alone, abandoned again by my mother and headed into foster care, I packed up the house on Queen Anne and kept only these few things, whatever could fit in this single box. The Firefly Lane box contains the few things that my mother and I collected in our brief time together. In my entire life, I lived with my mother only once, in 1974, in the house on Firefly Lane, until one day when she simply disappeared. I have always told people it was a blessing, that short time with my mother, because I met the girl who would become my best friend. And that's true. It was a blessing. It was also another abandonment.

I grab an old coverlet and kneel on it. Then I pull the box marked *Queen Anne* toward me.

My hands are shaking as I peel back the flaps. My pulse is washer-on-spin-cycle fast, heartbeats tumble over one another. I have trouble breathing. The last time I opened this box I was in my grandmother's house, kneeling in my bedroom. The social services lady had told me to be "ready" when she arrived to take me away from the house. I had packed carefully, but even after all the terrible years with my mother, I expected her to save me. I was seventeen, I think. All alone and waiting for a mother who wouldn't save me. Again.

I reach inside the box. The first thing I find in the shadowy interior is my old scrapbook.

I had forgotten all about this.

It is oversized, and slim, with Holly Hobbie on the cover, her profile hidden by a huge pioneer-girl bonnet. I run my fingertip over the white cover. Gran had given me this album on my eleventh birthday. Not long after, my mom had shown up, drunk and unannounced, and taken me to downtown Seattle.

I never knew what my mother intended to do that day. All I know is that she abandoned me on a doorstep in Pioneer Square in the middle of an antiwar protest.

Your mom has problems, Gran had said later, while I sat on the floor, crying.

Is that why she doesn't love me?

"Stop it," I say to myself. This is old news, old pain.

I open the scrapbook and see a picture of myself at eleven, posing for the camera already, leaning over a cake to blow out the candles.

Pasted on the other side is the first of hundreds of letters I'd written to my mother and never mailed. *Dear Mommy, today is my eleventh birthday—*

I close the scrapbook. I have barely looked through it, hardly glimpsed what is here, and already I am feeling worse than when I began. These words bring her alive, the me I have spent a lifetime outrunning, the girl with the broken heart.

If Katie were here, I could go through this box, pull up my pain, and examine it. She would be there to say, *Your mom, what a loser,* and *Look how pretty you are in that picture,* and all the other little things I need to hear. Without her, I don't have the strength.

I climb slowly to my feet, realizing that I have drunk too much wine.

Good.

Without bothering to close the box, I leave the storage unit, forgetting to even lock it. If I am lucky, maybe someone will steal these boxes before I have to go through them. I am halfway to the elevator when my cell phone rings. It is Margie.

"Hey, Margie," I answer quickly, grateful for the distraction.

"Hey, Tully. I'm making reservations for Saturday night in Los Angeles. What was the name of that restaurant you love?"

I smile. How had I forgotten, even for a moment? This weekend is Marah's high school graduation. I will be with the Mularkeys and the Ryans for two days. It is a gift I won't take for granted. Maybe I will even ask Johnny for help in getting a job. "Don't worry, Margie. I already made reservations for all of us. Seven o'clock at Madeo."

Fourteen

✦

This weekend, I am going to be my old self. I will pretend that my life is ordinary and that not everything has changed. I will laugh with Johnny and hold on to my goddaughter and play Xbox games with the boys.

I will not walk into their new house and see only empty chairs and missing people. I will focus on who is left. Like the Wordsworth poem, I will find strength in what remains.

But when the Town Car pulls up in front of a contemporary house on an uber-landscaped lot in Beverly Hills, I feel panic tug at my resolution.

Kate would hate this house.

A Xanax calms my runaway nerves.

I get out of the car and haul my single suitcase up the stone walkway. I go to the front door and ring the bell. When no one answers, I open the door and step inside, calling out.

The twins come bursting down a wide stone staircase like a pair of Great Dane puppies, bumping into each other, laughing loudly. At nine and a half, both have long, unruly brown hair and wide, toothy grins. They shriek at the sight of me. I have barely a moment to prepare before I am knocked back by the exuberance of their hug.

"I *knew* she'd come," Lucas says.

"You liar," Wills says with a laugh. "I said it." To me, he says, "What did you get Marah?"

"Probably a Ferrari," Johnny says, coming into the room.

In one look, our history rushes past like a river, tumbling images. I know we are both thinking of the woman who isn't here, and of the distance that has grown between us. He comes toward me.

I hip-bump him because I don't know what to say. Before he can respond, I hear Margie call out for me. In minutes, I am surrounded by them—the boys, Johnny, Bud, and Margie. Everyone is talking at once, smiling and laughing. When the twins drag their grandparents back up the stairs for some "sick Xbox game," Johnny and I are left alone again.

"How is Marah?" I ask.

"Fine. Doing well, I think," is what he says, but I hear more truth in his sigh. "How are you? I keep watching for *The Girlfriend Hour* to start back up."

This is my moment. I could tell him the truth, maybe even ask for help. I could tell him about my collapsed career and ask for advice.

I can't do it. Maybe it is his sorrow, or my pride, or a mixture of the two. All I know for sure is I can't tell Johnny how ruined my life is, not after what he has been through. I don't want his pity. "I'm fine," I say. "I'm writing a memoir. George tells me it is sure to be a best-seller."

"So you're fine," he says.

"Totally fine."

He nods and looks away. Later, even when I am swept away by the sheer joy of being with these people again, I can't help thinking about my lie to Johnny. I wonder if I am the kind of fine that Marah is.

✦

Marah is not fine. We learn that lesson the hard way. On Saturday, the day of her graduation, when we are gathered in the living room, Marah comes down the stairs. She looks—ghastly is all I can think of, or ghostly—pale and thin, with slumped shoulders and dull black hair that falls like a curtain in front of her face.

"I need help," she says at the bottom of the stairs, and lifts her arm. She is bleeding profusely. I rush to help her, and so does Johnny. Once again, we bang up against each other, say things we shouldn't; what I know is this: Marah needs help and I have promised to be there for her. I swear to Johnny that I will take care of her in Seattle, get her in to see Dr. Bloom.

Johnny doesn't like letting her go with me, but what choice does he have? I say I know how to help her and he has no idea what to do. In the end, he decides to let her live with me for the summer. But he doesn't like it. Not at all. And he makes sure I know it.

✦

In June of 2008, Marah moves into my condo on one of those scaldingly beautiful early summer days that make Seattleites come out of their darkened homes in last year's shorts, blinking like moles in the brightness, looking for sunglasses that have been lost and unused for months.

I feel proud; never have I fulfilled my promise to Katie more completely. It's true that I am not my best self these days, that panic often crouches in my peripheral vision, pouncing into the foreground when I least expect it. And, yes, I am drinking more than I should and taking a few too many Xanax. I can no longer sleep without sleeping pills.

But all of that will fade now that I have this obligation. I help her unpack her small suitcase and then, in our first evening together, we sit in the living room together, talking about her mother as if Kate is at the store and will return any moment. I know it is wrong, this pretense, but we need it, both of us.

"Are you ready for Monday?" I ask at last.

"For my appointment with Dr. Bloom?" she says. "No, not really."

"I'll be with you every step of the way," I promise. I don't know what else there is to say.

The next day, while Marah is in the meeting with Dr. Bloom, I move impatiently, pacing back and forth in the waiting room.

"You're wearing a groove in the carpet. Take a Xanax."

I stop dead in my tracks and turn.

A boy stands in the door. He is dressed all in black, with painted fingernails and enough macabre jewelry to fill a store on Bourbon Street. But he is strangely handsome beneath all the goth-ware. He moves forward in a gliding Richard-Gere-in-*American-Gigolo* way and slouches on the couch. He is holding a book of poetry.

I could use something to occupy my mind, so I go to him, sit down in the chair beside him. This close, I smell both marijuana and incense on him. "How long have you been seeing Dr. Bloom?"

He shrugs. "A while."

"She helping you?"

He gives me a sly smile. "Who says I need help? 'All that we see or seem is but a dream within a dream.'"

"Poe," I say. "Kind of cliché. I would have been *really* surprised if you'd quoted Rod McKuen."

"Who?"

I can't help smiling. It is a name I haven't thought of in years. As girls, Kate and I had read a lot of lovey-dovey-feel-good poetry from people like Rod McKuen and Kahlil Gibran. We had memorized "Desiderata." "Rod McKuen. Look him up."

Before he can answer, the door opens and I lurch to my feet. Marah comes out of the office looking pale and shaken. How can Johnny not have noticed how thin she is? I rush toward her. "How was it?"

Before she answers, Dr. Bloom appears beside her and asks me to step aside with her.

"I'll be right back," I say to Marah, and go to the doctor.

"I'll want to see her twice a week," Dr. Bloom says quietly. "At least until she starts school in the fall. And I have a teen grief support group that might help her. It meets on Wednesdays. Seven P.M."

"She'll do whatever you suggest," I promise.

"Will she?"

"Of course. So how did it go?" I ask. "Did she—"

"Marah's an adult, Tully. Our sessions are private."

"I know. I just wanted to know if she said—"

"Private."

"Oh. Well, what should I tell her father? He's expecting a report."

Dr. Bloom thinks carefully and then says, "Marah is fragile, Tully. My advice to you and to her father would be to treat her as such."

"What does that mean, fragile?"

"Webster's would say damaged, delicate, brittle. Easily broken. Vulnerable. I would watch her carefully, very carefully. Be there for her. She could all too easily make a bad decision in her current state."

"Worse than cutting herself?"

"As you can imagine, girls who cut themselves sometimes cut too deeply. As I said. Watch her carefully. Be there for her. She's fragile."

On the way home, I ask Marah how it went with Dr. Bloom.

What she says is, "Fine."

That night, I call Johnny and tell him everything. He is worried—I can hear it in his voice—but I promise that I am taking care of her. I am watching her closely.

✦

When Marah goes to her first teen grief therapy meeting, I decide to work on my book. At least, I try to. The blue screen bothers me so much, I walk away for a minute. I pour myself a glass of wine and stand at my window, staring out at the glittering nighttime cityscape.

The phone rings and I jump on it. George, my agent, is calling to tell me that he has had some interest in my book idea—no offers yet, but he thinks there's hope. Also, *Celebrity Apprentice* wants me to be on the show.

As if.

I am telling George how offended I am by this offer when Marah comes home from her meeting. I make us two cups of hot cocoa and we sit together in bed, just as we used to when she was little. It takes a while for the truth to come out, but finally Marah says, "I can't talk about my mom to her."

I have no answer to that, and I can't insult her with a lie. I have been urged to go to therapy several times in my life, and I am smart enough to know that my recent panic attacks are the result of more than a hormonal imbalance. There's a river of sadness in me; it's always been there, but now it is rising, spilling over its banks. I know there's a possibility that if I'm not careful, it will become the biggest part of me and I will drown in it. But I don't believe that words will make it back down; I don't believe that swimming in my memories will save me. I believe in sucking up, in going on.

And look where it has gotten me.

I put an arm around Marah and pull her close. We talk quietly about what scares her; I tell her that her mother would want her to stay in therapy. In the end, I pray I have done some good, but what do I know about what a teenager needs to hear?

We sit there a long time, both of us thinking of the ghost in the room, the woman who brought us together and left us alone.

The next day, Johnny arrives and tries to get Marah to change her mind about Seattle, to come home to Los Angeles, but she is firm in her resolve to stay with me.

✦

"Are you looking forward to the UW?" I say on the Friday afternoon after Marah's second appointment with Dr. Bloom. I am leaning against Marah. We are on my sofa, tucked together under a cream-colored cashmere throw. Johnny has gone back to Los Angeles and she and I are alone again.

"Scared, I'd say."

"Yeah, your mom was, too. But we loved it, and so will you."

"I am looking forward to my creative writing class."

"Like mother, like daughter."

"What do you mean?"

"Your mom was a talented writer. If you'd read her journal—"

"No," Marah says sharply. It is what she says to me each time I broach this tender subject. She is not ready to read the words her dying mother wrote. I can hardly blame her. It is like choosing to stab your own heart. But there's comfort there, too. Someday she will be ready.

Beside me, the cell phone rings. I lean over, check the caller ID. "Hi, George," I say. "I hope this isn't about some shitty reality show."

"And hello to you, too. I'm calling about your book deal. We have an offer."

My relief is staggering. I hadn't even known how much I was counting on this. I pull away from Marah and straighten. "Thank God."

"It's the only offer we got. And it's a good one."

I get up and begin to pace. When your agent starts to sell you, it's trouble. "How much, George?"

"Remember, Tully—"

"How much?"

"Fifty thousand dollars."

I stop. "Did you say fifty thousand?"

"I did. In advance. Against royalties."

I sit down so quickly it is almost like collapsing. Fortunately, there's a chair beneath me. "Oh." I know it is a lot of money in the ordinary world. I was hardly born with a silver spoon in my mouth. But I have spent so many years in an extraordinary world that it hits me hard, this proof that I have lost so much of my fame. You work like a dog for thirty years and think what you've built will last.

"It is what it is, Tully. But it can be your comeback. Yours is a Cinderella story. Make the world yours again."

I am feeling unsteady. My breathing is bottoming out. I want to scream or cry or snap or yell at the unfairness of everything. But I have only one choice and I know it. "I'll take it," I say.

✦

That night, I am too wired to sleep. At eleven o'clock, I give up on the pretense of it. For at least ten minutes I roam through my darkened condo. Once, I almost go to Marah's room and waken her, but I know that would be selfish of me, so I resist the urge to open her door. Finally, at about 11:20, I decide to work. Maybe writing will help.

I crawl back into bed and pull my computer into my lap, opening my most recent document. There it is: *Second Act*. And a blue screen. I stare at it, concentrating so intently I begin to imagine things. I think I hear footsteps in the hallway, a door opening and closing, but then it's quiet again.

Research. That's what I need. I have to go through the boxes in my storage unit.

I can't put it off anymore. After pouring myself a glass of wine, I go downstairs. Kneeling in front of the box, I tell myself to be strong. I remind myself that Random House has bought this memoir and paid for it. All I need to do is write down my life story. Certainly I can find the words.

I go to the *Queen Anne* box and open it. I pull the scrapbook out and place it on the floor beside me. I am not ready for it yet. I will work up to that collection of my dreams and heartaches.

I lean over and peer into the dark interior. The first thing I see is a ratty-looking stuffed rabbit.

Mathilda.

She is missing one shiny black eye and her whiskers look as if they've been cut off. This gift from my grandmother had been my best friend growing up.

I put Mathilda aside and reach in again. This time, I feel something soft and pull out a small gray Magilla Gorilla T-shirt.

My hand trembles just a little.

Why did I keep this?

But even as I ask the question, I know the answer. My mom bought it for me. It's the only thing I remember her giving to me.

A memory sears away everything else.

I am young—maybe four or five. I am in my chair at the kitchen table, playing with my spoon instead of eating my breakfast, when *she* comes in. A stranger.

My Tallulah, she says, lurching unsteadily toward me. She smells funny. Like sweet smoke. *Did you miss your mommy?*

Upstairs, a bell rings. *That's Grandpa,* I say.

The next thing I know, I am in the stranger's arms and she is running out of the house.

Gran is behind us, yelling, "Stop! Dorothy—"

The woman says something about *him* and adds a bunch of words I don't understand. Then she stumbles. I fall out of her arms and crack my head on the floor. My grandmother screams; I cry; the woman scoops me back into her arms. After that, the memory darkens, turns murky.

I remember her asking me to call her Mom. And I remember how hard the seat was in her car and how I was supposed to pee by the side of the road. I remember the smell of smoke in the car and her friends. They scared me.

I remember the brownies. She gave them to me and I ate them and she thought it was funny when I lost my balance and started throwing up.

I remember waking up in a hospital bed, with my name, TALLULAH ROSE, pinned to my chest.

Who was that lady? I asked Gran later when she came to pick me up.

Your mama, Gran said. I remember those two words as if I heard them yesterday.

"I don't like living in a car, Gran."

"Of course you don't."

I sigh and put the T-shirt back in the box. Maybe this memoir thing is a bad idea. I back away from the box and leave the storage unit, remembering to lock it this time.

Fifteen

✦

"You don't need to walk me to all of my therapy appointments, you know," Marah says to me on a bright and sunny Monday in late June as we walk up First Street toward the public market.

"I know. I want to," I say, linking my arm through hers.

Here's what I have learned in the two weeks she has lived with me: being responsible for a teenager is exhausting and terrifying. Every time she goes into the bathroom, I worry that she's cutting herself. I look through the trash and count the Band-Aids in every box. I am afraid to let her out of my sight. I am constantly trying to do the right thing, but let's face it, what I know about motherhood wouldn't fill a Jell-O shot.

Now, in Dr. Bloom's waiting room, I open up my laptop and stare at the blank blue screen. I have to get started on this thing, make some real progress. I *have* to.

I know how these things go. I've read a hundred memoirs in my life. They always begin in the same way; with the backstory. I need to set the stage, so to speak, to paint a picture of my life before I came into it. Introduce the players and the place.

And there it is. The thing that stops me this time, just as it has each time before: I can't write my story without knowing my own history. And my mother's.

I know almost nothing about her, and I know even less about my father. My history is this blank, yawning void. No wonder I can't write anything.

I have to talk to my mother.

At the thought, I open my purse and find the small orange container. I am down to my last Xanax. I swallow it without water and then, slowly, I pick up my cell phone and call my business manager.

"Frank," I say when he answers. "This is Tully. Is my mother still cashing her monthly checks?"

"I'm glad you called. I've left some messages. We need to talk about your finances—"

"Yeah, sure. But now I need to know about my mom. Is she still cashing her check?"

He tells me to hold, and then comes back onto the line. "Yes. Every month."

"And where is she living these days?"

There is another pause. "She's living in your house in Snohomish. Has been for a few years. We sent you notice. I think she moved in when your friend was sick."

"My mom's living in the house on Firefly Lane?" Did I know that, really?

"Yes. And now, can we talk about—"

I hang up. Before I can really process this information, work through it, Marah is coming out of Dr. Bloom's office.

That's when I notice the goth kid is beside me again. His black hair is streaked in magenta and green and safety pins hang from his earlobes. I see a glimpse of the script tattoo on his throat. I think it says madness, but there's more I can't see.

At Marah's entrance, he stands. Smiles. I don't like the way he looks at my goddaughter.

I get to my feet and edge around the coffee table, sweeping in protectively beside Marah. I take her arm in mine and lead her out of the office. When I look back from the door, gothie is watching us.

"Dr. Bloom thinks I should get a job," Marah says as the door closes behind us.

"Yeah, sure," I say, frowning. Really, all I can think about is my mother. "That's a great idea."

✦

All afternoon, I pace in my apartment, trying to think clearly.

My mother is living in one of the two houses I inherited from my grandmother; the house I have never been able to sell because it is across the street from the Mularkeys. This means that if I go to talk to her, I have to go back to the place where Kate and I met, where my whole life changed on a starry night when I was fourteen years old.

And I have to either take Marah with me or leave her alone. Neither choice seems particularly appealing. I am charged with watching her like a hawk, but I don't want her to see this meeting with my mother. Too often our reunions have been either humiliating or heartbreaking.

"Tully?"

I hear my name and turn. I think, vaguely, that Marah has called me before, but I can't be sure. "Yes, honey?" Do I look as distracted as I feel?

"I just heard from Ashley. A bunch of my high school friends are going to Luther Burbank beach park today for a picnic and waterskiing and stuff. Can I go?"

Relief comes in a sweet rush. It is the first time she has asked to spend time with her old friends. It is the sign I have been waiting for. She is returning to her old self; softening. I move toward her, smiling brightly. Maybe I can stop worrying so obsessively about her. "I think that's a great idea. When will you be home?"

She pauses. "Uh. There's this movie afterward. A nine o'clock show. *Wall-E*."

"So, you'll be home, by . . ."

"Eleven?"

That seems more than reasonable. And it gives me plenty of time. So why do I have a nagging sense that something is wrong? "And someone will walk you home?"

Marah laughs. "Of course."

I am overreacting. There's nothing to worry about. "Okay, then. I have a business thing to do, anyway, so I'll be gone most of the day. Be safe."

Marah surprises me by hugging me tightly. It is the best thank-you I've had in years, and it gives me the strength I need to do what I know needs to be done.

I am going to see my mother. For the first time in years—decades—I am going to ask her real questions, and I won't leave until I have some answers.

✦

Snohomish is one of those small western Washington communities that has changed with the times. Once a dairy farming community tucked in a verdant valley between the jagged peaks of the Cascade Mountain Range and the rushing silver water of the Snohomish and Pilchuck Rivers, it has blossomed into yet another of Seattle's bedroom communities. Old, comfortable farmhouses have been torn down and replaced with big stone and wood homes that boast magnificent mountain views. Farms have been sliced and diced and trimmed down to lots that fan along new roads that lead to new schools. I imagine you rarely see girls on horseback in the summer anymore, riding in cutoff shorts on the sides of the road, their bare feet swinging, their hair glinting in the sunlight. Now there are new cars and new houses and young trees, planted sometimes in the very place where older ones had been uprooted. Weedless lawns stretch up to painted porches, and well-maintained hedges make for good neighbors.

But even with the new views, the old town still shines through in places. Every now and then an old farmhouse stands defiantly between subdivisions, its fenced acres thick with tall grass and grazing cattle.

And then there is Firefly Lane. On this small ribbon of asphalt, outside of town, not far from the banks of the Pilchuck River, change has come slowly, if at all.

Now, coming back to this place that has always meant home, I ease my foot off of the accelerator. My car responds immediately and slows down.

It is a beautiful summer day; the unreliable sun is playing hide-and-seek among the wafting clouds. On either side of the road, green pastures roll lazily down toward the river. Giant trees stand guard, their arms outstretched to provide shade for the cattle gathered beneath.

How long has it been since I was here? Four years? Five? It is a sad, serrated reminder that time can move too fast sometimes, gathering regrets along the way.

Without thinking, I turn into the Mularkey driveway, seeing the FOR SALE sign planted by the mailbox. In this economy, it is no surprise that they haven't been able to sell the place. They are renting in Arizona now; when this house sells, they'll buy something.

The house looks exactly as it always did—a pretty, well-tended white farmhouse with a wraparound porch overlooking two sloped green acres that are outlined by mossy split-rail cedar fences.

My tires crunch on gravel as I drive up to the yard and park.

I see Kate's upstairs window, and in a blink I am fourteen again, standing here with my bike, throwing stones at her window.

I smile at the memory. The rebel and the rule-follower. That's what we'd seemed like in the beginning. Kate had followed me anywhere—or so it had seemed to me then, through my girl's eyes.

That night we'd ridden our bikes down Summer Hill in the darkness. Sailing. Flying. Arms outflung.

What I hadn't known until too late was that I was following her, all those years ago. I am the one who can't let go.

The drive from her childhood home to mine takes less than a minute, but to me it feels like a shift from one world to another.

My grandparents' old rental house looks different than I remember. The side yard is torn up; there are mounds of landscape debris piled in the middle of dirt fields. Before, giant juniper bushes had shielded the rambler from view. Now someone has ripped out the shrubs but not replaced them with anything, leaving piles of dirt and roots mounded in front of the house.

I can only imagine what I will find inside. In the thirty-some years of my adulthood, I have seen my mother a handful of times, always—only—when I have gone in search of her. In the late eighties, when Johnny, Katie, and I were the three musketeers at KCPO, I stumbled across my mom living in a campground in Yelm, a follower of J. Z. Knight, the housewife who claimed to channel a thirty-thousand-year-old-spirit named Ramtha. In 2003, I'd taken a camera crew and gone in search of her again, thinking—naïvely—that enough time had passed and maybe a new beginning could be forged. I'd found her living in a run-down trailer, looking as bad as I'd ever seen her. Starry-eyed with hope, I'd taken her home with me.

She'd stolen my jewelry and run off into the night.

The last time I'd seen her, only a few years ago, she had been in the hospital. She'd been beaten up and left for dead. That time, she sneaked out while I slept in a chair at her bedside.

And yet here I am.

I park the car and get out. Holding my laptop like a shield, I pick my way across the torn-up landscaping, stepping over trowels and spades and empty seed packets. The front door is wooden and has a faint green furring of moss. Taking a breath, releasing it slowly, I knock.

There is no answer.

She is probably passed out on the floor somewhere, dead drunk. How many times had I come home from school to find her lying on the sofa, half on and half off, with a bong not far from her outstretched hand, snoring loudly enough to wake the dead?

I test the knob and find that the house is unlocked.

Of course.

I open the door cautiously and go inside, calling out, "Hello," as I go.

The interior is gloomy and dark. Most of the light switches I find don't work. I feel my way into the living room and find a lamp and turn it on.

Someone has ripped up the shag carpeting and exposed the dirty black floorboards beneath. Gone is the seventies furniture. Instead, there is a single overstuffed chair positioned next to a garage-sale side table. In the corner a card table plays host to two folding chairs.

I almost leave. Deep inside, I know that nothing will come of this meeting, that once again I will get nothing but heartache and denial from my mother, but the truth is that I have never been able to walk away from her. Not in all our years together, not with all the times she's abandoned or disappointed me. I have spent each of my forty-eight years aching in some small way for a love that has never been mine. At least now I know better than to expect something different. That is a help, of sorts.

I sit down on the rickety folding chair to wait. It is not as comfortable as the other chair, but I am not certain of the fabric's cleanliness, so I choose the metal chair.

I wait for hours.

Finally at just past eight o'clock in the evening, I hear the crunching of tires on gravel.

I straighten.

The door opens and I see my mother for the first time in almost three years. Her skin has the wrinkled gray cast that comes with years of hardscrabble, drunken living. Her fingernails are brown with dirt. Clawing your way through life will do that.

"Tully," she says. It surprises me, both the strong, even tenor of her voice and the use of my nickname. All my life she has called me Tallulah, which I hate.

"Hi, Cloud," I say, standing.

"I'm Dorothy now."

Another name change. Before I can say anything, a man comes into the house and stands beside her. He is tall and whipcord-lean, with wrinkles in his tanned cheeks that look like furrows. I can read his story in his eyes—and it is not a pretty one.

My mother is high, I'm pretty sure. But since I don't think I've ever seen her sober, how would I know?

"I'm so glad to see you," she says, giving me an uncertain smile.

I believe her, but I *always* believe her. Believing her is my Achilles' heel. My faith is as constant as her rejection. No matter how successful I become, ten seconds in her presence will always turn me into poor little Tully again. Always hopeful.

Not today. I don't have the time—or the energy—to step on that Tilt-A-Whirl again.

"This is Edgar," my mother says.

"Hi," he says, giving my mother a frown. Her dealer, probably.

"Do you have any family photographs?" I say, a little impatiently. I am beginning to feel claustrophobic.

"What?"

"Family photos. Pictures of me as a girl, that kind of thing."

"No."

I wish it didn't hurt, but it does, and the hurt pisses me off. "You took no pictures of me as a baby?"

She shakes her head, saying nothing. There is no excuse and she knows it.

"Can you tell me *anything* about my childhood or who my dad was or where I was born?"

She flinches at each word, pales.

"Look, missy—" the pot dealer says, moving toward me.

"Stay out of this," I snap. To my mother, I say, "Who are you?"

"You don't want to know," she says, sounding scared. "Trust me."

I am wasting my time. Whatever I need for my book, I won't find it here. This woman isn't my mother. She might have given birth to me, but that's where her commitment to me ended.

"Yeah," I say, sighing. "Why would I want to know who you are? Who I am?" I grab my purse off the floor and push past her and leave the house.

I pick my way over the furrowed, upended piles of dirt and get in my car and drive home. All the way back to Seattle, I am replaying the scene with my mother over and over again in my head, trying to glean meaning from nuance, but there is nothing there.

I pull into my building and park.

I know I should go upstairs and work on my book—maybe today's outing will be a scene. At least it is something.

But I can't do it, can't walk up into my empty condominium. I need a drink.

I call Marah—she sounds sleepy when she answers—and tell her I'm going to be home late. She tells me she's already in bed and not to wake her when I get home.

I exit the elevator and go straight to the bar, where I allow myself only two dirty martinis, which calm my racing nerves and steady me again. It is almost one o'clock in the morning when I finally go upstairs and unlock the door to my condo.

All of the lights are on and I can hear the TV.

Frowning, I close the door behind me. It clicks shut.

I walk down the hallway, turning off lights as I go. Tomorrow I will have to have a talk with Marah. She needs to understand that light switches flip both ways.

As I pass her bedroom door, I pause.

Her light is on. I can see the strip of it beneath the closed door.

I knock gently, sure she has fallen asleep watching TV.

There is no answer, so I open the door quietly.

I am unprepared for what I see.

The room is empty. There are Coke cans on both nightstands, the TV is on, and the bed is unmade from this morning. Rumpled sheets are heaped in the middle of the bed.

"Wait a second."

Marah is not here. At one o'clock in the morning. She *lied* to me about being home and in bed.

"What do I do?" I am talking to myself now, or maybe to Kate, as I rush from room to room, flinging open doors.

I call her phone. There is no answer. I text: *Where are you???* and hit send.

Should I call Johnny? Or the police?

It is one-ten now. I am shaking as I pick up the phone. I have dialed 9-1 when I hear a key jiggling in the lock on my front door.

Marah comes in as if she is a cat burglar, trying to tiptoe, but even from here I can see that she is off balance, and she keeps giggling and shushing herself.

"Marah." My voice is so sharp I sound like a mother for the first time in my life.

She turns, trips, hits the door hard, and starts to laugh. Then she clamps a hand over her mouth and mumbles, "Shorry. Thass not funny."

I take her by the arm and lead her into her bedroom. She stumbles along beside me, trying not to laugh.

"So," I say when she collapses onto her bed. "You're drunk."

"I only had two beersh," she says.

"Uh-huh." I help her get undressed and then guide her into the bathroom. When she sees the toilet, she moans, "I'm gonna be shick—" and I barely have time to hold back her hair before the vomit flies.

When she is done puking, I put toothpaste on her toothbrush and hand it to her. She is pale now, and as weak as a rag doll. I can feel her trembling as I guide her into bed.

I crawl into bed beside her and put an arm around her. She leans against me and sighs. "I feel terrible."

"Consider this a life lesson. This is not two beers, by the way. So what were you really drinking?"

"Absinthe."

"Absinthe." That is not what I expected. "Is that even legal?"

She giggles.

"In my day girls like Ashley and Lindsey and Coral drank rum and Cokes," I say, frowning. Am I really so old that I don't know what kids are drinking these days? "I am going to call Ashley and—"

"No!" she cries.

"No, what?"

"I, uh . . . wasn't with them," she says.

Another lie. "Who were you with?"

She looks at me. "A bunch of kids from my therapy group."

I frown. "Oh."

"They're cooler than I thought," she says quickly. "And really, Tully, it's just drinking. Everyone does it."

That's true. And she's definitely drunk; I can smell it on her breath. Drugs would be different. What eighteen-year-old doesn't come home drunk at least once?

"I remember the first time I got drunk. I was with your mom, of course. We got caught, too. It wasn't pretty." I smile at the memory. It was 1977, on the day I was supposed to go in foster care. Instead, I'd run away—straight to Kate's house—and convinced her to go to a party with me. We'd gotten busted by the cops and been put in separate interrogation rooms.

Margie had come for me, in the middle of the night.

A girl who lived with us would have to follow the rules. That was what she said to me. After that, I got to see what a family was, even if I was on the outside, looking in.

"Paxton is way cool," Marah says quietly, leaning against me.

This worries me. "The goth kid?"

"That's harsh. I thought you didn't judge people." Marah sighs dreamily. "Sometimes, when he talks about his sister and how much he misses her, I start to cry. And he totally gets how much I miss my mom. He doesn't make me pretend. When I'm in a sad mood, he reads me his poetry and holds me until I feel better."

Poetry. Sorrow. Darkness. Of course Marah is drawn in. I get it. I've read *Interview with a Vampire.* I remember thinking Tim Curry was totally hot in *Rocky Horror,* spangly heels and corset and all.

But still, Marah is young and Dr. Bloom says she's fragile. "As long as you're with a group of kids—"

"Totally," Marah says earnestly. "And we're just friends, Tully. Me and Pax, I mean."

I am relieved by this.

"You won't tell my dad, right? I mean, he's not as cool as you are, and he wouldn't understand me being friends with someone like Pax."

"I'm glad you're just friends. Keep it that way, okay? You're not ready for anything more. How old is he, by the way?"

"My age."

"Oh. That's good. I guess every girl gets swept away by a brooding poet at least once in her life. I remember this weekend in Dublin, back in— Oh, wait. I can't tell you that story."

"You can tell me *anything,* Tully. You're my best friend."

She twists me around her little finger with that one; I love her so much right now it honestly hurts. But I can't let her glamour me. I need to take care of her.

"I won't tell your dad about Pax, because you're right, he'd freak. But I won't lie to him, so don't make me. Deal?"

"Deal."

"And Marah, if I come home to an empty house again, I'm calling your dad first and the cops second."

Her smile falls. "Okay."

✦

It changes something in me, that late-night talk with Marah.

You're my best friend.

I know it's not quite true, that really we are surrogates for each other, both of us standing in for Kate. But that truth fades in the sunshine of a beautiful Seattle summer. Marah's love for me—and my love for her—is the lifeline I have needed. For the first time in my life, I am really, truly *needed,* and my reaction to that surprises me. I want to be there for Marah in a way I've never really been there for anyone. Not even Kate. The truth is that Kate didn't need me. She had a family who loved her, a doting husband, and adoring parents. She brought me into the circle of her family and she loved me, but I was the one with the need.

Now, for once, I am the strong and stable one, or I intend to be. For Marah, I find the strength to be a better version of myself. I put my Xanax and sleeping pills away and cut back on the wine. Each morning I get up early to make her breakfast and make the calls for dinner takeout to be delivered.

Then I go to work on my memoir. After the dismal reunion with my mother, I decide to let go of the part of my story I don't know. It's not that I no longer care—I still care deeply. I am desperate to know my own life story, and my mother's, but I accept the reality. I will have to write a memoir based on what I know. So, on a gorgeous day in July, I sit down and simply begin.

Here's the thing: When you grow up as I have, a lost girl without any real past, you latch on to the people who seem to love you. At least that's what I did. It started early, my holding on too tightly and needing too much. I always craved love. The unconditional, even unearned kind. I needed someone to say it to me. Not to sound poor me, but my mother never said it. Neither did my grandmother. There was no one else.

Until 1974, when I moved into the house my grandparents bought as an investment. It was on a little street in the middle of nowhere. Did I know when I moved into a run-down house with my pothead mom that my world had just shifted? No. But from the moment I met Kathleen Scarlett Mularkey, I believed in myself because she believed in me.

Maybe you're wondering why my memoir begins with my best friend. Maybe you're speculating that I'm really a lesbian or just plain broken or that I don't understand what a memoir is.

I'm starting here, at what seems to be the end, because my story is really about our friendship. Once—not long ago—I had a TV show. The Girlfriend Hour. *I walked away from it when Katie was losing her battle with cancer.*

Apparently, walking away from a TV show without warning is bad. I am now unemployable.

How could I have done it differently, though?

I took so much from Kate and gave too little back. That was my time to be there for her.

At first, when we lost her, I didn't think I could go on. I was sure somehow that my heart would simply stop beating or my lungs would stop filling up with air.

People aren't as helpful as you'd think, either. Oh, they'll roll out the comfort mat when you've lost a spouse or a child or a parent, but a best friend is different. You're supposed to get over that.

"Tully?"

I look up from my laptop. How long have I been working? "Yeah?" I say distractedly, reading over what I've done.

"I'm leaving for work now," Marah says. She is dressed in all black and her makeup is a little heavy. She calls it a uniform for her new job as a barista in Pioneer Square.

I glance at my watch. "It's seven-thirty."

"I have the night shift. You know that."

Do I? Has she told me this before? She only got this job a week ago. Should I have some kind of chart somewhere? That sounds like something a mother would do. She has been gone a lot lately, hanging out with her old high school friends.

"Take a cab home. You need money?"

She smiles. "I'm fine, thanks. How's the book going?"

"Great. Thanks."

She comes over and gives me a kiss. As soon as she leaves, I go back to work.

Sixteen

✦

For the rest of the summer, I work seriously on my book. Unlike most memoirs, mine ignores my childhood and begins with my career. I start in the early days at KCPO, with Johnny and Kate, and then drift toward New York and the network. Recording the story of my ambition fuels me, reminds me that I can do anything I set my mind to. When I am not working, Marah and I act like best friends: going to movies and walking downtown and buying school supplies for the UW. She is doing so well that I have stopped worrying obsessively about her.

Until a sunny day in late August of 2008 changes everything.

On that afternoon, I am in the new King County Library, putting together a collection of the many magazine and newspaper articles written about me over the years.

I have planned on being here all day, but when I look up and see the sun shining through the expansive glass windows, I make a snap decision. Enough work for the day. I pack up my pages of notes and my laptop and I walk down the busy Seattle sidewalk toward Pioneer Square.

The Wicked Brew is a small, trendy place that seems loath to spend money on lighting. The interior smells like coffee mixed with incense and clove cigarettes. Kids sit huddled together at rickety tables, sipping coffee and talking quietly. The shop seems unconcerned with modern Seattle's no-smoking laws. The walls are layered with concert flyers for bands I have never heard of. I am pretty sure I'm the only one not dressed in black.

The kid at the cash register is wearing skinny black jeans and a vintage velvet jacket over a black T-shirt. His earlobes are the size of quarters and hold black hoops within. "Can I help you?"

"I'm looking for Marah."

"Huh?"

"Marah Ryan. She's working today."

"Dude, no one by that name works here."

"What?"

"What?" he parrots back at me.

I speak slowly. "I'm looking for Marah Ryan. Tall girl, dark hair. Beautiful."

"Definitely no one beautiful works here."

"Are you new?"

"I've been here forever, dude, like, half a year. No one named Marah works here. You want a latte?"

Marah has been lying to me all summer.

I spin on my heel and march out of the dingy, little place. By the time I reach my condo, I am fuming mad. I fling open the door and call out for her.

No answer. I look at my watch. It's 2:12 in the afternoon.

I go to her bedroom door, turn the knob, and go inside.

Marah is in bed with that boy, Paxton. Naked.

An ice-cold wave of pissed off overwhelms me and I shout at him to get off my goddaughter.

Marah scrambles back, pulls a pillow over her naked breasts. "Tully—"

The boy just lies there, smiling at me as if I owe him something.

"In the living room," I say. "Now. *Dressed.*"

I go to the living room to wait for them. Before they get there, I take a Xanax to calm my runaway nerves. I can't stop pacing. I feel a panic attack forming. What will I tell Johnny?

Like a mama hen, Johnny. You can trust me.

Marah walks in quickly, her hands clasped together, her mouth drawn into a frown. Her brown eyes are wide with worry. I see how much makeup she has on—heavy eyeliner, purplish black lipstick, pale foundation—and I know suddenly that she has been hiding this, too. There is no work uniform. She dresses like a goth when she goes out. She is wearing skinny black jeans and a black mesh top over a black cami. Paxton comes out beside her. He doesn't move so much as glide forward in his tight black jeans and black Converse tennis shoes. His chest is skinny and bare, so white it's almost blue. A scripty black tattoo unfurls from his collarbone to his throat.

"Y-you remember Pax," Marah says.

"Sit down," I snap.

Marah complies instantly.

Paxton moves closer to me. He really is beautiful up close. There is a sadness in his eyes, amid the defiance, and it is perversely seductive. Marah never had a chance with this kid. How did I not see that? Why did I romanticize it? It was my job to protect her and I failed.

"She's eighteen," he says, sitting down beside her.

So that's how he wants to play it.

"And I love her," he says quietly.

Marah gives him a look and I realize how deep this trouble runs. *Love.* I sit slowly, looking at them.

Love.

What in the hell am I supposed to say to that? One thing I know for sure. "I have to tell your dad."

Marah gasps. Tears flood her eyes. "He'll make me move back to L.A."

"Tell him," Paxton says, taking Marah's hand. "He can't do a thing. She's an adult."

"An adult with no money and no job," I point out.

She pulls away from Paxton and comes toward me, kneeling in

front of me. "You said my mom fell in love with Dad the first time she saw him."

"Yes, but—"

"And you had an affair with your professor. When you were my age, and everyone thought it was wrong, but you loved him and it was real."

I should not have told her so much. If I hadn't been caught up in my book and seduced by *you're my best friend,* I'm sure I wouldn't have. "Yes, but—"

"I love him, Tully. You're my best friend. You have to understand."

I want to tell her she's wrong, that she can't love a boy who wears guyliner and tells her what she feels, but what do I know about love? All I can do is try to undo the damage, to protect her. But how?

"Don't tell my dad. Please. It's not a lie," she adds. "Just don't say anything unless he asks."

It is a terrible and dangerous bargain I make. I know what will happen if Johnny finds out about this secret, and it will not bode well for me. But if I tell him, I will lose her; it's that simple. Johnny will blame me and take her away and she will never forgive either one of us.

"Fine," I say, and I know what I will do: I'll keep Marah so busy for the next three weeks she won't have time to see Paxton. Then she will start college and forget all about him. "But only if you promise not to lie to me anymore."

Marah smiles in a way that makes me feel uncomfortable, and I know why. She has been lying to me all this time.

What good is her promise?

✦

In September, I am Marah's shadow. I barely work on my book. I am determined to keep her away from Paxton. Making plans—and executing them—takes all my time. The only time we are apart is when we're sleeping, and I check on her at least once every night and I make sure she knows it. Johnny and the boys move back into the house on Bainbridge Island. He calls three nights a week and asks how she is doing—every time I tell him she is doing well. He pretends not to be hurt that his daughter doesn't visit and I pretend not to hear the hurt in his voice.

As my warden grip tightens, Marah pulls away from me. Our relationship begins to fray. I can see her chafing at the bit, straining to be free. She has decided I am not cool anymore, that I can't be trusted, and she withholds conversation as a punishment.

I try to rise above all of it and show her that still I love her. In this cold war atmosphere, my anxiety begins to grow again. I go see a new doctor and get prescriptions. I lie and say I've never been on Xanax before. By September twenty-first, I am beside myself with guilt and worry, but I am holding on. I am trying my best to keep my promise to Kate.

When Johnny shows up, ready to take Marah off to college, there is a moment of stunned silence as we stare at each other. I feel sick at the trust he has placed in me and my failure.

"I'm ready," Marah says at last, breaking the quiet, as she steps toward her dad. She is wearing artfully ripped black jeans, a black long-sleeved T-shirt, and about twenty silver bangles. Too much eyeliner and mascara accentuate her pallor and make her look tired. And scared. I am pretty sure she has powdered her face to look even more pale and gothlike.

I can see that Johnny is about to say the wrong thing—anything about her appearance is the wrong thing lately. Boy, do I know that.

I raise my voice to cover his. "Do you have everything you need?"

"I guess so," she says. Her shoulders slump, and in a second she turns into a kid again, hesitant and uncertain. My heart goes out to her. Before Katie's death, Marah was a bold, in-your-face-girl, and now she is someone else completely, vulnerable. Fragile.

"I should have picked a smaller school," she says, glancing out the window at the sunlit day, chewing on her black fingernail.

"You're ready," Johnny says from across the room. "Your mom said you were born ready."

Marah looks up sharply.

The moment feels charged. I feel Kate's presence in the air we're breathing, in the sunlight streaming through the window.

I know I am not alone in this feeling, either. In silence, we leave my condo and get into the car and drive north. I can almost hear Kate's off-key humming along with the radio.

"Your mom and I had so much fun here," I say as the gothic pink spires of the university come into view. I remember our toga parties and fraternity mixers and girls passing a candle at dinner to announce their engagements to boys who wore polo shirts and khaki pants and boat shoes without socks. Kate had thrown herself into sorority and collegiate life—she'd dated frat boys and planned social functions and pulled all-night study sessions.

Me, I'd had blinders on. I hadn't cared about anything except my future career.

"Tul?" Johnny says, leaning over. "Are you okay?"

"I'm fine," I say, managing a smile. "It brings back a lot of memories."

I get out of the car and help Marah with her luggage. The three of us walk through the campus toward the dorms. McMahon Hall rises up into the cloudless sky, a collection of jutting gray buildings with decks that stick out like broken teeth.

"It's not too late to sign you up for Rush," I say.

Marah rolls her eyes. "A sorority? Gross."

"You used to want to be in your mom's and my sorority."

"And gummy bears used to be my favorite food."

"Are you saying that you're too mature to join a sorority?"

Marah smiles for the first time all day. "No. Just too cool."

"You wish, goth girl. If you had seen us in our parachute pants and shoulder pads, you'd be screamin' jealous."

Even Johnny laughs at that.

We haul Marah's luggage into the elevator and ride up to her floor, where we enter a dank, dingy hallway that is crammed with kids and parents and suitcases.

Marah's "suite" is one of a collection of prison-cell-sized rooms fanned out around a small bathroom. In her bedroom, two twin beds take up most of the space; there are also two wooden desks.

"Well," I say, "this is homey." *Not.*

Marah sits down on the mattress nearest her. She looks so young and scared it breaks my heart.

Johnny sits down beside her. They look so much alike. He says, "We are proud of you."

"I wish I knew what she'd say to me now," Marah says.

I hear the way her voice breaks, and I sit down on her other side. "She would say that life is full of unexpected joy and to throw yourself into your college years."

The door behind us opens. We all turn, expecting to see one of Marah's new roommates.

Paxton stands there, dressed in black, holding a bouquet of dark purple roses. The streaks in his hair are scarlet now, and he is wearing enough chains to contain Houdini. He sees Johnny and stops.

"Who the hell are you?" Johnny says, getting to his feet.

"He's my friend," Marah says.

I see it all in a kind of slow motion. Johnny's anger—a thin layer over concern—and Marah's desperation and Paxton's not-so-subtle arrogance and disdain. Marah throws herself at her dad, clinging to his arm, trying to slow him down.

I step between Johnny and Paxton.

"Johnny," I say sternly. "This is Marah's day. She will remember it forever."

He pauses, frowns. I can see him working to reel in his anger. It takes longer than I would have expected. Slowly, he turns his back on Paxton. It is a comment, to be sure, one Paxton appreciates but Marah does not. I can see how much it costs Johnny to pretend that he doesn't mind Paxton being here.

Marah goes to stand by Paxton. Next to him, she looks even more dark-side, goth. They are both so tall and thin, like a pair of onyx candlesticks.

"Well," I say brightly to diffuse the tension in the room, "let's go out for lunch. You, too, Pax. I want to take Marah down memory lane. I'll show her where her mom and I used to study in Suzzallo Library, and our favorite place in the Quad, and the Department of Communication—"

"No," Marah says.

I frown. "No, what?"

"I don't want to go on your Firefly Lane memory tour."

This is a defiance I never saw coming. "I . . . I don't understand. We talked about this all summer."

Marah looks at Paxton, who nods encouragingly, and I feel my stomach tighten. This is *his* opinion. "My mom's dead," Marah says, and the flatness in her voice is devastating. "It doesn't help to keep talking about her all the time."

I am dumbstruck.

Johnny moves toward her. "Marah—"

"I appreciate you guys bringing me here, but I'm stressed out enough. Can we just call it a day?"

I wonder if this hurts Johnny as much as it does me. Or maybe parenthood builds calluses on your heart and I am simply unprepared for it.

"Sure," Johnny says gruffly. He ignores Paxton completely and muscles his way to his daughter, taking her in his arms. Paxton has no choice but to step back. Anger flares in his bourbon-colored eyes, but he banks it quickly. I'm pretty sure he knows I'm watching him.

This is my fault. I took her to Dr. Bloom's, where she met this obviously troubled young man, and when she told me about him, I acted as a kind of permission board. I should have reminded her that she was fragile and damaged, a girl who cuts herself on purpose. I should have protected her. And when I found out they were having sex, I should have told Johnny. I certainly would have told Kate.

When it is my turn to say goodbye, I want to say all the things I should have said before. It makes me angry at my useless mom all over again—if I'd had a mother, maybe I would have known *something* about acting like one.

In Marah's eyes, I see a carefully banked irritation. She wants us gone so that she can be alone with Paxton. How do we do this? How do we just leave her on this huge campus, an eighteen-year-old girl who cuts herself, with a boy who wears makeup and skull jewelry?

"Maybe you should live with me this quarter," I say.

I hear Paxton make a sound of contempt, and I want to smack him.

Marah barely smiles. "I'm ready to be on my own."

I pull her into a hug that lasts half as long as I would like.

"Keep in touch," Johnny says gruffly. Then he takes my arm and pulls me away. I stumble along beside him, blinded by tears. Regret and fear and worry braid together and become my spine, the things that hold me up.

The next thing I know, Johnny and I are at a bar on the Ave, surrounded by kids doing Jell-O shots in the middle of the day.

"That was brutal," he says when we sit down.

"Worse than brutal."

I order a tequila shot.

"When the hell did she make friends with that loser?"

I feel sick to my stomach. "Group therapy."

"Great. Money well spent."

I down my tequila and look away.

Johnny sighs. "God, I wish Katie were here. She'd know how to handle this."

"If Kate were here there'd be nothing to handle."

Johnny nods and orders us both another drink. "Let's talk about something less depressing. Tell me how your big-ass book deal is going . . ."

✦

When I get home, I pour myself a large glass of wine, which I carry from room to room. It takes me a while to realize that I am looking for her.

I am anxious, edgy, and a second glass of wine doesn't help. I need to do something. *Say* something.

My book.

I jump at the idea. I know exactly what to write. I get my laptop and open it up and find my document.

I have never known how to say goodbye. It is a failing that has been with me all of my life. It's especially problematic, given how often partings have come up. I suppose it all goes back to my childhood—doesn't everything? I was always waiting for my mother's return. How many times have I said that in this memoir? I'll have to go back and edit some of them out. But deleting the sentences won't delete the truth. When I care about someone, I hang on with a desperation that borders on mental illness. That's why I didn't tell Johnny about Paxton and Marah. I was afraid of disappointing him—losing him—but let's face it, he is already lost to me, isn't he? He was lost to me the moment Katie died. I know what he sees when he looks at me: the lesser half of a friendship.

Still, I should have told him the truth. If I had, maybe the goodbye to Marah wouldn't have felt so terribly, dangerously final . . .

✦

Christmas of 2008 surprises me.

It has been three months since Marah moved into her dorm, and in that short space of time, life has changed for all of us. I have been writing regularly—not managing to rack up a lot of pages, but I am steadily finding the words that tell my story. It energizes me, this new pursuit, gives me something to do in the long and empty hours of the day and night. I have become a hermit of sorts, one of those middle-aged women who live their lives at arm's length. I rarely leave my condo; there's no need. Everything can be delivered, and really, I don't know what to do with myself in the world these days. So I write.

Until Margie calls me one rainy day in late December. Have I been waiting for her call? I don't know. I just know that when it comes in, when I see her name on my caller ID, I almost start to cry.

"Hey, there," she says in that husky smoker's voice of hers, "what time are you getting over here on Friday?"

"Over here?" I ask.

"To Bainbridge Island. Johnny and the twins are home, so of course we're having Christmas here. We can't have the girlfriend hour without you."

And there it is. The thing I have been waiting for without even knowing it.

✦

It is a new beginning, that Christmas on Bainbridge Island; at least it seems like one. We are all together again for the first time in so long—Bud and Margie have come up from Arizona, Johnny and the twins have moved back into the home in which they belong. Even Marah comes home for a week. We all pretend not to notice how thin and sullen she is.

When we separate, we promise to stay in closer touch, to get together more often. Johnny hugs me tightly, and in the embrace I remember who we used to be to each other. Friends.

For the next few months, I am almost my old self, at least a paler, quieter version of her. I write almost every day; I make progress, not quickly, perhaps, but some progress is better than none and it helps anchor me, gives me a future. I call Marah every Monday night; it's true that she often doesn't pick up my call, and when she does deign to talk to me she exerts a strong rule: if I nag at her at all, she hangs up. And yet I find a way to be okay with that. It is something. We are talking. I believe that our fake, useless conversations will grow real over time. She will find her place at the UW, make friends, and mature. Soon I'm sure she will see Paxton for who he really is. But when her freshman year nears its end and he is still by her side, I begin to worry a little bit more.

In May of that year—2009—Lucas calls and invites me to the last baseball game of the season. I meet Johnny at the ballpark and sit with him in the stands. At first it is awkward being side by side; we are both uncertain of how to treat each other, but by the end of the third inning, we have found a way. As long as we don't mention Kate, we can laugh together again. For the rest of the summer and into that autumn, I visit often.

By the winter of 2009, I feel almost like my old self. I have even come up with a plan to bring Marah home from school early to decorate for the holidays.

"Are you ready?" Johnny says when I open the door to my condo. I can see that he is impatient, excited. We are all worried about Marah, and the idea of bringing her home from school early is a good one.

"I was born ready. You know that." I wrap the cashmere scarf around my throat and follow him down to his car.

On this cold, black, mid-December evening, heavy gray clouds collect above the buildings. Before we even reach the freeway, a few snowflakes begin to fall, so small that by the time they hit the windshield, all that is left is a starburst of water, plopping here and there, wiped away quickly, but still it lends a festive air. We talk about Marah on the way, her falling grades, and our hope that she will do better in this sophomore year than she did in her freshman.

The University of Washington's sprawling, gothic campus seems smaller in this weather; elegant buttressed buildings shimmer ghostlike beneath the stone gray sky. The snow is beginning to stick; a white sheen dusts the grassy lawns and concrete benches. Students move briskly between buildings, their hoods and backpacks slowly turning white. There is a hushed feeling here, a loneliness that is rarely felt on this giant campus. It is the last few days of Finals Week. On Monday, the school will close until January. Most of the students are already gone. In golden windows, professors rush to grade the last of their tests before the holiday begins.

McMahon Hall is particularly quiet. At Marah's room, we pause and look at each other. "Should we yell surprise?" I ask.

"I think it'll be obvious when she opens the door."

Johnny knocks on the door.

We hear footsteps and the door opens. Paxton is standing there, wearing boxer shorts and combat boots, holding a bong. He is paler than usual and the look in his eyes is glassy and blank. "Whoa . . ." he says.

Johnny pushes Paxton so hard the kid stumbles and falls. The place reeks of marijuana and something else. On the nightstand is a small crinkled piece of blackened foil with a dirty pipe beside it. *What the hell?*

Johnny kicks aside pizza boxes and empty Coke cans.

Marah is in bed, wearing only a bra and panties. At our entrance, she scrambles back, pulling the blanket up to her chest. "Wha' the hell are you doin' here?" she says. Her words come out mangled; her gaze is glassy. She is obviously high. Paxton moves toward her.

Johnny grabs Paxton as if he is a Frisbee and throws him sideways, then pins him to the wall. "You raped her," Johnny says. The tone in his voice is terrifying .

Marah climbs out of bed, falls to the floor. "Dad, don't . . ."

"Ask *her* if I raped your daughter," Paxton says, nodding at me.

When Johnny turns and looks at me, I open my mouth but nothing comes out.

"What?" Johnny yells at me. "What do you know about this?"

"She knew we were sleeping together," Paxton says with a small smile. He is tearing us apart; he knows it and enjoys it.

"Pax . . . doan . . ." Marah says, stumbling forward.

Johnny's gaze turns cold as ice. "What?"

I grab his arm and pull him to me. "Please, Johnny. Listen to me," I whisper. "She thinks she loves him."

"How *dare* you not tell me?"

I am almost too scared to answer. "She made me promise."

"She's a kid."

I shake my head. "I was trying—"

"Kate would not forgive you for this." He knows exactly how these words strip me bare. He pulls out of my grasp and spins to face his daughter.

She is on her feet, holding on to Paxton as if she would fall without his support. I see now that her eyebrow is pierced and her hair is streaked with purple. She pulls on a pair of jeans and grabs a dirty coat from the floor. "I'm sick of pretending to be who you want me to be," Marah says. Tears fill her eyes and she wipes them away impatiently. "I'm quitting school and getting the hell out of here. I need my own life." She is shaking as she puts on her shoes. I can see it from here.

Paxton nods encouragingly.

"This would break your mom's heart," Johnny says, looking as angry as I've ever seen him.

Marah stares at him. "She's dead."

"Come on, Marah," Paxton says. "Let's get the hell out of here."

"Don't go," I whisper. "Please. He'll ruin you."

Marah turns. She is so unsteady on her feet, she careens into the wall. "You said every girl needed a poet once in her life. I thought *you'd* understand. With all your my-job-is-to-love-you bullshit."

"She said *what*?" Johnny shouts. "Every girl needs a *poet*? Oh, for Chri—"

"He'll ruin you," I say again. "That's what I should have told you."

"Yeah," Marah says, her face tightening. "Tell me all about love, Tully. Cuz you know so much about it."

"She doesn't, but I do," Johnny says to Marah. "And so do you. Your mom wouldn't want you anywhere near this kid."

Marah's eyes go flat and blank. "Don't bring her into this."

"You come home with me *now*," Johnny says. "Or—"

"Or what? Don't come home at all?" Marah snaps back.

Johnny looks like he is falling. But he is angry, too. "Marah—"

She turns to Paxton, says, "Get me out of here."

"Fine, go," Johnny snaps.

I stand there, unable to draw a breath. How has everything gone wrong so fast? When I hear the door bang shut, I turn to Johnny. "Johnny, please—"

"Don't. You knew she was sleeping with . . . that kid . . ." His voice cracks. "I don't know how the hell Kate stayed with you all those years, but I know this: it's over now. This is YOUR fault. You stay the hell away from my family."

For the first time ever—*ever*—Johnny turns his back on me and walks away.

Seventeen

✦

O*h, Tully.*

Over the faint whir of the ventilator and the beep of the heart monitor, I hear the disappointment in Katie's voice. I forget where my body is—or try to—and live in the memory of where we are supposed to be. The Quad at the UW. Good times.

I lie back in the grass. I can almost feel it beneath me; tiny tips poking into my skin. I can hear the murmur of voices distinct and indistinct; they sound like waves washing up on a pebbled shore. That pure, beautiful light envelopes everything and gives me a sense of peace that is totally at odds with the memory I just shared with Kate.

You let them both walk away?

I roll onto my side and stare at this beautiful, incandescent vision of my best friend. In the pale glow of her, I see us as we once were—a pair of fourteen-year-old girls wearing too much makeup, with overplucked eyebrows, sitting on my bed, with an array of *Tiger Beat* magazines open between us. Or in the eighties, wearing shoulder pads the size of dinner plates and dancing to "We Got the Beat." "I ruined everything," I say.

She sighs quietly; I feel her breath like a whisper against my cheek. I get a whiff of the bubble gum she used to love, and the Baby Soft perfume that she hasn't worn in decades.

"I missed having you to talk to."

I'm here now, Tul. Talk to me.

"Maybe you want to talk to *me*, about what it's like where you are."

About the kind of missing that wakes you up at night, about forgetting how your son's hair smells right out of the bath or wondering if he's lost a tooth or how he'll grow up to be a man without a mother to guide him? She sighs quietly. *That's for another time. Tell me what happened after Marah ran away and Johnny said he didn't want to see you anymore. Do you remember?*

I remember, all right. December of 2009 was the beginning of the end. Last year. It feels like yesterday to me.

"After that horrible scene, I . . .

run out of the dorms and find myself alone on campus. It is a cold, snowy mess out here now; slush is furring the streets. I go to Forty-fifth Street, hail a cab, and get into the backseat.

At home, I am shaking so hard I slam my thumb in the door. I go straight to the bathroom and take two Xanax, but the pills don't stop me from falling apart. Not this time. I know it's because I deserve to feel bad. What had I been thinking, to say those things to Marah, to hide the truth from Johnny? He's right. This is my fault. How is it that I keep hurting the people I love?

I climb onto my big king-sized bed and curl into a ball on top of the silver silk coverlet. It absorbs my tears as if they'd never been.

I remember time passing in weird ways—in the slow charcoal darkening of the sky, in the lights coming on in high-rises around me, in the number of Xanax I take. In the middle of the night I eat everything in my fridge and am halfway through the pantry when I know I've overdone it. I stumble into the bathroom and puke it all up, along with the Xanax, and afterward I feel as weak as a kitten.

When the phone beside me rings, I waken, so groggy and lethargic that I forget where I am and why I feel like someone rolled over me with a dump truck. And then I remember.

I reach over and answer my phone.

"Hello?" I say, noticing how dry my mouth is.

"Hey."

"Margie." I whisper her name, afraid to say it out loud. I wish she didn't live in Arizona. I need to see her now.

"Hello, Tully."

I hear the disappointment in her voice and know why she is calling. "You heard?"

"I heard."

I am so ashamed I feel sick. "I screwed up."

"You were supposed to be taking care of her."

The truly pathetic thing is that I thought I was. "How do I fix it?"

"I don't know. Maybe when Marah comes home—"

"What if she doesn't?"

Margie draws in a sharp breath, and I think: *How much heartache can one family handle?*

"She'll come back," I say, but I don't believe it, and Margie knows. Instead of making me feel better, this conversation is making me feel worse. I make a mumbling excuse and hang up.

An Ambien helps me sleep.

✦

For the next two weeks, the weather matches my mood. Gray, swollen skies cry with me.

I know I am depressed. I can *feel* it, but the strange thing is that I find it comforting. All of my life I have run from my own emotions. Now, alone in my apartment, cut off from everyone, I revel in my pain, swim in its warm waters. I don't even pretend to work on my book. The sleeping pills I take at night leave me feeling fuzzy in the morning and slow-moving, and even with them in my system, I toss and turn at night; sweats and hot flashes have me alternately boiling and freezing.

Until Christmas Eve. Thirteen days after the fight at Marah's dorm room.

On that morning, I wake up with a plan.

I stumble out of bed and make my way to the bathroom, where a mirror reveals a middle-aged woman with bloodshot eyes and hair that needs to be colored.

I fumble with the Xanax container and take two. I need two because I'm going out, and just the idea of it sends me into a panic.

I should take a shower, but I am feeling so shaky and weak, I can't do it.

I gather the presents I bought weeks ago. Before.

I put them in a big gray Nordstrom bag and walk to the door.

I stop, unable suddenly to breathe. Pain spikes in my chest.

This is pathetic. *I* am pathetic. I haven't left my condo in almost two weeks. That's no time at all. When did I become *unable* to open a door?

I ignore my rising panic and reach for the doorknob. It feels ember-hot in my sweaty hand and I make a little sound—a yelp—and let go. Then I try again, more slowly. I open the door and step out into the hallway. When the door closes I fight an urge to turn around.

This is ridiculous. I know it's ridiculous. I just can't get ahold of myself. Still, I have made a plan. Today is Christmas Eve. A day of family and forgiveness.

I release my breath—how long have I been holding it in?—and walk resolutely toward the elevator. All the way there—fifteen feet of marble floor—my heart is skipping beats in my chest, stopping and starting.

The elevator ride to the parking garage is a test of my will. It feels heroic to make it to my car, to get in the driver's seat, to start the engine.

Outside, the streets of Seattle are dusted white with snow. Holiday decorations fill the windows on either side of the street. It is four o'clock on Christmas Eve. The only shoppers I see out are men in heavy coats, their faces hunched into flipped-up collars, shopping at the last possible moment.

I turn right on Columbia. It feels canyonlike in the snow, this hidden street, huddled as it is beneath the aging concrete viaduct overhead. Here, there are no people out and about in the falling snow. It is like driving through a black-and-white painting; my headlights are the only color I see.

I drive onto the ferry and park, deciding to stay in my car for the crossing. The movement of the ferry, the idle chugging, the occasional blaring of the foghorn, lull me into a kind of trance. I stare through the boat's open end at the snow falling in front of us; flakes disappear into the flat gray Sound.

I am going to apologize. I will throw myself to my knees if I have to, beg Johnny to forgive me.

"I'm sorry, Johnny," I say aloud, hearing the way my voice trembles. I want this so much. Need it. I can't go on the way I've been. The loneliness is unbearable, as is the guilt.

Kate would not forgive you.

On Bainbridge Island, I drive slowly off the ferry. The few blocks of downtown Winslow are dressed up for the holiday; white lights flicker in storefronts and wind up streetlamps. A red neon star hangs above Main Street. It looks like a Norman Rockwell painting, especially with the snow falling, sticking.

I drive down a road that is as familiar as my own hand but feels exotic in the snow. The nearer I get to their driveway, the looser my hold on panic becomes. At the last turn, my heart starts skipping beats again. I turn into the driveway and stop.

I take another Xanax. When did I take the last one? I can't remember.

I see a white Ford sedan in the driveway. That must be Bud and Margie's rental car.

I put the car in drive and inch forward. Through the curtain of falling snow, I see the Christmas lights strung along the eaves and the rectangular golden glow of the windows. Inside, the tree is lit up; shadowy people are gathered around it.

I park, turn off my lights and imagine it. I will go to the house, knock on the door and Johnny will answer.

I am so sorry, I will say. *Forgive me.*

No.

It hits me like a slap, so hard I snap back. He will not forgive me. Why should he? His daughter is gone. Gone. She has run away with a dangerous young man and disappeared because of me.

He will leave me standing there with my presents.

I can't do it, can't reach out and be smacked down again. I am barely holding myself together as it is.

I back out of the driveway, go back down to the ferry. In less than an hour, I am downtown again. Now the streets are really quiet; no one is walking on the slick sidewalks. The stores are closed. The roads are icy, and I slow down, just to be extra careful.

Then I am crying. I don't feel it coming on, this sadness, don't see it circling me, but suddenly I am sobbing even as my heart is racing and a hot flash sweeps through me in pins and needles. I try to wipe my eyes and to calm down, but I can't. My body is heavy, lethargic.

How many Xanax did I take?

This is the thing on my mind when the red lights flash behind me.

"Shit."

I put on my turn signal and pull off to the side of the road.

The police cruiser pulls up behind me. That damn red light blinks and flares and then stills.

The officer comes to my window and taps on the glass. It occurs to me a second too late that I should have lowered the window.

Smiling too brightly, I hit the button and the window slides soundlessly downward. "Hello, Officer," I say, waiting for recognition. *Oh, Ms. Hart. My wife-sister-daughter-mother loves your show.*

"License and registration, please," he says.

Oh. Right. Those days are over. I bolster my smile. "You sure you need my ID, Officer? I'm Tully Hart."

"License and registration, please."

I lean over to my purse and fish my license out of my wallet and retrieve the registration documents from my visor. I can see that my hand is trembling as I offer him what he's asked for.

He shines a flashlight onto my license, and then turns the light on me. I can't imagine I look good in that harsh light and it worries me. He stares into my eyes.

"Have you been drinking, Ms. Hart?"

"No. None," I say, and I think it's true. Isn't it? Have I had any wine tonight?

"Step out of the vehicle, please."

He takes a few steps back, moves to the rear of my car.

Now my hands are really shaking. My heart starts that wild samba beat again and my mouth goes dry. *Stay calm.*

I get out of my car and stand on the side of the road with my hands clasped tightly together.

"I'd like you to walk forty feet along this line, Ms. Hart. Heel to toe."

I want to do as he asks, quickly and easily, but I can't keep my balance. I keep taking too big a step and laughing nervously. "I've never been very coordinate . . . d," I say. Is that the right word? I'm so nervous I can't think straight, and I wish I hadn't taken those last two Xanax. My movements and thoughts are sluggish.

"Okay. You can stop. Stand here, in front of me. Tilt your head back and spread your arms out and touch your nose with one finger."

I fling my arms out and immediately lose my balance and stumble sideways. He catches me before I fall off the sidewalk. I try again, with all my will pulled in.

I poke myself in the eye.

He shoves a Breathalyzer at me and says, "Blow."

I am pretty sure I haven't been drinking, but honestly, I don't trust myself. My thoughts are too fuzzy, and I know I shouldn't blow into this thing if I have been drinking. "No," I say quietly, staring up at him. "I'm not drunk. I have panic attacks. I have a prescription—"

He pulls my arms together and puts me in handcuffs.

Handcuffs!

"Wait a second," I cry out, trying to think how I might explain this, but he isn't listening to me. He maneuvers me back to his cruiser.

"I have a prescription," I say in a small, scared voice. "For panic attacks."

He reads me my rights and tells me I'm under arrest and then pulls out my driver's license and punches a hole in it and forces me into the backseat of the cruiser.

"Come on," I plead when he slides into the driver's seat. "Don't do this. Please. It's Christmas Eve."

He doesn't say a word as we drive away.

At the police station, he helps me out of the cruiser and leads me by the elbow into the building.

There aren't a lot of people here on this snowy holiday night, and I'm glad of that. My shame is blossoming, widening. How could I have been so stupid? A woman built like a brick takes me into a room and searches me from head to toe, patting me down as if I am a terrorist.

They take my jewelry and all my belongings and then book and fingerprint me. Then they take my picture.

I feel the start of tears, and I know they're useless—raindrops on the desert floor—gone almost before they fall.

✦

Christmas Eve in a jail cell. A new low.

I sit on the painted concrete bench in some holding area, alone, huddled beneath a single glaring light fixture. Anything is better than looking at the bars. In the office on the other side of my cell, a few tired-looking men and women in uniform are seated at desks dotted with Styrofoam coffee cups and family photos and Christmas decorations, doing paperwork and talking to one another.

It is nearing eleven o'clock—these are the longest few hours of my life—when the brick-shaped woman comes to the cell door and unlocks it. "We've impounded your car. You can go if someone will pick you up."

"Can I take a cab?"

"Sorry, no. We haven't got your tox report back yet. We can't simply release you. There must be someone you can call."

Suddenly the floor I have been standing on gives way, and I realize that this whole thing has just gotten worse.

I will sit in jail overnight before I will call Margie on Christmas Eve and ask her to bail me out of jail.

I look up into the woman's lined, tired face. I can tell that she is a kind woman, but it is Christmas Eve and she is here and there is somewhere she'd rather be. "Do you have a family?" I ask.

She looks surprised by my question. "Yes," she says, after clearing her throat.

"It must be hard, to work tonight."

"I'm lucky to have a job."

"Yeah," I say with a sigh.

I can only think of one person to call, and I don't even know why his name comes to me. "Desmond Grant," I say. "He's an emergency room doctor at Sacred Heart. He might come. I have his number in my purse."

The woman nods. "Come on, then."

I get up slowly, feeling as worn down and dull as a piece of old chalk. We walk down the medicinal-green-painted hallway to a room full of empty desks.

The woman hands me my purse. I dig through it, ignoring the shaking in my hands (I could really use a Xanax now), and find both the phone number and my phone.

Under the woman's watchful eye, I punch in the number and wait, my breath held.

"Hello?"

"Desmond?" I can barely get any volume in my voice. I am already regretting this call. He won't help me; why should he?

"Tully?"

I don't want to say anything.

"Tully?" he says again, sounding concerned. "Are you okay?"

Tears gather in my eyes, sting. "I'm in the King County jail," I say softly. "DUI. But I didn't drink anything. It's a misunderstanding. They won't let me leave unless someone will be responsible for me. I know it's Christmas Eve and—"

"I'll be right there," he says, and I feel hot tears slide down my cheeks.

"Thanks."

I clear my throat and hang up.

"This way," the woman says. She prods me a little, just to remind me that I need to move. I follow her to another room; this one is big and busy, even on this holiday night.

I sit in a chair by the wall, ignoring the stream of drunks and hookers and street kids who are brought in every few minutes.

Finally the door opens and I see Desmond walk in; snow swirls in behind him. His long hair is grayed by melting snowflakes, his shoulders are blotched with moisture, and his sharp nose is red.

I stand, unsteady on my feet, feeling vulnerable and stupid and ashamed.

He crosses the room toward me, his long black coat flapping open like wings at the movement of his strides. "Are you okay?"

I look up. "I've been better. I'm sorry to call you so late. And on Christmas Eve. And for this." Shame tightens my throat until I can barely swallow.

"My shift ended in ten minutes anyway."

"You were working?"

"I cover for people who have families," he says. "Where can I take you?"

"Home," I say. All I want is to be in my own bed. I want to fall into a sleep so deep I forget about this entire night.

He takes me by the arm and leads me to his car, which is illegally parked out front. I tell him the address and we drive the few blocks to my building in silence.

He pulls up in front of the building. A liveried valet appears almost instantly at his door.

Desmond turns to me.

I see the question in his gaze when he looks at me. The truth is that I don't want to invite him up. I don't want to have to smile and make small talk and pretend to be fine, but how can I turn him away now, after he came for me?

"Would you like to come up for a drink?"

His gaze is questioning, unnerving. "Okay," he says at last.

I open my car door and get out so fast I almost fall. The doorman is there in an instant to steady me. "Thanks," I mutter, pulling away. Without waiting for Desmond, I walk across the lobby, my heels clicking on the stone floor, and press the up button at the elevator. In more silence, we ride up together, our images thrown back at us by the mirrored walls.

At my condo, I open the door and let him inside. He follows me down the hallway to the living room, with its outstanding view of the city at night, snow falling from the black sky, flakes turned colors by the muted city lights. "Wine?"

"How about some coffee for both of us?"

Do I hate him for the reminder of my night? Yes, a little, I do.

I go into the kitchen and make coffee. While it's brewing, I excuse myself. In the bathroom, I am appalled by my appearance—hair flattened and frizzed by the snow, face pale and tired, no makeup.

Good God.

I open the medicine cabinet, find my Xanax, and take one. Then

I return to the living room. He has found my CD player and put on Christmas music.

"I'm surprised you called me," he says.

The answer to that is so pathetic, I remain quiet. I sit on my sofa, kind of collapse. The full impact of this night is hitting me now; I am not strong enough to stand. The Xanax isn't working. I feel panic coming on. "Desmond Grant," I say. Anything to break the silence. "I slept with a guy named Grant for a few years."

"Wow." He comes over to me, sits down. He is so close I can smell the faintly metallic scent of melting snow on wool, and the aroma of coffee on his breath.

"Wow, what?" I say, unnerved by the way he is studying me.

"Most people would phrase it differently, use words like *love* or *dating* or *boyfriend* or *relationship* to describe someone you slept with for years."

"I'm a journalist. I pick words carefully. I slept with him. I neither dated him nor loved him."

"You said you'd been in love once. Maybe."

I do not like the turn this conversation has taken. Don't I already look pathetic enough with the DUI? I shrug. "I was nineteen. A kid."

"What happened?"

"I didn't realize I loved him until I was almost forty." I try to smile. "Story of my life. He married a woman named DeeAnna about six years ago."

"That must have been hard. So what was the other Grant like?"

"Flashy, I guess. I got a lot of flowers and jewelry, but not . . ."

"Not what?"

"Not the kind of present you give a woman you want to grow old with."

"What would that be?"

I shrug. How would I know? "Slippers, maybe, or a flannel nightgown." I sigh. "Look, Desmond, I'm really tired." It's been a terrible day. "Thanks for coming, though."

I see him set his cup down on the coffee table and turn slowly toward me. He takes me by the hand and pulls me to my feet. The way he looks at me makes it hard to breathe. He *sees* me somehow, impossibly, sees my vulnerability and my fear. "You're like the Lady of Shalott, Tully, watching the world from the safety of your high-rise tower. You've done it all, succeeded beyond most people's wildest dreams. So why don't you have anyone to call on Christmas Eve or anywhere to be?"

"Leave," I say tiredly. I hate him for his question, for exposing my loneliness and my fear, and for acting like I could do something differently. "Please." My voice breaks a little, cracks. All I want to do is crawl into bed and sleep.

Tomorrow will be a better day.

Eighteen

✦

By June of 2010, I know I am in trouble, but I don't know how to care. Depression has descended like a bell jar around me. I feel detached from everything and everyone. Even my weekly Wednesday night phone calls from Margie fail to lift my spirits.

I climb wearily out of bed and find that I'm lethargic as I walk to my bathroom. How many sleeping pills did I take last night? It scares me that I can't remember.

I take a Xanax to calm my nerves and get in the shower. Honestly, the Xanax isn't working so well anymore; I need to take more and more to get the same calming effect. I know this should bother me, and it does, in a distant, intellectual way.

Afterward, I pull my wet hair into a ponytail and dress in a pair of sweats. My head is throbbing now.

I try to eat something—it will be good for me—but my stomach is in such a knot I'm afraid I'll throw it back up.

The morning crawls by slowly. I try reading a book and watching TV and even vacuuming. Nothing diverts my attention from how bad I feel.

Maybe a glass of wine will help. Just one. And it is past noon.

It does help, a little. So does the second.

I am deciding—again—to quit drinking when my cell phone rings. I see the caller ID and dive for the phone as if it is Jesus Christ calling.

"Margie!"

"Hello, Tully."

I sink down to the sofa, realizing how much I needed to hear from a friend. "It's so good to hear from you!"

"I'm in the city. I thought I'd drop by. I'll be there in ten minutes. Let me in."

I lurch to my feet, almost crying at how much this means to me. I really am a mess. I will talk to Margie—my almost-mom. Maybe she can help me. "I'd love that."

I disconnect the call and rush into the bathroom, where I dry my hair quickly and put on enough product to bend steel. Then I put on makeup and dress in jeans and a short-sleeved top. I am pathetically eager to see someone who loves me, to be welcomed and wanted. I slip into a pair of flats. (I shouldn't have had those two glasses of wine; my balance isn't quite good enough for heels.)

The doorbell rings and I run for it, opening the door.

There stands my mother, looking as thin and ragged as a piece of twine. She is dressed like a refugee from a seventies commune: baggy pants, Birkenstock sandals, and one of those embroidered Mexican tunic tops that I haven't seen in years. Her gray hair is fighting the leather strap she's pulled it into; wisps float around her narrow, wrinkled face. I am so bewildered by the sight of her that I don't know what to say.

"Margie sent me," she says. "But it was my idea. I wanted to see you."

"Where is she?"

"She's not coming. I'm the one who wanted to see you. I knew you wouldn't open the door for me."

"Why are you here?"

She walks past me, comes into my home as if she has a right to be here.

In the living room, she turns to me. In a hesitant, gravelly voice, she says, "You have a drug or alcohol problem."

For a second, my mind goes utterly, terribly blank. I think, *I've been caught.* It's horrifying and humiliating and I feel stripped bare and vulnerable and broken. I back away, shaking my head. "No," I say. "*No*. My medications are *prescribed* for me. You make it sound like I'm a drug addict." I laugh at the idea of that. Does she think I hang around street corners and score drugs and inject them into my veins and slump to the street? I go to a *doctor*. I buy my drugs at Walmart, for God's sake. And then I consider the source of this accusation.

My mother steps forward. She looks out of place in my designer room. I can see all the disappointments of my life in her wrinkles, in the sun spots on her cheeks. I cannot remember a single time she held me or kissed me or told me she loved me. But now she's going to call me an addict and *help* me.

"I've been through rehab," she says in a timid, uncertain voice. "I think—"

"You have no right to say anything to me," I yell at her. "Not a thing, you understand me? How *dare* you come to judge me?"

"Tully," my mother says. "Margie says your voice has been slurred the last few times she's talked to you. I saw your mug shot on TV. I know what you're going through."

"Go away," I say, my voice breaking.

"Why did you come to see me in Snohomish?"

"I'm writing a book about my life. Not that *you* know anything about it."

"You had questions."

I laugh and feel the start of tears, which makes me angry. "Yeah. A lot of good it did me."

"Tully, maybe—"

"No maybes. Not from you. Not again. I can't take it." I grab her by the arm and drag her out of the condo—she weighs nothing. Before she can say anything, I shove her out into the hall and slam the door shut. Then I go into my bedroom and climb into bed, pulling the covers over my head. I hear my own breathing in the dark.

She is wrong. I don't have a problem. So what if I need Xanax to keep the panic attacks at bay and Ambien to sleep? So what if I like a few glasses of wine at night? I can control all of it, stop whenever I want to.

But, damn, I have a headache now. It's *her* fault I'm in pain. My mother. She and Margie have betrayed me. That is the cruelest part of all. I expect nothing from my mother, less than nothing, but Margie has been one of the few safe harbors of my life. To have her betray me like this is a blow I can't handle. At the thought, my anger dissolves into a bleak despair.

I roll sideways and open my nightstand drawer and reach for the Xanax.

✦

You think it was a betrayal? Kate says beside me, and her voice brings me out of my memories, pulls me up like a leash snap.

I remember where I really am. In a hospital bed, connected to a ventilator, a hole drilled in my head, watching my life flash before my eyes.

"I was in trouble," I say quietly. And they tried to help me.

How did I not know that? How did I miss the obvious?

You see now, don't you?

"Stop stop stop. I don't want to do this anymore." I roll onto my side and close my eyes.

You need to remember.

"No. I need to forget."

✦

September 3, 2010
2:10 P.M.

In the hospital conference room, the police detective stood with his legs spread far enough apart to hold him steady if an earthquake struck. He had a small notepad open and was reviewing his notes.

Johnny glanced around the quiet room. Most of the chairs were empty, pushed in close to the table. Two Kleenex boxes stood at the ready in the middle of the table. Beside him, Margie was trying her best to sit tall and straight, but this had been a tiring vigil; she kept slumping in defeat. He'd called her early this morning; she and Bud had been on a plane from Arizona by nine-fifteen. Now Bud was at Johnny's house, waiting for the boys to come home from school. Marah was in with Tully.

He and Margie had been in this room before. Here, they'd been told that the surgeons had failed to get clean margins on Kate's cancer and that it had spread to her lymph nodes and that there were quality-of-life decisions to be made. He reached over to hold Margie's cold, big-knuckled hand.

The detective cleared his throat.

Johnny looked up.

"The toxicology report won't be in for a while, but a search of Ms. Hart's residence revealed several prescription drugs—Vicodin, Xanax, and Ambien, primarily. We haven't found any witnesses to the accident yet, but our estimate, based on the crime scene analysis, is that she was driving in excess of fifty miles per hour on Columbia Street, heading toward the waterfront, in the rain. She hit a concrete stanchion at a high rate of speed."

"Were there skid marks?" Johnny asked. He heard Margie draw in a breath, and he knew that this question hadn't occurred to her. Skid marks before a collision meant that the driver had tried to stop. No skid marks meant something else.

The detective looked at Johnny. "I don't know."

Johnny nodded. "Thanks, Detective."

After the detective left, Margie turned to Johnny. He saw the tears in her eyes and regretted his question. His mother-in-law had already suffered so much. "I'm sorry, Margie."

"Are you saying . . . Do you think she drove into it on purpose?"

The question stripped Johnny of his strength, left him exposed.

"Johnny?"

"You've seen her more recently than I have. What do you think?"

Margie sighed. "I think she felt very alone in the last year."

Johnny got to his feet and mumbled an excuse about needing to use the bathroom and left the room.

In the hallway, he leaned against the wall and hung his head. When he finally looked up, he saw a door across the hall from him, and a sign: CHAPEL.

When was the last time he'd been in a church?

Kate's funeral.

He crossed the hall and opened the door. It was a small, narrow room, utilitarian-looking at best, with a few pews and a makeshift altar at the front. The first thing he noticed was the quiet. The second was the girl seated off to the right in the front pew. She was slumped down so far, all he could see was a tuft of gelled pink hair.

He moved forward slowly, his footsteps lost on the carpeted floor. "May I join you?"

Marah looked up sharply. He could see that she'd been crying. "Like I could stop you."

"Do you want to stop me?" he asked quietly. He had made so many mistakes with her, he didn't want to add to the pile by pushing her too hard when she'd come here to be alone.

She stared at him a long time and then slowly shook her head. She looked so young right now, like a kid at Halloween, dressing up for attention.

He sat down cautiously, waited a while before he said, "Does praying help you?"

"Not so far." Tears filled her eyes. "Do you know what I did to Tully last week?"

"No."

"It's my fault she's here."

"It's not your fault, baby. It was a car accident. There's nothing you could have done—"

"It's your fault, too," Marah said, sounding miserable.

To that, Johnny didn't know what to say. He knew what his daughter meant; he felt the same thing. They'd let Tully down, cast her out of their life, made her feel alone, and here she was.

"I can't *stand* this," Marah cried. She bolted to her feet and headed for the door.

"Marah!" he yelled.

At the door, she paused and looked back.

"Don't hurt yourself," he said.

"Too late," she said quietly, and left the room. The door banged shut behind her.

Johnny got slowly to his feet. Feeling every one of his fifty-five years, he went back out to the waiting room, where he found Margie seated in the corner, knitting.

He sat down beside her.

"I tried calling Dorothy again," she said after a while. "No answer."

"Will she get the note you had Bud put on her door?"

Margie seemed to hunch down at that. "Sooner or later," she said quietly. And then, "I hope it's sooner."

✦

September 3, 2010
2:59 P.M.

On this cool September afternoon, leaves were falling all over the town of Snohomish, on the roadsides and in parking lots and on riverbanks. As Dorothy Hart stood in her stall at the farmers' market, staring out over the view that had become her life, she saw little bits of beauty. The last wild roses for sale in Erika's red buckets across the way, a young woman with a plump, curly-haired baby on her hip tasting some of Kent's smoked salmon, a little boy sipping homemade cider from a Dixie cup. The farmers' market was a bustle of color and activity and sights and sounds. Only a few short blocks from the historic center of town, this lively market sprang up on a patch of pavement every Friday from noon to five: white tent roofs rose above it all like ice-cream peaks; beneath them, a dazzling, glittering array of fruits and nuts, berries, herbs, vegetables, crafts, and honey. The patchwork colors were gorgeous in this fading autumnal light.

In the small booth, Dorothy was coming to the bottom of her limited supply of produce. She had a long, low table set up, draped in newspaper—the Sunday comics this week—and dotted with boxes that held this week's crop: bright red apples, plump raspberries, baskets full of herbs, and the vegetables: green beans, tomatoes, broccoli, and summer squash. Of those, only a few remained; lonely apples in the bottom of an otherwise empty box, a handful of green beans.

She was out of almost everything. The sky—cloudless and blue—was a bright backdrop to the melee as she packed up her boxes and carried them across the aisle to the Cascade Farms stall.

The owner, a big, wild-haired man with a potbelly and a hook of a nose, gave her a smile. "Looks like a good day for you, Dorothy."

"Really good, Owen. Thanks again for letting me use part of your booth. The raspberries were gone in a nanosecond."

She handed him the stack of wooden boxes. He took them from her and put them in the back of his rusted pickup truck. He would drop them off at her house later. "You sure we can't give you a ride home?"

"Naw. I'm good, but thanks. Tell Erika hi. See you guys later."

She walked back to her part of the shared stall, feeling a slight tingle of sweat along the back of her neck. A bead slid down her spine, dampening the waistband of her baggy pants. She unbuttoned the ragged plaid shirt that was basically her uniform—she had at least six of them—and took it off, tying it around her waist by the sleeves. The ribbed red tank she had on underneath was blotched with sweat beneath her arms, but there was nothing she could do about it.

She was sixty-nine years old, with long gray hair, skin that looked like ten miles of dry riverbed, and eyes that held all the sorrow she'd experienced in her life. The last thing she cared about was whether she smelled. She retied the red bandanna across her forehead and climbed onto the rusted bike that was her only mode of transportation.

One day at a time.

The guiding tenet of this new life of hers. In the past five years, she'd turned her life around, pared down and stripped away until only what mattered remained. She left almost no carbon imprint on the planet. She composted everything. She grew and tended and sold her organically grown produce, and she ate only organic food. Fruits, nuts, vegetables, and grains. She was not pretty anymore, and she was as thin and stringy as her beans, but none of that bothered her. In fact, it pleased her. The life she'd led showed on her face.

She was alone now. It was how it always should have been. How many times had her father told her that? *You're cold as ice, Dotty. You'll end up alone if you can't thaw.* It was criminal that his voice was still in her head after all these years.

She put a rubber band around her pant leg and climbed onto the bike. With a flourish, she was off, pedaling through town with her cash box banging around in the basket between her handlebars. Cars honked at her and came too close, but she barely noticed. She'd learned that people were uncomfortable with old hippies in general, but especially those on bicycles.

At the corner, she held her arm out to indicate her intention and turned onto Main Street. It gave her a small bit of pleasure, just following the rules, indicating her turn. She knew it sounded odd and most people wouldn't understand, but her whole life had been spent in the wildlands of anarchy, and the peace that came with rules and fences and society had proven to be unexpectedly comforting. She parked her bike in one of the stands outside the pharmacy. The newer residents of town, the hipper suburbanites who'd chosen this once-sleepy town as their home because it was thirty-some miles from downtown Seattle, would lock their bikes up in bright red tubing and protect their investment.

It always made Dorothy smile, seeing that sort of care being taken for *things*. Someday, if they were lucky, they'd learn what needed to be held close in life, and what wasn't worth worrying over. Retying her bandanna as she walked down the cracked, uneven sidewalk, she was surprised by the number of people in town today. Tourists moved in flocks in and out of the antique stores that had become Snohomish's raison d'être. On this street, once the only one in town, banked on one side by the wide, flat ribbon of the Snohomish River and on the other by the start of the new part of town, the storefronts retained the frontier look of the old days.

She went into a brightly lit pharmacy and strode directly to the prescription counter. Along the way there were plenty of pretty things that caught her eye—brightly colored barrettes, coffee mugs with inspirational sayings, greeting cards—but she knew that less was more. Besides, she had no money left and her check from Tully hadn't come in yet this month.

"Hey, Dorothy," the pharmacist said.

"Hey, Scott."

"How was the farmers' market today?"

"Great. I have some honey for you and Lori. I'll bring it by."

He handed her the medication that had made such a difference in her life. "Thanks."

She paid for her pills, pocketed the small orange bottle, and headed out. She went back out to the busy street, climbed onto her bicycle, and pedaled the three miles home.

As always, going up Summer Hill kicked her ass, and by the time she reached the top and turned onto Firefly Lane, she was sweating hard and breathing heavily. At her driveway, she wheeled left and hung on tightly as the old bike rattled down toward the house.

There was a note pinned to her front door. Frowning, she got off her bike, let it clatter to the ground. When was the last time someone had left her a note?

> *D—*
>
> *Tully is in Sacred Heart Hospital. Johnny says to hurry. Cab fare under mat. 426 E.*
>
> *M*

Dorothy bent down and lifted up the black rubber doormat. A dirty white envelope lay on the damp potato-bug-dotted cement beneath. Inside the envelope was a one-hundred-dollar bill.

Dorothy hurried through the rambler that had once belonged to her parents and now was owned by her daughter—the same house a much younger Dorothy had once lived in with a fourteen-year-old Tully. The only place they'd ever lived together.

In the last few years, Dorothy had done a little work on the place, but not much. The exterior was still beige and in need of paint; the roof still grew a green moss in places. Inside, she'd ripped up the avocado shag carpeting and found hardwood floors beneath, which someday she intended to refinish. The kitchen was still the Pepto-Bismol-colored apocalypse some renter had chosen in the early seventies, but the hideous gingham curtains were gone. The only room Dorothy had really gutted was the master bedroom. She'd ripped down the cheap blinds, pulled up the gold sculpted carpeting, and painted the walls a pretty cream color.

Dorothy opened her prescription bottle and took her pill, washing it down with a handful of warm tap water. Picking up the old-fashioned corded phone in the kitchen—an antique in this cell phone era—she opened the phone book, looked up the number, and called a cab. There was no time to take a shower, so she just brushed her hair and teeth. Braiding her stringy gray hair as she walked into the bedroom, she caught sight of herself in the oval mirror above her dresser.

She looked like Gandalf after a bender.

A cab horn honked out front. She grabbed her purse and ran out. It wasn't until she was in the smelly brown velour seat, staring through a dirty window, that she realized one pant leg was still rubber-banded to her ankle.

She stared at her farm as the cab pulled out of the driveway. More than four years ago—when she'd finally accepted the idea of true change—this place had saved her. She often thought that her tears had been the moisture that made her vegetables grow.

She was grateful for the prescription drugs in her system. The veil they provided was chiffonlike, a softening of the world around her. Just a little. Enough so that her emotions—her unreliable and dangerous moods—were calmed. Without them, she knew she could spiral downward now, into the darkness that had been home for most of her life.

Memories clamored at her, pushing, demanding until she couldn't hear the cabdriver breathing or the engine purring or the traffic zipping past them.

Time unspooled and wrapped around her and she had no will to resist. She gave up, gave in, and for a split second the world went utterly, completely still.

Then she heard a dog barking, a chain snapping taut, and she knew where she was, *when* she was: 2005. November. She was sixty-four years old, a woman who called herself Cloud, and her daughter was one of the most famous people on TV. Cloud lived in a broken-down trailer on a muddy lot off a logging road near Eatonville. The sweet, cloying smell of . . .

marijuana engulfed her. She was high, but not high enough. Lately, there wasn't enough weed in the world to protect her.

Maybe a drink would help. She climbed out of the ripped brown Barcalounger and stumbled into the Formica coffee table. Pain bit deep into her shin and beer cans rattled and fell to the floor.

She moved cautiously through the mobile home, wondering if the floors were slanted suddenly or she was higher than she thought. In the kitchen, she paused. What had she come in here for?

She glanced dully around, noticing the stack of dirty dishes on the stove. She should do those before Truc got home. He hated it when she didn't clean up . . . Were those *flies* buzzing around the pizza boxes?

She shuffled over to the fridge and opened the door. The light came on, illuminating some leftover sandwiches, a case of beer, and milk that looked vaguely green. She slammed it shut and opened the freezer. A fifth of vodka lay in the rack on the door. She was reaching for it with a trembling hand when she heard the throaty purr of a diesel engine.

Shit.

She should start cleaning, but she was shaking badly and she felt sick to her stomach.

Outside, the dogs were barking, snarling. She could hear them leaping toward him, straining their collars, snapping against long coils of chain.

She had to meet him. She ran shaking hands through her long, tangled hair. When had she showered last? Did she smell bad? He hated that.

She shuffled to the door and opened it. At first, all she saw was a gray afternoon that smelled of diesel smoke and dog crap and wet dirt.

She blinked, focused.

There was his big red truck parked by the woodpile.

Truc climbed out of the cab, his steel-toed boot splashing down in a pothole. He was a big man, with a belly that entered the room first and straggly brown hair that framed a boxy, well-traveled face.

The truth was in his eyes. They were small and black and the light in them could go dark in an instant.

"H-hey, Truc," she said, snapping open a beer for him. "I didn't think you'd be home until Tuesday."

He came into the light and she knew he'd been drinking. There was a glassy look in his eyes, a slackness in his mouth. He paused to pet his beloved Dobermans, fishing dog treats out of his pockets. The snapping of their jaws seemed terrifyingly loud in the quiet night. She winced, tried to keep smiling.

Truc took the beer from her and stood there in the pale rectangle of light. The dogs were quiet beside him now, servile, slobbering their affection. Just the way he liked them. Behind them, the grassy field disappeared into a fog that cleansed the yard of its rusted cars and broken refrigerators and discarded furniture.

"It is Tuesday," Truc growled. He finished the beer and tossed the can to the dogs, who immediately began fighting over it. He reached out and pulled her into his big arms and held her tightly. "I missed you," he whispered in his gravelly, slurred voice, and she wondered where he'd been since his shift ended. At the Lucky Spot, probably, drinking boilermakers and complaining about cutbacks at the paper plant. He smelled of pulpwood and grease and smoke and whiskey.

She tried to stand very still, hardly daring to breathe. He was touchy lately, and getting touchier all the time. She never knew what would set him off. "I missed you, too," she said, hearing the slur in her voice. Her mind was moving slowly, thoughts pushing through sludge.

"You're not wearing the blouse I bought you."

She drew back slowly. What blouse? Honestly, she couldn't remember. "I . . . I'm sorry. I'm saving it for nice. It's so pretty."

He made a sound, maybe disgust, maybe acceptance, maybe apathy. She couldn't tell. Her thoughts were too fuzzy, and that was bad bad bad. She held on to his hand, squeezing it as she led him into the mobile home.

The place reeked of pot, she realized suddenly. And something else; garbage, maybe.

"Cloud," he said, so quietly that the hair on the back of her neck stood up. What had he seen? What had she done or not done?

Cleaning. She'd forgotten to clean. He hated dirty dishes in the sink.

She turned slowly, unable to even think of an excuse.

He kissed her lightly on the lips, so lovingly that she released a sigh of relief. "You know I hate a mess like this. With all I give you—"

She pulled back. "Please—"

Before she could even lift her hands in defense, he punched her in the face. She felt her nose crumple beneath his fist; blood sprayed everywhere and she stood there, bleeding down her shirt. Crying only made it worse.

✦

She woke to the sound of heavy breathing. For a second she didn't remember anything, and then pain reminded her. She pried open one eye and immediately winced. Pale light from the TV stabbed at her, made her blink. Her mouth was dry; she was trembling uncontrollably and everything hurt.

Take stock.

She'd woken up in this condition more times than she could count. She knew what to do.

She was in bed, with Truc sprawled beside her, his bulbous belly pointed skyward, his hairy arms outflung. It was dark out now. Night had fallen.

She inched out of bed and winced as she put her weight on her left ankle. Sprained in one of her falls, obviously.

She limped to the bathroom and saw herself in the full-length mirror on the back of the door. Her hair was a tangled mess and matted with blood. Her eye was swollen shut and the bruising around it was a sickening stew of purple, brown, and yellow. Her nose was in the wrong shape—flattened—and dried blood caked her chin and cheeks.

Hurting too badly to clean up, she dressed in what she could find, yesterday's clothes or last night's clothes, she couldn't remember, and it hurt too much to look down to see if there was blood on the fabric.

She had to get out of here, away from Truc, before he killed her. She had thought this before, dozens of times, every time he beat the shit out of her, and once, about a year ago, she'd even left for a while, made it as far as Tacoma, but in the end he found her and she came back because she had nowhere else to go, and really, this was what she expected in her life. It was what she'd always had.

But she wasn't young anymore, was old, in fact. Her bones broke so easily these days, and what if one of these times she hit the wall and her spine just snapped?

Do it.

She crept past him to the bedside table and fumbled shakily through his wallet, where she found three twenties. Fisting the money, she knew it would only make it worse for her if she didn't get away, but she *would* get away this time. She had to.

As quietly as she could, she took a step.

The floor squeaked and Truc made a sound in his sleep and rolled toward her.

She froze, her heart pounding, but he didn't wake up. Releasing her breath, she gathered up her two important belongings—a ragged, falling-apart macaroni-and-bead necklace and an old black-and-white photograph. She put the necklace on and tucked the photograph into the pocket of her flannel shirt, buttoning the pocket to protect it.

She turned quietly on her unhurt foot and limped out of the room.

Outside, the dogs immediately sat up, watching her intently. Mount Rainer loomed not far away, its snowy peak lit by the moon.

"Shhh, boys," she said, edging past them.

She was picking her way around the ripped old Barcalounger when the first one barked. She kept going, didn't look back.

It was dark out here in the woods, so dark that only with patience and slow going could she find her way, and the pain of each step reverberated up through her body. Her neck ached like hell and her face literally pulsed with pain, but she didn't stop or slow down until she got to the bus station in Eatonville. There, hidden on three sides by dirty Plexiglas, she slumped onto the bench and finally breathed.

She pulled out a joint—her last one—and smoked it as she sat there in the dark, and it helped, but not enough. Her pain was still unbearable, as was her regret. Already she feared she would go back.

She climbed onto the bus when it arrived, ignoring the driver's judgmental look.

Two and a half hours later, at just past ten P.M., she got off the bus in downtown Seattle. Pioneer Square, to be exact. It was where you could disappear in Seattle. She knew all about being invisible. It was what she needed now, to become an insubstantial shadow in a blurry world.

But as she moved in this place that should have welcomed her with its dark corners and blind alleys, her headache intensified. It felt like hammer blows to the skull. She heard the small whimpering sound she made and thought that it couldn't be coming from her. She'd learned how to suffer through pain quietly, hadn't she? He'd taught her how a long time ago.

She hurt so much she couldn't think straight.

The next thing she knew, she was falling.

Nineteen

✦

Cloud came awake in stages. First came the realization of her pain, then of her breathing, then that she smelled clean. That told her where she was.

Hospital. She'd been in enough of them in her life to recognize the sights and smells and sounds. It was November 2005, and she was running away.

She lay quietly, afraid to open her eyes. She remembered the night before in staccato images—a red flashing light, being lifted onto a gurney and wheeled into a bright white room. Doctors and nurses buzzing around her, asking who had beaten her up and who they could call for her. She'd closed her eyes and ignored them. Her mouth had been so dry she couldn't talk even if she had had something to say, and now the shaking in her hands was back.

There was someone in the room with her. She could hear breathing, and the flipping of pages on a chart. Cautiously, she opened her good eye. The other felt swollen shut.

"Hello, Dorothy," said a plump black woman with dreadlocks and a smattering of dark freckles across her fleshy cheeks.

Cloud swallowed hard. She could have corrected this earnest-looking young woman, told her that Dorothy had died in 1973, but really, who cared? "Go away," she said, wishing she could lift a hand to gesture. She was afraid to reveal how shaky she was. You never wanted to show weakness in a hospital. One wrong move and you could find yourself in the psych ward.

"I'm Dr. Karen Moody. I don't know if you remember, but you tried to hit one of the paramedics who brought you in here."

Cloud sighed. "You're here to eval me. Let me make it easy: I'm not a threat to myself or others. If I lashed out it was an accident."

"I take it this isn't your first psych evaluation. You know the rules."

Cloud shrugged.

"I've got your medical records, Dorothy. And I've spoken to the police. It all tells quite a story."

Cloud stared at her, saying nothing.

"The number of broken bones is certainly not normal. And I saw the cigarette burns on your collarbone. I'm guessing there are more."

"I'm clumsy."

The doctor closed the chart. "I doubt that, Dorothy. And I'm guessing you self-medicate to forget."

"Is that your way of calling me a drunk and a stoner? If it is, you're right. I'm both. Have been for decades."

The doctor stared down at her, eyes narrowed and assessing. Then she reached into her pocket and pulled out a card. "Take this, Dorothy. I work at a rehab facility. If you're ready to change your life, I'd like to help you."

Cloud took the card, studied it. "I guess you know who my daughter is. You figure she'll pay for anything."

"I want to help you, Dorothy. That's what I do."

"Why? Why would you want to help me?"

The doctor slowly lifted her sleeve.

Cloud saw the series of small, puckering pink starburst scars that coiled up the dark flesh. Cigarette burns. "I know about drinking to forget."

Cloud didn't know what to say.

"It stops working. Well, actually, it never worked, but after a while the drinking makes it worse. I *know*. I could help you. Or I'd like to try. It's up to you."

Cloud watched the woman walk out of the hospital room and shut the door behind her. In the quiet darkness, she found it difficult to breathe. She hadn't thought about those scars in years.

Sit still, damn it, you know you have this coming.

She swallowed hard. On the wall in front of her, the clock ticked forward the minutes. It was 12:01. Just past midnight.

A new day.

She closed her eyes and fell asleep.

✦

Someone was touching her, stroking her forehead.

It had to be a dream.

She forced her gritty eyes open. At first there was only darkness. Then, gradually, her good eye adjusted. She saw the charcoal square of a window, with a pale exterior light casting a golden glow into her room. The door was open; beyond it, the nurses' station was brightly lit and quiet.

It was the middle of the night. She could tell by the quiet.

"Hey," someone said.

Tully.

She would know her daughter's voice anywhere, even in this antiseptic darkness.

Cloud turned her head on the pillow, wincing at the pain it caused.

Her daughter stood there, frowning slightly. Even at this hour, Tully looked gorgeous—sleek auburn hair, beautiful chocolate brown eyes, mouth that should have been too big but somehow fit her perfectly. She was, what—forty-four now? Forty-five?

"What happened?" Tully asked, pulling her hand away from Cloud's forehead.

She missed the comfort of that touch more than she had any right to. "I got beat up," she said, adding, "by a stranger," so she looked slightly less pathetic.

"I wasn't asking what put you here. I was asking what happened to you."

"I guess your precious grandmother never told you, huh?" She wished she could find the anger that had fueled her for so many years, but it was just gone. All she had left was sadness and regret and exhaustion. How could she explain to her daughter what she'd never been able to understand for herself? There was a darkness in her, a weakness that had swallowed her whole. All her life she had tried to protect Tully from the truth of it, keeping her away the way you'd tell a child to stand back from a cliff's edge. It was too late to undo all that damage now.

None of it mattered anymore, and knowing the truth wouldn't help either of them. Maybe there had been a time, long ago, when talking would have made a difference, but not anymore. Tully was still talking—of course—but Cloud wasn't listening. She knew what Tully wanted, what she needed, but Cloud didn't have the strength or the clarity to be what her daughter needed. She never had. "Forget about me."

"I wish I could, but you're my mother."

"You break my heart," Cloud said quietly.

"You break mine, too."

"I wish . . ." Cloud began, and stopped. What was the point of all this pain?

"What?"

"I wish I could be what you need, but I can't. You need to let me go."

"I don't know how to do that. After everything, you're still my mother."

"I was never your mother. We both know that."

"I'll always keep coming back. Someday you'll be ready for me."

And there it was, the whole of their relationship boiled down to its essence. Her daughter's unending need and Cloud's equally overwhelming failure. They were a broken toy that couldn't be repaired. Now Tully was talking, saying something about dreams and motherhood and holding on. All of it just made Cloud feel worse.

She closed her eyes and said, "Go away."

She could feel Tully beside her, hear her daughter breathing in the dark.

Time passed in sounds: the creaking of the floor beneath Tully's feet, the heaviness of a sigh.

Finally, after what seemed like hours of pretense, the room went quiet.

Cloud opened her one good eye and saw that Tully had fallen asleep in the chair by the wall. She pushed the covers back and got out of bed, wincing when she put weight on her bad ankle. Limping to the closet, she opened the door, hoping her belongings were there.

Luckily, she saw a brown paper bag. Her hands were shaking as she reached for it and opened it up. Inside lay the clothes she'd been wearing—torn brown painter's pants, a stained gray T-shirt, a flannel shirt, worn boots, and her underpants. No bra, no socks.

At the bottom, coiled like a little snail, lay her necklace.

Well, it wasn't really a necklace anymore, just a few bits of dried macaroni and a single bead strung on a ragged strand of string.

Cloud picked it up. The poor, pathetic little thing lay in her wrinkled palm and made her remember.

Happy birthday. I made this for you . . .

Ten-year-old Tully had held it out in her pudgy pink palms as if it were the Hope diamond. *Here, Mommy.*

What would have happened if Cloud had said, *It's perfect. I love it. I love you,* all those years ago?

She felt a fresh surge of pain. Pocketing the barely-there necklace, she dressed quickly and then glanced back at her daughter.

She limped closer and began to reach out, but when she saw her hand, pale and veiny and knobby and shaking—a witch's hand—she drew it back without even touching her daughter's sleeve.

She had no right to touch this woman, no right to yearn for what had never been, no right even to regret.

At that, she thought: *I need a drink.* She glanced at her daughter one last time and then opened the door. Moving cautiously down one hallway and then another, she made her way to an exit.

Outside, the darkness of Seattle swallowed her, and once again she was invisible.

✦

Reaching into her pocket, Cloud found the wadded-up sixty dollars she'd taken from Truc.

He'd be waking up soon, growling like a bear, stretching his arms, calling for her to bring him coffee.

She pushed the thought away and kept walking. Limping. It was dawn now. Breaks of pale gray light fell falteringly between the buildings on either side of her. When rain began to fall, spittingly, then angrily, she climbed up onto the stoop of a vacant-looking building and sat down, pulling her feet in close to her body.

Her headache was getting worse. So was the shaking in her hands. But the bars weren't open yet and neither were the liquor stores.

Across the street, dawn lit the sky behind a row of old brick buildings. Sagging sheets hung in broken windows. Beside her, a scrawny-looking cat prowled between stinking, overfull garbage cans. Rain studded bits of paper and trash to the sidewalk.

How many times in her life had she slept in a place just like this? And this was a better choice than others she'd made. Men like Truc. In the dark, they were all the same, the men she'd chosen in her life, and those who had been chosen for her. Fists and booze and anger.

She dug through her gritty pocket for the money she'd taken from Truc's wallet. Maybe, if she let it go, just dropped it into the rain, it would be an untangling of some kind, a do-over.

But what she pulled out was a business card with a dog-eared edge.

Dr. Karen Moody [funny name for a shrink]
Occidental Rehab

Written across the bottom was: *When you're ready to make a change.*

Cloud had heard these words a thousand times in her life from doctors and social workers. Even from her daughter. People pretended all the time that they could help, that they wanted to.

Cloud had never trusted them, not even back when she was Dorothy and young enough to believe in the kindness of strangers. She had thrown away dozens of cards and flyers and pamphlets like this over the years.

But now, this time, as she sat on the garbage-stinking stoop, with rain nipping at her heels, the word—*change*—filled her with longing. She glimpsed the pit of her own loneliness, saw how deep it ran, how dark it was.

Occidental.

The street was less than a block away. Was it a sign?

There had been a time when she lived her life believing in signs. The *est* and Unitarian years. She'd thrown herself into one belief system after another. The jumps into faith had always been followed by depression, moods so dark and low she could only belly-crawl her way out. Each time she had failed, and each failure had taken something from her.

The one god she'd never turned to was herself. Rehab. Sobriety. One day at a time. These words and phrases had always terrified her. What if she really *tried* to be better—saner—and she failed at that? Would there be enough of her left to save?

And yet here she was. Sixty-some years old, the girlfriend of a mean drunk, a punching bag, essentially homeless, unemployed, a drunk and a pothead. A mother and not a mother.

There already wasn't enough of her to save. This was the rock bottom she'd feared all of her life. She was beaten and down. The only way she could stand was if someone helped her up.

She was so tired of this life . . . exhausted.

It was that, the exhaustion, that did it.

She grabbed hold of the wobbly handrail and hauled herself to a shaking, unsteady stand. Gritting her teeth, she limped out into the rain and kept going.

The rehab center was housed in a small, flat-roofed brick building that dated back to Seattle's gritty pioneer beginning. The blackened concrete viaduct thundered with traffic nearby. She took a deep breath and reached for the door handle.

It was locked.

She sat down on the concrete stoop, this time unprotected by an overhang. Rain hammered her, drenched her. Her headache continued, and so did the pain in her neck and her ankle, and the shaking grew worse, but she didn't move. She sat there, coiled up like a sword fern, shivering and cold and shaking, until a sound roused her. She looked up and saw Dr. Moody standing in front of the steps, beneath a blossoming umbrella.

"I'll fail," Cloud said dully, shivering hard.

Dr. Moody came up the steps and reached out. "Come on, Dorothy. Let's go inside where it's dry."

"I guess dry is the point."

Dr. Moody laughed. "A sense of humor. That's good. You'll need it."

✦

Cloud Hart went into rehab, and forty-five days later Dorothy Hart emerged. Now she stood in her small room and packed up her few belongings: a loosely-held-together macaroni necklace and a creased, slightly blurry photograph with the date *October 1962* stamped on its scalloped white edge.

They had seemed like nothing when she walked into this building, these two small personal items. Trinkets, she would have said, but now she understood their value. They were her treasures; somehow, through all her years of alcoholism and addiction, she'd held on to them. Dr. Moody claimed that it was the Real Dorothy who'd kept them, the slivered, thin, healthy part of her who had somehow been strong enough to survive it all.

Dorothy didn't know about that. Honestly, she tried never to think about the girl she'd once been, and her life in that tract house in Rancho Flamingo. Sobriety didn't make it easier to look back. The opposite was true, in fact. Now she lived her life in moments, in breaths drawn and released, in drinks not sipped and bowls of pot not smoked. Every dry second was a triumph.

It had begun like all of her Hail Mary passes at normalcy—with a feeling of relief. Nothing was more comforting in the beginning than relinquishing control. She'd shuffled through the center and followed the rules. She'd had no mouthwash or other alcohols or drugs to give up, no bags to be searched. She'd let Dr. Moody lead her to a small room with barred windows that overlooked the gray concrete curl of the viaduct.

When the shaking started, and then the headaches intensified, she glimpsed the truth of the decision she'd made for the first time, and she'd gone crazy. There was no other word for it, although she hated the word. Her craziness had been epic—throwing chairs, pounding her head on the wall until she bled, screaming to be let go.

She'd ended up in a detox ward for seventy-two of the longest hours of her life. She remembered it in images that crawled over one another, pulled each other out of shape until nothing made sense. She remembered the smell of her own sweat, and the feel of bile rising in her throat. She'd cursed and writhed and puked and cried. She'd begged to be let out, to be given just one drink.

And then, miraculously, she'd fallen asleep and wakened in another world, washed ashore. Disorientated, still shaking, weak as a newborn puppy.

Dry.

It was hard to describe how vulnerable she'd felt, how fragile and delicate. She sat in the group therapy sessions like a ghost day after day, listening to her neighbors start their whining speeches with, *Hi, I'm Barb and I'm an alcoholic. Hi, Barb!*

It was like some horrible Kumbaya camp moment, and she'd zoned out, biting her nails until they bled, tapping her foot, thinking about how soon she could get drunk and that she didn't belong here—these guys had had overdoses and killed people in cars and been fired from jobs. They were Big-Time drunks; she was just a loser who drank too much.

She remembered when it had changed for her. It had been in morning group, about three weeks after her detox. She'd been staring down at her ragged, bleeding thumbnail, listening—barely—to fat girl Gilda complain about the time she'd been raped at a fraternity party, crying hard, spewing snot, and Dr. Moody had looked right at Cloud.

"How does that make you feel, Cloud?"

She started to laugh at the idea that the story meant anything at all to her, and then a memory floated up, bobbing to the black surface of her thoughts like a dead body.

It's dark. He's smoking. The red tip is terrible-looking. I smell smoke. Why won't you be good? You make me look bad. I'm not bad.

I know you're not.

"Cloud?"

"I used to be Dorothy" was how she'd answered, even though it made no sense.

"You can be her again," Dr. Moody had said.

"I want that," she'd said, realizing right then how true it was, how long it had been true, and how scared she was that it couldn't be.

"I know it's scary," Dr. Moody said. The bobbleheads in group nodded, murmured their agreement.

"I'm Dorothy," she'd said slowly, "and I'm an addict . . ."

That had been the beginning, maybe the only real one ever. From then on, recovery had been her addiction; honesty her drug of choice. She talked and talked and talked, told anyone who would listen about her blackouts and her mistakes and the men she'd been with—they were all the same, she saw now, a string of mean drunks with something to prove. This pattern came as no surprise when she thought about it, which she did. Endlessly. But even with her new sober-zealotry, she never named her daughter or talked about her youth. Some pains ran too deep for sharing with strangers.

"Are you ready to leave us?"

She heard Dr. Moody's kind voice and Dorothy turned.

Dr. Moody stood in the doorway. In her high-waisted, straight-legged jeans and ethnic-embroidered tunic top, she looked like exactly who she was—a woman who gave all her time and energy to helping others. Dorothy wished she had money to give to this woman who had saved her.

"I think I'm ready, but I don't feel like I am. What if—"

"One day at a time," Dr. Moody said.

It should have screamed cliché, like the words of the Serenity Prayer. Both had once made her roll her eyes. Now she knew that some things could be cliché and true at the same time.

"One day at a time," Dorothy said, nodding. She could do it that way, she hoped. Break her life into bite-sized pieces.

Dr. Moody held out a small envelope. "This is for you."

Dorothy took it, stared down at the picture of bright red cherry tomatoes on it. "Tomato seeds."

"For your organic garden."

Dorothy looked up. In the past weeks, this "plan" had come to her. She'd studied it, imagined it, dreamed it. But could she do it? Could she really move back into her parents' old investment property on Firefly Lane and rip up the overgrown rhododendrons and junipers and till the small plat of land and grow things?

She'd never successfully cared for anything in her life. She'd never succeeded, period. Not at anything. Panic began its slow, popping bubbling up inside of her.

"I'll come out on Friday," Dr. Moody said. "I'll bring my boys. We'll help you start clearing."

"Really?"

"You can do this, Dorothy. You're stronger than you think."

No. I'm not. But what choice did she have? She couldn't go back again.

"Will you contact your daughter?"

Dorothy released a heavy sigh. A parade of memories sidled into the room. All the times "Cloud" had abandoned Tully. She could change her name back to Dorothy, but Cloud was still a part of her, and she had broken her daughter's heart more times than she could count. "Not yet."

"When?"

"When I believe."

"In what?"

Dorothy looked at her counselor and saw the sadness in her dark eyes. It was understandable. Dr. Moody wanted to cure Dorothy; that was her goal. In pursuit of that cure, the doctor had put Dorothy through detox, talked her through the worst of her withdrawal, and convinced her to go on medication for mood swings. All of it had helped.

But it wasn't a cure for the past. There was no pill that offered redemption. All Dorothy could do was change and atone and hope that someday she would be strong enough to face her daughter and apologize. "In me," she said at last, and Dr. Moody nodded. It was a good answer. Something they talked about in group all the time. Believing in yourself was important—and hard for people who'd perfected the art of disappointing their friends and family. Truthfully, Dorothy said the words and tried to sound sincere, but she didn't believe in the possibility of redemption. Not for her.

✦

One day at a time, one breath at a time, one moment at a time. That was how Dorothy learned to live this new life of hers. She didn't lose her craving for drugs and alcohol and the forgetfulness they offered, nor did she forget the bad things she'd done or the hearts she'd broken. In fact, she made a point of remembering them. She became evangelical about her change. She reveled in her pain, swam in the icy waters of clarity.

She started slowly, and did things in order. She wrote to her daughter's business manager and told him she was moving into her parents' old rental house on Firefly Lane. It had been vacant for years, so she saw no reason not to claim it. As soon as she'd mailed the letter, she felt a slim thread of hope. Each day when she went to the mailbox she thought: *She'll answer.* But in January of 2006, the first year of her sober life, she heard a businesslike, *I'll forward your monthly allowance to Seventeen Firefly Lane,* from the manager and not a word from her daughter.

Of course.

Her days that first winter were a confusing mix of despair, discipline, and exhaustion. She pushed herself harder than she'd ever pushed herself before. She rose at dawn and worked in the big, flat field until nightfall, when she fell into bed so tired she sometimes forgot to brush her teeth. She ate breakfast (a banana and an organic muffin) and lunch (a turkey sandwich and an apple) in the field every day, sitting cross-legged in the tilled black earth that smelled like fecund possibility. In the evenings she rode her bike into town and attended meetings. *Hi, I'm Dorothy and I'm an addict. Hi, Dorothy!*

As odd as it sounded, the roteness of it soothed and comforted her. The strangers who stood around after the meeting, drinking bad coffee in Styrofoam cups and eating stale store-bought cookies, became friends. She'd met Myron there, and through Myron, Peggy, and through Peggy, Edgar and Owen and the organic farming community.

By June of 2006, she had cleared a quarter of an acre and rototilled a small patch of earth. She bought rabbits and built them a hutch and learned to mix their droppings with dying leaves and what little food leftovers she had into compost. She stopped chewing on her fingernails and traded her obsession for marijuana and alcohol into one for organic fruits and vegetables. She had sworn off much of the world, thinking that a life without modern choices would suit her newfound self-discipline best.

She was kneeling in the dirt, tilling with a gardening trowel, when she heard someone call out.

She put down her trowel and stood up, brushing the dirt off her oversized gloves.

A small, older woman was crossing the street, coming toward the gate. She was dressed in dark-washed jeans and a white sweatshirt that had been bedazzled to read: WORLD'S BEST GRANDMA. Her black hair had a skunklike streak of stark white along the part, and framed a round, apple-cheeked face with a pointed chin.

"Oh," the woman said, stopping abruptly. "It's you."

Dorothy peeled the gloves off and tucked them into her sagging waistband. Wiping the sweat from her forehead, she walked to the fence line. She was about to say, *I don't know you,* when a memory struck.

I'm lying on the sofa, spread-eagled, with a mound of weed on my stomach. I try to smile at the do-gooder who has just walked into the house, but I am so high all I can do is laugh and swear. Tallulah is bright red with embarrassment.

"You're oven-mitt-girl's mom," Dorothy said quietly. "From across the street."

"Margie Mularkey. And yes, to my daughter's horror, I sent her over here with a hot casserole in about 1974. You were . . . indisposed."

"High. And probably drunk."

Margie nodded. "I came to see what was going on over here. I didn't know you'd moved in. The house has been empty for a long time. I should have noticed, but . . . we've had a tough year. Been gone a lot."

"I could keep an eye on the place for you. Collect your mail." The moment the offer slipped out, Dorothy felt exposed. A nice woman like Margie Mularkey, who welcomed neighbors and probably quilted, would never accept help from someone like Dorothy.

"That would be nice. I'd appreciate it. There's a milk box on the porch. Maybe you could put the mail in there."

"I could do that."

Margie glanced away. She was looking down the empty road, staring right into the sun through her big tinted glasses. "The girls used to sneak out at night and ride their bikes on this road. They thought I didn't know." At that, her legs seemed to give out on her and Margie crumpled to the ground.

Dorothy opened the gate and went to the woman, helping her to stand. Holding on to her elbow, she guided the woman down to the patio area in the backyard, and into a dirty birchwood chair. "I . . . uh . . . haven't cleaned the outdoor furniture yet."

Margie laughed dully. "It's June. Summer just started." She reached into her pocket and pulled out a pack of cigarettes.

Dorothy sat cross-legged on the weed-choked cement patio, watching a tear slip down the woman's round cheek and splash on her veiny hand.

"Don't mind me," Margie said. "I've been holding this in too long."

"Oh."

"Katie, my daughter," Margie said, "has cancer."

Dorothy had no idea what people said at a time like this. *I'm sorry* seemed pathetic and obvious, and what else was there?

"Thank you," Margie said into the silence.

Dorothy breathed in some of the secondhand menthol smoke. "What for?"

"Not saying, 'She'll be fine,' or, worse, 'I'm sorry.'"

"Bad shit happens," Dorothy said.

"Yeah. I didn't used to know that."

"How's Tully?"

"She's with Katie now." Margie looked up. "I think she'd like it if you went to see her. She just quit her TV show."

Dorothy tried to smile but couldn't. "I'm not ready. I've hurt her a few times too many. Don't want to do it again."

"Yes," Margie said. "She's always been more fragile than she seems."

They sat there a little longer, saying nothing. Finally, Margie stood. "Well. I have to get back."

Dorothy nodded. She rose slowly and walked Margie off the patio and up to Firefly Lane. As Margie started across the street, Dorothy said, "Margie?"

Margie turned back. "Yes?"

"I'll bet she knows how much you love her. Your Katie. That would mean a lot."

Margie nodded and wiped her eyes. "Thanks, Cloud."

"I'm Dorothy now."

Margie smiled tiredly. "Dorothy, I hope you don't mind me saying this: time passes. Trust me. Strong girls suddenly get sick. Don't wait too long to see your daughter."

Twenty

✦

In October of 2006, rain fell from swollen clouds day after day, turning Dorothy's carefully tilled fields into a black and muddy mess full of cloudy puddles. Still, she went out every day, rain or shine, to care for this ground that had become the whole of her focus. She planted garlic and a mixture of winter rye and hairy vetch to cover the wet ground. She prepped the beds for crops she would plant in the spring, lining them with dolomite and layering compost down. She was busy planting when a floral delivery van turned into the driveway across the street.

Dorothy sat back on her heels and looked up at the Mularkey house. Rain threaded the view, fell from the brim of her hat in fat beads that obscured the black ribbon of Firefly Lane.

The house was empty now, she knew. The Mularkeys were either at the hospital or Kate's house every day. Dorothy had picked up their mail and stacked it carefully into piles and placed it in the silver milk delivery box. Several times she'd found the box empty and the mail gone, so she knew Bud and Margie were home occasionally, but she'd not seen either of them or their car in the past month.

She put down her trowel and stood up slowly, peeling off her gloves. Tucking them into her waistband, she picked her way out of the garden and walked across the patio and along the side yard toward the driveway.

She was at her mailbox when the delivery truck chugged back down the Mularkeys' driveway and turned left onto Firefly Lane.

She walked across the street and up the gravel driveway in her oversized rubber boots. To her right, the rolling green pasture fell away from the farmhouse and ended at the split-rail fence that delineated the property. As she approached the white farmhouse's welcoming front porch, she couldn't help thinking that this was the house that came closest to home for her daughter and Dorothy had never even been inside.

The porch was full of flower arrangements. They were on the floor, on the tables; one was even on the milk box. Dorothy felt a sinking feeling in the pit of her stomach. She plucked the envelope from a bouquet near her and opened it.

We are so sorry for your loss.
Kate will be missed.
Love, the Goldstein family

Dorothy had no idea why she felt such loss. She couldn't even summon a picture of Kate Ryan in her mind. Nothing came to her but a memory of stringy blond hair and a quiet smile.

Pot and alcohol. They'd stolen so much from her, and never had she missed her memories more.

This would break Tully's heart, pure and simple. Dorothy might not know much about her daughter, but she knew this: Kate was the ground beneath her daughter's feet, the rail that kept her from falling. She was the sister Tully had yearned for and never had; the family her daughter had wanted so desperately.

Dorothy prayed the Mularkeys didn't come home to a porch full of dead flowers—how depressing would *that* be? But what could she do to help?

She could reach out to her daughter at last.

The thought filled her with a tenuous, unexpected hope. Maybe this terrible moment would be the time to show Tully that she had changed. She hurried back down the driveway to her house. It took less than thirty minutes on the phone to find out the funeral plans. It would be held in a few days, at the Catholic church on Bainbridge Island. In a town as small as Snohomish, the news of a death of one of their own moved quickly.

For the first time in as long as Dorothy could remember, she prepared for an event. She rode her bike into town on October fifth—in the pouring rain—and had her hair cut. She could tell by the way the young girl clucked and *tsk*ed that she thought Dorothy's hair was too long and too gray, but Dorothy had a long history of being too something and she was okay with that. She didn't need to come out looking like Jane Fonda, all impossibly young and fit. She just wanted not to embarrass Tully, to show her daughter that she'd changed.

So she had her hair cut to shoulder-length and let the blackbird girl in the motorcycle boots dry it until it fell in pretty waves. Then she went to one of the small local boutiques on First Street (where she endured more clucking and *tsk*ing) and purchased a pair of simple black pants and a matching turtleneck. She had the clothes wrapped up in plastic bags and carried them out to her bicycle. By the time she got there, her hair was ruined again, but she hardly noticed. She was too consumed with the conversation going on in her head.

It's good to see you again.

I'm so sorry for your loss.

I know what she meant to you.

I'm sober now. Two hundred and ninety-seven days.

She bought a book on how to help a loved one through grief. Most of the sentences would sound ridiculous coming from her: *She's in a better place. Time will help. Prayer can be a comfort.* But some of it she could try: *I know how much she meant to you. You were lucky to have her.* She underlined some of the sentiments and practiced saying them to a mirror, pretending all the while not to see how old and broken-down she looked, the toll drugs and alcohol had taken on her skin.

On the day of the funeral, she woke to a surprisingly bright and sunny morning. She showered carefully and conditioned her hair, although she was hopeless at styling it and, really, that cut had made little difference. She still had a vague Albert-Einstein-meets-old-hippie vibe going on. What could she do about it, though? Her wrinkled face and tired-looking eyes could not be helped by makeup. With her fading eyesight and unsteady hand, she'd probably end up looking like Bette Davis in *What Ever Happened to Baby Jane?*

Still, she did her best. She brushed her teeth and dressed in her new clothes. She looked a little—very little—like Blythe Danner after a bad night with tequila, but her clothes were respectable.

She climbed onto her bike and rode into town, grateful beyond measure for the sunshine, but it was cold out.

Downtown, she splurged on a soy milk chai tea latte and waited impatiently for the bus, going through those sentences in her head again. When the bus pulled up, she got on.

She could do this. She could go to her daughter and help her. At last.

She stared out the window, seeing a ghostly version of her own face. Beyond was the freeway, and beyond that, an unexpected memory.

A parking lot full of cars. Maple trees providing shade, a city park with kids playing . . .

I am stoned out of my mind. It's the only way.

I am here because my mother has died.

"Mom. Thank God you're here."

My daughter is so beautiful, and the sight of her makes me impossibly sad. Is she sixteen? How can I not know for sure? The darkness swells, slops over the edges, and I feel myself getting smaller, weaker.

"You knew I'd need you."

Tully is smiling. Smiling.

I think of how often I have tried to be what this girl needed, and how often and how profoundly I have failed. Tully is talking, saying more, and I feel the start of tears. I stumble forward, say, "Look at me."

"I'm looking."

"No. Look. I can't help you."

Tully frowns and steps back. "But I need you."

Dorothy turned away from the window. What had she said to her daughter on that day of her own mother's funeral? She couldn't remember now. All she remembered was leaving . . . and the dark, dark days—months, years—that followed. The men. The drugs.

She'd let her daughter become a ward of the state that day.

The bus pulled up to the ferry terminal and came to a wheezing stop. Dorothy disembarked and boarded the ferry for Bainbridge.

Had she ever been there before? She didn't think so; or, if she had, she must have been drunk or high, because she couldn't remember it.

The island was pretty in a well-tended way, with quaint shops and quiet streets. Definitely the kind of place where everybody knew everybody and someone like her would stand out, even in new, clean clothes.

She knew that if she weren't on her meds she'd be whack right now. But with her meds she was okay. Fuzzy-thinking, a little dull in the mind, but steady, and that was what mattered. For years she'd hated the fuzziness of meds enough to suffer through the Ferris Wheel highs and subterranean lows. But now she would take steady any day.

Although, honestly, she wanted a drink. Just one.

She put her hand in her coat pocket and clutched the nine-month-clean chip she had earned at the last meeting. Soon, she'd get the ten-month. One day at a time.

She moved with the steady stream of locals and tourists, off the boat, up the terminal, and out into the sunshine. Following her directions, she walked through town, which was quiet on this early October day. The distance to the Catholic church was farther than she'd thought and so when she arrived, she was late. The service had already begun. The big double doors were closed. She had crashed a lot of things in her life, but she wasn't about to go into that church alone.

She found a bench beneath a pair of maple trees at the edge of the parking lot and sat beneath their multicolored canopy. Above her, an autumn leaf released its last tenuous hold on life and fluttered to the ground. Dorothy brushed it from her face and stared down at her hands, thinking.

When she looked up again, Tully stood alone in front of the church. Dorothy got to her feet and started to move forward, but then she stopped.

The parking lot was filling up with people. Mourners poured out of the church. Several of them collected around Tully.

Kate's family, probably. A gorgeous man, a beautiful teenaged girl, and two mop-headed boys.

Margie hugged Tully, who sobbed in her arms.

Dorothy stepped back into the shadows beneath the tree. She'd been an idiot to think she had a place here, that her presence would help.

Her daughter *had* people who cared about her, and about whom she cared. They would gather together on this day and ease their grief by sharing it. Wasn't that what people did? What families did?

It made Dorothy feel inestimably sad and old and tired. She'd come all this way, following a beam of light that couldn't be grasped.

✦

It's no good to pretend, you know. And we don't have all the time in the world. I hear Kate's voice, and honestly, I wish I didn't. *You see now, don't you?*

I am like a little kid, squeezing my eyes shut, certain that in my self-imposed darkness I can't be seen. That's what I want right now: to disappear. I don't want to do this whole going-into-the-light/looking-back-on-your-life thing anymore. It hurts too much.

You're hiding from me.

"Yeah. No shit. You dead people don't miss a thing."

I feel her coming closer; it is like firelight drawing near. Tiny yellow white stars burst across the black expanse of my vision. I smell lavender and Love's Baby Soft spray and . . . pot smoke.

That takes me back.

Open your eyes.

The way she says it breaks my resolve. I slowly do as she asks, but even before I see the poster of David Cassidy and hear Elton John singing "Goodbye Yellow Brick Road," I know where I am. Back in my bedroom in the house on Firefly Lane. My old Close 'n Play is on the bedside table, along with a stack of 45s.

Dorothy. "Goodbye Yellow Brick Road." The Emerald City. How had I missed all the obvious clues in my life? I was always a little girl, lost in Oz, looking for a way to believe that there was no place like home . . .

Kate is beside me. We are sitting on my bed in the house on Firefly Lane, leaning against the rickety headboard. A yellow poster that reads WAR IS NOT HEALTHY FOR CHILDREN AND OTHER LIVING THINGS fills my vision.

You see now, don't you? Kate says again, more quietly this time.

I don't want to think about it all—the day my mother showed up to "help" me with my "addiction" and how badly I handled it. What else have I been wrong about? But before I can answer her, there is another voice, whispering in my ear. *I'm sorry.*

Oh, my God.

It is my mother. The bedroom dissolves around me. I smell disinfectant.

I turn to look at Kate. "She's here? Or there? At the hospital, I mean?"

Listen, Kate says gently. *Close your eyes.*

✦

September 3, 2010
4:57 P.M.

"Lady? Lady? Are you getting out?"

Dorothy came back to the present with a start. She was in the cab, parked in front of the hospital's emergency entrance. She paid the cabbie, giving much too big a tip, and then she opened the door and stepped out into the rain.

The walk to the front door unnerved her. Every footstep felt like an act of unimaginable will, and God knew her will had always had the strength of warm wax.

As she moved into the austere lobby, she felt self-conscious, a ragged old hippie in a high-tech world.

At the reception desk, she stopped, cleared her throat. "I'm Doro— Cloud Hart," she said quietly. The old name pinched like a bad bra, but it was how Tully knew her. "Tully Hart's mother."

The woman at the desk nodded, gave her the room number.

Gritting her teeth, fisting her cold hands, Dorothy headed for the elevator and rode it up to the fourth floor. There, feeling her nerves tightening with every step, she followed the whitish linoleum floor to the waiting room, which was mostly empty—mustard-colored chairs, a woman at a desk, a pair of TVs on without sound. Vanna White turned the letter R on-screen.

The smell of the place—disinfectant and cafeteria food and despair—hit her hard. She'd spent a considerable effort in her life to stay away from hospitals, although she'd awakened in them a few times.

Margie sat in the waiting room. At Dorothy's arrival, she put down her knitting and stood.

Beside her was that good-looking man who'd been Kate's husband. He saw Margie stand, followed her gaze, and frowned. Then he slowly got to his feet, too. Dorothy had seen him from a distance at the funeral; he looked grayer now. Thinner.

Margie came forward, her hands outstretched. "I'm glad you got my note. I had to have Bud pin it on the door. I didn't have time to go looking for you."

"Thank you," Dorothy said. "How is she?"

"Our girl is a fighter," Margie said.

Dorothy felt a squeeze of emotion—longing, maybe. *Our* girl. As if she and Margie were both mothers to Tully. Dorothy wished it were true—but only Margie could claim that connection, really. She started to say something—she had no idea what—when *he* approached them. At the shuttered anger in his eyes, Dorothy's voice turned to ash.

"You remember Johnny," Margie said. "Katie's husband and Tully's friend."

"We met years ago," Dorothy said quietly. It was not a good memory.

"You've never done anything but hurt her," he said in a soft voice.

"I know."

"If you hurt her now, it's me you'll be dealing with. You got that?"

Dorothy swallowed hard but didn't look away. "Thank you."

He frowned. "For what?"

"Loving her."

He looked surprised by that.

Margie took Dorothy by the arm and led her down the hallway, and into a bright ICU enclave with glass-walled rooms that fanned out behind a central nurses' station desk. There, Margie let go of her long enough to go speak to the woman at the desk.

"Okay," Margie said when she returned. "That's her room right there. You can go talk to her."

"She won't want me here."

"Just talk to her, Dorothy. The doctors think it helps."

Dorothy glanced over at the glass window; inside, a utilitarian curtain shielded the bed from view.

"Just *talk* to her."

Dorothy nodded. She stepped forward, shuffling like an invalid, her fear expanding with every step, filling her lungs, aching. Invalid. In valid. That was her.

Her hand was literally shaking as she opened the door.

Dorothy took a deep breath and went toward the bed.

Tully lay there, surrounded by buzzing, thumping, whooshing machines. A clear plastic tube invaded her slack mouth. Her face was misshapen and scraped and bruised. She was bald and a plastic tube went into her head. One arm was in a cast.

Dorothy pulled a chair up to the bed and sat down. She knew what Tully would want to hear. It was what her daughter had come to Snohomish for, what she'd asked for in a thousand ways over the years. The truth. Dorothy's story. Their story.

She could do this. At last. She *could*. This was what her daughter needed from her. She drew in a deep breath.

"When I was a kid, California was beautiful citrus groves instead of parking lots and freeways. Oil derricks pumping continually up and down on the hillsides, like giant rusty praying mantises. The first Golden Arches. I remember when they started building Disneyland and my father thought Walt was 'bat shit crazy' for pumping so much money into a kids' carnival," she said quietly, slowly, finding her way word by word.

"We were Ukrainian.

"Did you know that?

"No, of course you didn't. I never told you anything about my life or your heritage. I guess it's time now.

"You've always wanted to know my story. So here goes.

"As a girl, I . . .

thought it meant "ugly"—Ukrainian—and it might as well have. It was the first of the secrets I learned to keep.

Fitting in. Not standing out. Being Americans. This is what mattered to my parents in the plastic, shiny world of the fifties.

You can't understand how this could be, I'll bet. You are a child of the seventies, wild and free. You grew up around people who wore a whole different kind of headband.

In the fifties, girls were like dolls.

Extensions of our parents. Belongings. We were expected to be perfect, with nothing on our minds except pleasing our parents, getting good grades, and marrying the right boy. It's hard to think now, in this modern world, how much it mattered that you marry well.

We were to be nice and pliable and make cocktails and babies, but neither until after marriage.

We lived in one of the first cul-de-sacs in Orange County. Rancho Flamingo, it was called, a horseshoe plan of ranch-style houses set on identical lots, with green, well-tended lawns out front. If you had *really* made it, you had a swimming pool.

Pool parties were all the rage. I remember seeing my mother's friends clustered by the pool, wearing bathing suits and flower-dabbed rubber swim caps, smoking and drinking as the men drank martinis by the barbecue. They were all drunk by the time someone finally jumped in.

Weekends were a movable feast; one tropical-themed pool party after another. The weird thing is, I only remember watching the adults. Children were to be seen and not heard back then.

Honestly, I never thought much about it when I was little. I blended into the woodwork. No one paid me any mind. I was an awkward girl, with frizzy hair and thick eyebrows that overshadowed my face. My dad used to say I looked like a Jew—he would swear when he said it, and I had no idea why it bothered him—why *I* bothered him—but it was obvious I did. Mom told me to just stay quiet and be a good girl.

I did.

I kept quiet, so quiet I lost the few friends I'd had in grade school. By junior high I was an outcast, or maybe not an outcast, maybe just invisible. By then the world was changing, but we didn't know it. Terrible things—injustices—were happening all around us, but we didn't see. We looked away. *They*—black people, Hispanics, Jews—were "them," not "us." My parents never mentioned our own ethnicity as they spewed their racism over cocktails. The first time I asked if Ukrainians were like Communists, I was fourteen years old. My dad smacked me across the face.

I ran to my mother. She was in the kitchen, standing at the avocado-green Formica counter, wearing an apron over her pale blue housedress, smoking a cigarette as she poured onion soup mix into a bowl of sour cream.

I was crying so hard snot was leaking into my mouth and I knew a bruise was forming on my cheek. *Dad hit me,* I said.

She turned slowly, a cigarette in one hand and that empty soup mix packet in the other. She stared at me through her jeweled, cat's-eye black glasses and asked, *What did you do?*

Me? I drew in a great, gulping breath. She took a drag of her Lucky Strike in its holder and exhaled.

That's when I understood it was my fault. I'd done something bad. Wrong. And I'd been punished. No matter how much I thought about it, though, I couldn't figure out what I'd done that was so bad.

But I knew I couldn't tell anyone.

That was the start of me falling. I don't know how else to describe it. And then it got worse. In the summer, I began to change physically. I started my period (*You're a woman now,* my mother said, handing me a pad and belt, *don't embarrass us or get in trouble*), and my breasts developed and I lost layers of baby fat. The first time I showed up at a pool party in an Annette Funicello two-piece, I heard Mr. Orrowan from next door drop his martini glass. My father grabbed me by the arm so hard it felt as if the bone snapped as he hauled me into the house and pushed me into a corner and told me I looked like a tramp.

The way he looked at me was worse than the slap across the face. I knew he wanted something from me, something dark and inexplicable, but I didn't understand.

Then.

✦

He came into my room one night when I was fifteen. He was drunk and smelled like cigarettes and he hurt me. I don't think I have to say any more about that.

Afterward, he said it was my fault for dressing like a tramp. I believed him. He was my dad. I was used to believing him.

I tried to tell my mom—more than once—but she avoided me now, snapped at me over the smallest things. She was constantly telling me to go to my room or go for a walk. She couldn't stand the sight of me. That was obvious.

After that, I tried to disappear. I buttoned my sweaters to my throat and wore no makeup at all. I talked to no one, made no new friends, and lost the few I'd had.

My life went like that for months. My dad got drunker and angrier and meaner, and I got quieter and more depressed and more hopeless, but I thought I was okay. You know, handling it, until one day in class when a boy pointed at me and laughed and everyone joined in. Or I thought they did. It felt like that scene in *Suddenly, Last Summer* where the boys turn on Liz Taylor and the guy she's with. Ravenous and hungry and pushing. I started screaming and crying and pulling at my hair. The classroom went silent. I heard the quiet and looked up, horrified at what I'd done. The teacher asked what was wrong with me and I just stared up at her until she snorted in disapproval and sent me to the principal's office.

Appearances. That's what mattered to my parents. They didn't care *why* I'd cried in class, or pulled out my own hair, just that I'd done it in public.

Twenty-one

✦

They said the hospital was for my own good.

You're a bad girl, Dorothy. Everyone has problems, why are you so selfish? Of course your father loves you. Why would you say such terrible things?

You think there aren't parallel universes, but there are. They can exist inside of you. You can be an ordinary girl one minute, and an empty shell the next. You can turn a corner—or open your eyes in your own dark bedroom—and step into a world that looks like yours but isn't.

The hospital—they called it a sanatorium—was in another city. Even now I couldn't tell you where. It could have been Mars.

They put me in a straitjacket. Wouldn't want me hurting myself, or so said the men in white who came for me.

So there I was. A sixteen-year-old girl with bald spots, trussed up like a goose and screaming. My mom cried every time she looked at me but not because I was in pain. Because I was so loud. My dad wouldn't even come with us.

Take care of it, Ma, he said.

It.

When we got to the place, it looked like a prison on a hill.

Will you be good? We'll take off the straitjacket if you'll be good.

I promised to be good, which I knew meant quiet. In the fifties, good girls were quiet girls. They unwrapped me and let me walk up these wide stone steps. Mom walked beside me, but not close enough to touch me, as if I'd contracted some disease she thought might be communicable. I walked in this fog where I was both awake and asleep. I learned later that they'd drugged me. I don't remember it, though. I just remember going up those steps; it was like being underwater. I knew where I was and what I was seeing, but it was all hazy and the proportions were wrong.

I wanted so much for my mom to hold my hand. I'm pretty sure I kept whimpering at her, which only made her walk faster. Click, click, click. That's the sound her heels made on the stone steps. She was holding on to the patent leather strap of her handbag so tightly I thought the leather would rip.

Inside, everyone wore white and looked grim. I think that's when I noticed the bars on the windows. I remember thinking I was so insubstantial I could float away, through the bars, if I really wanted to.

The doctor's name was Corduroy. Or Velvet. Some fabric. He had a pinched mouth and an alcoholic's nose. When I saw him I started to laugh. I thought his nose looked like a red parachute opening up and I laughed so hard I started to cry, and my mother hissed at me to *behave, for God's sake,* and her fingers clenched around the strap again.

Sit down, Miss Hart.

I did as I was told, and as I did it, I stopped laughing. I became aware of the hushed silence in the office, and then of the weird light. There were no windows. I guessed too many people had looked at Mr. Cotton's parachute nose and jumped.

Do you know why you're here? Dr. Silk asked me.

I'm fine now.

No, Dorothy. "Fine" girls don't pull their own hair and scream and make wild accusations about people who love them.

That's right, my mother said crisply. *Poor Winston is beside himself. What's wrong with her?*

I looked helplessly at Dr. Wool. He said, *We can help you feel better if you're a good girl.*

I didn't believe him. I turned to my mom and begged to be taken home, where I swore I'd be better.

I ended up on my knees beside her, yelling. I told her I didn't mean to do it and that I was sorry. *You see?* she said to Dr. Silk. *You see?*

I couldn't make her understand how sorry I was, and how scared, and I started screaming and crying. I knew it was wrong—bad, too loud. I fell forward, hit my head on the hard wooden arm of my mother's chair.

I heard my mother scream, MAKE HER STOP DOING THAT.

I felt someone—people—come up behind me, grabbing me, holding me.

When I woke up, however much later it was, I was in a bed, with my wrists and ankles strapped down so tightly I couldn't move.

People in white began appearing around me, springing into place like those targets on a wheel in a carnival. I remember wanting to scream, trying to, but no sound came out. They were working on me and around me without even really seeing me.

I heard a rolling sound and realized I could still turn my head, although it took effort. A nurse—I later learned her name was Helen—wheeled a machine into the room, up to the bed.

Someone touched my head, smeared a cold goo into my temples. I turned my head away and heard a voice say, *Shit,* and felt fingers tangle in my hair.

Helen leaned over me, so close I could see the tiny black hairs in her nostrils. *Don't be afraid. It'll be over in no time.*

I felt the sting of tears. Pathetic, that such a small kindness could make me cry.

Dr. Seersucker came in next, his face pursed up, his nose preceding him. He leaned over me without a word and fit cold, flat metal plates to either side of my head. It felt like rounds of ice, both freezing and burning, and I started to sing.

Sing.

What the hell was I thinking? No wonder they thought I was crazy. I lay there, tears leaking out of my eyes, singing "Rock Around the Clock" at the top of my lungs.

The doctor clamped a strap around my head. I tried to tell him he was hurting me, scaring me, but I couldn't seem to stop singing. He jammed something in my mouth and I gagged.

Everyone stepped back from me and I remembered thinking, *Bomb! They've strapped a bomb to my head and I'm going to blow up.* I tried to spit out the thing in my mouth and then . . .

The jolt is impossible to describe. I know now it was a bolt of electricity burning through me. I shook like a rag doll and peed my pants. The noise was a high, piercing *whirrrrrr.* I thought my bones would snap. When it finally let me go, I sagged onto the bed lifelessly, feeling as close to dead as I could imagine. I heard a tiny *drip-drip-drip* of my urine falling onto the linoleum floor.

There, Helen said, *that wasn't so bad, now, was it?*

I closed my eyes and prayed to Jesus to take me. I had no idea what I'd done that was terrible enough to warrant this punishment, and I wanted a mom, but not *my* mom, and I certainly didn't want my dad. I guess I wanted someone to hold me and love me and tell me it would be okay.

But . . . well, if wishes were horses, all beggars would ride, right?

You might think I am stupid because you've seen me high so much of the time, but I'm smart. It took no time for me to learn where I'd screwed up. Oh, I knew what had been expected of me before I arrived at the hospital, but I hadn't known the cost of changing lanes. I learned. Boy, did I learn.

Be good. Be quiet. Do as you're told. Answer direct questions with answers, never say you don't know, never say your father hurts you. Don't tell them that your mother knows what's happening to you and doesn't care. Oh, no. And never say you're sorry. He hates that most of all.

I'd gone into the hospital broken. But I learned how to gather up the pieces and hold them tightly to my chest. I nodded and smiled and took whatever pills they gave me and asked when my mother was coming. I didn't make friends because the other girls were "bad" and damaged. My mother would never approve. How could I be friends with a girl who'd slit her wrists or set her family dog on fire?

I kept to myself. Kept quiet. Smiled.

Time passed oddly in there. I remember seeing the leaves turn color and fall to the ground, but that's my only way to judge the passing of the days. One day, after another shock treatment, I was in the "game room"—they called it that because there were checkerboards on the tables, I guess. I was in a wheelchair, facing the window. My hands had started shaking and I was trying to hide it from everyone.

Dorothy Jean?

Never had my mother's voice sounded so sweet. I turned slowly and lifted my chin so I could see her.

She looked thinner than I remembered, with her hair so precisely styled that it looked shellacked. She had on a full plaid skirt and a prim sweater with a Peter Pan collar and black horn-rimmed glasses. She was holding her purse strap in both hands, and this time she was wearing gloves.

Mommy, I said, doing my best not to cry.

How are you?

Better. I swear. Can I come home now? I'll be good.

The doctors say you can. I hope they're right. I can't believe you belong with . . . these people. She looked around, frowning.

That's why she was wearing the gloves. She didn't want to catch crazy. I guess I should have been happy that she felt okay to touch me, to breathe the air that I exhaled between us. And I tried to be happy after that, I really did. I was polite when I said goodbye to Dr. Gabardine and I shook Helen's hand and tried to smile when she told my mother what a joy I'd been to have around. I followed my mother out to her big blue Chrysler and slid into the leather bench seat. She immediately lit up a cigarette, and as she moved the car into gear, ash sprayed down onto the seat. That's how I knew she was upset. My mother didn't believe in mess.

When I got home, I saw the place. Really saw it. The one-story house, decorated to look like it was a part of a ranch, complete with a horsey weather vane and barnlike garage doors and western fretwork around the windows. Out in front, a black-faced metal jockey held out a welcome sign.

It was all such a lie, and a lie pokes through that parallel universe. Once you glimpse it, you're changed. You can't not see it.

My mom wouldn't let me get out of the car in the driveway. Not out in the open where the neighbors could see. *Stay there,* she hissed, slamming the car door and opening the garage. Once we were in the garage, I got out. I walked through the darkness and stepped into the brightness of our space-age living room with its aerodynamic, futuristic look. The ceiling slanted sharply upward and had been decorated with tiny colored rocks. Huge glass windows looked out on the Polynesian-themed backyard pool. The fireplace was set into a wall of giant rough white rocks. The furniture was sleek and silver.

My father stood by the fireplace, still dressed in his Frank Sinatra suit, holding a martini in one hand and a lit Camel cigarette in the other. The kind of cigarette John Wayne smoked—a good American smoke. He looked at me through his wire-and-tortoiseshell-framed glasses. *So you're back.*

The doctors say she's fine, Winston, my mother said.

Is she?

I should have told the old prick to go screw himself, but I just stood there, wilting like a flower beneath the punishment of his gaze. I knew now the price of making a spectacle. I was clear on who had the power in this world, and it wasn't me.

She's crying, for God's sake.

I hadn't even known it, not until he said it. But still I kept quiet. I knew now what was expected of me.

✦

When I came home from the loony bin, I was an untouchable. I had done the unthinkable in Rancho Flamingo—made a messy scene, embarrassed my parents—and after that, I was like some dangerous animal only allowed to live in your neighborhood at the end of a sturdy chain.

Nowadays, shows like yours and Dr. Phil's tell people that you need to talk about the wounds you bear and the loads you carry. In my time, it was the opposite. Some things were never spoken of and my breakdown fell in that category. On the rare occasion when my mother did accidentally refer to my time away—which she tried never to do—it was called my vacation. The only time she ever looked me in the eye and said the word *hospital* was on the very first day I came home.

I remember setting the table for dinner that night, trying to grasp what I was supposed to be. I turned slowly to look at my mother, who was in the kitchen, stirring something. Chicken à la king, I think. Her hair, still brown then—dyed, I think—was a cap of carefully controlled curls that wouldn't have looked good on anyone. Her face was what you'd call handsome today; sharp and just a little masculine, with a broad forehead and high cheekbones. She wore cat's-eye black horned-rimmed glasses and a charcoal-gray sweater set. There was not an ounce of softness in her.

Mom? I said quietly, coming up beside her.

She cocked her head just enough to look at me. *When life gives you lemons, Dorothy Jean, you make lemonade.*

But he—

Enough, she snapped. *I won't hear about it. You have to forget. Forget all of it and you'll learn to smile again in no time. As I have.* Her eyes widened behind the lenses, pleaded with me. *Please, Dorothy. Your father won't put up with this.*

I couldn't tell if she wanted to help me and didn't know how or if she didn't care. What I did know was that if I told the truth again, or showed my pain in any way, my father would send me away and she would let him do it.

And there were worse places than where I'd been. I knew that now. There had been talk in the hospital from kids with eyes as blank as chalkboards and shaking hands, talk of ice-water baths and much worse. Lobotomies.

I understood.

✦

That night, without even changing clothes, I climbed into my little-girl bed and fell into a deep and troubled sleep.

He woke me up, of course. He must have been waiting all that time. While I was away, his anger had spread out tentacles and wound around everything, growing until I could see how it was strangling him. I had humiliated him with my "lies."

He would teach me a lesson.

I told him I was sorry—a terrible mistake. He burned me with a cigarette and told me to keep my mouth shut. I just stared at him. It made him even angrier, my silence. But it was all I had. I'd learned my lesson, remember. I couldn't stop him from hurting me, but when he looked at me that night, he saw something new, too. I might tell on him again. *Girls have babies, you know,* I whispered softly. *Proof.*

He backed away and slammed the door shut. It was the last time he came to my bed, but not the last time he hurt me. All I had to do was look at him and he hit me. And I lay in bed every night now, waiting, worrying, wondering when he would change his mind and go back to his old ways.

School was worse when I got back from the sanatorium, too.

I survived it, though. I kept my head down and ignored the pointing and the snickering. I was damaged goods and everyone knew it. There was an odd comfort in it. I no longer had to pretend.

My mother couldn't stand the new me, with my baggy clothes and untended hair and sleepy eyes. Whenever she saw me, she would purse her lips and mutter, *Ach, Dorothy Jean, have you no pride?*

But I liked being on the outside, looking in. I saw so much more clearly.

We were poised on the cusp of a new world in California at the end of the plastic decade. The suburbs were opening up; forming a new American dream. Everything was spic-and-span, Mr. Clean, wash-and-wear. We had shopping malls with Tomorrowland-style rooftops, and hamburger drive-ins. As an outsider, I saw things with the clarity that distance provides. It wasn't until I lost my way that I noticed the factions that inhabited our school hallways. There were the "it" kids, the popular ones who dressed in the latest fashion and popped gum bubbles as they talked to one another and drove their parents' shiny new cars along the strip on Saturday night. They gathered in bubbling, laughing pods at Bob's Big Boy and drove up and down the street at night, waving and racing and laughing. They were the kids the teachers loved; boys who threw the winning touchdowns and girls who talked of college and spent their parents' money. They followed the rules, or seemed to, anyway, and to me they seemed golden somehow, as if their skin and hearts were impervious to the pains that assaulted me.

But by the spring of my junior year, I started noticing the other kids, the ones I hadn't seen before, the ones who lived on the wrong side of the tracks. One day they were invisible like me, and the next day they were everywhere, dressing like James Dean in *Rebel Without a Cause,* greasing their hair back, rolling packs of cigarettes in their T-shirt sleeves. Black leather jackets moved in alongside the lettermen's sweaters.

Hoods, we called them at first, and then greasers. It was supposed to be an insult, but they only laughed and lit their cigarettes and mocked their "betters." Almost overnight, rumors started swirling of fights and rumbles.

Then a "nice" boy was killed in a drag race and our community erupted with the kind of swirling, ugly anger I hadn't imagined was there before.

It spoke to me, that anger. I didn't realize how angry I'd been until it was in the air, infecting everyone. But as always, I held it inside. While I walked down the hallways—alone in a crowd, my books held close—I listened to the two groups taunting each other, the boys in black leather yelling out, *Here, chicky-chicky,* to the girls in pleated skirts, who bristled and walked away faster, their gazes hot with superiority.

On the Monday after the accident, I remember being in home ec, listening to Mrs. Peabody drone on about the importance of a stocked cupboard for a young housewife. She positively glowed when she told us how we could impress our drop-in guests with only Vienna sausages and a few other handy ingredients. She promised to show us how to make a white sauce, whatever that was.

I barely listened. I mean, who cared? But the "it" girls—the ones who spent their days draped in lettermen's sweaters and tossing their heads like horses in the starting gate, they were perched on the edges of their seats, taking notes.

When the bell rang, I was the last to leave the classroom. It was always better that way. The popular kids rarely bothered to look behind them.

I made my way cautiously through the minefield that high school hallways could be for the unpopular.

It sounded like traffic buzzing around me, only it wasn't cars making all that racket, it was the popular kids, talking all at once, making fun of everyone else.

I walked woodenly to my locker, hearing their voices raise. Not far away Judy Morgan stood by the water fountain, surrounded as she always was by her bouffant-haired pep-squad friends. A golden virgin pin decorated her Peter Pan collar.

"Hey, Hart, nice to see your hair is growing back in."

My cheeks flamed in embarrassment. I put my head down and fumbled with my lock.

I felt someone come up behind me. Suddenly the hallway went quiet. I turned.

He was tall and broad-shouldered, with enough curly black hair to set my mother's teeth on edge. He'd slicked it back, but still it wouldn't be controlled. His skin was dark—unacceptably so—and he had strong white teeth and a square jaw. He wore a white T-shirt and faded jeans. A black leather jacket hung negligently from one hand, sleeves draping on the floor.

He reached for the pack of smokes in his rolled-up sleeve. *You don't care what a bitch like her thinks, do yah?*

He lit his cigarette, right there in the hallway. The glowing tip sent fear slicing through me, but still I couldn't look away.

She's crazy, Judy said. *Perfect for you, greaser.*

Principal Moro came bustling down the hallway, pushing through the crowd, blowing her silver whistle and telling everyone to get to his or her classroom.

The boy touched my chin, made me look up, and it was like seeing a different guy altogether. He was just a kid with slicked-back black hair, smoking a cigarette in a high school hallway. *I'm Rafe Montoya,* he said.

Dorothy Jean, was all I could get out.

You don't look crazy to me, Dorothy, he said. *Are you?*

It was the first time someone had asked, really asked, and my first thought was to lie. Then I saw how he was looking at me and I said, *Maybe.*

The smile he gave me was sadder than anything I'd seen in a long while and it made this ache start up in my chest. *That just means you're paying attention, Dorothy.*

Before I could answer, Principal Moro was taking me by the arm, pulling me away from Rafe, dragging me down the hall. I stumbled along beside her.

I didn't know much about life back then, but I knew one thing for sure: good girls from Rancho Flamingo did not talk to boys with dark skin named Montoya.

But from the second I saw him, I couldn't think about anything else.

It sounds cliché, but Rafael Montoya changed the course of my life when he said those words to me. *It just means you're paying attention.*

I said them over and over in my mind as I walked home from school, studying them from every possible angle. For the first time ever, I wondered if maybe I wasn't crazy or alien. Maybe the world was as unbalanced as it felt to me.

For the whole next week, I moved through my ordinary routine in a daze. I slept, I woke, I dressed and went to school, but all of that was a camouflage. I was always thinking of him, looking for him. I knew it was wrong, dangerous, even, but I didn't care. No. That's not right. I *embraced* the wrongness of it.

I wanted to be a bad girl, suddenly. The good-girl thing had been such a disaster. I thought that being bad might break me out.

I agonized over my hair, straining to make it look like the popular girls'. I ironed it and curled it and teased it. I plucked my heavy brows until they were perfect arches above my eyes. I wore one pretty Peter Pan–collared dress after another, with coordinating sweaters tied casually around my shoulders and belts cinched tight to show off my small waist. I bleached my tennis shoes until they were so white they hurt to look at. Instead of being the first into every classroom and the last out, I did the opposite, not caring that kids stared at me when I rushed into class with the bell. Everyone noticed the change. My father's eyes darkened every time he saw me, but he kept his distance. He was afraid of me now, as afraid of me as I'd once been of him. I was unstable and I let him know it—I was crazy enough to do or say anything.

Boys started following me around, but I barely cared. I didn't want the kind of boy who wanted a girl like me. I hovered in the hallways, looking for him.

I felt myself changing. It was as if, in his absence, I took myself apart and reorganized the pieces in the image of what I imagined he would want. It sounds crazy—hell, I *was* crazy—but it felt perfectly sane to me. Saner than I'd been in years.

My father watched me closely. I felt his observation and refused to wilt beneath it. Desire had given me a new strength. I remember having dinner one night, sitting at that mustard-flecked green Formica table, eating my mother's tasteless Welsh rarebit with tomato slices and little sausages. My dad smoked through the whole meal—alternating a drag of his cigarette with a reach of the fork. He talked in staccato sentences that sounded like gunfire.

My mother chatted into every silence, as if to prove how happy and normal we were. When she said the wrong thing—asked me about my new hairdo—my dad slammed his fist on the table, rattling the white Corningware plates that were my mother's latest purchase.

Don't encourage her, he hissed. *She looks like a tramp.*

I almost said, *You'd like that, wouldn't you?* and the thought of saying it scared me so much I lurched to my feet. I knew that one wrong word could send me back to Loonyville. Just *wanting* to speak scared me.

I ducked my chin into my neck and began clearing the table. As soon as the dishes were done, I mumbled something about homework and bolted into my room, shutting the door behind me.

I can't remember now how long it went on, me waiting and hoping and looking. Two weeks at least, maybe longer. And then one day I was standing by my locker, concentrating on the numbers, when I heard him say, *I've been looking for you.*

I froze. My mouth went dry. As slowly as I've ever done anything, I turned around and found him standing too close, towering over me. *You looked for me?*

And you looked for me. Admit it.

H-how do you know that?

In answer to my question he closed the space between us. The black leather jacket he wore made a crinkling sound as he slowly lifted his arm and used one finger to tuck the hair behind my ear. At his touch, I felt this flare of longing. It was as if, for the first time, someone *saw* me. Until that second, I didn't know how much my invisibility had hurt. I wanted to be seen. More than that, I wanted his touch, and wanting it terrified me. All I'd known of sex was pain and degradation.

I knew it was bad to feel the way he made me feel, and dangerous to be excited by this boy who was wrong for me. I should have wanted to turn it off, to look away, to mumble something about it being wrong, but when he touched my chin and made me look at him, it was already too late.

His face was all hollows and planes beneath the hallway's harsh light. His hair was too long—greaser long—and almost blue in places, and his skin was too dark, but I didn't care. Before I met Rafe, a suburban-wife future lay open to me.

And then it closed. Just like that. Anyone who says that one second can't change your whole life is a fool. I wanted to break the rules. Anything for him.

He was the picture of cool, standing there smiling cockily down at me, but in him I saw the same emotions that had turned me into someone new.

Dangerous. That's what we would be together. I knew it to my bones. We would push each other every second to feel like this again.

Be with me, he said, reaching out. *Don't care about what they think.*

"They" were everyone—my parents, the neighbors, the teachers, the doctors who had treated me. None of them would approve of us. It would scare them all, and I was crazy, too.

Dangerous, I thought again.

Can we keep it quiet? I asked.

I could tell my question hurt him, and I hated that. It wasn't until later, when he took me to bed and taught me about love and passion and sex, that I told him all of it, every sordid detail of my barren, ugly life. He held me and let me cry and told me he'd never let anyone hurt me again. He kissed the tiny constellation of starburst scars on my chest and arms. Then he understood.

For months, we kept our relationship quiet and hidden . . . until I realized I was pregnant.

Twenty-two

✦

People think high school girls didn't get pregnant in my day, but we did. Some things in this world are givens, and teens having sex is one of them. The difference was that we disappeared. There were always rumors and innuendos. Girls were simply gone one day—off to visit an elderly aunt or an ill cousin—and back sometime later, thinner, usually, and quieter. Where they really went, I never knew or cared.

I loved Rafe; not in the breathless schoolgirl way of our first meeting, but thoroughly, utterly. I didn't yet know that love was fragile and your future could turn on a dime. One night in late May of my junior year, my father came home, uncharacteristically smiling, and informed my mother and me that he'd been promoted and that we were moving to Seattle. He showed us a picture of the house he'd purchased and gave my mother a peck on the cheek. She looked as stunned as I felt.

On a dime.

July first, Dad said. *That's the day we will be leaving.*

I had to tell Rafe everything. There was no more time to worry or plan. My future—unless Rafe changed it—would be in a place called Queen Anne Hill in Seattle.

As scared as I was to tell him, I was excited, too. Maybe even a little proud. We had made this, created a child out of our love, and wasn't that what I'd been raised to do?

He didn't loosen his hold on me, that night I finally told him. We were seventeen and eighteen, respectively; kids. He had less than a month of high school left. I had more than a year. We lay in "our" place, in a bower we'd made in Old Man Kreske's orange grove. There, we'd left out an old sleeping bag and a pillow. We kept our bed in a garbage bag and tucked it into a hedge when we weren't there. After school, we laid out our sleeping bag and crawled into it. On our backs, always touching, we stared up at the sky. The air smelled of ripening oranges and fertile soil and dirt baked by the sun.

A baby, he said, and suddenly I was imagining you: ten fingers, ten toes, a mop of black hair. In an instant, I fashioned a dream life for the three of us, but then he was quiet and my doubt set in. How could he want me like that, me, who was so damaged?

I can go away, I said into the silence. *To . . . wherever girls go. When I come back—*

No. This is our baby, he said fiercely. *We'll be a family.*

I had never loved anyone as much as I loved him then.

On that orange-scented afternoon, we started to plan. I knew I couldn't tell my parents. If they could lock me up and give away my child, I knew they'd do it. And I didn't think twice about quitting school, either. I was no scholar and I hadn't even begun to realize how big the world could be or how long a life could last. I was a girl of my time. I wanted to be a wife and mother.

We would leave right after his graduation. He was alone, essentially, too. His mother had died at his birth; he'd come to Southern California with an uncle, after his father deserted the family. They were migrant workers. Rafe wanted something more for himself and we were naïve enough to think we could find it together.

On the date we'd chosen for our escape, I was crazy nervous. At dinner, I couldn't get a word out. The last thing I wanted was dessert; I couldn't choke down even a bite of my mother's Ritz-cracker pie.

What's wrong with her, Ma? my dad said, frowning at me through the blue smoke of his cigarette.

Homework, I mumbled, then shot to my feet. I washed and dried the dishes while my father smoked his cigarette in between bites of pie and my mother tended to some needlework sampler with a sentimental saying. I didn't hear them talk to each other, which was hardly unusual. And really, my heart was pounding so loudly I'm not sure I could have heard their voices anyway.

I made sure everything was done perfectly, up to my father's exacting standards, before I hung the gingham dish towel over the stove's metal handle. By then, my parents had moved into the living room. They sat in their respective favorite seats—Dad in the olive-green mohair club chair with a fringe hem, and Mom at one end of the cream-colored sofa. Behind them both, bark cloth drapes in an abstract olive green, white, and red pattern framed the view of the neighbor's house.

I have a lot of homework to do tonight, I said, standing at the edge of the room like a penitent, my hands gripping together, my shoulders hunched. I was trying so hard to be good. I didn't want to anger my father even the slightest bit.

You'd best go then, he said, lighting one cigarette with another.

I rushed out of the room. Behind my closed door, I waited for them to turn off the lights, pacing, my packed suitcase stowed under the bed.

Every second felt like an hour. Through the thin walls, I heard Danny Thomas's voice singing something on the television, and from under the door I smelled my father's cigarette smoke.

At nine-fifteen, I heard them turn off the TV and lock up the house. I waited another twenty minutes, long enough for my mom to slather Noxzema on her face and pin up her hair and cover it in a net.

I was scared when I positioned pillows and stuffed animals in my bed and pulled the covers up over them. I dressed carefully in the dark. It was June, and even in Southern California it could get chilly at night. I put on a boldly colored plaid skirt and a black button-up sweater with three-quarter sleeves. I teased my hair and pulled it back in a ponytail and I opened my door.

The hallway was quiet and dark. No light shone from beneath my parents' bedroom door.

I crept through the hallway, scared by the sound of my own footsteps on the carpeting. I kept expecting to be stopped, grabbed, hit, every step, but no one followed me and no lights came on. At the back door, with its crisscross faux-barn exterior, I paused and looked back at the house.

I swore silently that I would never come back. Then I turned, saw the headlights waiting at the end of the cul-de-sac, and I ran toward my future.

✦

It wasn't until we burned through the first tank of gas that the fear set in. What would we do? How would we live, *really*? I was seventeen years old and pregnant, with no high school diploma and no job skills. Rafe was eighteen, with no family or money to fall back on. In the end, the money we had took us only as far as Northern California. Rafe did the only thing he knew. He worked on one farm after another, picking whatever was in season. We lived in tents or shacks or cabins. Whatever we could find.

I remember always being tired and broke and dusty and lonely. He wouldn't let me work in my condition, and I didn't mind. Instead, I stayed in whatever hovel we'd found and tried to make it homey. We meant to get married. At first I wasn't old enough, and later, after I'd turned eighteen, the world had begun to change around us, and it swept us into the chaos. We told ourselves that no piece of paper mattered to people in love.

We were happy. I remember that. I loved your father. Even when we both started to change, I hung on.

The day you were born—in a tent in a field in Salinas, by the way—I felt empowered and overwhelmed by love. We named you

Tallulah because we knew you would be extraordinary, and Rose because your pink skin was the softest, sweetest thing I'd ever touched.

I did love you. I *do*.

But something happened to me when you were born. I started having nightmares about my father. Nowadays, someone would tell a young mother about postpartum depression, but not back then, at least not in a migrant camp in Salinas. In our cramped, dusty little tent, I would wake in the middle of the night, screaming. The scars of my cigarette burns seemed to throb in pain. Sometimes I thought I saw them glowing through my clothes. Rafe couldn't understand.

I started to remember how crazy felt and to feel that way again. It scared me so badly I shut up and just tried to be good. But Rafe didn't want me to be good, to be quiet; he kept grabbing me, shaking me, begging me to tell him what was wrong. One night, when he was crazed with worry, we started fighting. Our first real fight. He wanted something from me I couldn't give. He pulled away from me, or I pushed him away. I can't remember. Anyway, he stormed out, and in his absence I fell apart. I knew I'd been bad, that I'd lost him, that he'd never really loved me—how could he? When he finally came home you were naked and screaming and you'd pooped all over the floor, and I just sat there, dazed, staring at you. He called me crazy and I . . . snapped. I slapped him in the face as hard as I could.

It was awful. The police were called. They put handcuffs on Rafe and took him away and made me give them my driver's license. That was 1962, remember. I was an adult, a mother, but they called my father. In those days, my mother didn't even have her own credit card. My father said hold me and they did.

I sat in a stinky dirty cell in the jail for hours. Long enough for Rafe to be fingerprinted and booked for assault (I was a white girl, remember). Some sour-faced woman from social services took you away from me, clucking at how dirty you were. I should have been screaming for you, reaching out my empty arms, demanding my child's return. But I sat there, weighed down by a despair so bleak I couldn't breathe, by a sorrow that seemed impossible to dispel. I was crazy. I knew that now.

How long was I there? I still don't know. In the morning I tried to tell the police I'd lied about Rafe hitting me, but they didn't care. They kept me locked up "for my own safety" until my father came for me.

✦

The hospital they sent me to the second time was much worse than the first. I should have screamed and fought and clawed to get away. I don't know why I didn't. I just stood by my mother as she led me up the stone steps and into a building that smelled like death and rubbing alcohol and old urine.

Dorothy ran away and had a baby and beat up her boyfriend. Now she won't speak.

That was when I started to lose big chunks of time, somewhere in that white, smelly building with the barred-and-chicken-wired windows.

I have memories of that place, but I can't talk about them. Still. After all this time. The gist of it is this: medications. Elavil for depression, chloral hydrate for sleep, something I can't remember for anxiety. And electroshock and ice baths . . . and . . . anyway, they said it was for my own good. I knew better at first, but Thorazine turned me into a zombie; light began to hurt my eyes and my skin dried up and started to wrinkle, and my face swelled. When I found the energy to get up and look in the mirror, I knew they were right. I was sick and needed help. They only wanted to make me better. All I had to do to get better was be a good girl again. Stop swearing and fighting and lying about my father and demanding my child.

I was there for two years.

✦

I left the hospital a different person. Drained. That's the best way I can put it. I thought I had known fear before those doors banged shut behind me, before I'd learned to see the sky through metal bars and chicken wire, but I was wrong in that. When I came out, my memory was shaky—time leapt away from me sometimes and there were chunks of my life I couldn't remember.

What I remembered was love. It was the slimmest of strands, my memory of it, but it kept me alive in there. I clung to my memories in the dark, fingering them like a rosary. *He loves me.* I told myself this over and over. *I'm not alone.*

And there was you.

I kept an image of you in my mind through all of it—your pink cheeks and chocolate brown eyes—Rafe's eyes—and the way you launched forward when you were trying to crawl.

When they let me out—finally—I shuffled out of the hospital ward in clothes that I didn't recognize as my own.

My mother stood waiting for me, her gloved hands holding the strap of her purse. She wore a staid brown short-sleeve dress with a tiny white belt at her waist. Her hair looked like a swim cap. She pursed her lips and peered at me through her cat's-eye glasses.

Are you better now?

The question exhausted me, but I held that tiredness in. *I am. How's Tallulah?*

My mother gave a little sigh of displeasure and I knew I wasn't supposed to ask. *We've told everyone she's our niece. They know we went to court to get custody, so don't say anything.*

You took her away from me?

Look at you. Your father was right. You have no business raising a child.

My father, was all I said, but it was enough. My mother's hackles rose up.

Don't start that again. She took me by the arm and led me out of the hospital and down the steps and into a new sky-blue Chevrolet Impala. All I could think about was saving you from that terrible house where *he* lived, but I knew I would have to be smart. If I screwed up again, they might find a way to make sure I never gave them trouble again. I'd seen how they did it, in those places back then. The bald heads and scars of surgery; the blank eyes and shuffling feet of patients who drooled and peed where they stood.

The drive home took more than two hours. I remember watching the freeway pass beside me and realizing that I didn't know this city at all. My parents lived in the shadow of this weird new thing called a Space Needle that looked like an alien ship stuck on top of a tower. I don't remember a single word passing between us until we pulled into the garage.

It helped you, didn't it? my mom said, and I saw a glimmer of worry in her eyes. *They told us you needed help.*

I knew I could never tell her the truth—if I could even find it anymore. *I'm better,* I said dully.

But when I walked into their new house, full of the furniture of my youth, and smelling of my dad's Old Spice aftershave and Camel cigarettes, I felt so sick I ran to the kitchen sink and threw up.

✦

When I first saw you again, I started to cry.

Dorothy, don't upset her, my mother said sharply. *She doesn't know you.*

She wouldn't let me touch you. My mother was sure my poison would infect you somehow, and how could I disagree?

You seemed happy with her, and she smiled around you, even laughed. I couldn't remember ever making her as happy as you did. You had your own room and lots of toys, and she rocked you to sleep. That first night home, I stood in the doorway of your room and watched her sing "Hush, Little Baby" to you.

I felt my father come up behind me; the air turned cold. He eased up too close, put a hand on my hip, and whispered in my ear, *She's going to be a looker. Your little wetback.*

I spun around. *Don't you even* look *at my daughter.*

He smiled. *I'll do what I want. Don't you know that by now?*

I screamed in rage and pushed him away from me. His eyes widened as he lost his balance. He reached out for me and I backed away, watching him tumble down the hardwood stairs—rolling, thumping, cracking, banisters breaking. When he was still, I went down to stand beside him. Blood seeped out from the back of his head.

I felt a pale gray coldness descend around me; it cut me off, separated me. I dropped to my knees in the blood beside him. "I hate you," I said, hoping these were the last words he'd ever hear. When I heard my mother's voice, I looked up.

What have you done? my mother screamed. She had you in her arms; you were sleeping. Even her cries didn't waken you.

He's dead, I said.

Oh, my Lord. Winston! My mother ran back into the room and I could hear her calling the police.

I ran up after her, caught her as she was hanging up.

She turned. *I'll get you help,* she said.

Help.

I knew what that meant. Electroshock and ice baths and barred windows and medications that made me forget everything and everyone.

Give her to me, I pleaded.

She's not safe with you. My mother's arms tightened around you. I saw how she was fighting for you and it hurt me so much I couldn't breathe.

Why didn't you fight him for me?

How?

You know how. You know what he did to me.

She shook her head, saying something I couldn't hear. Then, very quietly: *I'll protect her.*

You didn't protect me.

No, she said.

I heard the sirens coming. *Give her to me,* I begged again, but I knew it was too late.

Please.

My mother shook her head.

If they found me here, they'd arrest me. I was a murderer now. My own mother had called the police, and God knew she wouldn't protect me.

I'll be back for her, I promised, crying now. *I'll find Rafe and we'll be back.*

✦

I ran out of my parents' house and crouched behind a giant rhododendron in their yard. I was still there when the police and the ambulance showed up, and the neighbors.

I wanted to hate who I'd become—a murderer—but I couldn't feel anything but happy about his death. I had saved you from him, at least. I wanted to save you from my mother, too, but really, how could I care for you alone? I was nothing. I had no job, no money, no high school diploma.

We needed Rafe to make us a family.

Rafe. His name became everything—my religion, my mantra, my destination.

I walked down to First Avenue and stuck out my thumb. When a VW bus covered in flower decals pulled over, the driver asked me where I was going.

Salinas, I said. It was all I could think of. The last place I'd seen him.

Get in.

I did. I climbed aboard and stared out the window and listened to the music coming from his scratchy radio: "Blowin' in the Wind."

You get high? he asked me, and I thought: *Why not?*

✦

They say pot isn't addictive. It was for me. Once I smoked my first joint, I couldn't stop. I needed the calm it gave me. That was when I started to live like a vampire, up all night, high all the time. I slept with men I can't remember on dirty mattresses. But everywhere I went, I asked about Rafe. In every town in California, I hitchhiked out to the local farms and asked for him in my broken Spanish, showing the only photograph I had to workers who eyed me warily.

I drifted that way for months, until I made it to Los Angeles. Alone, I hitchhiked out to Rancho Flamingo and saw the house I'd grown up in. Then I made my way to Rafe's old house. I'd never been there before, so it took me a long time to find it. I didn't expect to find him there, and I wasn't wrong. Still, someone answered the door.

His uncle. I knew the moment I saw him. He had Rafe's dark eyes—your eyes, Tully—and the same wavy hair. He looked incredibly old to me, lined and wrinkled and faded by a lifetime of hard work under a hot sun.

I'm Dorothy Hart, I said, wiping my sweaty brow.

He pushed the battered straw cowboy hat back on his head. *I know who you are. You got him put in jail.* He said it like: *Ju got heem.*

What could I say to that? *Would you tell me where he is?*

He looked at me for so long I started to feel sick. Then he made a little follow-me motion with his gnarled hand.

I let hope bloom just a little and lurched forward, up the uneven porch steps. I followed him into the clean, shadow-filled house, which smelled of lemons and something else, cigars, maybe, and roasting meat.

At a small, soot-stained fireplace, the old man stopped. His shoulders sagged and he turned to me. *He loved you.*

I saw Rafe in that man's black, sad eyes, and love tightened like a clamp around my heart. How could I tell this man my shame—that

I'd been chained like an animal for years? That I would have cut off my arm to get free? *I love him, too. I do. I know he thinks I ran away, but—*

Then it sank in.

Loved you. *Loved.*

I shook my head. I didn't want to hear what he would say next.

He looked for you. Very long.

I blinked back tears.

Vietnam, he said at last.

That's when I noticed the flag folded into a small triangle and framed in wood sitting on the mantel.

We couldn't even bury him in land that he loved. There wasn't enough of him left.

Vietnam. I couldn't imagine him going there, my Rafe, with his long hair and flashing smile and tender hands.

He knew you would come looking for him, he tell me give you this.

The old man reached behind the flag and pulled out a piece of ordinary notebook paper—the kind you use in high school. It had been folded into a small square. Time and dust had turned it the color of tobacco.

My hands were shaking as I opened it.

Querida, he'd written, and my heart stopped at that. I swore I heard his voice and smelled the scent of oranges. *I love you and will always love you. When I come back, I will find you and Tallulah and we will begin again. Wait for me, querida, as I wait for you.*

I looked at the old man and saw my pain reflected in his eyes. I clutched the note—it felt like ash in my hands, impossibly fragile. I stumbled out of his house and walked until it got dark, and even then I kept walking.

The next day, when I went to the protest rally that had brought me to Los Angeles, I was still crying. My tears mixed with the dust and the dirt and turned into a war paint of loss. I stood in the middle of that huge crowd—mostly kids like me, there had to be a thousand of us—and I heard their chanting and protesting about the war, and it hit me. People were *dying* over there. And the anger that was always inside of me found a place to go.

That day was the first time I was arrested.

✦

That was the start of me losing time again. Days, weeks, even a month one time. Now I know it was because I was doing so many drugs. Pot and quaaludes and LSD. Everything seemed safe back then, and I was desperate to turn on and tune out.

You haunted me, Tully; you and your daddy. I began to see you both in the hot air rising up from the desert floor at the Mojave commune where I lived. I heard you crying when I washed dishes or got water from the cistern. Sometimes I felt your little hand touch mine and I would scream out in fear and jump. My friends just laughed and warned me about bad trips and thought LSD would help.

When I looked back—finally, when I got sober—I thought, *Of course.* It was the sixties, I was barely an adult; I'd been molested and abused and I thought it was my fault. No wonder I lost myself so completely to drugs. I became like a piece of string on some cold-water river, just bobbing along. High all the time.

Then one night, when it was so hot I couldn't get comfortable in my sleeping bag, I dreamed about my father. In my nightmare he was alive and coming for you. Once the nightmare descended into my life, nothing could get rid of it. No drugs or sex or meditation. Finally I couldn't stand it anymore. I told this guy—Pooh Bear, we called him—that I would blow him all the way to Seattle if he'd take me home. I gave him the address. The next thing I knew, there were five of us in an old VW bus, banging our way north, singing along to the Doors in a cloud of smoke. We camped out along the way, made pot brownies in a cast-iron skillet over an open fire, and dropped acid.

My nightmares turned uglier and more intense. I started seeing Rafe in the daylight, too, started thinking his ghost was following me. I heard his voice calling me a tramp and a terrible mother. I cried in my sleep all the time.

And then one day I woke up, still high, and found that we were parked in front of my mother's house. The bus was half on the street and half on the sidewalk. I don't think any of us remember parking. I climbed over the carpeted floor and jumped out of the van and onto the street. I knew I looked bad and smelled bad, but what could I do?

I stumbled across the street and went into the house.

You were right there at the kitchen table, playing with a spoon, when I opened the screen door and went inside. Somewhere upstairs, a bell tinkled.

That's Grandpa, you said, and I felt rage explode inside of me. How could he be alive? And what had he done to you?

I went up the stairs, banging into the walls, screaming for my mother. She was in her bedroom, with my father, who looked like a cadaver in a twin bed. His face was slack, gray; drool slid down his chin.

He's alive? I screamed.

Paralyzed, she said, getting to her feet.

I wanted to tell my mother I was taking you; I wanted to see the pain in her eyes. But I was so crazy, I couldn't think straight. I ran downstairs and I scooped you into my arms.

My mother ran down behind me. *He's paralyzed, Dorothy Jean. I told the police he had a stroke. I swear. You're safe. No one knows you pushed him. You can stay.*

Can your grandpa move? I asked you.

You shook your head and popped your thumb in your mouth.

Still. I had you in my arms and I couldn't let you go. I imagined redemption for myself, a new beginning for us. I imagined a life with picket fences and bikes with training wheels and Campfire Girl meetings.

So I took you.

And nearly killed you by letting you eat a brownie filled with marijuana.

It wasn't even my idea to take you to the hospital when you started flipping out. It was Pooh Bear's.

I don't know, Dot. That's, like, way too much weed for a kid. She looks . . . green.

I carried you into the emergency room and said you'd gotten into the neighbor's stash. No one believed me.

It wasn't until later, when you were asleep, that I sneaked back in and pinned your name on your shirt with my mother's phone number. It was all I could think of to do. I got it finally: I didn't deserve you.

I kissed you before I left.

I bet you don't remember any of this. I hope you don't.

✦

After that, I fell. Time became as elastic as rubber for me. Pot and 'ludes dulled my mind and stripped me of my ability to care about anything. I spent the next six years in communes and on painted-up school buses and hitchhiking by the side of the road. Mostly I was too high to even know where I was. I made it to San Francisco. The epicenter. Sex. Drugs. Rock 'n' roll. Jimi at the Fillmore. Joan and Bob at the Avalon. I don't remember anything much . . . until one day in 1970, when I looked out the van's dirty window on the way to a peace rally and saw the Space Needle.

I didn't even know we'd left California. I yelled out, *Wait! My kid lives near here.*

When we parked in front of my mother's house, I knew I shouldn't get out of the car. You were better off without me, but I was too high to care.

I stumbled out of the van and pot smoke tumbled out with me, circling me, protecting me. I went up to the front door and knocked hard. Then I tried to stand still. The effort was such a failure that I couldn't help laughing. I was so stoned, I—

✦

September 3, 2010
6:15 P.M.

Beeeeep . . .

The noise sliced through Dorothy's memories, brought her back to the present. She'd been so deep in her story that it took her a moment to clear her head. An alarm was sounding.

She lurched to her feet.

"Help!" she screamed. "Someone get in here! Please. I think her heart is stopping. Please! Now! Someone save my daughter!"

✦

The brightness around me is gorgeous; like lying inside of a star. Beside me, I hear Katie breathing. Lavender scents the night air. "She's there . . . here," I say, awed, by the very idea that my mother would come to see me.

I am listening to her voice, trying to make sense of her words. There's something about a picture, and a word—*querida*—that doesn't make sense. None of it makes sense, actually. It's sounds and pauses jumbled together. A voice that is both forgotten and etched into my very soul.

Then I hear something else. A noise that doesn't belong in this beautiful place. A beep.

No, a drone. An airplane high in the sky . . . or a mosquito buzzing by my ear.

I hear a scuffing sound. People walking on thick-soled shoes. A door clicking shut.

But there is no door. Is there?

Maybe.

An alarm goes off, blaring.

"Katie?"

I look sideways and see that I am alone. I shiver with an unexpected cold. What's wrong? Something is changing . . .

I concentrate hard, will myself to see where I really am—I know I'm in that hospital room, hooked up to life support. A grid engraves itself into existence above me. Acoustical tiles. A white ceiling, pocked with gray pinholes. Rough. Like a pumice stone or old concrete.

And suddenly I'm back in my body. I'm in a narrow bed, with metal railings that undulate like eels, flashing silver as they move. I see my mother beside me. She is screaming something about her daughter—me—and then she is stumbling away. Nurses and doctors rush in and push her aside.

The machines go silent all at once and look expectantly at me, their anthropomorphic forms straightening. They whisper among themselves, but I can't make out their words. A green line moves across a black, square face, smiling and frowning, beeping. Beside me, something whooshes and thunks.

Pain explodes in my chest, coming so fast I don't even have time to yell for Kate.

Then the green line goes flat.

Twenty-three

✦

September 3, 2010
6:26 P.M.

"She's dead. Why are we still here?"

Marah turned to Paxton. He sat on the floor in the waiting room with his long legs stretched out, crossed at the ankles. Beside him lay a brightly colored heap of food wrappers—cookies, cakes, potato chips, candy bars; he'd bought whatever was for sale in the vending machine by the elevator. He kept sending Marah to her dad for more money. She frowned at him.

"Why are you looking at me like that? On TV, when someone flat-lines, it's over. Your dad texted you, like, ten minutes ago that her heart stopped. Then the doctor wanted a meeting. We know what that's about. She's toast."

All at once, she *saw* him. It was like having the house lights go up on a decrepit theater that had looked magical in the dark. She noticed his pale skin and pierced eyebrows and blackened fingernails, and the dirt that discolored his throat.

She scrambled to her feet, almost fell in her haste, righted herself, and started to run. She skidded into Tully's ICU room just as Dr. Bevan was saying, "We've stabilized her again. Her brain activity is good, but of course we can't know anything for sure until she wakes up." He paused. "If she wakes up."

Marah pressed back against the wall. Her father and grandmother were standing by the doctor. Dorothy stood off by herself, her arms crossed tightly, her mouth crimped shut.

"We've begun warming her body temperature and we're bringing her out of the coma, but that's a slow process. Tomorrow we'll reconvene and assess her progress. We'll take her off the ventilator and see."

"Will she die when you take her off the machine?" Marah asked, surprising herself by speaking aloud. Everyone in the room looked at her.

"Come here," Dad said. She understood suddenly why he didn't want her brothers to be here.

She moved cautiously toward him. They'd been at odds for so long it felt weird, going to him for comfort, but when he lifted his arm, she sidled in close, and for a beautiful second, the bad years fell away.

"The truth is that we don't know," Dr. Bevan said. "Brain injuries are impossible to predict. She may wake up and breathe on her own, or she may breathe on her own and not wake up. Or she may not be able to breathe on her own. When she's off the medications and her body temperature is back to normal, we'll be able to assess her brain activity better." He looked from face to face. "She has been very unstable, as you know. On several occasions her heart has stopped. This is not necessarily indicative of her chances for survival, but it is worrisome." He closed the chart. "Let's meet again tomorrow and reassess."

Marah looked up at her dad. "I want to go get her iPod—the one Mom gave her. Maybe if she hears her music . . ." She couldn't finish. Hope was such a dangerous thing, so ephemeral and amorphous; it didn't fit in the concrete world of words spoken aloud.

"There's my girl," he said, squeezing her upper arm.

She remembered being his girl suddenly, how safe she used to feel. "Remember how they used to dance to 'Dancing Queen'?" She tried to smile. "They had so much fun."

"I remember," he said in a voice that was tight. She knew he was thinking of it, too: how Mom and Tully used to sit together on the deck, even when it got bad and Mom was as pale and thin as a sheet of paper, listening to their eighties music and singing along. He looked away for a moment, then smiled down at her. "Will the doorman let you into her apartment?"

"I still have a key. I'll take Pax to her house and get the iPod. Then . . ." She looked up. "We could come back to the house. If that's okay."

"Okay? We moved back to Bainbridge for you, Marah. I've kept the light on every night since you left."

✦

An hour later, Marah and Pax were in a cab, heading toward the waterfront.

"What are we, *servants*?" Paxton sat slumped beside her. He found a thread coming loose on his black T-shirt and pulled on it until a corkscrew of used thread lay in his lap and the neckline of his shirt gaped.

It was at least the tenth time he'd asked Marah this question in the last eight blocks.

She didn't answer. A moment or so later, he said, "I'm hungry. How much money did the old man give you? Can we stop at Kidd Valley for a hamburger on the way?"

Marah didn't look at him. They both knew full well that her dad had given her enough money for a burger and that Paxton would spend every cent she'd been given.

The cab pulled to a stop in front of Tully's building. Marah leaned forward in her seat and paid the cabbie, and then she followed Paxton out into the cool Seattle evening. The blue of the sky was darkening by degrees.

"I don't see why we have to do this. She can't hear shit."

Marah waved at the doorman, who frowned at her and Paxton, as almost all adults did. She led Pax through the elegant cream-colored marble lobby and into the mirrored elevator. On the top floor, they exited the elevator and went to Tully's condo.

She unlocked the door and opened it. The hush inside felt weird. There was always music playing in Tully's place. She turned on lights as she made her way down the hall.

In the living room, Paxton picked up a glass sculpture and turned it over in his hands. She almost said, *Be careful, that's a Chihuly,* but bit the warning back. It never did any good to criticize Pax. He was sensitive to the point of edgy and he could get angry in no time.

"I'm hungry," Pax said, already bored. "Is that Red Robin still down the block? A cheeseburger would be good."

Marah was happy to give him enough money to get rid of him.

"You want anything?"

"No. I'm fine."

He palmed the twenty from her dad. When he was gone, and the place was quiet again, she walked past the coffee table, where piles of mail lay strewn about. On the floor beside it lay the newest *Star* magazine, its pages open to the story.

Marah's legs almost gave out on her. Tully had been reading the magazine last night . . . before she got in her car. Here was the proof.

She looked away from the evidence of her betrayal and kept walking. The iPod station in the living room was empty, so Marah went to Tully's bedroom and looked around. Nothing by the bed. She went into Tully's big walk-in closet and came to a sudden stop.

Here, try this on, Marah. You look like a princess in that. I love dress-up, don't you?

Guilt swirled around her like dark black smoke, rising, tainting the air she breathed. She could smell it, feel it wafting over her exposed skin, raising gooseflesh. She dropped slowly to her knees, unable suddenly to stand.

He'll ruin you. That's the last thing Tully had said to her on that terrible December night when Marah had chosen Paxton over everyone else who loved her. She closed her eyes, remembering. Had it really only been nine months ago that Dad and Tully had stormed into her dorm room? It felt like a lifetime. Paxton had taken her hand and led her out into the snowy night, laughing—laughing—calling them . . .

Romeo and Juliet.

It seemed romantic at first, all that "us against them." Marah quit college and moved into the run-down apartment Paxton shared with six other kids. It was a fifth-floor walk-up in a vermin-infested building in Pioneer Square, but somehow it didn't matter that they rarely had electricity or hot water and that the toilet didn't flush. What mattered was that Paxton loved her and they could spend the night together and come and go as they wanted. She didn't mind that he had no money and no job. His poetry would make them rich someday. Besides, Marah had money. She'd saved all of her high school graduation-gift money in a savings account. During college, her dad had given her enough money that she'd never needed to crack into her own savings.

It wasn't until the money in Marah's account ran out that everything began to change. Paxton decided that marijuana was "lame" and that meth and even sometimes heroin were "where it's at." Money began to disappear from Marah's wallet—small amounts; she was never one hundred percent sure, not enough to accuse him, but it seemed to go more quickly than she expected.

She'd worked from the start. Paxton couldn't hold down a job because he needed nights to slam poetry in the clubs and days to work on his verses. She'd been happy to be his muse. Her first job had been as a night clerk at a seedy hotel, but it hadn't lasted long. After that, she'd gone from one job to the next, never able to keep one for long.

A few months ago, in June, Paxton had come home from a club one night, late, high, and told her that Seattle was "over." They packed up the next day and followed one of Paxton's new friends to Portland, where they moved into a sagging, dirty apartment with three other kids. She'd gotten her job at Dark Magick within the week. The bookstore job was different from her other jobs, but it was also the same. Long hours on her feet, helping rude people, coming home with very little money. Months passed like that.

It wasn't until ten days ago that Marah really understood the precariousness of their life together.

That night she came home to an eviction notice nailed onto the door of their apartment. She pushed open the broken door—the lock hadn't worked when they moved in and the super never cared enough to fix it—and found her roommates sitting on the living room floor, passing a pipe back and forth.

"We're being evicted," she said.

They laughed at her. Paxton rolled sideways and stared up at her through glassy, unfocused eyes. "You've got a job . . ."

For days, Marah walked around in a fog; fear set in like an iceberg, deep and solid. She didn't want to be homeless. She'd seen the street kids in Portland, panhandling, sleeping in dirty blankets on stoops, rifling through Dumpsters for food, using their money for drugs.

There was no one she could talk to about her fear, either. No mom. No best friend. The realization made her feel even more alone.

Until she remembered: *My job is to love you.*

Once she had the thought, she couldn't shake it. How many times had Tully offered to help her? *I don't judge people. I know how hard it is to be human.*

At that, she knew where she had to go.

The next day, without telling Paxton, she called in sick to work, took her last few precious dollars, and bought a bus ticket to Seattle.

She arrived at Tully's apartment at just past seven o'clock at night. She stood outside the door for a long time, fifteen minutes at least, trying to work up the nerve to knock. When she finally did, she could hardly breathe.

There was no answer.

Marah reached in her pocket and pulled out the spare key. Unlocking the door, she went inside. The place was quiet and well lit, with music playing softly from Tully's iPod in the living room. Marah could tell by the song—"Diamonds and Rust"—that it was the iPod Mom had made for Tully when she was sick. *Their songs*. Tullyand-Kate's. When had Tully played anything else?

"Tully?"

Tully came out of the bedroom, looking like a street person, with messy hair and ill-fitting clothes and tired eyes. "Marah," she said, coming to a dead stop. She seemed . . . weird. Shaky and pale. She kept blinking as if she couldn't focus.

She's high. Marah had seen it often enough in the past two years to know.

Marah knew instantly that Tully wouldn't help her. Not this Tully, who couldn't even stand up straight.

Still, Marah tried. She begged, she pleaded, she asked for money.

Tully said a lot of pretty things and her eyes filled with tears, but in the end, the answer was no.

Marah wanted to cry, she was so disappointed. "My mom said I could count on you. When she was dying, she said you'd help me and love me no matter what."

"I'm trying to, Marah. I want to help you—"

"As long as I do what you want. Paxton was right." Marah said the last words in a jangle of pain. Without even waiting for Tully's response, she ran out of the condominium. It wasn't until she was in the bus station in downtown Seattle, sitting on a cold bench, that she knew how to solve her problem. Beside her was one of those celebrity magazines. It was open to a story about Lindsay Lohan, who'd been pulled over driving a Maserati while she was on probation. The headline read STAR OUT OF CONTROL ONLY DAYS AFTER LEAVING REHAB.

Marah picked up the magazine, called the hotline number, and said, *I'm Marah Ryan, Tully Hart's goddaughter. How much would you pay for a story about her drug problem?* Even as she asked the question, she felt sick. Some things, some choices, you just knew were wrong.

"Marah? Check this out."

She heard her name as if from far away. She came to slowly, remembering where she was: kneeling in Tully's closet.

Her godmother was in the hospital, in a coma. Marah had come here to find the iPod that held all of Tully's favorite songs so that maybe—just maybe—the music could reach through the darkness and help Tully to wake up.

Marah turned slowly, saw Paxton holding a half-eaten hamburger in one hand while he pawed through Tully's jewelry box with the other. She got slowly to her feet.

"Pax—"

"No, really. Check it out." He held up a single diamond stud earring nearly the size of a pencil eraser. It flashed colored light, even in the dark closet.

"Put it back, Paxton," she said tiredly.

He gave her his best smile. "Oh, come on. Your godmother wouldn't even notice if this went missing. Think of it, Marah. We could go to San Francisco, like we've been dreaming of. You know how stuck I've been in my poetry. It's because of our money and how we don't have any. How can I be creative when you're gone all day, working?" He moved toward her. Reaching out, he pulled her close to him, pressed his hips into hers, moving suggestively. His hands slid down her back and settled on her butt, then tugged hard. "This could be our future, Mar." The intensity in his black-rimmed eyes scared her just a little.

She pulled out of his arms and stepped back. For the first time, she noticed the selfishness in his gaze, the thin rebellion in his mouth, the pale hands that were softened by laziness, the vanity in his dress.

He took the silver and black skull earring out of his earlobe and put Tully's diamond in its place. "Let's go."

He was so sure of her, so certain she would fold her will into his own. And why wouldn't he be? That was what she'd done from the beginning. In Dr. Bloom's office she'd seen a gorgeous, troubled, wrist-slashed poet who'd promised her a way through her pain. He'd let her cry in his arms and told her that song lyrics and poems could change her life. He'd told her it was okay to cut herself—more than okay, he said; it was beautiful. She'd dyed her hair and cut it with a razor blade and painted her face white in grief. Then she'd followed him into the underbelly of the world she'd known and let its darkness seduce and conceal her.

"Why do you love me, Pax?"

He looked at her.

It felt as if her heart were hanging from a thin, silver hook.

"You're my muse. You know that." He gave her a lazy smile and went back to pawing through the jewelry box.

"But you hardly write anymore."

He turned to her. She saw the anger flash in his eyes. "What do you know about it?"

And there went her heart, tearing free, falling. She couldn't help thinking about the love she'd grown up around. The way her parents loved each other and their kids. She took a step forward, feeling strangely as if she were both breaking free and growing up at the same time. She imagined the view from the living room, of Bainbridge Island, and suddenly she ached for the life she once had, for the girl she'd once been. It was all still there for her, just across the bay.

She let out a deep breath and said his name.

He looked over at her, impatience etched in his jaw, darkening his eyes. She knew how much he hated it when she questioned his art. Come to think of it, he hated to be questioned about anything. He loved her most when she was quiet and broken and cutting herself. What kind of love was that? "Yeah?"

"Kiss me, Pax," she said, moving close enough for him to take her in his arms.

He kissed her quickly; she held on to him, pulled him close, waited for his kiss to consume her as it always had.

It didn't.

She learned then that some relationships ended without fireworks or tears or regret. They ended in silence. It scared her, this unexpected choice, showed her the depth of her loneliness. No wonder she'd been running from it for years.

She knew how wounded he had been by his sister's death and his parents' abandonment. She knew that he sometimes cried in his sleep and that certain songs could turn his mood as black as ink. She knew that just saying his sister's name—Emma—could unsteady his hand. There was more to him than the poet or the goth or even the thief. Or, someday, there could be more. But he wasn't enough for her now.

"I loved you," she said.

"And I love you." He took her hand and led her out of the condo.

Marah wondered if love—or the end of it—would always hurt like this.

"I forgot something," she said at the front door, tugging free, coming to a stop. "Meet me at the elevator."

"Sure." He walked over to the elevator, pushed the button.

Marah backed into the condo, closing the door behind her. She hesitated a second, no more than that, and then she locked the door.

He came running back for her, banging on the door, screaming and shouting. Tears stung her eyes and she let them fall until he yelled, "Screw you, then, you fake bitch," and stomped away. Even after that, she sat there, slumped on the floor, her back pressed against the door. As the sound of his footsteps faded away, she pushed up her sleeve and counted the tiny white scars on the inside of her arms, wondering what in the hell she was going to do now.

✦

Marah found the iPod and packed it in a shopping bag with its portable docking station. Afterward, she moved through the condominium slowly, allowing herself to remember a thousand small moments with Tully. She found her mom's journal, too, and packed that in the bag. For someday.

When she couldn't stand it anymore—couldn't stand the oppressive silence of this place without Tully's easy laughter and endless talking—she left the condo and went down to the ferry terminal. Boarding the next boat, she took a seat in one of the booths and pulled out the iPod. She put the tiny buds in her ears and hit play. Elton John sang to her. *Goodbye . . . yellow brick ro . . . ad . . .*

She turned her head and stared out at the black Sound, watching the tiny golden lights of Bainbridge Island appear. When the ferry docked, she put the iPod back in the box and walked out to the terminal, where she caught a bus and rode it out to the turnoff to her road.

She saw her house for the first time in more than a year, and the sight of it stopped her in her tracks. The cedar shingles, stained the color of homemade caramel, looked dark on this cool night; the snow-white trim practically glowed in the golden light that shone from within.

On the porch, she paused, expecting for just a second to hear her mother's voice. *Hey, baby girl, how was your day?*

She opened the door and went inside. The house welcomed her in the way it had since she'd first come home from kindergarten, with light and sound and comfortable, overstuffed furniture. Before she could even think of what to say, she heard a door *whack* open upstairs.

"She's here! Move it or lose it, Skywalker!"

Her brothers careened out of their upstairs bedroom and came thundering down the stairs in tandem. They were both dressed in football sweats and wore identical skater-boy haircuts and had silver braces on their teeth. Wills's face was ruddy and clear and showed the first sprouts of a mustache. Lucas's face was red with acne.

They pushed each other out of the way and came together to pick her up. They laughed at her feeble efforts to get free. When she'd last seen them they'd been *boys*; now they were almost twelve, but they hugged her with the fierceness of little boys who'd missed their big sister. And she had missed them, too. She hadn't known how much until right now.

"Where's Paxton?" Wills asked when they finally let her go.

"Gone," she said quietly. "It's just me."

"Excellent," Wills said in his best stoner-boy voice, nodding his mop of hair. "That kid was a douchebag."

Marah couldn't help laughing at that.

"We missed you, Mar," Lucas said earnestly. "It was a boner move to run away."

She pulled them into another hug, this one so tight they squealed and wiggled free.

"How's Tully?" Lucas said when he drew back. "Did you see her? Dad says we can go tomorrow. She'll be awake by then, right?"

Marah's mouth went dry. She didn't know what to say, so she gave a little smile and a shrug. "Sure. Yeah."

"Cool," Wills said.

Within moments they were thundering up the stairs again, calling dibs on something.

Marah picked up the shopping bag and climbed the stairs to her old room, opening the door slowly.

Inside, nothing had changed. Her camp pictures were still on the dresser, her yearbooks were stacked alongside her Harry Potter books. She tossed the bag on the bed and walked over to her desk. She wasn't surprised to find that her hands were shaking as she picked up her old, tattered, often-read copy of *The Hobbit*. The book Mom had given her so many years ago.

I don't think you're quite ready for The Hobbit *yet, but someday soon, maybe in a few years, something will happen to hurt your feelings again. Maybe you'll feel alone with your sadness, not ready to share it with me or Daddy, and if that happens, you'll remember this book in your nightstand. You can read it then, let it take you away. It sounds silly, but it really helped me when I was thirteen.*

"I love you, Mommy," Marah had said, and her mom had laughed and said, "I just hope you remember that when you're a teenager."

But Marah had forgotten. How?

She traced the embossed gold lettering with her fingertips. *Maybe you'll feel alone with your sadness.*

Marah felt a surge of loss so keen it brought tears to her eyes and thought: *She knew me.*

Twenty-four

✦

I am back in my make-believe world, my once-upon-a-time world, with my best friend beside me. I can't picture where exactly, but I am lying in grass, staring up at a starlit sky. I hear strains of a song. I think it's Pat Benatar, reminding me that love is a battlefield. I don't know how it's possible, all this coming and going, but theology was never my strong suit. Pretty much everything I know about religion comes from *Jesus Christ Superstar.*

My pain is gone; the memory of it remains, though, like a remembered melody, distant, quiet, but there, in the back of your mind.

"Katie, how can it be raining?"

I feel drops, soft as the brush of a butterfly wing against my cheek, and for no reason that makes sense, I feel sad. This world around me—as strange as it is—made sense before. Now something is changing and I don't like it. I don't feel safe anymore. Something essential and important is wrong.

It's not raining.

Her voice has a gentleness I haven't heard before. Another change.

It's your mother. She's crying. Look.

Were my eyes closed?

I open them slowly. The blackness fades unevenly; images drizzle down, drawing light into them. Tiny grains of darkness are drawn together like metal shavings and form themselves into shapes. Light appears suddenly, and I see where I am.

The hospital room. Of course. I'm always here; it is the other places that are mirages. This is real. I can see my banged-up body in the bed; my chest rises and falls in time to the bedside machine that makes a *whiz-thunk* sound at every exhalation. A graph shows the mountainous green line that is my heartbeat. Up and down, up and down.

My mother is beside the bed. She is smaller than I remember, thinner, and her shoulders sag as if she has spent a lifetime carrying a heavy burden. She is still dressed for another era—that time of Flower Power and Maui Wowie and Woodstock. She is wearing white socks and Birkenstock sandals. But none of that is what matters.

She is crying. For me.

I don't know how to believe in her, but I don't know how to let go, either. She's my mother. After all of it, all the times she's held on to me and all the times she's let me go, she's still woven through me, a part of the fabric of my soul, and it means something, that she's here.

I feel myself straining forward, listening for her voice. It seems loud in the quiet of this room. I can tell that it is the middle of the night. Beyond the windows, it is jet-black outside.

"I've never seen you in pain," she says to my body. Her voice is almost a whisper. "I never saw you fall down the stairs or scrape your knee or fall off a bike." Tears are falling from her eyes.

"I'll tell you everything. How I became Cloud, how I tried to be good enough for you and failed. How I survived all those bad years. I'll tell you everything you want to know, but I can't do any of it if you don't wake up." She leans over the bed, looks down at me.

"I'm so proud of you," my mother says. "I never told you that, did I?"

She doesn't wipe her tears away. They fall onto my face. Leaning closer, she is almost close enough to kiss my cheek. A thing I can't ever remember her doing. "I love you, Tully." On this, her voice breaks. "Maybe you don't care, and maybe I'm too late, but I love you."

I have waited my whole life to hear those words from my mother.

Tul?

I turn to Kate, see her glowing face and her beautiful green eyes. In them, I see my whole life. Everything I've ever been, and ever wanted to be. That's what your best friend is: a mirror.

It's time, she says, and I understand at last. I have been coasting with Kate, drifting lazily down the river of my life with her beside me, but there are rapids up ahead.

I have to make a choice, but first I have to remember. I know instinctively that it will hurt.

"Will you stay with me?"

Forever, if I could.

It is time, at last, to face why my body is here, broken and hooked up to machines in this white, white room.

"Okay, then," I say, gathering my courage. "It starts with Marah. How long ago did she come to visit me? A week? Ten days? I don't know. It's late August of 2010, well after my mother's so-called intervention, and honestly, time is not my friend. I have been . . .

*trying to write my memoir, but it isn't working. A headache seems to be my con-*stant companion.

How long has it been since I left my condo? I am ashamed to admit that I can't do it anymore. I can't open the door. When I even touch the doorknob, panic washes over me and I start to tremble and shake and hyperventilate. I hate this weakness in me, am ashamed by it, but I can't make myself overcome it. For the first time in my life, my will is gone. Without it, I have nothing.

Each morning, I make a vow to myself: I will stop taking Xanax and I will leave my home and venture out into the world. I will look for Marah. Or a job. Or a life. I imagine different scenarios in which I go to Bainbridge Island and beg Johnny for forgiveness and receive it.

Today is no different. I wake late in the day and realize instantly that I must have taken too many sleeping pills. I feel terrible. My mouth is tar-pit-sticky and it tastes like I forgot to brush my teeth last night. I roll over in bed, see my bedside clock. I smack my lips together and rub my eyes, which feel gritty and bloodshot. No doubt I cried in my sleep. And again, I have slept the day away.

I get up and try to focus. In my bathroom, I find a mountain of clothes on the floor.

Yeah. Yesterday I tried to go out. I thought it was the outfit stopping me. Makeup lies scattered across the counter.

This is really getting out of control.

Today I will change my life.

I start with a shower. The hot water pounds down on me, but instead of washing away my lethargy, it somehow makes me feel worse. In the steamy enclosure, I relive too much: Johnny's anger, Kate's death, Marah's running away.

The next thing I know, the water is cold. I blink slowly, wondering what the hell has happened to me. Freezing now, shaking, I get out of the shower and dry off.

Eat.

Yes.

That will help.

I dress slowly, in sweats I find on the floor of my bedroom. I am shaky and headachy. Eating will help. And one Xanax.

Only one.

I walk through my dark condo, turning on lights as I go, ignoring the mail scattered on my coffee table. As I am pouring a cup of coffee, my cell phone rings. I answer it quickly. "Yes?"

"Tully? It's George. I've gotten you a ticket to a screening of *The American*, with George Clooney. I'll e-mail you the details. It's a charitable event at a theater in downtown Seattle. The network guys will be there. This is your chance to wow them. September second. Eight P.M. Don't be late, and look good."

"Thanks, George," I say, smiling for the first time in days.

I feel hope stir inside of me. I need this so much. I'm cried out, as dry as sawdust. I can't live this way anymore.

Then it hits me: I have to leave my condo and go out in public. I start to panic, try to tamp it down.

No.

I can do this. I can. I take another Xanax (I will quit tomorrow) as I head back to my closet to pick out some clothes for the event.

I will need . . .

What? Why am I standing here in my closet?

Oh. A hair appointment.

"Tully?"

Am I imagining Marah's voice? I turn so quickly I stumble, bang into the door of my closet. I am unsteady on my feet as I make my way through the condo, toward a voice I don't really believe is even there.

But she is there, in my living room, standing in front of the wall of windows. She is dressed in black, with her hair short and spiked and pink; she has silver charms hanging from her eyebrow. She looks dangerously thin; her cheekbones are like knife blades above her pale, hollow cheeks.

She is going to give me another chance. "Marah," I say softly, loving her so much it hurts. "I'm glad you're back."

She shifts nervously from foot to foot. She looks, not scared, exactly, but uncomfortable.

I wish my head were clearer, that this damn headache would loosen its grip. I feel restless, a little impatient for her to speak.

"I need . . ." she begins.

I move toward her, a little off balance. I am embarrassed by my unsteadiness. Does she notice?

"What do you need, baby girl?" Did I say all of that, or only think it? I wish I hadn't taken that second Xanax. Is she running away from Paxton? "Are you okay?"

"I'm fine. Pax and I need money."

I stop. "You came to me for money?"

"That's how you can help me."

I press two fingers to my temple, trying to still the pain. My little fairy tale collapses around me. She doesn't want *me,* isn't here for my help. She wants money and then she will leave again. Money for Paxton, most likely. He has put her up to this. I'm sure of it. And what would Johnny say if he found out I gave her money and let her go again?

As gently as I can, I take hold of her wrist and push her sleeve up. Her forearm is pale and crisscrossed with a web of scars, some silvery and old, some new and red and sore-looking.

She pulls her hand away.

My heart breaks for her. I can see that she is hurting. It is what we have in common these days, but now we will come together again, be there for each other. I will never let her down again. I will be the godmother Kate wanted me to be. I will not let her or Johnny down again. "If you're okay, why are you still hurting yourself?" I try to ask it gently, but I am really shaking. I feel headachy and nauseated. The blood is pounding in my ears. It's like a panic attack is coming on, but why? "I want to help you, you know I do—"

"Are you going to give me money or not?"

"What's it for?"

"None of your business."

The words hurt me as deeply as she obviously intended. "So you came to me for money." I look at this girl whom I barely recognize. "Look at me," I say, wanting desperately to make her understand how dangerous her choices are. "I've screwed up my life, Marah. I don't have any family; no husband and no kids. The one thing I did have—my career—I lost. Don't end up like me. Alone. You have a family that loves you. Go home. Johnny will help you."

"I have Pax."

"Some men are worse than being alone, Marah."

"Like you would know. Will you help me or not?"

Even in my precarious state, I know I can't do what she is asking. I want to, want it like air, but I can't make it easy for her to run away again. I have made a lot of mistakes with this girl over the years, none worse than romanticizing Paxton and concealing their relationship from Johnny, but I have learned. "I'll give you a place to live and set you up with Dr. Bloom, but I won't make the same mistake again. I won't go behind your dad's back and give you money so you can live in some hovel with that weirdo who doesn't care that you cut yourself."

After that, we say terrible things to each other, things I want to forget. This girl I love as much as my own life gives me a look that could shatter wood. Then she leaves, slamming the door behind her.

✦

The day of the movie premiere sneaks up on me. How that could be, I don't really know. All I know is that on the evening of September second, I am moving listlessly from room to room, doing nothing, pretending to work on my memoir, when my cell phone bleats out an appointment alert.

I look down at the entry. *Movie. Eight P.M. Network brass.* Then I look at the time.

It is 7:03.

I will go. I *must* go. This is my opportunity. I will not let fear or panic or desperation stop me. I will dress up, look good, and retake my place in the spotlight. This is America, after all, the land of second chances, especially for celebrities. Oh, perhaps I'll have to do the Hugh Grant talk show walk of shame, apologize with a smile, come clean about my anxieties and my depression, but people will understand. Who doesn't have anxieties, these days, in this economy? Who hasn't lost a job they love?

I am a little panicked as I make my way back to my bedroom, but a Xanax will help, so I take two. I can't worry about an anxiety attack tonight. I have to be perfect. And I can be. I am not the kind of woman who hides out beneath warm covers and behind locked doors.

I go into my closet, stepping over clothes I don't remember buying, let alone wearing, and stand in front of my dresses. I am too overweight to make a fashion statement, so I pluck an old standby off the rack: a vintage black Valentino with an asymmetrical neckline and patterned black hose. It used to hang beautifully on me; now it fits me like a sausage casing, but it's black and it's the best I can do.

My hands are unsteady; I can't do much with my hair beyond pulling it back into a sleek ponytail. Huge gold and black pearl earrings draw the attention away from my sallow face (I hope). I put on more makeup than I've ever worn in my life and still I look tired. Old. Trying not to think about that, I slip into an expensive pair of bright pink patent leather pumps and grab an evening bag.

I am reaching for my doorknob when panic hits, but I grit my teeth and push through it. I open the door, step out into the hallway.

By the time I reach the lobby, I am hyperventilating, but I refuse to rush back to the safety of my condo.

The doorman hails the Town Car and I collapse in the backseat.

Youcandothisyoucandothis.

I close my eyes and survive this panic one second at a time, but when the car pulls up in front of the theater, I feel light-headed enough to pass out.

"You getting out, lady?"

Yes. Of course.

I climb out. It feels as if I am wading through mud as I approach the red carpet. The klieg lights burn my eyes, make me blink.

It is raining, I notice. When did that start?

Eerie red light cascades down from the marquee, flashing in puddles of rainwater on the street. Beyond the roped-off area, a giant, jostling crowd of onlookers is waiting for a celebrity to arrive.

My hands are shaking now; my mouth is so dry I can hardly swallow.

I tilt my chin and force myself to walk the red carpet. A few flashbulbs go off—then they see it is me and the photographers turn away.

Inside the theater, I have the debilitating thought that I am the oldest woman here. I worry about having a hot flash, turning red suddenly and sweating. I should look for the network executives, but I can't. Instead, I make my way into the theater and collapse into one of the velvet seats.

The house light dims, the movie begins. All around me people are breathing, moving quietly, their seats creaking.

I try to stay calm and pay attention, but I can't do it. Anxiety is a living, breathing entity inside of me. I need to get out of here, just for a second.

I find a sign for the restroom and follow it. The bathroom is so bright it scalds my eyes. Ignoring the mirror, I stumble into a stall and sink down onto the closed seat, kicking the door shut. I slump back, trying to calm down, and close my eyes. *Relax, Tully. Relax.*

The next thing I know, I am waking up. How long have I been here, passed out in a toilet stall in a movie theater?

Pushing out of the stall so hard the door cracks against the next stall, I lurch out into a line of women. They stare at me, their mouths open. The movie must be over.

Downstairs, I see the way people look at me. They step out of my way, as if I am rigged with dynamite or carrying a contagious disease. My DUI mug shot is what they are seeing when they look at me. And suddenly I know: I can't do it. I can't meet the network brass and plead my case and get my job back. It's too late. I have lost my chance. The realization is a pit of quicksand that pulls me under. I elbow my way through the crowd, muttering apologies I don't mean, until I can breathe again. I end up in a quiet alleyway in the pouring rain.

✦

Sometime later, a man tries to pick me up in a bar. I almost let him. I see him looking at me, smiling, saying something that makes me ache with longing—not for him, of course, for my lost life, but he is there and the life is gone. I hear myself begging—begging—him to kiss me and I cry when he does because it feels so good and not nearly good enough.

After the bar closes, I walk home (or take a cab or get a ride—who knows?—at least I arrive home). My condo is dark when I get there. No lights are on. I turn them all on as I stumble past, ricocheting off the walls and tables as I go.

I am so ashamed I could cry, but what is the point? I slump onto my sofa and close my eyes.

When I open my eyes again, I see the pile of mail on my coffee table. Bleary-eyed, I stare at the remnants of my former life. I am about to look away when a picture catches my attention. *My* picture.

I lean forward and push the stack of envelopes and catalogs aside; there, beneath the bills and junk mail, is a *Star* magazine with my mug shot in the upper left corner. Beneath it is a single, terrible word. *Addict.*

I pick up the magazine and open it to the article. It's not the cover story, just a little tidbit on the side.

The words blur before my eyes, dance and jump, but I tackle them one by one.

THE REAL STORY BEHIND THE RUMORS

> Aging isn't easy for any woman in the public eye, but it may be proving especially difficult for Tully Hart, the ex-star of the once-phenom talk show *The Girlfriend Hour.* Ms. Hart's goddaughter, Marah Ryan, contacted *Star* exclusively. Ms. Ryan, 20, confirms that the fifty-year-old Hart has been struggling lately with demons that she's had all her life. In recent months, she has "gained an alarming amount of weight" and been abusing drugs and alcohol, according to Ms. Ryan.

> Tully Hart once appeared to have it all, but the aging talk show host, who has openly spoken of the difficult childhood she survived, and who has never been married or had children, appears to be crumbling under the pressure of her recent failures.
>
> Dr. Lorri Mull, a Beverly Hills psychiatrist, who hasn't treated the star, says, "Miss Hart is exhibiting classic addict behavior. She's clearly spiraling out of control."
>
> Most drug addicts . . .

I let the magazine slide to the floor. The pain I have been holding at bay for months, years, roars to life, sucks me into the bleakest, loneliest place I've ever been. I will never be able to crawl out of it.

I stumble out of the living room and leave my condo, grabbing my car keys as I go. I don't know where I'm going. Just out. Away.

I can't live like this anymore. I have tried to go on alone; God knows I've tried. But the world is so big and I feel so incredibly small, not myself at all. I am like a charcoal drawing of the woman I once was, just black lines and white space, a silhouette. My heart can't hold this loss. I can't . . . look away anymore. Now all I see is the emptiness around me, beside me. Inside of me.

A strong wind would blow me away, that's how weak I am, and it's okay. I don't want to be strong anymore. I want to be . . . gone.

In the elevator I push the down button. As I careen through the underground parking lot, I fish the Xanax out of my evening bag and swallow two, gagging at the bitter taste.

I get into my car, rev the engine, and drive away. I turn onto First Street without even looking to my left. Tears and rain blur my view, turn my familiar city into a landscape I've never seen before, a jagged, misshapen blur of silvery skyscrapers and distorted neon signs and lamplight burned into impossible, watery shapes. My despair is spilling over, obliterating everything else. I swerve to the right to miss something—a pedestrian, a bicyclist, a figment of my imagination—

and there it is: a hulking concrete stanchion that supports the aging, dangerous viaduct, looming in front of me.

I see that huge black post and I think: *End it.*

End it.

The simplicity of it takes my breath away. Has the thought been there all along? Have I been circling it in the obscurity of my subconscious, watching it? I don't know. All I know is it's there now, as seductive as a kiss in the dark.

I don't have to be in pain anymore. All it takes is a turn of the wheel.

Twenty-five

✦

"Oh, my God." I turn to Kate. "I tried to turn at the last second to avoid hitting the stanchion."

I know.

"I had one split second where I thought, *Who would care?* and I kept my foot on the gas, but then I turned. Only . . . it was too late."

Look.

The moment she says the word, I see that we are in the hospital room again. It is bright and white and there are people around my bed.

I'm hovering above it all, looking down on them.

I see Johnny with his arms crossed tightly, moving back and forth. His mouth is drawn into a frown, and Margie is crying quietly, a handkerchief held to her mouth, and my mother looks devastated. The twins are there, standing close together. What I see are the tears in Lucas's eyes and the defiant, angry jutting out of Wills's small chin. They look insubstantial somehow, boys who have been partially erased.

They have spent too much time in hospitals already, these boys. It breaks my heart that I have brought them back here again.

My boys, Kate says, and the softness in her voice takes me aside. *Will they remember me?* This she says so quietly I think I may have imagined it. Or maybe I am reading her mind like best friends do.

"Do you want to talk about it?"

My boys, growing up without me? No. She shakes her head; silvery blond hair shivers at the movement. *What is there to say?*

In the silence that falls between us, I hear strains of a song, coming from the iPod on the bedside table; the volume is so low I can barely hear it. *Hello darkness my old friend . . .*

And then I hear voices.

". . . it's time . . . not hopeful . . ."

". . . temperature normal . . . remove ventilator."

". . . we've removed the shunt, but . . ."

". . . drained . . ."

". . . on her own, we'll see . . ."

The man in white seems menacing somehow; I shiver when he says, ". . . Are you ready?"

They are talking about my body, about *me*, about taking me off life support. They are here, my friends and family, to watch me die.

Or breathe, Kate says. Then: *It's time. Do you want to go back?*

I get it. Everything has been leading up to this moment. I see that with a clarity that should have been there before.

I see Marah walk into the hospital room. She looks so thin and frail as she stands by Johnny, who puts an arm around her.

She needs you, Kate says to me. *And so do my boys.* There is a hitch in her voice; an emotion I know runs deep. I made her a promise to be there for her children and I failed. In a way, the proof is in the piercings. I feel my old nemesis—longing—uncoil from its place deep, deep inside me and spread out.

They love me. Even from where I am, through the mist of worlds, I can see that. Why didn't I see it when I was standing beside them? Maybe we see what we expect to. I *do* want to undo what I've done—this terrible, selfish thing—I want to undo it and have a chance to be another version of myself. A better version.

And I *love* them. How was it that I have believed I was incapable of love, all these years, when I feel it so deeply? I turn to say this to Kate, and she smiles at me, my best friend, with her long, tangled blond hair and thick eyelashes and her smile that lights up any room.

My other half. The girl who took my hand all those years ago and didn't let go until she had to.

In her eyes, I see our lives: dancing to our music, riding our bikes in the dark, sitting in chairs on her beach, talking and laughing. She is my heart; the one who lets me soar and keeps me grounded. No wonder I went crazy without her. She was the glue that held us all together.

Say goodbye to me, she says quietly.

In the hospital room—and now it feels far, far away—I hear someone—the doctor—say, "Does anyone want to say anything first?"

But I am listening to Kate now: *I'll always be with you, Tul. Always. Friends no matter what. This time you won't stop believing.*

I *had* stopped believing—in her, in me, in us. In everything.

I look at her, see through the brightness to the face I know as well as my own.

When someone hip-bumps you or tells you that it's not all about you or when our music plays. Listen and you'll hear me in all of it. I'm in your memories.

I know she's right. Maybe I've known it all along. She is gone. I lost her a long time ago, but I didn't know how to let go. How do you release your other half? But I have to . . . for both of our sakes. I see that now. Still, I can't say the word.

"Ah, Katie . . ." I say, feeling the hot sting of tears.

See? she says. *You're saying goodbye.*

She moves toward me, and I feel a heat shimmering off her, and then, like a touch of flame, I feel a brush of skin against mine and goose bumps break out across my flesh, the hair on the back of my neck stands up. *Slip out the back, Jack,* she says. *Make a new plan, Stan.*

The music. Always the music.

"I love you," I say quietly, and finally it is enough. Love is what lasts. I understand that now. "Goodbye."

At that, just the single heartfelt word, I am plunged back into the darkness.

✦

I can see myself, I think, from a distance. I am in pain. A headache blinds me, it hurts so much.

Move. It is an old word, one I used to know, and it comes to me now. There is a black velvet curtain in front of me. I am backstage, maybe. Somewhere out there are lights . . .

I have to get to my feet . . . walk . . . but I am tired. So tired.

Still, I try. I get up. Each step sends pain ringing up my spine, but I don't let it stop me. There is a light out there, onstage. Like a lighthouse beam, it flashes bright, shows me the way, and then disappears again. I keep walking, trudging forward, thinking, *Please,* but my mind is so muddy I don't know to whom I am praying. And then suddenly there is a hill above me, growing fast, reaching upward, climbing out from the blackness in front of me.

I can't make it.

From far away, I hear: "Wake up, Tully, please—"

And pieces of a song, something about about sweet dreams that I almost recognize.

I try to take another step, but my lungs ache from the exertion and I hurt all over. My legs give out and I pitch to my knees, landing hard enough to rattle bones and break my resolve.

"I can't do it, Katie."

I almost ask her *why,* almost scream the question in frustration. But I know why.

Faith.

It is something I have never had.

"Come back, Tully."

I follow the line of my goddaughter's voice. In this black world, it shimmers like gossamer, just beyond my reach. I reach for it, follow it. Then I take a deep, painful breath and try to stand.

✦

September 4, 2010
11:21 A.M.

"Are you ready?" Dr. Bevan asked. "Does anyone want to say anything first?"

Marah couldn't even nod. She didn't want this. It was better to keep her godmother plugged in, breathing, than to take her off the machines. What if she died?

Tully's mom moved closer to the bed. Her cracked, colorless lips moved silently, forming words that Marah couldn't hear. They were all here, gathered around the hospital bed: Dad, Grandma and Grandpa, the twins, and Tully's mom. Dad had spoken to Marah and the boys this morning on the ferry, explained to them what this all meant. They had raised Tully's body temperature and taken her off the heavy meds. Now they were going to unplug her from the ventilator. Hopefully she would wake up and breathe on her own.

Dr. Bevan put Tully's chart in a sleeve at the end of the bed. A nurse came in and removed the breathing tube from Tully's mouth. Time seemed to screech to a halt.

Tully took a rattling, phlegmy breath and released it. Beneath the white cotton blanket, her chest rose and fell, rose and fell.

"Tallulah," Dr. Bevan said, leaning over Tully. He pried open her eyelids and shone a beam of light in her eyes. Her pupils reacted. "Can you hear me?"

"Don't call her that," Dorothy said in a cracked voice. Then, more softly, as if she thought she shouldn't have spoken, "She hates that name."

Grandma reached out and held Dorothy's hand.

Marah pulled away from her dad and inched toward the side of the bed. Tully was breathing on her own, but she still looked pretty much dead, all bruised and black and blue and bandaged and bald. "Come on, Tully," she said. "Come back to us."

Nothing happened.

How long did Marah stand there, gripping the bedrails, waiting for her godmother to wake up? It felt like hours had passed when she finally heard Dr. Bevan say:

"Well. Time will tell, I guess. Brain injuries are tricky. We'll monitor her closely over the next few hours. Hopefully she'll wake up."

"Hopefully?" Grandma said. They'd all learned to be wary of that word from doctors.

"That's all there is now," Dr. Bevan said. "Hope. But her brain activity is normal and her pupils are reactive. And she's breathing on her own. Those are very good signs."

"So we wait," Dad said.

Dr. Bevan nodded. "We wait."

The next time Marah glanced at the clock, she saw that the thin black hands were still moving, still gobbling minutes and moving on.

She heard the adults whispering behind her, talking among themselves. She spun to face them. "What? *What?*"

Dad came forward. He reached out and held her hand, and she knew it was bad.

"Do you think she's going to die?" Marah asked.

He sighed, and it sounded so sad that she almost started to cry. "I don't know."

His hand was a lifeline suddenly. How had she forgotten that, how her dad could hold her steady? He'd always been able to, even back in the old days when Marah had fought with her mom constantly.

"She's going to wake up," Marah said, trying to believe it. Her mom used to say, *Don't stop believing until you have to, and certainly don't stop then.* Of course, she'd died anyway. "Do we just wait?"

Dad nodded. "I'm going to take the boys and your grandpa out for lunch. You know Wills has to eat every hour or he has a melt-down. You hungry?"

Marah shook her head.

"Dorothy and I are going for some coffee," Grandma said, moving toward Marah. "It's been a tough last few hours. You want to come with us? I'll buy you a hot chocolate."

"I'll stay with her," Marah said.

After everyone left, she stood at her godmother's bedside, gripping the bedrails. Memories slipped in to stand beside her, crowded her on all sides. In almost all of her best childhood memories, Tully was there. She remembered Tully and Mom at Marah's high school play, when Mom was so sick, all bald and hunched down in the wheelchair. From her place onstage, Marah had looked down at the two best friends and seen that they were both crying. Tully had leaned over and wiped the tears from Mom's eyes.

"Tully?" Marah said. "*Please* hear me. I'm right here. It's Marah, and I'm so sorry for what I did. I want you to wake up and yell at me. Please."

✦

September 12, 2010
10:17 A.M.

"I'm sorry," Dr. Bevan said quietly.

Dorothy wondered if the man knew how often he'd said these words in the past week. If there was one thing they were all certain of, it was this: Dr. Bevan was sorry that Tully hadn't wakened from her coma. He still handed out hope as if it were a bit of hard candy he kept in his pocket for emergencies, but the hope in his eyes had begun to dim. He'd ordered a tracheotomy on day two to maintain something called efficient aeration of the lungs; a nasogastric feeding tube had been inserted into her nostril and taped in place.

Tully looked like she was sleeping. That was what bothered Dorothy the most as she sat in this room, hour after hour. Every single second felt charged with possibility.

Each of the last eight days, she'd thought: *Today.*

Today Tully will wake up.

But each evening came, sweeping darkness into the room, and each evening her daughter's unnatural sleep went on.

Now Dr. Bevan had called them here for a meeting. It could hardly be a good sign.

Dorothy stood in the corner, with her back to the wall. In her wrinkled clothes and orange clogs, she felt like the least important person in the room.

Johnny stood tall, with his arms crossed at his chest and his sons standing close. His grief revealed itself in tiny things—the places he'd missed shaving this morning and the way he'd misbuttoned his shirt. Margie looked smaller, hunched. This past week had whittled her down, added pain to a heart that had already been full of it. And Bud had hardly taken off his sunglasses. Dorothy often felt he was teary-eyed behind the dark lenses. But it was Marah, of all of them, who looked the worst. She was the walking wounded: thin, unbalanced. She moved as if each footstep needed to be calculated with care. Most people would look at the girl, with her freshly dyed black hair and baggy jeans and sweatshirt and pale skin, and see a grieving young woman, but Dorothy, who knew regret so well, saw guilt in Marah's gaze, and she hoped—as they all did—that this half life of Tully's would end with good news. Dorothy wasn't sure that any of them could handle the opposite.

"It's time," Dr. Bevan said, clearing his throat to get their attention again, "to talk about the future. Tully has been primarily unresponsive for eight days. She has recovered adequately from her acute injuries and shows no substantial evidence of brain injury, but the evidence of cognitive awareness fails to meet the medical criteria for intensive ongoing rehabilitation. In layman's terms, this means that although there have been some reports of her opening her eyes or—once—coughing, we believe it's time to consider custodial care. A hospital is no longer the place for her."

"She can afford—" Johnny began, but the doctor shook his head.

"Money isn't the point, John. We treat critically ill patients. That's what we do here."

Margie flinched at that, edged closer to Bud, who put an arm around her.

"There are several exceptional nursing homes in the area. I have a list—"

"No," Dorothy said sharply. She looked up slowly. Everyone was staring at her.

She swallowed hard. "Can . . . I take care of her at home?"

It was difficult not to squirm uncomfortably under the doctor's pointed perusal. She knew what he saw when he looked at her. An old hippie with moderate-to-poor hygiene skills.

But he had no idea what she'd survived just to be here. She lifted her chin, met the neurosurgeon's narrowed gaze. "Is it possible? Can I care for her at home?"

"It's possible, Ms. Hart," he said slowly. "But you hardly seem . . ."

Margie pulled away from Bud, moved to stand by Dorothy. "She hardly seems what?"

A frown tugged at the doctor's mouth. "It's a complicated, difficult job, caring for a comatose patient. And single caretakers often find themselves overwhelmed. That's all I meant."

Johnny moved in to stand beside his mother-in-law. "I could come every weekend to help out."

"Me, too," Marah said, moving to Dorothy's other side.

The twins stepped forward together, their gazes earnest and grown-up beneath the floppy overhang of their hair. "Us, too."

Dorothy was surprised by the swell of emotion that filled her. She had never stood up for her daughter before, and no one had ever stood up for her. She wanted to turn to Tully and say, *See, you are loved.* Instead, she fisted her hands and nodded, holding back the stinging tears that blurred her vision.

"There's a local company that specializes in care of comatose patients at home. It can be prohibitively expensive for most patients—and their families—but if money is not an issue, you could engage their services. A registered nurse could come to the house every day, or every other day, to change Tully's catheter and check her corneas for ulceration and run some tests, but even so, it will take a lot of work, Ms. Hart. You'd have to follow a pretty rigorous routine. I won't discharge her into your care unless you're certain you're up to it."

Dorothy remembered all the times she'd let go of her daughter's hand, or let her go in a crowd; all the birthdays she'd missed and all the questions she hadn't answered. Everyone in this room knew Dorothy's sad, pathetic history as a mother. She'd never packed Tully a school lunch or talked to her about life or said, "I love you."

If she didn't change now, reach out now, that would be their story.

"I'll take care of her," Dorothy said quietly.

"I'll research the insurance and take care of all the financial and medical arrangements," Johnny said. "Tully will have the best in home care possible."

"The costs—and the coma—may go on for quite some time. It's my understanding that she doesn't have a living will, and that Kathleen Ryan is the executrix of her estate and has the power of attorney to make medical decisions on her behalf, and that Ms. Ryan is deceased."

Johnny nodded. "We'll take care of all of that as a family." He looked at Dorothy, who nodded. "We can reassess later if we need to. I'll talk to her business manager this week. Her condo is worth several million, even in this economy. We can sell it if we need to, but my guess is that she has the maximum insurance coverage."

Marge reached over and held Dorothy's hand. The two women looked solemnly at each other. "The house in Snohomish hasn't sold yet. Bud and I could move back to help you."

"You are amazing," Dorothy said quietly. "But if you're there, it will be too easy for me to let you be her mother. I need to be the person who is responsible. I hope you understand."

Margie's look said it all. "I'm only a phone call away."

Dorothy released a heavy sigh.

There. It was done. For the first time in her life, she was going to be Tully's mother.

✦

September 12, 2010
6:17 P.M.

Johnny had spent most of the day with Tully's business manager, Frank, going over her finances. Now he sat alone in his car on the ferry, with a stack of her financial records in the seat beside him.

He'd had no idea how her life had unraveled in the years since Kate's death. He'd imagined her retirement from TV had been her choice, that the "book deal" had been lucrative and the beginning of yet another high-profile career. He would have found the truth easily—if he'd cared enough to look.

He hadn't.

Ah, Katie, he thought tiredly. *You are going to kick my ass for this . . .*

Leaning back into his leather seat, he stared out through the ferry's wide bow opening as the sandy hook of Wing Point came into view. When they docked, he drove over the bumpy metal ramp and onto the smooth asphalt of the road.

At the end of his driveway, the house was drenched in late afternoon light. It was the golden hour, that beautiful, crystalline time before sunset, when every color was crisp and clear. September was a good month in the Northwest, a repayment season for all the gray rainy days that were to come.

For the briefest of moments, he saw this place as it once had been. The house and yard—like everything else—had changed since Kate's passing. Before, the yard had had a wild, untended look. His wife had always been "about to" start taming it. Back then, every plant and flower and shrub had grown too tall and spread too wide. Flowers had crowded in on each other like schoolyard bullies fighting for turf. There had always been toys strewn about—skateboards and helmets and plastic dinosaurs.

These days, the yard was orderly. A gardener came once a week and raked and clipped and mowed. The plants were healthier, the flowers bigger and brighter.

He pulled into the dark garage and sat there a minute collecting his thoughts. When he felt strong again, he went into the house.

As he stepped inside, the boys came running down the stairs, banging into each other, pushing and shoving. It was like watching *Rollerball* on a hill. He'd long ago stopped yelling at them about it or worrying that one of them would fall. This was just who they were. They were both dressed in blue and gold Bainbridge Island sweats and were wearing skater shoes that he swore were two sizes too big.

In the past few years they'd become a trio, he and the twins. Their time in Los Angeles had brought them closer together, and they'd been happy to move back here. And yet, he could see fissures forming in their relationship. Both of them, but especially Wills, had begun to keep secrets. Wills had begun to answer ordinary questions evasively. "Who was that on the phone?" was a good example. "No one." "Oh, so you're talking to no one?" Like that.

"Hey, Dad," Wills said, jumping down the last three steps. Lucas was a second behind. They landed together hard enough to rattle the floorboards.

God, he loved these boys. And yet he'd let them down in a million tiny ways without Kate to guide him. Alone, he hadn't been as good a parent as his sons—or Marah—deserved. He reached out to hold on to the entry table beside him. He had made so many mistakes in the years without Kate. How was it he saw his failings so clearly now?

Would they forgive him someday?

"Are you okay, Dad?" Lucas asked. Lucas, of course. *Take care of Lucas . . . he won't understand. He may miss me most of all . . .*

Johnny nodded. "We're going out to clean Dorothy's house tomorrow and paint. Get ready for Tully to go home. I know how much you'll want to help."

"She and Mom liked blue," Wills said. "That would be a good color for her room."

Lucas took a step forward, looked up at Johnny. "It's not your fault, Dad," he said quietly. "Tully, I mean."

Johnny reached out, touched Lucas's cheek. "You're so much like your mom," he said.

"And Wills is like you," Lucas said. The family myth, reiterated, passed along, repeated often. And true.

Johnny smiled. Maybe that's how they would make it in the future, by keeping Kate alive in a thousand small ways while they moved on. He was ready, at last, to do that. Ironically, Tully's accident had shown him what really mattered. "Where's your sister?"

"Gee, Dad. Guess," Wills said.

"In her room?"

"What does she do in there all the time?"

"She's going through a hard time right now. Let's cut her a little slack, okay, Conqueror?"

"Okay," they said together.

He moved past them and went up the stairs. Although he paused at Marah's closed door, he neither knocked nor said anything. He was trying like hell to give her space. Today, in the hospital, he'd seen how deep her pain ran, and he'd learned a good lesson in the past few years: Listening mattered as much as talking. When she was ready to talk, he would be the best version of himself. He wouldn't fail her again.

He went into his room, tossed the pile of paperwork on his bed, and then took a long, hot shower. He was towel-drying his hair when there was a knock on his bedroom door.

He dressed quickly in jeans and a T-shirt and called out, "Come in."

The door opened. Marah stood there, her hands clasped tightly together. He still got a little jolt of sadness every time he saw her. She was so thin and pale, a kind of grieving doppelgänger of the girl she used to be. "Can I talk to you?"

"Of course."

She glanced away. "Not in here." Turning, she left his room and walked downstairs. In the mudroom, she grabbed one of the heavy sweaters from the hooks by the washing machine and put it on as she pushed through the door.

Out on the deck, she sat down in her mother's favorite Adirondack chair. Above them, the sprawling branches of the maple tree were plush with autumn. Scarlet, tangerine, and lemon-yellow leaves lay scattered across the deck and were stuck here and there on the railing. How often had he and Katie sat out here at night, after the kids were in bed, with night at their feet and candles glowing in the air above them, listening to each other and the waves?

He shook the memory aside and sat down in the chair beside her. The old, weathered wood creaked as he settled into place.

"I sold a story to *Star* magazine," she said quietly. "I told them Tully was a drug addict and an alcoholic. They paid me eight hundred and fifty dollars. It came out last week. I . . . saw it at Tully's condo. She read it before she got in the car."

Johnny took a deep breath and exhaled it. Then he did it again, thinking: *Help me, Katie.* When he was sure his voice would be even, he said, "That's what you meant when you said this was your fault."

She turned to him. The anguish in her eyes was heart-wrenching. "It *is* my fault."

Johnny stared at his daughter, saw the pain in her eyes. "We fell apart without your mom," he said. "And that's on me. It hurt too much to be around Tully, so I walked away. Hell, I ran away. You aren't the only one who hurt her."

"That doesn't help much," she said miserably.

He said quietly, "I've thought about that day in your dorm room a thousand times. I was wrong to blow such a gasket. I would do anything to have a do-over and to tell you that I love you no matter what choice you make and that you can always count on me to love you."

"I needed that," she said, wiping her eyes.

"And I would tell Tully I'm sorry, too. I was wrong to blame her."

Marah nodded but said nothing.

Johnny thought of all the mistakes he'd made with this girl, the times he'd walked away when he should have stayed; the times he'd remained silent when he should have spoken. All the wrong turns a single father makes when he's in over his head. "Can you forgive me?"

She gazed at him steadily. "I love you, Dad," she said.

"I love you, too, Munchkin."

Marah's smile was weak and a little sad. "What about Tully? She probably thinks—"

"What would you say to her right now?"

"I'd tell her how much I love her, but I won't get a chance."

"You'll get a chance. You can tell her when she wakes up."

"I have a little trouble believing in miracles these days."

What he wanted to say was, *Don't we all?* What he said was, "Your mom would hate to hear that. She would tell you that everything works out the way it's supposed to and not to give up hope until you have to, and—"

"Certainly not then," Marah said quietly, her voice an echo of his.

For a beautiful second, he felt Katie beside him. The leaves rustled overhead.

"I want to see Dr. Bloom again, if that's okay."

Johnny looked up briefly, saw a movement of the shadowy Mason jar. *Thank you, Katie.* "I'll make an appointment."

Twenty-six

✦

September 14, 2010
9:13 A.M.

On the day before Tully was to be brought home, the Ryans and Mularkeys descended on the house on Firefly Lane like a professional cleaning crew. Dorothy had never seen people work so hard or get along so well.

The back bedroom—Tully's at fourteen and now again at fifty—had been stripped down and scrubbed and painted a beautiful sky blue. The hospital bed had been delivered and set up to face the room's only window. From her place in bed, Tully would be able to look through the open sash window, across the vegetable field, to her once-best-friend's old house. The new bedding—picked out by Marah—was pretty white matelassé with a raised floral pattern, and the twin boys had chosen pictures to put on the dresser—there were at least a dozen of them, all told; pictures of Kate and Tully throughout their lives, of Tully holding a pink-faced infant, of Johnny and Tully accepting some award onstage. Dorothy wished she had a picture of herself and Tully to add to the collection, but there simply were none. In the middle of it all, a nurse showed up from the coma care company and talked to Dorothy for at least two hours about how to handle Tully's daily care.

When everyone finally left, Dorothy walked from room to room, telling herself she could do this. She read through the nurse's handouts and materials twice, making notes in the margins.

Twice, she'd almost gone for a drink, but in the end she'd made it through, and now she was in the hospital again, walking down the bright corridor toward her daughter's room. Smiling at one of the floor nurses, she opened the door and went inside.

There was a man sitting by her daughter's bed, reading. At Dorothy's entrance, he looked up. She noticed several things about him at once: he was young, probably not more than forty-five, and there was an exotic, multicultural look to him. His hair was drawn back into a ponytail and she was pretty sure that beneath his white doctor's coat would be worn, faded jeans and a T-shirt from some rock band. He wore the same plastic clogs that were her favorite.

"I'm sorry," he said, rising, setting the book aside. She saw it was something called *Shantaram*. It was a thick book and he was halfway through it.

"Are you reading to her?"

He nodded, coming forward, extending his hand. "I'm Desmond Grant, an ER doc."

"Dorothy. I'm her mother."

"Well. I should be getting back to work."

"You visit her often?"

"I try to come in either before or after my shifts. I see her a lot in the middle of the night." He smiled. "I hear she's going home today."

"Yes. In about an hour."

"It was nice to meet you." He headed for the door.

"Desmond?"

He turned back. "Yes?"

"Seventeen Firefly Lane. In Snohomish. That's where we'll be. If you want to finish reading her that book."

"Thanks, Dorothy. I'd like that."

She watched him leave and then walked over to the bed. In the eleven days since the accident, Tully's facial bruising had changed color, gone from a deep plum color to a rotten-banana brown. The dozens of tiny lacerations had scabbed over; only a few oozed yellow pus. Her full lips were cracked and dry.

Dorothy reached into her baggy smock pocket, pulling out a small jar of bee cream. Using the pad of her forefinger, she glazed the soft mixture across Tully's slack lips. "That will make them feel better, I think. How did you sleep last night?

"Me? Not so good," she went on, as if they were conversing. "I was nervous about your homecoming. I don't want to let you down. You don't think I will? I'm glad of that."

She placed a hand on her daughter's dry, bald scalp. "You'll wake up when you're ready. Healing takes time. Don't I know that?"

Just as she finished the sentence, the door opened and Dr. Bevan and Johnny came into the room.

"There you are, Dorothy," the doctor said, stepping aside to allow several nurses and two paramedics into the room.

She managed a smile. If it took all these people just to transport Tully, how in heaven did Dorothy think she could care for her alone?

"Breathe, Dorothy," Johnny said, coming up beside her.

She gave him a grateful look.

After that, everything moved quickly. Tully was transported from the bed to a gurney, disconnected from the IV and machines, and wheeled away. At the front desk, Dorothy signed a bunch of paperwork, collected some discharge papers and care procedure brochures and a set of notes from Dr. Bevan. By the time she was in Johnny's car, following the ambulance, she felt sick with worry.

On Columbia, they drove downhill—and there was the rough gray stanchion Tully had hit. Beneath it, on the pavement, a makeshift memorial had sprung up. Balloons and dying flowers and candles created a little shrine of sorts. A sign read WAKE UP, TULLY. Another read WE'RE PRAYING 4 U.

"Do you think she knows how many people are praying for her?" she asked.

"I hope so."

Dorothy fell silent after that. She sat back in the comfortable leather seat and watched the scenery go from city to town to country, from high-rises to low fences, from bumper-to-bumper traffic to slow, winding tree-lined roads with only a few other cars in sight. At home, they pulled up behind the ambulance and parked.

Dorothy hustled ahead to open the front door and turn on the lights and led the paramedics to Tully's bedroom, where the Ryan kids had tacked up a huge WELCOME HOME, TULLY poster.

Dorothy shadowed the paramedics, asked them questions, and studiously wrote down their answers.

All too quickly, it was done. Tully was in her room, apparently sleeping, and the ambulance was gone.

"Do you want me to stay?" Johnny asked.

Dorothy had been so lost in her own thoughts that his voice surprised her. "Oh. No. But thank you."

"Marah will be here Thursday. She's bringing food. And I'll be here for the weekend with the boys. Margie and Bud gave us the keys to the house across the street."

Today was Monday.

"And Margie wanted me to remind you that she's only a few hours away. If you change your mind and need help, she'll be on the next flight."

Dorothy forced a smile. "I can do this," she said, as much to herself as to him.

They walked to the door. There, Johnny paused and looked down at her.

"I wonder if you know how much this would mean to her."

"I know how much it means to me. How often do second chances come around?"

"If you get overwhelmed—"

"I won't drink. Don't worry."

"That wasn't my worry. I want you to know that we're all here for her. And for you. That's what I was going to say."

She stared up at this gorgeous man and said, "I wonder if she knows how lucky she is."

"We didn't," he said quietly, and Dorothy saw regret etch itself into the lines of his face.

Dorothy knew better than to say anything. Sometimes you simply made the wrong choice and you had to live with it. You could only change the future. She walked him out of the house and watched him drive away. Then she closed the door and went back to stand by her daughter's bedside.

An hour later, the nurse showed up and handed Dorothy a care list and said, "Come with me."

For the next three hours, Dorothy shadowed the woman's every move; she learned step by step what to do to care for her daughter. By the end of the visit, she had a notebook full of notations and reminders.

"You're ready," the nurse said at last.

Dorothy swallowed hard. "I don't know."

The nurse smiled gently. "It's just like when she was little," she said. "Remember how they constantly needed something—diaper changes, a little time in your arms, a bedtime story—and you never knew what it was until they quieted? It's like that. Just go through your list. You'll be fine."

"I wasn't much of a mother to her," Dorothy said.

The nurse gave her a little pat. "We all think that, hon. You'll be fine. And don't you forget. She can probably hear you. So talk, sing, tell jokes. Anything."

That night, when she was alone with her daughter for the first time, Dorothy slipped quietly into the bedroom and lit a gardenia-scented candle and turned on the bedside lamp.

She hit the bed's controls and elevated it to an exact angle of thirty-five degrees. She paused it there and then lowered it. Then she raised it again. "I hope this isn't making you dizzy. I'm supposed to elevate and lower your head for fifteen minutes every two hours." When she was done with that, Dorothy gently peeled back the blankets and began massaging Tully's hands and forearms. All the while, as she massaged her daughter's limbs and gently put her through passive exercises, she talked.

Afterward, she had no idea what she'd even said. She just knew that when she touched her daughter's feet, smoothing lotion onto the dry, cracked skin, she started to cry.

✦

Two weeks after Tully left the hospital, Marah had her first meeting with Dr. Bloom. As she walked through the empty waiting room, she couldn't help imagining Paxton there, with his sad and soulful eyes, and the black hair that continually fell across his face.

"Marah," Dr. Bloom said, welcoming her with a smile. "It's good to see you again."

"Thanks."

Marah sat down in the chair facing the polished wooden desk. The office seemed smaller than she remembered, and more intimate. The view of Elliott Bay was beautiful, even on this gray and rainy day.

Dr. Bloom sat down. "What would you like to talk about today?"

There were so many choices; so many mistakes to work through and things to figure out and so much guilt and grief. She wanted to fidget and look away, or count the leaves on the plant. Instead, she said, "I miss my mom and Tully's in a coma and I've screwed up my life so badly I just want to crawl in a hole somewhere and hide."

"You've done that already," Dr. Bloom said. Had her voice always been that gentle? "With Paxton. And here you are."

Marah felt a shock of recognition at the words; a new understanding muscled its way in. Bloom was right. It had all been a way of hiding—the pink hair, the piercings, the drugs, the sex. But she had loved Paxton. That, at least, had been real. Broken, maybe, and unhealthy, and dangerous, but real.

"What were you hiding from?"

"Then? Missing my mom."

"There is pain you can't outrun, Marah. Maybe you know that now. Some pains you have to look in the eye. What do you miss most about your mom?"

"Her voice," she answered. And then, "The way she hugged me. The way she loved me."

"You will always miss her. I know that from experience. There will be days—even years from now—when the missing will be so sharp it takes your breath away. But there will be good days, too; months and years of them. In one way or another, you'll be searching for her all your life. You'll find her, too. As you grow up, you'll understand her more and more. I promise you that."

"She would hate how I treated Tully," she said softly.

"I think you'd be amazed at how easily a mother forgives. And a godmother, too. The question is: Can you forgive yourself?"

Marah looked up sharply, her eyes stinging with tears. "I need to."

"Okay, then. That's where we will start."

It helped, Marah learned, all that looking back, all that talking about her mom and Tully and guilt and forgiveness. Sometimes she lay in bed at night, drawing her memories close and trying to imagine her mother talking to her in the dark.

Because that's what she missed most: her mother's voice. And through it all, she knew what she would someday have to do; she knew there was a place where she could find her mother's voice when she was strong enough to go looking.

But she needed Tully to be with her. That was the promise Marah had made to her mom.

✦

For weeks afterward, Dorothy fell into bed at night exhausted and woke tired. The to-do care list was never far from her grasp; she held it almost continuously and reread it over and over, afraid always that she had missed something. The tasks ran like a litany through her head. Elevate and lower, fifteen minutes every two hours; check fluids and food, check nasogastric tube, massage her hands and feet; apply lotion; brush her teeth; exercise her limbs through a gentle range of motion; keep bed dry and sheets clean; turn her from side to side every few hours; check tracheobronchial suction.

It took her more than a month to stop being afraid, and it was more than six weeks before the visiting nurse stopped adding to the notations on her list.

By late November, when the leaves had begun to fall and drop their bits of color onto her black, muddy, overgrown garden, she began to think—at last—that she could really do this, and by her first Christmas with her daughter, she had begun to leave her to-do list behind. The cycle of her days became routine. The nurse—Nora, a grandmother to twelve kids who ranged in age from six months to twenty-four—came by four times a week. Only last week she'd said, "Why, Dot, I couldn't do better myself. Honest!"

As Christmas Day 2010 dawned crisp and clear over the town of Snohomish, she finally felt at peace, or as at peace as a woman with a daughter in a coma could feel. She woke earlier than usual and set about readying the house to feel like a holiday home. There were no ornaments in the back storage closet, of course, and she had no problem with that. Making do was one of her life skills, but when she was in that dark closet, she stumbled across the two cardboard boxes full of Tully's mementos.

She paused, straightening, and stared down at them. A gray layer of dust covered the top.

When Johnny had delivered these boxes, along with Tully's clothes and toiletries and photos, Dorothy had thought they seemed sacrosanct, for Tully's eyes alone, but now she wondered if the contents could help Tully. She bent down and picked up the box marked *Queen Anne*. It was light—of course. How much would a seventeen-year-old Tully have thought to save?

Dorothy wiped away the dust and carried the box up to Tully's bedroom.

Tully lay still, her eyes closed, her breathing even. Pale silvery light shone through the window, pooling and writhing on the floor, the pattern shifting with the movement of the trees outside. Ribbons of light and dark chased each other across the floor, amplified by the glass beads in the dream catcher hung at the window.

"I brought up your things," she said to Tully. "I thought maybe, for Christmas, I could talk to you about what's in here." She set the box down by the bed.

Tully didn't move. A fuzz of graying mahogany hair had begun to grow back in, giving her a chicklike appearance. The bruises and lacerations had healed; only a few silvery scars marked where they'd been. Dorothy put some bee cream on her daughter's dry lips.

Then she pulled up the chair and sat down at the bedside. Leaning over, she opened the box. The first thing she pulled out was a small Magilla Gorilla T-shirt; at its touch, she felt slammed by a memory.

Mommy, can I have a brownie?

Sure. A little pot never hurt anyone. Clem, pass me the brownies.

And then: *Dot, your kid is flopping all over . . .*

She stared down at the T-shirt. It was so small . . .

She realized how long she'd been silent. "Oh. Sorry. You probably think I left, but I'm still here. Someday you'll know it meant something, that I kept coming back. I always knew where I belonged. I just couldn't . . . do it." She set the shirt aside, folded it carefully.

The next thing she pulled out was a large, flat photo-type album, its plastic cover dotted with blue forget-me-nots and a pioneer-type girl. Someone had written *Tully's Scrapbook* across the top.

Dorothy's hands were shaking as she opened the book to the first page, where there was a small, scallop-edged photograph of a skinny girl blowing out a candle. On the opposite page was a letter. She began reading it aloud.

Dear Mommy, today is my 11th birthday.

How are you? I am fine. I bet you're on your way to see me because you miss me as much as I miss you.

Love, your daughter, Tully

Dear Mommy,

Do you miss me? I miss you.

Love, your daughter, Tully

She turned the page and kept reading. More letters.

Dear Mommy,

Today at school we got to ride a pony. Do you like ponies? I do. Gran says maybe you're lergic, but I hope not. When you come to get me maybe we can get a pony.

Love, your daughter, Tully

"You sign them all *your daughter, Tully.* Did you wonder if I even knew who you were?"

In bed, Tully made a sound. Her eyes fluttered open. Dorothy rose quickly. "Tully? Can you hear me?"

Tully made a sound, like a tired sigh, and closed her eyes again.

Dorothy stood there a long time, waiting for more. It wasn't unusual, Tully opening her eyes, but it always felt meaningful. "I'll keep reading," Dorothy said, sitting down again, turning the page.

There were hundreds of letters, written at first in a wobbly child's hand, and then, as the years went on, in a more confident young woman's handwriting. Dorothy read them all.

I tried out for cheerleader today, to China Grove.
Do you know that song?

I know all of the presidents. Do you still want me to be president?

How come you never came back?

She longed to quit reading—each word of each letter was like a stab to the heart—but she couldn't stop. Here was her child's life, all laid out in letters. She read through her tears, each letter and postcard and piece from the school newspaper.

In about 1972, the letters stopped. They never turned angry or accusatory or blaming; they just ended.

Dorothy turned the last page. There, taped to the back page, she found a small blue envelope, sealed, that was addressed to *Dorothy Jean.*

She caught her breath. Only one person called her Dorothy Jean.

Slowly, she opened the envelope, saying in a nervous voice, "There's a letter here from my mom. Did you know it was here, Tully? Or did she put it here after you'd given up on me?"

She pulled out a single sheet of stationery, as thin as parchment, and crinkled, as if maybe it had been wadded up once and then resmoothed.

Dear Dorothy Jean,

I always thought you'd come home. For years I prayed. I begged God to send you back to me. I told Him that if He granted me just one more chance I would not be blind again.

But neither God nor you listened to an old woman's prayers. I can't say as I blame either one of you. Some wrongs can't be forgiven, can they? The preachers are wrong about that. I must have made a million samplers for God. A single word to you would have served me better.

Sorry. It is so small. Just five letters and I was never strong enough to say it. I never even tried to stop your father. I couldn't. I was too afraid. We both know how he liked his lit cigarettes, didn't we?

I am dying now, fading despite my best intentions to wait for you. I was better for Tully. I want you to know that. I was a better grandmother than I ever was a mother. This is the sin I take with me.

I won't dare to ask for your forgiveness, Dorothy Jean. But I am sorry. I want you to know that.

If only we could try again.

If only.

Dorothy stared down at the words; they danced and blurred in front of her. She'd always thought of herself as the only victim in that house. Maybe there had been two of them.

Three if you counted Tully, who had certainly been ruined by her grandfather's evil, not directly, perhaps, but ruined just the same. Three generations of women broken by a single man.

She let out a deep breath and thought: *Okay.*

Just that, a simple, single word. *Okay.* This was her past.

Her past.

She looked at her daughter, who looked like a sleeping princess, made young by her fuzzy new growth of hair. "No more secrets," she said—whispered, really. She would tell Tully everything, including the regret in her mother's letter. That would be her Christmas gift to her daughter. Dorothy would say the words at this bedside, begin from where she left off at the hospital. Then she would write it down, her entire story, so that Tully would have it all for her memoir, whatever she needed. There would be no more secret shame, no more running from the things that were her fault or the things that weren't. Maybe then, someday, they could heal.

"Would you like that, Tully?" she asked quietly, praying hard for an answer.

Beside her, Tully breathed evenly, in and out.

Twenty-seven

✦

That year, winter seemed to last forever. Gray days followed one another like dirty sheets on a line. Swollen clouds darkened the sky, releasing intermittent rain until the fields turned black and viscous and the cedar boughs drooped like wet sleeves. When the first sunny days of spring came, green swept across the fields in the Snohomish Valley, and the trees straightened again, straining toward the light, their tips lime-green with new growth. The birds returned overnight, squawking and diving for the fat pink worms that poked up from the damp earth.

By June, locals had forgotten all about the dismal winter and the disappointing spring. In July, when the farmers' markets started up again, there were already complaints about how hot it had grown in the summer of 2011.

Like the flowers in her yard, Marah had spent the long gray months gathering strength, or finding that which had been in her all along.

Now, though, it was late August. Time to look forward instead of back.

"Are you sure you want to do this alone?" her dad asked, coming up behind her. She closed her eyes and leaned back against him. His arms curled around her, held her steady.

"Yeah," she said, and it was the one thing in all of this about which she was sure. She had things to say to Tully, things she'd held back, waiting for a miracle; but there was not going to be a miracle. It had been almost a year since the accident, and Marah was preparing now to go off to college. Just last night, she'd helped her dad with his street kids documentary—and the images of those poor lost kids with their hollow cheeks and empty eyes and fake bravado had chilled her to the bone. She knew how lucky she was to be here, at home. Safe. And that was what she'd said when her dad filmed her. *I'm glad to be back.* But still, she had something left to do.

"I promised Mom something and I have to keep that promise," she said.

He kissed the top of her head. "I'm really proud of you. Have I told you that lately?"

She smiled. "Every day since I got rid of the pink hair and the piercing in my eyebrow."

"That's not why."

"I know."

He took her hand and walked her out of the house and to the car parked in the driveway. "Drive safely."

It was a sentence that meant a lot more to her these days. Nodding, she climbed into the driver's seat and started the car.

It was a gorgeous late summer day. On the island, tourists thronged onto and off the ferry, filling the sidewalks of downtown Winslow. On the other side of the water, the traffic was typically bumper-to-bumper, and Marah followed the crowd north.

In Snohomish, she turned off the highway and drove out to Firefly Lane.

She sat in the driveway for a moment, staring at the gray Nordstrom bag beside her. Finally, she picked it up and went to the front door.

The air smelled fresh and crisp, of apples and peaches ripening in the sunshine. From here, she could see that Dorothy's small vegetable garden was teeming with growth: bright red tomatoes, green beans, rows of leafy broccoli.

The door opened before she knocked. Dorothy stood there, wearing a flowery tunic and baggy cargo pants. "Marah! She's been waiting for you," she said, pulling Marah into a tight hug. It was what Dorothy had said to Marah every Thursday for nearly twelve months. "She opened her eyes twice this week. That's a good sign, I think. Don't you?"

"Sure," Marah said in a tight voice. She *had* thought that a few months ago, back when it started to happen. The first time it happened, in fact, it had taken her breath away. She'd called for Dorothy and waited, leaning forward, saying, *Come on, Tully, come back . . .*

She lifted the gray bag. "I brought her something to read."

"Great! Great! I could use some time in the garden. The weeds are bullying me around this month. You want some lemonade? It's homemade."

"Sure." She followed Dorothy through the scrupulously clean rambler. Drying lavender hung from the rafters overhead, scented the air. Bouquets of fragrant roses displayed in cracked water pitchers and metal pans decorated the counters and tabletops.

Dorothy disappeared into the kitchen and came back with an icy glass of lemonade.

"Thanks."

They stared at each other for a moment, and then Marah nodded and went down the long hallway to Tully's room. Sunlight poured through the window, making the blue walls shimmer like seawater.

Tully lay in her hospital bed, angled up, her eyes closed, her brown hair dusted with gray threads and curled riotously around her pale, thin face. A creamy coverlet was tucked up to just below her collarbone. Her chest rose and fell in a steady, easy rhythm. She looked so peaceful. As always, for a split second, Marah thought Tully would just open her eyes and give her that wide, toothy smile and say, *Hey.*

Marah forced herself to move forward. The room smelled of the gardenia hand lotion Dorothy loved. On the bedside table was a worn paperback copy of *Anna Karenina* that Desmond had been reading to Tully for months.

"Hey," Marah said to her godmother. "I'm going off to college. I know you know that, I've been talking about it for months. Loyola Marymount. In Los Angeles. Ironic, right? I think a smaller school will be good for me." She wrung her hands together. This wasn't what she'd come for. Not today.

For months and months, she'd believed in a miracle. Now, though, it was time to say goodbye.

And something else.

The ache in her chest was big and getting bigger. She reached for the chair by the bed and sat down, scooting close. "I'm the reason you crashed your car, aren't I? Because I was a bitch and sold that story to the magazine. I told the world you were a drug addict."

The silence after her statement dragged her down. Dr. Bloom had tried to convince her that Tully's condition wasn't her fault—everyone had—but it was one more thing Marah couldn't make herself believe. She couldn't help apologizing every time she visited.

"I wish we could start over, you and me. I miss you so much." Marah's voice was soft, uncertain.

In the quiet, she sighed and reached down for the gray bag on the floor beside her. She pulled out her most prized possession. Her mother's journal.

Her hands shook a little as she opened the journal, saw *Katie's Story* written in Tully's bold, scrawling handwriting.

Marah stared down at those two words. How was it possible that she was still afraid to read what was written on these pages? She should *want* to read her mother's last thoughts, but the idea of it made her queasy. "I promised her I'd read this with you when I was ready. I'm not really ready, and you're not really you, but I'm leaving and Dr. Bloom tells me it's time. And she's right. It is time."

Marah said quietly, "Here goes," and started to read aloud.

Panic always comes to me in the same way. First, I get a knot in the pit of my stomach that turns to nausea, then a fluttery breathlessness that no amount of deep breathing can cure. But what causes my fear is different every day; I never know what will set me off. It could be a kiss from my husband, or the lingering look of sadness in his eyes when he draws back. Sometimes I know he's already grieving for me, missing me even while I'm still here. Worse yet is Marah's quiet acceptance of everything I say. I would give anything for another of our old knock-down, drag-out fights. That's one of the first things I'd say to you now, Marah: Those fights were real life. You were struggling to break free of being my daughter but unsure of how to be yourself, while I was afraid to let you go. It's the circle of love. I only wish I'd recognized it then. Your grandmother told me I'd know you were sorry for those years before you did, and she was right. I know you regret some of the things you said to me, as I regret my own words. None of that matters, though. I want you to know that. I love you and I know you love me.

But these are just more words, aren't they? I want to go deeper than that. So, if you'll bear with me (I haven't really written anything in years), I have a story to tell you. It's my story, and yours, too. It starts in 1960 in a small farming town up north, in a clapboard house on a hill above a horse pasture. When it gets good, though, is 1974, when the coolest girl in the world moved into the house across the street . . .

Marah lost herself in the story of a lonely fourteen-year-old girl who got made fun of on the bus and lived through her favorite fictional characters. *They called me Kootie and laughed at my clothes and asked me where the flood was and I never said a word, just hugged my brown-paper-wrapped schoolbooks closer to my chest. Frodo was my best friend that year, and Gandalf and Sam and Aragon. I imagined myself on some mythical quest.* Marah could picture it perfectly: an unpopular girl who sat out one night under the stars and happened to meet another lonely girl. A few chance words that night became the start of a friendship that changed both of their lives.

And we thought we looked good. Have you gone there yet, Marah? Followed fashion to a ridiculous place that makes no sense and still looked in the mirror and seen a cool, magical version of yourself? That was the eighties for me. Of course, Tully was in full control of my wardrobe . . .

Marah touched her short black hair, remembering when it was pink and gelled . . .

When I met your father, it was magic. Not for him—not then—but for me. Sometimes, if you're lucky, you can look into a pair of eyes and see your whole future. I wish that kind of love for you kids—don't accept anything less.

When I held my babies and looked into their murky eyes, I found my life's work. My passion. My purpose. It may not be trendy, but I was born to be a mother, and I loved every single second of it. You and your brothers taught me everything there was to know about love, and it breaks my heart to leave you.

The journal kept going, winding and turning and bending through the years of her mother's life; by the time Marah came to the end, the sun was gone; night had fallen and Marah hadn't even noticed. Orange exterior light came through the windowpanes. Marah clicked on the bedside lamp and kept reading aloud.

Here's what you need to know, Marah. You are a struggler, a railer-against-the-machine. I know losing me will wound you deeply. You'll remember our arguments and fights.

Forget them, baby girl. That was just you being you and me being me. Remember the rest of it—the hugs, the kisses, the sandcastles we made, the cupcakes we decorated, the stories we told each other. Remember how I loved you, every single bit of you. Remember I loved your fire and your passion. You are the best of me, Marah, and I hope that someday you'll discover that I am the best of you, too. Let everything else go. Just remember how we loved each other.

Love. Family. Laughter. That's what I remember when it's all said and done. For so much of my life I thought I didn't do enough or want enough. I guess I can be forgiven for my stupidity. I was young. I want my children to know how proud I am of them, and how proud I am of me. We were everything we needed—you and Daddy and the boys and I. I had everything I ever wanted.

Love.

That's what we remember.

Marah stared down at the last word—*remember*—through a glaze of tears that burned her eyes and blurred the text. In that watery haze, she pictured her mother down to the minutest detail—her blond hair that never seemed to fall right, her green eyes that looked right into your soul and knew exactly what you were thinking, the way she knew when a slammed door was an invitation and when it wasn't, the way she laughed in fits and starts, the way she brushed the hair from Marah's eyes and whispered, "Always, baby girl," just before a kiss good night.

"Oh, my God, Tully . . . I remember her . . ."

✦

I can feel my heart beating. In it, I hear the rise and fall of the tides, the whoosh of a summer breeze, the beat of a drum.

Memories of sound.

But now there is something else in my darkness, tapping at me, prodding me, unsettling the beat of my heart.

I open my eyes, not even realizing that they've been closed, but it makes no difference; there is nothing to see except the endless black around me.

"Tully."

That's me. Or it was me. I hear it again, my name, and as the letters coalesce, echo with sound, I become aware of tiny bits of light, fireflies maybe, or flashlight beams, dancing around me, darting like fish.

Words. The starlight points are words, floating down to me.

". . . coolest girl in the world . . ."

". . . the sandcastles we made . . ."

". . . the best of you . . ."

I draw in a sharp breath of discovery; it rattles in my chest like a pair of dice.

Marah.

It is her voice I hear, but the words are Kate's. Her journal. I read it so many times over the years I have memorized it. I find myself straining forward, reaching out. Darkness presses back, restrains me; starlight is falling past me.

Someone takes my hand. Marah. I *feel* it, the warm strength of her grip, the curl of her fingers around mine; the only real thing in this world that makes no sense.

You can hear her, Kate says.

I turn and there she is, bathed in gorgeous, impossible light. I see her inside the glow, her green eyes, her blond hair, her wide smile.

Through the darkness I hear: "Oh, my God, Tully. I remember her."

And just like that, I remember *me*. The life I lived, the lessons I didn't learn, the way I failed the people I loved and how much I loved them. I remember watching them gather around my bedside, hearing them pray for me. I want them back. I want me back.

I stare at Katie and see it all in her eyes: our past. There's more, too: longing. I see the love she has for all of us—me, her husband, her children, her parents—and how that love is shiny with both hope and loss.

What do you want, Tully?

Marah's words fall around us, glimmering in the water, landing on my skin like kisses. "I want another chance," I say, and as I say it, the power of my choice pulses through me, gives strength to my tired, listless limbs.

I came to say goodbye. I need to move on, Tul. So do you. I need you to say goodbye to me and smile. That's all I need. A smile to let me know you're going to be okay.

"I'm afraid."

Fly away.

"But—"

I'm gone, Tul. But I'll always be with you. Go . . .

"I'll never forget us."

I know that. Now, go. Live. It's such a gift . . . and . . . tell my boys—

"I know," I say quietly. She has given me messages. I hold the words close to my heart, tuck them into my soul. I will tell Lucas that his mother comes to him at night and whispers in his ear and watches over his sleep, that she is happy and wants the same for him . . . I'll tell Wills it's okay to be sad and to stop fighting to fill that empty space where his mom used to be. *I'm not gone,* that was her message. *Just away.* I'll teach them all the things she would have, and make sure they know how much she loves them.

Turning away from her is the hardest thing I've ever done. Instantly I am cold, and my body feels heavy. There is a huge black hill in front of me, so steep it seems to push me back when I try to climb it.

At the top, there is a flash of light. I strain forward, lean into it, take another step.

The light is moving away from me.

I have to get to the top, where the world is, but I am so tired, so tired. Still, I keep trying. I climb slowly. Each step fights me. The darkness pushes back. Starlight turns to snow and each falling flake burns my skin. But there is a light, and it's getting stronger. It is like a lighthouse beam, flashing every now and then to show me the way.

I am breathing hard now, thinking, *Please,* realizing it is a prayer. The first real one of my life.

I am not going to make it.

No.

I *will* make it. I imagine Katie beside me, just like the old days, pushing our bikes up Summer Hill with only moonlight to guide us. I surge forward, and suddenly I am cresting the hill. I smell gardenia and dried lavender.

Light is everywhere now, hurting my eyes, blinding me. It comes from a small conical thing beside me.

I blink, trying to control my breathing.

"I did it, Katie," I whisper, my voice too small to be heard. Maybe I don't even say it aloud. I wait for her to say, *I know,* but there is only the sound of my breathing.

I open my eyes again, try to focus. There is someone beside me; I see her in slashes of light and shadow. A face, looking down at me.

Marah. She looks like she used to, beautiful and healthy. "Tully?" she says cautiously, as if I am a spirit or an illusion.

If I am dreaming, I welcome it. I am back. "Marah," takes me forever to say.

✦

I try to hold on, to stay, but I can't do it. Time falls away from me. I open my eyes—see Marah and Margie—and I try to smile, but I am so weak. And is that my mother's face? I try to say something; all that comes out is a croak of sound. And maybe I imagine it.

The next thing I know, I am asleep again.

Twenty-eight

Dorothy sat in the hospital waiting room, hands clasped in her lap, knees pressed together so closely the knobby bones bumped each other every time she moved. They were all here now: Johnny and his twin sons; Marah, who looked glazed and nervous and couldn't seem to sit still; Margie and Bud. It had been three days since Tully opened her eyes and tried to speak. They had immediately moved her back to the hospital, where the waiting game had begun again.

It had seemed like a miracle, at first, but now Dorothy wasn't so sure. She knew better than to believe in miracles, anyway, didn't she?

Dr. Bevan assured them that Tully was truly waking; he told them that it often took time to become fully conscious after so long a sleep. He warned them that there would probably be some lasting effects, and that certainly made sense. You couldn't sleep for a year and then wake up and ask for coffee and a donut.

For months, Dorothy had prayed for this. She'd knelt at her daughter's bedside every evening. It was uncomfortable, painful on her aging joints, but she was pretty sure that the pain was part of the price. So she knelt and she prayed, night after night, as autumn darkened into winter and then brightened again into spring. She prayed while her vegetables put down their roots and gathered the strength to grow; she prayed while the apples budded on her trees and began to ripen. Her prayer was always the same: *Please, God, let her wake up.*

In all that time, through the journey of her desperate words, she'd never allowed herself to really think about this moment. She'd been afraid to imagine an answer to her prayers, as if her need could jinx it.

That was what she'd told herself, anyway. Now she saw that it was another in the long string of lies she'd told herself over the years. She hadn't dared to imagine this moment because it terrified her.

What if Tully woke up and wanted nothing to do with her?

It was certainly a likely scenario. Dorothy had been a terrible parent for so long, and now, when she'd finally learned to be better, finally dared to let herself tumble into motherhood, it was not real. Not for Tully, anyway, who had slept through the whole thing.

"You're humming again," Margie said gently.

Dorothy pressed her lips together. "Nervous habit."

Margie reached over and held Dorothy's hand. It still surprised her sometimes, the easy intimacy she'd found with Margie; it surprised her, too, how much it could mean to simply be touched by another human being who understood you. "I'm afraid," she said.

"Of course you are. You're a mother. Fear is the job description."

Dorothy turned to look at Margie. "What do I know about motherhood?"

"You're a fast learner."

"What if she doesn't want anything to do with me when she wakes up? I don't know how to go back to who I was without her. I can't just walk up to her bed and say hi."

Margie's smile was sad, as tired as the look in her eyes. "She always wanted something to do with you, Dorothy. I remember the first time she asked me what was wrong with her, why you didn't love her. It broke my heart, honest to God. I told her that sometimes life didn't work out the way you expected, but that you never gave up hope. She was seventeen then. Your mother had just died and she was afraid of where she would live. We took her in, gave her a place to live. That very first night, when she was in bed in Katie's room, I sat down beside her and told her good night. She looked up at me and said,

'She'll miss me someday,' and I said, 'How could she not?' and Tully said—so quietly I almost couldn't hear: 'I'll wait.' And she did, Dorothy. She waited for you in a thousand different ways."

Dorothy wished she were the kind of woman who could believe a thing like that.

✦

Time passed for Tully in blurry images and nonsensical vignettes—a white car, a woman in pink saying something about feeling better now, a moving bed, a TV tucked up in the corner of a white room, voices that were a distant drone. Now there was only one voice. Sounds came at her, breaking apart, forming . . . words.

"Hello, Tully."

She blinked slowly and opened her eyes. There was a man standing beside her. A man in a white coat. She couldn't really focus on him; the light in here was so dim. She missed light. What did that mean? And she was cold.

"I'm Dr. Bevan. You're in Sacred Heart Hospital. You got here about five days ago. Do you remember?"

She frowned, trying to think. She felt as if she'd been in darkness for hours, years, lifetimes. She couldn't remember anything. Just something about a light . . . the sound of running water . . . the smell of green spring grass.

She tried to wet her lips—they felt painfully dry—and her throat was fricking on FIRE. "Wha . . ."

"You were in a car accident and sustained a serious head trauma. Your left arm was broken in three places, as was your left ankle—though that was a clean, simple break. Both bones healed nicely."

Car accident?

"No, Tully, don't try to move."

Had she been trying to move? "How . . . long?" She didn't even know what she was asking, and by the time he said something—she had no idea what—she was closing her eyes again. She would just sleep for a minute . . .

✦

She heard something. Felt something. She wasn't alone. She took a deep breath, released it slowly, and opened her eyes.

"Hey."

Johnny. He was here, beside her. Behind him stood Margie and Marah and . . . Cloud? What was her mother doing here?

"You're back," Johnny said quietly, his voice uneven. "We thought we'd lost you."

She tried to find her voice, but even with her best effort, her words came out garbled. She couldn't think clearly.

He touched her face. "We're here. All of us."

She worked hard to focus, desperate suddenly to tell him something. "Johnny . . . I . . ."

Saw her.

What did that mean? Saw who?

"Don't worry, Tul," he said. "We have time now."

She closed her eyes and drifted back to sleep. Sometime later, she thought she heard voices—Johnny and some other man. Words drifted toward her—*remarkable recovery, brain activity normal, give her time*—but none of it meant anything to her so she let it go.

✦

Johnny was still there when she woke up again. So was Margie. They stood by her bedside, talking quietly, as she opened her eyes. It felt different, this waking; she knew it instantly.

Margie saw her open her eyes and she started to cry. "There you are."

"Hey," Tully croaked. It took concentration to find that simple word, to find *herself* in words. She said something—she didn't know what, and she was pretty sure it didn't make sense. She could tell that her speech was slow, a little slurry, but the way they smiled took all that away, made it meaningless.

Johnny moved closer. "We missed you."

Margie came closer. "There's my girl."

"How long . . . here?" She knew there were more words that belonged in her question, but she couldn't grab hold of them.

Margie looked at Johnny.

"You got here six days ago," Johnny said evenly. He drew in a breath. "Your accident was on September third, 2010."

Margie said, "Today is August twenty-seventh, 2011."

"But. Wait."

"You were in a coma for almost a year," Johnny said.

A year.

She closed her eyes, feeling a little flutter of panic. She couldn't remember anything about a car accident or being in a coma, or—

Hey, Tul.

Suddenly, it was there in the darkness with her, a beautiful singular memory. Two grown women on bikes, riding side by side, their arms outstretched and . . . starlight . . . Katie beside her saying, *Who says you get to die?*

It couldn't be real. She'd imagined it. That had to be the answer.

"They had me on some big drugs, I guess, right?" Tully said, opening her eyes slowly.

"Yes," Margie said. "To save your life."

So that was it. In a drugged-out, half-dead state, she'd imagined her best friend. It was hardly a surprise.

"You have some physical and occupational therapy to do. Dr. Bevan has recommended an excellent therapist who will work with you. He doesn't think it will be too long before you're ready to live at home by yourself."

"Home," she said quietly, wondering exactly where that was.

✦

In her dream, she was in an Adirondack chair by the beach and Katie was beside her. But it wasn't the gray, pebbled shore of Bainbridge Island stretched out in front of them, nor was it the choppy blue waters of the bay.

Where are we? her dream self asked, and as she waited for an answer, light spilled across the turquoise water, illuminated everything until it was so bright Tully couldn't see.

When someone hip-bumps you or tells you that it's not all about you or when our music plays. Listen and you'll hear me in all of it.

Tully woke with a start. She sat up so quickly her breath caught and the pain in her head intensified.

Katie.

The memory of being in the light rushed at her, bowled her over. She'd been with Katie somewhere—over there—she'd held her hand, heard her say: *I'll always be with you. Whenever you hear our music or laugh so hard you cry, I'll be there. When you close your eyes at night and remember, I'll be there. Always.*

It was real. Somehow. Impossibly.

It wasn't drugs, or her brain injury, or wishful thinking. It was real.

Twenty-nine

✦

The next day was an endless series of medical tests: Tully was poked and prodded and zapped and X-rayed. It surprised her—and everyone else—how quickly she was improving.

"Are you ready?" Johnny said when she'd finally been discharged.

"Where is everyone?"

"Preparing for your homecoming. It's a pretty big deal. Are you ready?"

She sat in a wheelchair by the room's only window, wearing a helmet in case of a fall. Her reflexes were a little impaired and no one wanted her landing on her head.

"Yeah." She had trouble finding words sometimes, so she kept her answers simple.

"How many of them are out there?"

She frowned. "How many of what?"

"Your fans."

She gave a sigh. "No fans for me."

He crossed the room and came up beside her, turning her wheelchair toward the window. "Look more closely."

She followed the direction of his glance. A crowd of people stood in the parking lot below, huddled beneath brightly colored umbrellas. There were at least three dozen of them. "I don't see . . ." she began, and then she saw the signs.

WE ♥ U TULLY ♥!

GET WELL TULLY

UR GIRLFRIENDS NEVER GAVE UP!

"They're for me?"

"Your recovery is big news. Fans and reporters started gathering as soon as word leaked."

The crowd blurred before Tully's eyes. At first she thought the rain had picked up. Then she realized she was remembering all that she'd gone through in the last few years and crying for this evidence that she hadn't been forgotten after all.

"They love you, Tul. I hear Barbara Walters wants an interview."

She didn't even know what to say to that. It didn't matter anyway; Johnny was on the move. He grabbed the chair's rubberized handles and wheeled her out of the hospital room. She gave one last thoughtful look as she left.

In the lobby, he stopped and set the brake. "I won't be long. I'll just send your fans and the reporters on their way."

He positioned her against the wall, with the lobby behind her, and went through the glass pneumatic doors.

On this late August afternoon, a light rain drizzled down even as the sun shone. This was what locals called sun breaks.

As Johnny came forward, cameras pointed at him, flashes blinked on and off. The signs—WE ♥ YOU TULLY ♥; GET WELL; WE'RE PRAYING FOR YOU—lowered slowly.

"I know you have been apprised of Tully Hart's miraculous recovery. And it is miraculous. The doctors here at Sacred Heart, especially Dr. Reginald Bevan, gave Tully exceptional care and I know she'd want me to thank them for her. I know she'd want me to thank her fans, too, many of whom prayed for this recovery."

"Where is she?" someone yelled.

"We want to see her!"

Johnny held up a hand for silence. "I'm sure you can all understand that Tully is focused on her recovery right now. She—"

A gasp went through the crowd. The people in front of Johnny turned as one, faced the hospital doors. The photographers began jostling into one another, their flashes erupting.

Tully sat just outside the hospital doors, which kept whooshing open and closed behind her. She was out of breath, and the chair was cockeyed, no doubt because she was too weak to roll herself steadily forward. A gentle rain fell on her helmet and splotched her blouse. He went to her.

"Are you sure?" he asked her.

"Abso . . . lutely not. Let's do it."

He wheeled her forward; the crowd quieted.

She smiled uneasily at them, said, "I've looked better."

The roar of approval almost knocked Johnny back. Signs shot back up into the air.

"Thank you," she said when the crowd finally quieted.

"When will you go back on air?" one of the reporters yelled.

She looked out across the crowd, and then at Johnny, who knew her so well, who'd been with her from the beginning of her career. She saw the way he looked at her: Was he remembering her at twenty-one, when she'd been a firebrand who sent him a résumé a day for months and worked for free? He knew how desperately she had always needed to be *someone*. Hell, she'd given up everything to be loved by strangers.

She drew in a deep breath and said, "No more." She wanted to explain herself, to say that she was done with fame, that she didn't need it anymore, but it was just too hard to gather all those words together and put them in order. She knew what mattered now.

The crowd erupted in noise; questions were hurled at Tully.

She turned to Johnny.

"I've never been more proud of you," he said, too softly for anyone to hear.

"For quitting?"

He touched her face with a gentleness that made her breath catch. "For never quitting."

With the crowd still yelling questions, Johnny took control of the wheelchair and steered her back into the hospital lobby.

In no time, they were in the car and heading north on I-5.

Where were they going? She was supposed to be going home. "Wrong way."

"Are you in the driver's seat?" Johnny asked. He didn't glance at her, but she could tell he was smiling. "No. You're not. You're in the passenger seat. I know you've recently suffered a brain injury, but I'm sure you remember that the driver drives the car and the passenger enjoys the view."

"Where . . . we going?"

"Snohomish."

For the first time, Tully thought about her year-long coma. How come no one had told her where she'd been all that time? Were they keeping it from her? And why hadn't the question occurred to her before this? "Have Bud and Margie been taking care of me?"

"Nope."

"You?"

"No."

She frowned. "Nursing home?"

He indicated a turn and exited the highway toward Snohomish. "You've been staying at your house in Snohomish. With your mother."

"My *mother*?"

His gaze softened. "There have been more than a few miracles in all of this."

Tully didn't even know what to say. It would have been less surprising to hear that Johnny Depp had nursed her through the long dark months.

And yet, a memory teased her, came close, and then darted away.

A slippery combination of words and light. The smell of lavender and Love's Baby Soft . . . *Billy, don't be a hero . . .*

Katie saying, *Listen. It's your mother.*

Johnny pulled up in front of the house on Firefly Lane and stopped, turning toward Tully. After a long pause, he said, "I don't know how to tell you how sorry I am."

The tenderness she felt for this man was so sharp it was almost pain. How could she make him understand what she'd learned in that darkness—and in the light? "I saw her," she said quietly.

He frowned. "Her?"

She saw when he understood.

"Katie."

"Oh."

"Call me crazy or brain-damaged or drugged. Whatever. I saw her and she held my hand and she told me to tell you, 'You did fine and there's nothing for the kids to forgive you for.'"

He frowned.

"She thought you'd been kicking your ass about not being strong enough for her. You wish you'd let her tell you she was afraid. She said, 'Tell him he was all I ever needed and he said everything I needed to hear.'"

Tully reached over and held his hand, and there it was, between them again, all the years they'd spent together, all the times they'd laughed and cried and hoped and dreamed. "I'll forgive you for breaking my heart if you forgive me, too. For all of it."

He nodded slowly, his eyes glazed with tears. "I missed you, Tul."

"Yeah, Johnny boy. I missed you, too."

✦

Marah threw herself into the decorations for Tully's homecoming, but even as she talked to her grandparents and teased with her brothers, she felt as if she were walking on eggshells. Her stomach was tight with anxiety. She wanted Tully's forgiveness desperately, but she didn't deserve it. The only other person who looked uncomfortable with the upcoming celebration was Dorothy. Tully's mother had seemed to lose mass in the past few days, to grow smaller somehow. Marah knew that the older woman had begun to pack her few things into a bag. While everyone had busied themselves with decorating, Dorothy had said something about needing supplies at the nursery. She'd been gone for hours and hadn't yet returned.

At Tully's homecoming, everyone cheered and clapped and welcomed her back to the house. Grandma and Grandpa hugged her carefully and the boys shrieked at her return.

"I *knew* you'd be okay," Lucas said to Tully. "I prayed every night."

"*I* prayed every night, too," Wills said, not to be outdone.

Tully looked exhausted, sitting there, her head cocked in a strange way; the clunky silver helmet made her look almost childlike. "I know . . . two boys . . . who have a birthday coming up. I missed a year. Buy *two* presents now." Tully had to work really hard to say all that, and when she was done, her cheeks were bright and she was out of breath.

"Probably matching Porsches," Dad said.

Grandma laughed and scooted the boys into the kitchen to get the cake.

Marah made it through the party on false smiles and mumbled comments. Fortunately for her, Tully tired easily and said her good nights at about eight o'clock.

"Roll me to bed?" Tully said, taking hold of Marah's hand, squeezing.

"Sure." Marah grabbed the chair's handles and wheeled her godmother down the long, narrow hallway toward the back bedroom. There, she maneuvered Tully through the open doorway and into the room, where there was a hospital bed, and flowers everywhere, and pictures cluttered on the tables. An IV stand stood beside the bed.

"This is where I've been," Tully said. "For a year . . ."

"Yes."

"Gardenias," Tully said. "I remember . . ."

Marah helped her into the bathroom, where Tully brushed her teeth and slipped into the white lawn nightgown hanging from a hook on the back of the door. Then she got back into the wheelchair and Marah maneuvered her to the bed. There, she helped Tully to her feet.

Tully faced her. In one look, Marah saw all of it: *my job is to love you* . . . the fight . . . *you're my best friend* . . . and the lies.

"I missed you," Tully said.

Marah burst into tears. Suddenly she was crying for all of it—for the loss of her mom, and for finding her in the journal, for the way she'd betrayed Tully and all the wounds she'd inflicted on people who loved her. "I'm so sorry, Tully."

Tully brought her hands up slowly, cupped Marah's cheeks in her dry, papery palms. "Your voice brought me back."

"The *Star* article—"

"Old news. Here, help me into bed. I'm exhausted."

Marah wiped her eyes and pulled back the covers and helped Tully into bed. Then she climbed up into bed beside her, just like in the old days.

Tully was quiet for a long moment before she said, "It's true, all that going-into-the-light/your-life-flashing-before-your-eyes stuff. When I was in the coma, I . . . left my body. I could see your dad in the hospital room with me. It was like I was hovering in the corner, looking down on what happened to this woman who looked just like me but wasn't me. And I couldn't take it, so I turned, and there was this . . . light, and I followed it, and the next thing I knew I was on my bike, on Summer Hill, riding in the dark. With your mom beside me."

Marah drew in a sharp breath, clamped a hand over her mouth.

"She's with us, Marah. She will *always* be watching over you and loving you."

"I want to believe that."

"It's a choice." Tully smiled. "She's glad you ditched the pink hair, by the way. I was supposed to tell you that. Oh, and there was one more thing . . ." She frowned, as if trying to remember. "Oh. Yeah. She said, 'All things come to an end, even this story.' Does that make sense?"

"It's from *The Hobbit*," Marah said. *Maybe someday you'll feel alone with your sadness, not ready to share it with me or Daddy, and you'll remember this book in your nightstand.*

"The kids' book? That's weird."

Marah smiled. She didn't think it was weird at all.

✦

"I'm Dorothy, and I'm an addict."

"Hi, Dorothy!"

She stood in the middle of the ragtag circle of people who had come to tonight's Narcotics Anonymous meeting. As usual, the meeting took place in the old church on Front Street in Snohomish.

In the cool, dimly lit room that smelled of stale coffee and drying donuts, she talked about her recovery and how long it had taken her and what a dark road it had sometimes been. She needed this tonight, of all nights.

At the close of the meeting, she left the small wooden church and got onto her bicycle. For the first time in ages, she didn't stop to talk to anyone after the meeting. She was too edgy to play nice.

It was a blue-black evening, full of swaying trees and tiny stars. She rode along the main street, indicated her turn, and headed out of town.

At her place, she veered down onto the driveway and came to a stop. Balancing her bike carefully against the side of the house, she went to the front door and turned the knob. Inside, everything was quiet. There was a leftover aroma in the air—spaghetti, maybe—and some fresh basil. A few lights had been left on, but mostly it was quiet.

She reslung her purse over her shoulder and closed the door

behind her. The sharp, pungent smell of drying lavender filled her nostrils. She moved silently through the house. Everywhere she looked she saw evidence of the party she'd missed—the WELCOME HOME banner, the stack of brightly colored napkins on the counter, the wineglasses drying by the sink.

What a coward she was.

In the kitchen, she poured herself a glass of water from the sink and then leaned back against the counter, gulping the liquid as if she were dying of thirst. In front of her, the shadowy hallway unfurled. On one side was her bedroom door; on the other was Tully's.

Coward, she thought again. Instead of going down the hallway, doing what needed to be done, she found herself drifting through the house, heading toward the back door, going out onto the deck.

She smelled cigarette smoke.

"You were waiting for me?" she said quietly.

Margie stood up. "Of course. I knew how hard this would be for you. But you've been hiding long enough."

Dorothy felt her knees almost give out. She had never had a good friend in her life, not one of those women who would be there for you if you needed them. Until now. She reached out for the wooden chair beside her, held on to it.

There were three chairs out here. Dorothy had spent months restoring these wooden rockers that she'd found at the Goodwill. When she'd finished sanding and painting them—a wild array of colors—she'd painted names on the back. *Dorothy. Tully. Kate.*

At the time, it had seemed romantic and optimistic. As she held the paintbrush and smeared the bright colors along the rough wood, she'd imagined what Tully would say when she woke up. Now, though, all she saw was the presumption of her actions. What made her think that Tully would want to sit with her mother in the morning and have a cup of tea . . . or that it wouldn't break her heart to sit next to a chair that was always empty, its seat waiting for a woman who would never return?

"Do you remember what I told you about motherhood?" Margie said in the darkness, exhaling smoke.

Dorothy eased around an empty basket and sat down in the chair with her name on it. Margie, she noticed, was sitting in Tully's chair.

"You told me a lot of things," Dorothy said, leaning back with a sigh.

"When you're a mom, you learn about fear. You're always afraid. Always. About everything from cupboard doors to kidnappers to weather. There is nothing that can't hurt our kids, I swear." She turned. "The irony is they need us to be strong."

Dorothy swallowed hard.

"I was strong for my Katie," Margie said.

Dorothy heard the way her friend's voice broke on that, and without even thinking, she got up from her chair, crossed the small space between them, and pulled Margie up into her arms. She felt how thin the woman was, how she trembled at this touch, and Dorothy understood. Sometimes it hurt worse to be comforted than to be left alone.

"Johnny wants to scatter her ashes in the summer. I don't know how to do it, but I know it's time."

Dorothy had no idea what to say, so she just held on.

When Margie drew back, her eyes were wet with tears. "You helped me get through it, you know that, right? In case I never told you. All those times you let me sit over here and smoke my cigarettes while you planted your seeds and pulled up your weeds."

"I didn't say anything."

"You were there for me, Dorothy. Like you were there for Tully." She wiped her eyes and tried to smile, then said quietly, "Go see your daughter."

✦

Tully woke from a deep sleep, disoriented. She sat up quickly—too quickly; dizziness made the unfamiliar room spin around her for just a moment.

"Tully, are you okay?"

She blinked slowly and remembered where she was. In her old bedroom, in the house on Firefly Lane. She turned on the bedside lamp.

Her mother sat in a chair against the wall. She got up awkwardly, clasping her hands together. She was wearing bag-lady clothes, white socks, and Birkenstock sandals. And the tattered remnant of that macaroni necklace Tully had made for her in Bible camp. All these years later, her mother had kept it.

"I . . . was worried," her mother said. "Your first night here and all. I hope you don't mind that I'm here."

"Hey, Cloud," Tully said quietly.

"I'm Dorothy now," her mother said. She gave a hitching, apologetic smile and moved toward the bed. "I picked the name 'Cloud' at a commune in the early seventies. We were high all the time, and naked. A lot of bad ideas seemed good back then." She looked down at Tully.

"I'm told you took care of me."

"It was nothing."

"A year of caring for a woman in a coma? That's not nothing."

Her mother reached into her pocket and pulled out a small token. It was goldish in color, and round, a little bigger than a quarter. A triangle was stamped onto the coin; on the left side of the triangle was the word *sobriety* in black, on the right side was the word *anniversary.* Inside the triangle was the Roman numeral X. "Remember that night you saw me in the hospital, back in '05?"

Tully remembered every time she'd ever seen her mother. "Yes."

"That was rock bottom for me. A woman gets tired of being hit. I went into rehab not long after that. You paid for it, by the way, so thanks for that."

"And you stayed sober?"

"Yes."

Tully was afraid to believe in the unexpected hope that unfurled at her mother's confession. And she was afraid not to. "That's why you came to my condo and tried to help me."

"As interventions go, it was pretty lame. Just one old lady and a pissed-off daughter." She smiled, a little crookedly. "You see life a lot more clearly when you're sober. I took care of you to make up for all the times I didn't take care of you."

Her mother leaned forward, touching the macaroni necklace at her throat. There was a softness in her gaze that surprised Tully. "I know it was only a year. I don't expect anything."

"I heard your voice," Tully said. She remembered it in pieces, moments. Darkness and light. This: *I'm so proud of you. I never told you that, did I?* The memory was like the soft, creamy center of an expensive chocolate. "You stood by my bed and told me a story, didn't you?"

Her mother looked startled, and then a little sad. "I should have told it to you years ago."

"You said you were proud of me."

She reached out at last, touched Tully's cheek with a mother's tenderness. "How could I not be proud of you?"

Her mother's eyes filled with tears. "I always loved you, Tully. It was my own life I was running from." Slowly, she reached into the nightstand drawer and pulled out a photograph. "Maybe this will be our beginning." She handed the picture to Tully.

Tully reached for the photograph that shimmied in her mother's slim, shaking fingers.

It was square and small, about the size of a playing card, with white scalloped edges that were bent and mangled. The years had left a crackle-like patina on the black-and-white print.

It was a photograph of a man, a young man, sitting on a dirty porch step, with one booted foot pushed out to reveal a long leg. His hair was long and black and dirty, too. Splotches of sweat darkened the white T-shirt he wore; his cowboy boots had seen better days and his hands were dark with grime.

But his smile was wide and white and should have been too big for his angular face, but wasn't, and it was tilted the slightest bit to one side. His eyes were as black as night and seemed to hold a thousand secrets. Beside him, on the porch step, a brown-haired baby lay sleeping in a baggy, grayed diaper. The man's big hand lay possessively on the infant's small, bare back.

"You and your father," her mother said softly.

"My father? You said you didn't know who—"

"I lied. I fell in love with him in high school."

Tully looked back down at the picture. She ran her fingertip over it, studying every line and shadow, barely able to breathe. She had never seen even a hint of her own features in a relative's face. But here was her *dad,* and she looked like him. "I have his smile."

"Yes. And you laugh just like he did."

Tully felt something deep inside of her click into place.

"He loved you," her mother said. "And me, too."

Tully heard the break in her mother's voice. When she looked up, the tears in her mother's voice matched her own.

"Rafael Benecio Montoya."

Tully said the name reverently. "Rafael."

"Rafe."

Tully couldn't hold on to the emotion swelling inside her heart. This changed *everything,* changed her. She had a father. A dad. And he *loved* her. "Can I—"

"Rafe died in Vietnam."

Tully didn't realize that she'd even constructed a dreamscape, but with that one word, she felt it fall to pieces around her. "Oh."

"I'll tell you all about him, though," her mother said. "How he used to sing songs to you in Spanish and throw you into the air to hear you laugh. He picked your name because it was Choctaw and he said that made you a *real* American. That's why I always called you Tallulah. To remember him."

Tully looked up into her mother's watery eyes and saw love and loss and heartache. And hope, too. The whole of their lives. "I've waited so long."

Dorothy gently touched Tully's cheek. "I know," she said softly.

It was the touch Tully had waited for all of her life.

✦

In her dreams, Tully is sitting in one of the Adirondack chairs on my deck. I am beside her, of course; we are as we used to be: young and laughing. Always talking. In the branches of that old maple tree, dressed now in the scarlet and gold of autumn, several Mason jars hang from lengths of twine; in them, votive candles burn brightly over our heads, casting drops of flickering light to the floor.

I know that sometimes, when Tully sits in her chair out here, she thinks about me. She remembers the two of us flying down Summer Hill on bikes, our arms outflung, both of us believing the world was impossibly big and bright.

Here, in her dreams, we will be friends forever, together. Growing old, wearing purple, and singing along to silly songs that mean nothing and everything. Here, there will be no cancer, no growing old, no lost chances, no arguments.

I'm always with you, *I say to her in her sleep, and she knows it's true.*

I turn—barely a movement at all—just a sideways glance, and I am somewhere else, some when else. Inside my house on Bainbridge Island. My family is gathered together, laughing over some joke I can't hear. Marah is home from college for winter break; she has made the kind of friend that lasts through a lifetime—and my father is healthy. Johnny has begun to smile again—soon he will find himself falling in love. He will fight it . . . and he will give in. And my boys—my beautiful sons—are becoming men before my very eyes. Wills still goes through life in fifth gear, loud and booming and defiant, while Lucas slips along behind, barely noticed in a crowd until you see his smile. But it is Lucas I hear at night, Lucas who talks to me in his sleep, afraid that he will forget me. The way I miss them all is sometimes unbearable. But they are going to be fine. I know it, and now they do, too.

Soon, my mom will be with me, although she doesn't know it yet.

I look away for an instant, and I am back on Firefly Lane. It is morning. Tully limps out into the kitchen and has tea with her mother and they work in the garden, and I can see how strong she is growing. No more wheelchair for her. Not even a cane now.

Time passes. How much?

In her world, maybe days. Weeks . . .

And suddenly there is a man in the orchard, talking to Dorothy.

Tully puts down her coffee cup and moves toward him; her steps are slow and uncertain on the tilled, rough dirt of the garden. Her balance is still a little tenuous these days. She passes her mother and goes to the man, who holds a pair of—

Slippers?

"Des," Tully says. She reaches out for him and he takes her hand in his. When they touch, I glimpse their future—a gray, pebbled beach with a pair of wooden chairs set near the tide line . . . a table set for some holiday dinner, with my family and hers gathered around it and a high chair pushed up close . . . an aging house with a wraparound porch that overlooks the sea. I see all of this in the time it takes my best friend's heart to take a single beat.

I know in that moment she will be okay. Life will go on for her as it must; hearts will be broken and dreams will be fulfilled and risks will be taken, but she will always remember us—two girls who'd taken a chance on each other a lifetime ago and become best friends.

I move closer to her; I know she feels me. At last, *I whisper in her ear. She hears me, or maybe she only thinks she knows what I would say now. It doesn't matter.*

It is time for me to let go.

Not of TullyandKate. We will always be a part of each other. Best friends.

But I have to move on, as she has.

When I look back one last time, from far, far away, she is smiling.

Firefly Lane

by

KRISTIN HANNAH

It is 1974 and the summer of love is finally drawing to a close. The flower children are starting to realize that you cannot survive on peace and love alone.

Kate Mularkey has accepted her place at the bottom of the secondary-school social food chain. Then, to her amazement, the 'coolest girl in the world', Tully Hart – the girl all the boys want to know – moves in across the street and wants to be her best friend. Tully and Kate become inseparable and by summer's end they make a pact to be 'best friends forever'.

For thirty years Tully and Kate buoy each other through life, weathering the storms of friendship, jealousy, anger, hurt and resentment. Tully will follow her ambition to find fame and success. Kate knows that all she wants is to fall in love and have a family. What she doesn't know is how being a wife and a mother will change her.

They think they've survived it all until a single act of betrayal tears them apart. But when tragedy strikes, can the bonds of friendship survive? Or is it the one hurdle that even a lifelong friendship cannot overcome?

Firefly Lane **is a book for every woman who knows that her best friend is the only person who really, truly, understands her. And it is a book no one will ever forget.**

Home Front

By

KRISTIN HANNAH

'I don't love you any more'

One woman's fight for her marriage, and her life . . .

From a distance, Michael and Jolene Zarkades seem to have it all: a solid dependable marriage, exciting careers and children they adore. But after twelve blissful years together, the couple have lost their way. They are unhappy and edging towards divorce. Then an unexpected deployment tears their already fragile family apart, sending one of them deep into harm's way and leaving the other at home, caring for the children and waiting for news. When the worst happens, each must face their darkest fear and fight for the future of their family.

An intimate look at the inner landscape of a disintegrating marriage and a dramatic exploration of the price of war, *Home Front* is a provocative and timely portrait of hope, honour, loss, forgiveness – and the elusive nature of love.

Night Road

By

KRISTIN HANNAH

Selected for the TV Book Club Summer Read 2011

Why do we always hurt those we love the most?

Lexi and Mia are inseparable from the moment they start high school. Different in so many ways – Lexi is an orphan and lives with her aunt on a trailer park, while Mia is a golden girl blessed with a loving family, and a beautiful home. Yet they recognize something in each other which sets them apart from the crowd, and Mia comes to rely heavily on Lexi's steadfast friendship.

Mia's beloved, and incredibly good-looking, twin brother Zach, finds life much less complicated than his sister. Jude thought she'd never have to worry about her son, that he'd always sail through life easily achieving whatever he, and his family, wanted and expected – but then he fell in love.

The summer they graduated is a time they will always remember, and one they could never forget. It is a summer of love, best friends, shared confidences and promises. Then one moment one night changes them all forever. As hearts are broken, loyalties challenged and hopes dashed, the time has come to leave childhood behind and learn to face the future.